The Headlong God of War:

A Tale of Ancient Greece and the Battle of Marathon

By Jon Edward Martin

PublishAmerica
Baltimore

First printing

At the specific preference of the author, PublishAmerica allowed this work to remain exactly as the author intended, verbatim, without editorial input.

ISBN: 1-4241-9504-7
PUBLISHED BY PUBLISHAMERICA, LLLP
www.publishamerica.com
Baltimore

Printed in the United States of America

Historical Note

Founded by Cyrus circa 550 BC, the Persian Empire was the world's first Super Power. Its frontiers stretched from India in the east to Egypt in the west, subjecting millions to its rule. In the latter part of the 6th century BC, Darios, the new emperor, embarked on the invasion of Europe by launching a campaign against the European Skythians, a tribe of nomadic horsemen from what is now Romania and the Ukraine.

At this same time, the small independent city-states of Greece were evolving from monarchies and tyrannies to various forms of rule that distributed power. All of these city-states restricted participation in government to some extent. In Sparta adult males who were part of the ruling class, called Spartiates, constituted the people's assembly. In Athens too, only the elite upper class or aristocracy, exercised true citizens' rights. But soon a new form of government would evolve—Demokratia, or rule by the people.

Across the Aegean, Ionian Greeks had settled along the coast of Asia Minor, coming into contact with the great nations of the East. During Persia's expansion they too became subjects of Cyrus then his successors Cambyses and Darios. Co-existence proved short-lived. The Greeks, or more accurately the Hellenes, hardly proved compliant subjects, for this new idea of democracy, born in Athens, began to spread. Men would now fight, but not for land, power nor wealth, but for ideas.

There is no exaggeration necessary to define their struggle—if successful generations would be bestowed with the gifts of liberty, theater, art, architecture, philosophy, and science. In defeat, the world would have entered a true Dark Age from which there might have been no release.

Acknowledgments

I would like to thank Dr. Nicholas Sekunda from the University of Gdansk for answering my many questions regarding the battle of Marathon and the preceding events. His input has proved invaluable.

A special thanks goes out to Howard David Johnson for providing the cover art for my novel. He is a prolific artist, with a keen interest in history and an equally keen eye for reproducing it in a breathtaking manner.

And I extend my gratitude to Spiros Halkides, my friend in Athens, who patiently drives me to all the archaeological sites, battlefields, and museums while managing to always find the best tavernas, no matter what part of Greece we are in.

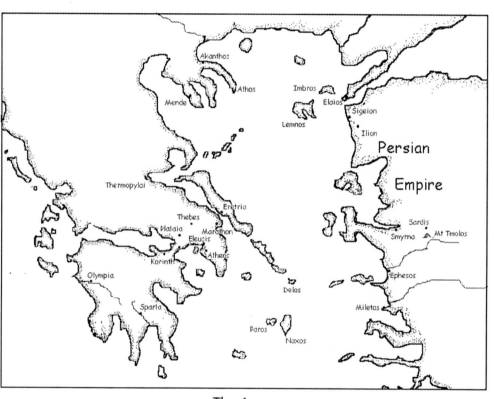

The Aegean

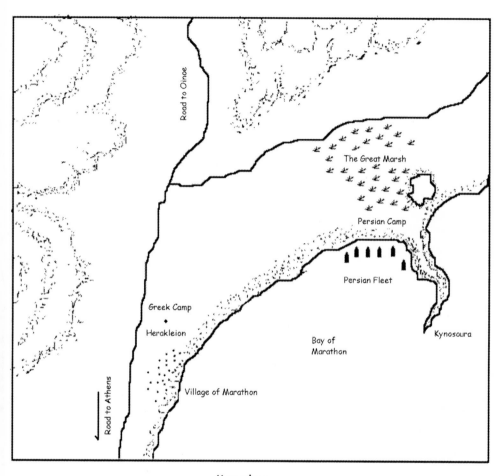

Marathon

Selected Chronology

550 BC – Kyros (Cyrus) becomes first king of the Persian Empire

528 BC – Hippias becomes tyrant of Athens

522 BC – Darios becomes king of Persia

521 BC – Kleomenes becomes king of Sparta

513 BC – Darios, king of Persia, invades Skythia

510 BC – Spartans oust Hippias from Athens

507 BC – Democratic reforms of Kleisthenes at Athens

499 BC – Ionian revolt begins

494 BC – Persian Empire defeats Greek Ionian fleet at Lade Gulf

491 BC – Demaratos exiled from Sparta; Leotykhidas becomes king

490 BC – Kleomenes dies; Leonidas becomes king of Sparta

490 BC – Persians invade Attika at Marathon

480 BC – Battles of Thermopylae and Salamis

479 BC – Battles of Plataia and Mykale

Main Characters

Aiskhylos
hoplite infantryman at Marathon and later a renowned playwright

Arimnestos
commander of the Plataian army at Marathon

Aristagoras
tyrant of Miletos and cousin to Histiaios

Aristides
commander of the Athenian division Antiokhis at Marathon

Artaphernes (the Elder)
Persian noble and one of the Six that put Darios on the throne

Artaphernes (the Younger)
son of the Elder and second in command of the Persian invasion forces at Marathon

Belos
uncle to Arimnestos the Plataian

Darios
King of the Persian Empire

Datis
supreme commander of the Persian invasion forces at Marathon

Hegesipyle
wife to Miltiades

Hippias
tyrant of Athens

Histiaios
tyrant of Miltetos and subject to Darios

Illyrios
slave to Miltiades

Kallimakhos
polemarkhos (warleader) of the Athenian army at Marathon

Kimon
son to Miltiades

Kleomenes
king of Sparta

Koinos
father to Arimnestos the Plataian

Kyra
sister to Arimnestos the Plataian

Lampon
best friend to Arimnestos

Metiokhos
son to Miltiades

Mikkos
younger brother to Arimnestos

Miltiades
commander of the Athenian division Oineis at Marathon

Themistokles
commander of the Athenian division Leontis at Marathon

Why sit you Doomed Ones?…all is ruined for fire and the headlong god of War, speeding in a Persian chariot, shall bring you low. – Prediction of the Delphic Oracle to the Athenians, 5th century BC

Chapter 1

The River Ister (Danube)—513 BC

Even in the middle of the day this country looked black to him: black trees swirling in black shadows and the raging waters of the wide, black Ister cleaving this landscape. Miltiades stood on the bank, rigged for battle in his bronze thorax and greaves, helmet pushed up to clear his face, watching the ships as they shivered in the current. Lashed together to span the river, they formed the only avenue of escape for the grand army of King Darios, Lord of Asia and Emperor of Persia; he had marched across two months prior in pursuit of the Skythians, a race of mounted warriors who had ravaged the frontier of his empire, and who now must submit to Darios' will or suffer annihilation. Miltiades laughed to himself as he untied the final knot in the leather strap that Darios had given him to count the days. He recalled the king's words as though he spoke them yesterday: "Sixty knots for sixty days. Untie one each day and if you should loosen the final one before I return, you Greeks may return home, your obligations to me fulfilled." He had debated with the others to cut the bridge of boats. Cut the bridge and his worries would be over. Cut the bridge and it would be the army of Darios that would suffer annihilation. But the others, Greeks though they may be, owed much to the Great King. Set up as tyrants along the coast of Asia, the Persians assured their rule. No, they would hardly chance leaving their fate up to the people of their cities. But with Miltiades it was different. Yes, he was lord of the Thrakian Peninsula, but he was placed in this land that his family had settled, and sent to rule it by his native city of Athens. The armies of Darios had swarmed over all the cities of the coast, his included, and asked only one thing of them—fight the Skythians. Darios had lectured them, "We Persians are of an ancient and noble race. Our rule is benign, like that of a father to his children, but if the Skythians ride against you, you will be nothing more to them than deer in the hunt. Any civilized man would follow me." Miltiades admired their culture and their refined ways, but he knew the Persians. They were all like a vast and powerful team of oxen yoked and under one whip— a whip wielded by a single man. They would drive under any who stood in his path. Athens' time would come.

"Riders!" bellowed Lykomedes from his perch in a towering pine. "Skythians!"

Miltiades grinned.

"Seems we will not have to cut the bridge," said Histiaios. "Perhaps the Skythians will do it for you."

Aristagoras moved next to them, shading his eyes as he peered out to the road on the far bank. He counted eight Skythians, and only eight, moving from the body of their cavalry toward the Greeks guarding the bridge, with which they conversed for a short while before trotting up and onto the bobbing pontoons. Miltiades bounded upon his horse, followed by Histiaios, Aristagoras and Strattis, the four Greek commanders on watch this afternoon, and rode out to greet them.

They wore high pointed hats, bright red leather trousers and goatskin boots that hugged their knees, riding horses that stood taller than Greek breeds. Their formidable bows were safely stowed in cases that bounced on their hips as they cantered into speaking range. Seven of the eight Skythians reined up, allowing a single rider to approach Miltiades. "I am known as Skopasis," the man announced in impeccable Greek, his speech incongruous with his appearance. "I bring you freedom. Leave this bridge, and its master Darios, to me. I know you pledged to guard it for him, but the sixty days has passed, and with it your oath."

Miltiades leaned towards Histiaios and whispered. "We must consent, if only for this moment, to avoid battle."

Histiaios peered across the Ister to the swarming barbarian horsemen. "Agreed," he admitted loudly for all to hear.

Miltiades looked to Skopasis. "How can any sensible man refuse such advice?"

These words brought a grin to the Skythian, revealing his peg-like yellow teeth framed by a flame red beard. His blue eyes gleamed like sapphires sunk deep into his leathery face. His knuckles, until this very moment whitened by a nervous grip on the reins, relaxed; he stroked the mane of his horse, caressing the chestnut hair before letting it fall from his fingers. "The man who taught me to speak your language was shrewd too, as it seems all you Greeks are." Now with a quick tug he spun his horse around then peered back over his shoulder to Miltiades. "I will remember you, Greek." Quickly he led the seven others off the bridge and to the body of anxious cavalry.

Miltiades trotted his horse beyond the midpoint of the bridge. He studied the barbarians as they counseled, hoping they would take him at his word and simply depart. From the shore he watched the modest shadows of afternoon stretch long then meld as the sun slipped behind the dark trees. The wind, a breath of Boreas, swept in from the north, reminding him how far he was from his true home. For over ten years he had lived in the north—on the Peninsula—and during times such as these would gladly trade all his land for a townhouse in Athens. But he thought again of Hippias the tyrant, master of his native Athens. At one time they were close, brothers-in-law in fact. A most politic marriage had been arranged between these two most politic families. Miltiades dutifully wedded the sister of Hippias, but soon after obligations compelled him to stand in for his brother as leader of the colony on the Peninsula. His new bride sailed with him, and persisted longer than any would have guessed, but after six years of yearning for her native city she abandoned husband and son. The divorce soon followed. Not long after Miltiades fortuitously arranged to marry the Thrakian princess Hegesipyle. An alliance with Oloros, her father, could only strengthen his hold on the Peninsula.

The thunder of hooves returned him to the present. Skopasis galloped off with his seven companions. Over five hundred Skythians, though, lingered at the far end of the bridge.

✳✳✳✳✳

Gobryas, commander of the first hazarabam of Persian cavalry, yelled for his men to reform. The dust smothered them, limiting vision to only a few meters, while the screams of frightened, disoriented men and the awful wails of dying horses magnified the chaos. The deadly hiss of a Skythian arrow slicing by his head compelled him to duck. Another one drilled by, thudding into a cavalryman riding next to him, who tumbled from his mount into certain death in the tumult of hooves below. Beyond the yellow haze that engulfed them he heard the hoots and war cries of the enemy, the thunder of charging steeds, the thwang of bowstrings and the sizzle of bronze arrowheads lacerating the air. Suddenly the pounding hooves of the Skythian warhorses faded. A breeze began to whisk away the dust. Around him dozens of his men lie dead in the trampled meadow, while beyond, far out into the plain, a fleeing cloud marked the Skythians. They struck quickly. And quickly they withdrew. Now he scanned the meadow, overlooking his own dead, searching for the unmistakable garb of a Skythian horseman. He trotted his mount in an ever-widening circle. Not one. Not a single Skythian corpse lie in this field laden with death.

"Lord Gobryas, the king calls for you. He calls for you now!" The rider's eyes gleamed wide and white, framed by the black scarf that covered his mouth, ears and head. Gobryas swung his whip hard into the horse's flank, breaking into a gallop, forcing men to leap out of his path. All through the meadows that bracketed this section of the road he passed the wounded, the dead, and the many that lingered in between, while still others collapsed from their burden of exhaustion. The attack had penetrated far into their column, to the Royal carriages and the bodyguard of Darios. The Immortals, the king's elite infantry numbering ten thousand, had formed a perimeter far out into the plain, enclosing them. One of the king's eunuchs raced toward Gobryas then tugged him on the arm, pulling him toward the Royal entourage. Linen parasols wobbled and jostled above the center of the gathering. Gold bands and jeweled necklaces jingled as the gaudily clad Persian nobles leaned inward, all trying to catch a glimpse of the Great King. The eunuch slapped at the onlookers with a horsetail flyswatter, parting them. Gobryas followed. Two young Spearbearers of the Immortals blocked their way forward.

Gobryas yelled, "Mardonios, step aside. You also Datis." The pair of Royal guards moved to open a path to Darios, who still braced himself on his war chariot, its four white Nisaean steeds being held to station by a pair of servants gripping their golden spiked war-bits. Gobryas bowed, touching his fingers to his lip as he knelt. All around stared at him in silence.

The king clapped his hands and a slave slunk forward clutching a hide-wrapped bundle. Carefully, he peeled away the covering to reveal a bird, a mouse, a frog and a clutch of five arrows.

"Gobryas, what do you make of these Skythian gifts?"

Gobryas slowly uncoiled from his crouch of obeisance, while reaching into the bundle with a gauntleted hand. He plucked up the dead bird, turned it over, doing the same with the mouse and frog, finally taking one of the arrows, and running his finger along its razored edge. He imagined its twin drilling into one of his cavalrymen. Artaphernes the Elder, advisor to the king, stepped forward. "Everyone here thinks these gifts are a sign that the Skythians are finished. What do you see, Gobryas?"

"I am no Magus, no soothsayer, no peddler of star-crossed predications, but after today's battle the meaning is clear, at least to me." Gobryas continued to study the arrow.

Artaphernes bobbed his head knowingly. "Enlighten us, then."

Gobryas grasped the arrow like a dagger and began to point at each item cradled in the slave's arms. "Unless we are birds and fly up into the air, or mice and burrow into the earth, or frogs and jump into the lakes and rivers, we will be shot dead with Skythian arrows."

All within earshot began to grumble at these words. Others loudly challenged Gobryas, shouting out that he was indeed no Magus but a soldier, and possessed no talents of augury or interpretation. Artaphernes bowed to Darios. "Truth may not always sound agreeable, but it must be heard."

Darios turned and began walking toward the cauldron that held the sacred fire of Ahura Mazda, god of light and truth. He was still a young man, physically powerful, with iron-gray eyes peering down at all who approached. The priests surrounded him as he stood astride the altar. He chanted his devotion and a prayer for guidance. Everyone gazed at the ceremony—everyone except Artaphernes. "Come with me Gobryas." The two men threaded their way through the hundreds of courtiers, servants and sycophants of the Great King and continued walking until they came to the outermost ring of soldiers formed by the Immortals. The setting sun set the plain ablaze and stretched their shadows, while to the east the night's first stars flickered low in the purple sky. The smell of wood-smoke wafted through the chilly air as the Persian army settled in. Hundreds of torches, spiked into the ground, ringed the colossal tent of Darios, while mules brayed, and horses snorted and neighed as farriers worked to tether them for the night. For a moment the battle faded from Gobryas' mind.

"They will return, and soon." Artaphernes' growling voice shook him. "And we must deliver our king from this cursed land."

"Lord Artaphernes, we as soldiers may do our part, but what will happen when we reach the Ister? We are not birds and cannot fly across, nor frogs and cannot swim to safety. Neither do I think we can burrow like mice. Without a bridge what hope have we?" He shook his head. "Do you really think the Greeks will remain a moment past the sixty days, a sixty days that passed with today's sun?"

"Gobryas, as long as we are alive there is hope. Fear not, for I have a plan, but it will take the both of us to convince Darios." He stroked his perfumed beard. "Are you with me?"

*****

"I must speak with the king," Gobryas pleaded. The two Spearbearers, Datis, and his own son Mardonios, stood at the entrance to the pavilion at attention, left foot forward, the golden, apple-shaped pommel of each spear resting upon the insteps of their felt slippers, bejeweled hands clamped fiercely upon the shafts. Neither would answer. "Mardonios!" he bellowed, standing but a hand's breadth away, "Do you heed the wishes of that eunuch before those of your own father—one of the Six?"

Datis glanced sideways at Mardonios, his fingers clenching the shaft of his spear tighter. Finally he broke from his stance. "Let him through. Bupares will never know." That was all Mardonios needed. He too moved away from the entrance. Gobryas breezed past them without another glance.

"Without doubt we will be punished." Mardonios warned, shaking his head at Datis.

"Why? Who will tell Bupares? Certainly not your father." Datis' composure began to slip away. He twisted his spear again.

"He would be the first to tell the King that we let him pass without proper orders. Each and every day he repeats to me what the great King Kyros told all his men—'learn to ride, shoot the bow, but above all else learn to tell the truth.'"

"Then what of our appointment to the Royal Cavalry?"

Mardonios face grew dark and grave. "That is a minor concern, for I am sure if we clash with these Skythians again, I will make a reputation that will erase such a minor offense. Then I pray, we fight again. And again. And each time my reputation will grow."

Datis, hardly unsettled by these words, smiled genuinely. "Truly now, our king will have two contenders for his praise. But do not stumble, for both my hands are full, and I cannot spare one to lift you up."

Gobryas suddenly flew from the pavilion, men rushing after him. The war drum pounded out the order to break camp, sending servants scurrying. Within moments, as though the command had preceded the messengers, tents collapsed as laborers withdrew their ridge-poles, while farriers tugged on the reins of prancing horses, queuing them up to receive riders. From the darkness beyond the ring of torches jogged Artaphernes toward the shrinking royal pavilion. Gobryas intercepted him mid-course and without a word squeezed both his shoulders as he looked eye to eye. They whispered together for a while, in words so hushed that neither Datis nor Mardonios could hear. Finally Artaphernes stepped away from Gobryas. "Tell the wounded what you please!" He stormed off leaving Gobryas standing and staring.

Datis trotted to him, maintaining the stiff aspect of a royal bodyguard. "What is happening?"

Oddly, instead of the attendants rushing about to extinguish all the cooking fires, they nurtured them—and kindled more. Only a very few tents, the ones belonging to the surgeons, still stood erect. Slaves scrambled to load the mules and oxen carts with the paraphernalia of the encampment. Dathaba, squads of ten soldiers, formed up, and marched to join their companies of 100. These, in turn, coalesced neatly into regiments numbering 1,000.

Gobryas finally turned away from the commotion of decampment to face Datis. "We leave tonight. But we must induce the Skythians to think otherwise. That is why they are lighting more fires."

"What of the surgeons' tents?" Datis pointed with his spear tip at the few canopies still billowing in the chilled night wind.

"They stay for the wounded."

Mardonios stepped close to Datis and whispered, "Things are more desperate than we could guess."

✳✳✳✳✳

"We have been all through this before," barked Histiaios. The feeble tongues of lamp-flame sputtered as the wind shook the tent. He leaned upon his left arm and swung both his feet onto the dining couch. The Thasian wine was running low so he ordered it to be thinned even more. It brought a muted smile to his face as he sipped. "Darios will return, and we must be here."

"We have kept our word to this king," countered Miltiades. "Leave him to Skopasis." Miltiades poked the olives in the bowl with an impatient finger, inspecting each one until he found the plumpest. He slipped it between his lips, chewing deliberately. *I miss Athens*, he thought to himself, as he tossed the pit onto the carpeted floor of the tent.

"And then what? You may have a hold on your city, but many of us would lose ours." Histiaios looked around, while most everyone else nodded in agreement. "Without Darios and his army behind us, I dare say the gates to our very cities would be bolted against us on our return." The tent flap snapped open suddenly. In strode Xenias the engineer attended by Illyrios, his servant and bodyguard. Histiaios shook his head. "Does that brute follow you everywhere?"

Xenias slid onto a dining couch while Illyrios loomed over him, his weaponless arms crossed, feet spread, as though the huge slave prepared to challenge any approach. "Are we still debating the fate of my bridge?" Xenias bobbed his head back and forth, trying to gain the attention of the wine servant. Before he knew what happened the wine servant was off the ground and gliding toward Xenias, the single hand of Illyrios depositing him before his master and his empty cup. Now all the other servants scurried forward, each presenting a platter, bowl or pitcher to Xenias.

"Now I see why," said Histiaios, chuckling. "Maybe your slave can work his persuasion on Miltiades here, and convince him not to destroy your bridge."

Miltiades raised his hands, as if to admit defeat. "It matters not to me if we stay here a while longer. The Skythians think we are dismantling the bridge. But do not ask me to send any of my men to fight them. Darios can have his bridge. Remember though, it is more than we owe him."

The night wore on like the sixty nights before: the flute players' enthusiasm faded along with the fires in the braziers; the drinking songs' lyrics plummeted to the ribald; the Thasian wine was replaced by a potent local vintage. By morning, the stench of vomit, stale wine, and discarded food scraps that littered the carpeted floor forced even the dogs out into the chill. Miltiades staggered to the entrance, and after minutes fumbling with the cord, finally freed the tent flap. The cold, clear air smacked him solidly as he stepped outside, reminding him of his forgotten cloak. Another step and a belly full of wine rushed up and out of his mouth in spasms. He bent over, hands clamped on his thighs as he convulsed, vomit roaring, until he was empty. Finished, he spit to clear his mouth and swiped his thick, dark beard clean with his forearm. By the faint light of the setting moon he spotted his felt hat upon the ground before him, plucked it up, sniffed at it before pulling it tight to his head. By the time he had reached the bridge the camp had come to life: chatter mingled with the sound of rushing water; his nostrils filled with the aroma of wood-smoke as it hung in the breezeless morning air; the yellow flames of cook-fires pierced the cold, blue shadows. Across the Ister smoke rose also, and the flames of a hundred fires sparkled in the camp of the Skythians. As Miltiades lowered himself into a crouch he scanned the ground before him. He plucked up several pebbles, and began to shake his hands as if he held two pair of knucklebones, finally tossing them out onto the earth before him. He shrugged his shoulders, as if to concede a poor throw, and then shouted to Xenias.

"Too much wine?" Xenias said through a tight-lipped grin.

"Not enough!" Miltiades, with an arm around Xenias' shoulder walked him out onto the shivering pontoons. "Our friends over there," he shouted above the roar of the great river below his feet, "unsettle me. We should give them good cause to depart." Miltiades spoke at length with Xenias, explaining how the bridge demolition should appear to take place. The Greeks would disassemble the far side of the bridge, ensuring first their own safety, and slowly continue on, removing pontoon after pontoon.

"Look," bellowed Xenias, as he pointed to the east and the golden disc of the sun with the tip of his spear.

"Now my friend, I must hurry to the morning sacrifice, while you must hurry to your task."

Outside the tent of Histiaios' they gathered where the mantis led a small procession toward the commanders. Behind him a young boy clad in a white chiton solemnly followed, clutching the tether of the white goat, while two servants cradling bowls, a wad of linen and a pitcher completed the retinue. Miltiades slipped in with the others, standing across the circle from Histiaios and his cousin Aristagoras—the two never separated. The mantis reached into a bowl and grabbed some barley, which he sprinkled atop the goat's head. He repeated this with water. Both times the victim obliged by shaking its head in affirmation. Histiaios wrapped his forearm around the beast's neck, yanking it tight to his chest while it kicked and bucked, until he could pins its rear legs with a knee. With an open hand he called for the knife. A smooth draw of the blade. He held tight while the beast convulsed and shivered before at last surrendering its final bit of life with an ominous hiss. The carcass fell from his arm as the earth turned black beneath it, blood coursing from the yawning slice in its throat. Miltiades peered over his shoulder at the altar and the crackling flames that roared up as the two slaves fed it. It worried him a little that he had given his order to Xenias before the morning sacrifice. It certainly would have worried him a great deal if the signs had been less than propitious. As the smoke of the sacrifice billowed skyward, to Zeus they all hoped, the gathering began to dissolve, each man wishing to take the akratisma meal prior to morning exercise. Before Histiaios could depart, Miltiades approached him. "I have ordered the demolition of the bridge." Histiaios' mouth opened, but not a word followed. Before he could speak Miltiades added, "Do not worry, my friend. When Darios arrives he will have his bridge to cross, and you will still have Miletos."

Histiaios was not one to be lectured to. "And you will have Elaios."
Miltiades shook his head. "In time Darios will have both—more."

* * * * *

They had marched throughout most of the night, but now, with the coming of a new day Darios the Great King, king of kings, lord of Persia and Media, master of nations, the son of Hytaspes, the grandson of Arsames the Achaemenid, prayed before the sacred fire of his god, the god of Zoroastra, Ahura Mazda. All around knelt, leaving Darios alone standing before the flaming altar. Datis craned his neck to watch the ceremony. The orange flames reflected wildly on the golden torques, jeweled bracelets and glittering rings that adorned the Great King. Reminded of the power of Ahura Mazda by this ritual, he began to stare at the scores of eight-rayed circles stitched upon his cloak, an emblem of his god and his allegiance to him. Above the chanting of Darios, the drumming hoof-beats of a single rider induced him to look back over his shoulder. Gobryas reined up at the perimeter of Immortals, waiting. Plumes of smoke and sparkling embers wafted up as Darios tossed a handful of incense into the flames. He raised both hands, as if to embrace the heavens, and then stepped up into his gold-posted carriage where Artaphernes drew the purple curtains, sealing the Great King from view. Gobryas' smile beamed. Artaphernes hurried to him.

"Splendid news, my friend," announced Gobryas. "We are less than a day from the bridge."

Artaphernes grin suddenly dissolved beneath his beard. He sighed. "This day would possess the most danger for us, I would think. Once we are across the Ister, the Skythians would be hard-pressed to follow."

Gobryas still smiled. He knelt, brushing away the stones and twigs to clear a bit of earth. The throat of his sword scabbard thwanged as he withdrew his akinakes, its golden blade gleaming, the ruby-eyed twin lions that formed its pommel snarling defiantly at him. He commenced to scratch out some lines upon the dark soil. "Look," he said to Artaphernes. "The road we took at the outset passes through these low hills, but my scouts have found another. They have ridden all the way to the Ister. That way, at least for now, is clear."

The Skythians had hoped to trap the Persians in these low hills between their main army and Skopasis' advance guard on the Ister. With the help of Ahura Mazda they could by-pass the ambuscade using this new route. The terrain would be difficult for the horses and wagons, but hardly so for the Persian infantry—men born to the mountains. The new orders were passed from the command staff of Darios to each regiment. Datis, along with

Mardonios and the hazarabam of Spearbearers, stood before Artaphernes awaiting their orders.

"Mardonios will command," barked out Artaphernes. "Spearbearers of the king, you will hold this end of the pass."

Datis' envy vanished quickly as the meaning of the order was realized. They would be the rearguard, the final sacrifice, all of whom would perish like their wounded the night previous to effect the retreat of Darios. His heart began to lighten. *His will be a brief command,* he thought, as he looked at a grinning Mardonios. They formed up by dathabam, units of ten men deep, and a hundred across, sealing the road that laced its way south between the cliffs. These Persian warriors stood in a gloomy defile, buried in shadows that only briefly departed at the height of day. After an hour, the last clang of yoke chains, the final hoof-beats, and the muffled chatter of men faded into the abyss of trees; only the rustle of the tree tops in the north wind cut the silence. Datis rested his scallop edged shield upon the ground, its royal emblem—the falcon—staring up at him with black, soulless eyes. Without thinking he bent to brush the dust from his blue felt slippers, and then lifted the shield again, satisfied that his appearance suited his station; if he should die, then he should die outfitted nobly, as an Immortal and kinsman to Darios. It was an honor to die for his king.

By evening the stiff stance of combat had been replaced by one of casualness. Men, here and there, sat upon the ground, while others trotted away from their files to piss away their fears, or simply restore movement to stiff limbs. Mardonios now looked to the standard-bearer, who raised the falcon pennant high above his head, while the drummer pounded out the signal. The two flanks poured rearward into the narrow pass, each file peeling away until only the three central dathaba remained. Datis stared long and hard northward, straining to hear the sounds of Skythian horse as they bore down on them. Instead, only the wind played upon his ears. His turn now come, he led his file southward, through the pass and toward the river, the bridge, and the safety of his homeland.

✳✳✳✳✳

Miltiades stood upon the bridge barking out orders to the workmen. "Slowly, now!" A squad of laborers tugged the leg thick flax rope free of the bobbing penteconter, while its pilot steered the ship, tracing the remaining sections of the bridge back to the southern bank. Far off, the rumble of horsemen echoed through the valley, marking by sound what the thick mist rising from the river tried to mask. Miltiades strained to see beyond this mist, both dreading and welcoming what might be thundering toward them. He kept to his task, shouting encouragements and instructions, feeling secure in the hundred-meter gap in the bridge that separated his men from the Skythian archers. Still, he could not see to the far side of the river, but knew by the roar of cavalry that the enemy began to line its bank. Now his attention was drawn to his side of the Ister and the labored breathing of a man as he splashed out of the river and up the embankment. The dark figure of a man jogged toward him. He reached for his spear, plucking it from the soggy turf, and lowered it.

"Put that away," barked the naked figure as he swept the point aside. "Those horsemen," said Xenias, as he slicked back his sopping curls, "are Persians. Seems the Skythians have departed."

Miltiades forced a smile. "Xenias, my friend, get the boats back in line. I am sure Darios will be in a hurry."

Xenias scraped the water from his arms and chest with the palms of his hands. "Illyrios!" His huge slave came lumbering out of the fog; he was clothed in hides, with a massive bear-fur cloak draped across equally massive shoulders. As soon as he caught sight of Xenias he trotted off toward their camp, soon returning with a cloak and chiton, both choked in the palm of a single hand.

"Cease strangling my clothes," yelled Xenias as he yanked them out his slave's grip. The slave stood there. Not a word. Not a shrug, nor a grin nor grimace. Not even a grunt. After Xenias slipped his chiton over his head, he looked to Miltiades. "We can have it back in place before midday." Xenias hurried off to the bridge with Illyrios following no faster than a plow after an apathetic ox, and with even less interest, it seemed, in his destination.

Miltiades watched the pair melt into the glowing fog before hurrying after. Before he could spot them shouts marked out where undoubtedly Xenias had found his workers. "Put it back together?" barked one of the Karian laborers. "I spent all night taking it apart." Another bridge man moved next to him nodding his head. Soon Xenias stood surrounded by a dozen burly laborers, all refusing to follow his command. Silently Illyrios shouldered his way through the ring of malcontents, moving to Xenias' right, all the while squeezing his paw-like hands into knuckle-whitening fists. The loud Karian suddenly fell silent. Illyrios edged closer to him. The Karian backed up, and so too did his companions.

"Are we prepared to get back to work, gentlemen?" Xenias waved his open hand toward the bridge as though he was introducing a guest at a symposion. Illyrios crossed his arms, elbows coming to eye-level with the Karian.

"Let's get to it!" yelled the Karian, as he turned away, carrying his band of malcontents with him.

Xenias walked to the very end of the bridge, then measured with his eye the distance to be spanned. The sun rose higher, and the day's heat with it, but the fog retreated reluctantly; by mid-morning he could begin to see the glitter of spears and war-bridles of the Persian cavalry on the far bank. A few of the Persians, the ones who knew Greek, had been shouting across the Ister the entire morning. Even with all their entreaties to hurry, his men worked as they always did—with purpose and precision. The helmsman on the penteconter warship yelled to the crewmen who scrambled over the bridge, cursing when they missed the lines cast to them, or exalting them when they finally tied off their ship in the long string of ships that bobbed and swayed in the swirling current of the Ister. Xenias watched as the last vessel slipped between the shore and the bridge. Men scampered aboard even before it was secured, dragging planks to form a temporary road, while others hurried to hang the huge hides that would screen the skittish horses and sumpter beasts from the spectacle of the fearsome waters of the river.

The Imperial cavalry crossed initially, followed by a company of Immortals, before the Royal carriages at long last rolled eagerly over the bridge. Miltiades, Histiaios, Aristagoras and the other generals gathered at the egress of the bridge, watching with pride as their work held. Darios and his entourage passed them by, with Gobryas the only one among the Persians who even dignified them with a nod of acknowledgment.

"See Histiaios, the gratitude of Darios." Miltiades rubbed the dust from his eyes. Aristagoras glared at his cousin.

✳✳✳✳✳

Datis pulled the bowstring back till it touched his ear. The arrow tip wavered with each breath as he honed in on the target, a small pomegranate wedged into the crook of a branch in a weather-twisted pine. He held his breath. The arrowhead pointed true. As he exhaled he withdrew his fingers from the string, liberating the eager arrow. It sliced through the air with a whisper, drilling dead-centered through the pomegranate, propelling it from the tree in a spray of crimson seeds. He smiled for a moment, satisfied with his aim, but the chill of the north wind on his bare chest and back quickly stole any pleasant thoughts.

Mardonios looked on. He did not smile before, during, or after the shot, but only when Datis' own smile was replaced with a scowl. "Come Datis. Our king has invited us to dine with the Greeks tonight."

Datis snatched up a piece of his target and began sucking the juicy seeds into his mouth. He chewed as he slowly twirled the crimson tipped arrow, then dropped it back into his gyrtos quiver, while Paramenes, his body-servant, approached with a sleeved cloak draped carefully over a palm-up arm. Datis waved him off. "I shall bathe first." Now he ambled toward Mardonios. "Shall I meet you there?"

"I have nothing better to do my friend, so I will wait in your tent, perhaps try a little of your wine, before accompanying you to the feast."

Paramenes shuffled ahead of them, snapping open the tent flap as he bowed. The two marched in. Before Datis could lower himself into a chair, the slave hurried to him. He knelt before his master, and pried each of his blue slippers off, and gathered up the trousers that Datis stepped out of as he moved to his bath. The tub itself had been a gift to his father, given by the Great King Kyros before he was born, and passed on to Datis for this expedition. He plunged one leg, then the next into the tepid water before lowering himself to a seat in the tub. Paramenes left the tent for only a moment, to return quickly with a steamy bronze pitcher. He poured the pitcher empty over Datis' back, shaking the lingering drops out, and before the any chill could afflict his master, began to stroke him dry with a lilac scented sponge. Datis closed his eyes as Paramenes emptied another pitcher of hot water over his head, leaving his imagination to return him to Persis and the estate of his father. It was the first day he had come upon the great bronze bathtub. Even though he now sat within it, his memory conjured accurate images of the crouched silver lions that served as feet to set the tub level. The likenesses incised and encircling it told the story of Kyros the Great, first king of the Persian Empire, and his victory over Kroisos the Lydian. He opened his eyes thinking there will be no bathtubs with Skythians carved upon them. Mardonios reclined quietly upon a divan, sipping wine from a plain wooden cup.

"Have one more cup, and I should be ready," Datis assured him as he stepped from the tub. Paramenes tipped a small flask, releasing a puddle of lilac oil into the palm of his hand, which he patted daintily onto Datis' back. He donned his leather trousers and sleeved cloak quickly. The slave deftly outlined his master's eyes with kohl before daubing a bit of ochre on his cheeks. Datis left all but two bands of gold still within the jewel chest, slipping on his favorites, one to each arm, but still had a ring for each finger and one for each ear also. "Paramenes, you shall stay here," is all he said as both Mardonios and he departed. He paused on the way to the king's pavilion, staring off into the darkness toward the unseen Ister. "Truly Mardonios, I did not think we would see this side of the river."

"I knew, without doubt, that we would be delivered," Mardonios boasted. Datis arched his eyebrows. "And how did you come to realize this?

"When I was born, a Magus read the stars at my mother's insistence. He revealed to her that I would lead a great army, defeat the undefeated, and be victorious so long as I could ride." Mardonios smiled confidently. "So the intentions of heaven protect me, and I you, my dearest friend."

Datis tried not to wince at these words. By no means were they dearest friends. They, by their families' high station, had become companions in arms in the Great King's bodyguard, two men who excelled at war, but two men who would defer to no other man but their king. They clung to each other knowing that without a rival, there can be no victory.

The feast was well under way by the time they had entered, the Greeks having brought with them musicians: flute-boys who cheeks bulged unbecomingly as they played; girl slaves who plucked solemnly on their kitheras, smiling but daring not to look up; garlanded women called *companions* tapping the krotala cymbals; thick-armed slaves banging out the rhythm on the tympano; the singers chanting the enkomion. Their music, although entertaining, sounded odd to him, but Datis took his couch, a goblet of wine, then began to peruse the sumptuous platters that servants presented to him, each accompanied by solicitous grins. The seating, as always, had been arranged by rank in the nobility of Persia. Gobryas, Artaphernes the Elder and the four other nobles who had helped restore the throne to the family of Kyros, sat closest to the Royal Presence. These men, the most trusted in the Empire, had been drawn to the Great King by a deed of murder. Darios and his six companions had uncovered an imposter, Smerdis the Magus, on the throne of Persia, and had quickly drawn their plans. They would, without compunction, kill him, but when the act had been finally committed it was Darios himself that plunged the blade of his akinakes deep into the belly of Smerdis, a victim held fast from escape by Gobryas. Even after these many years passed, anyone could see these Six formed an impenetrable circle that no man or god could undermine. Only these men sat in close proximity to Darios. A score of Greeks possessed the couches of honor, no doubt for their loyalty and in thanks for their robust bridge. Most of them smiled, except for one whose vacant expression glared from the chaos of revelers. "What is his name?" Datis whispered as he leaned toward Mardonios.

"The dark-browed Greek with curly hair?" Mardonios asked as he pointed with an empty goblet while wiping the wine from his beard with the swipe of his hand. "He is an Athenian. Miltiades, son of Kimon."

"By the look of him, you would think Skythians dined with him." Datis snatched a date from a passing platter. He touched it to his lips for a moment, to savor its sweetness, before slipping it into his mouth.

"It is said he wished to abandon the bridge," said Mardonios

Datis shook his head. "And where did you hear this? Another Greek, perhaps? Hardly a trustworthy race." He stared long and hard at the Greek called Miltiades.

Mardonios turned to Xenias as though he had ignored the conversation so far. "Greek, those bones you roll around in your hands. I understand they are employed in wagering…"

✳✳✳✳✳

Miltiades, never one to let an opportunity slip by, approached Xenias slowly. The engineer sat on the bank of the Ister, staring at the star-filled sky, his vaporous breath rolling from his lips and dissolving into the icy night air

"Upset by the wager?" Miltiades lowered himself onto the wet grass, taking a reluctant seat. It would be a small inconvenience.

Xenias turned. "A perfect throw!" He shook his head and repeated in a mumble, "a perfect throw." He rattled the knucklebones in his hand.

"Good god man, did you not think the Persians had played knucklebones?" Miltiades extended an open hand. "Let me see those."

Xenias poured the four bones into Miltiades' palm. He clamped his knees with his hands and stared once more at the sky. "We should have heeded your counsel, Miltiades. If we had, that damned Persian Mardonios would be turning on a Skythian spit, and I would be none the poorer."

"What's done is done," said Miltiades. "Pay up and forget about Mardonios." Xenias kept gazing up in silence. "You can pay it?"

"That is the issue, isn't it? I do not have two gold darics."

"An issue indeed." Miltiades tugged on Xenias' shoulder. "You do understand he is Mardonios, son of Gobryas, not some Sogdian herdsman. If he discovers you wagered in bad faith, well, maybe after twenty years of shoveling stable shit for him, he may consider the debt reconciled."

Xenias, his spirit roused, turned to face Miltiades. "What can I do?"

"Now my friend, compose yourself. I have the means to help you. I would ask a small favor in return."

"You would help?" Now Xenias' face transformed, momentarily dispatching dread and replacing it with desperate hope. "Name the favor, and it is yours."

"We will walk to my tent and I will give you two gold darics. You will return to yours and send Illyrios to me." Miltiades extended a hand, and without hesitation Xenias took it. "And give me those." He pointed to the knucklebones in Xenias' hand.

Chapter 2

Plataia, north of Athens—510 BC

The town hugged the foothills of Kithairon like a dog at his master's feet, its wall peering north toward the trickle of a river named the Asopos. A few miles further, and beyond sight, loomed the city of Thebes, and all around smaller villages loyal to her. Plataia stood alone. And when the Spartans under King Kleomenes marched to their town in years gone by, the Plataians asked him for Sparta's protection. Mighty Sparta, the land of invincible warriors! Kleomenes, a king but as practical a man as any other Spartan, proclaimed he was honored by this request, but in truth could not help them, for his own city was far off in the heart of the Peloponnese. He endorsed the Athenians. They were nearby, not much more than a day's walk away, and indeed they had even less affection for the Thebans. But thorny crested Kithairon rose like a great stonewall separating these two allies. It was only on rare occasions that Plataians wended their way over the Oaks-Head Pass and to the city of Athena. And today was certainly special. Arimnestos, now entering his sixth year, would leave the care of his mother and sisters to join the world of men. His father and uncle had loaded the wagon with several bales of sheep's wool and he would ride with them to the agora of Athens.

To him it seemed like he had not slept at all, for the sky revealed not the slightest hint of day as he searched the east beyond the village of Erythrai. Persephone had been abducted, pulled beneath the earth by gloomy Hades and with her went the warm, long days of summer; her bright smile had been replaced by winter's dark, and the icy breath of Boreas. The journey would be long, and daylight precious, so they hoped not to spend any of it until they cleared the head of the pass. Arimnestos tugged on the necklace of amulets and charms that his aunt had hung around his neck before leaving home. He fancied the one of blue glass, the one, he had been told that matched the color of his own eyes. "It wards off the Evil Eye," she said as she caught him staring at the magic bobble. His uncle Belos walked in front of the donkeys, tugging on the single lead as his father chatted with him; Arimnestos sat on the front edge of the wagon, nestled between the warm bales of fleece, for it was designed for cargo, not passengers and had no seat and afforded little comfort. At the outset he had declined the wagon, insisting on strolling with the men, but his protest had been short-lived; his father whirled him off the ground and tossed him in with the wool as soon as they rolled onto the road. As they crawled higher into the pass, he grew thankful, for now he sat wedged between the bales, insulated from the gnawing wind, soothing sleep finally recapturing him.

"Wake up." His father nudged him with the thumb-stick he had been using to encourage the donkey. "The sun!"

The wagon wheels groaned on the hard packed road as his uncle and father worked to steady the donkey. He stood up, his bare feet wobbling on the narrow strip of wood that spanned the front of the wagon. The plain below glowed in the red-gold light of dawn while the ridge of Mount Aigilaos underlined the brightening sky. Amongst the trees he recognized the handiwork of men, the striated fields, and the warm, orange roof tiles of the scattered farmhouses poking above the frosty mists.

"Is that it? " Arimnestos covered his brow with a salute, searching out the plain. He had spotted the painted marble of temples in the midst of more densely packed houses, all not far from the glistening sea.

"That is sacred Eleusis," instructed his father. "Well beyond that is Athens."

Now the descent from the pass proved treacherous and far more taxing than their climb. Both men had to work the wheels, acting as brakes, but even still the donkeys skidded and stumbled every so often when gravity overmatched them all. It was here that one of the animals, in a fit of panic, caught Belos with a reflexive kick just below the knee. He crumbled to the road in pain, but would not let on. He sat for a moment and rubbed his leg.

"Stupid, am I," he mumbled as Koinos knelt to help him. His brother tried to peel away Belos' hand from the wound, but he snapped, "It's nothing. Just a reminder to be smarter than a donkey." Belos eased himself up, using the wagon's frame and Arimnestos' shoulder to steady him. "Try that again, and I'll rap you," he growled at the beast as he feigned a kick of his own.

When they approached a level portion of the road, both his father and uncle would let loose the wheels and the donkeys, sending Arimnestos and the wagon careening until the grind of the stony road and the lack of slope slowed them. As they continued their descent they lost sight of Eleusis and soon the entire Thriasian plain, becoming engulfed in the forest of plane, ash and oak that extended over the lower slopes. Once upon the plain they fell in with others, some who like them, had wagons of fleece, which they assessed with furtive glances, while others plied carts crammed with amphorai of oil or wine, but many of them walked along with nothing to sell. *Maybe buyers*, thought Koinos, *but more likely they were on their way to the festival of Pompaia.*

The road swerved lazily into the sacred town of Eleusis, skirting the precinct of the holy place of the Mysteries where a high wall and gated road keeps out the curious traveler or casual passer-by. By the time they had arrived in the town, the festival of Pompaia had been long underway—the ram had been sacrificed, its blood had stained the altar of Zeus Meilikhios, and the procession had wended its way to the western hill of the acropolis.

"We'll take the wagon over there," instructed his father as snapped the reins to quicken the donkeys, while Belos and Arimnestos pushed lazily from behind. Eleusis was not a large town, smaller even than their modest home of Plataia, but its buildings sparkled with richly painted columns, pediments and antefixes—even the inns, constructed mostly for pilgrims to the Well of Maidens, were finely appointed. Belos hobbled off to inquire about beds and a meal for the trio while Koinos and Arimnestos led their team and wagon into the gated stable-yard.

A young boy, maybe a year or two older than Arimnestos, hurried to assist. He scrambled on all fours to unhitch the animals then led them, one by one, to a water trough and manger. "You missed it," he said as he passed by Arimnestos, "but you can stand on the fleece. The sun is still up." He looked up quickly to the still bright evening sky.

"Why would I want to do that?" Arimnestos shouted after the boy. "I have been with fleece all day long."

The stable boy executed a single exaggerated step. "It brings good luck to stand on it. Blessed by Zeus himself, it is." Now he slapped his thigh and stomped his bare left foot. "But only if you step on it with this one."

Belos limped slowly out of the inn, and yelled, "They have a bed for us." As he stood next to Arimnestos he placed a well-callused hand on the boy's shoulder, partly out of affection, but partly to take a bit of weight off his injured leg. "I will be back for our dinner." Belos hobbled off toward the acropolis and the pilgrims queued up to be blessed by the fleece.

"Father, can we go too?" said Koinos.

Koinos smiled. "Why not? I think we all can do with a little help from Zeus the Kindly."

At that Arimnestos raced after his uncle, catching up quite soon. From behind, he could see his uncle's shaky limp and also see a huge red lump swelling on his calf. "Come uncle," he said as he slipped a shoulder under Belos' arm as a crutch. "The fleece will heal your leg."

Belos leaned a bit more than he wanted to upon his nephew's shoulder, for the pain was worsening. "The fleece didn't do much for him," he mumbled beneath his breath as they passed the blood stained altar and the black-eyed head of the sacrificed ram.

"Did you say something, uncle?" Arimnestos craned his neck. His uncle shook his head. They slowly made their way up the hill, following the other pilgrims. Now he could see the sacred fleece, pegged to the earth and flanked by two incense burners. The resinous scent filled his nostrils as they approached. "Remember uncle, only your left foot."

Belos kicked his sandal off and a boy pulled his bare foot gently into a basin of water as he done a hundred times or more this day. But he interrupted his cadence as he spotted the bruised leg of Belos, keeping his foot submerged noticeably longer than any other, finally pulling it free of the basin. Arimnestos snapped up the sandal and shouldered his uncle along. Belos peered down and mumbled a prayer while hesitatingly lowering his foot onto the fleece, as though he expected it to be very hot, or very cold, imbued with something from the world of the gods and foreign to the touch of men. The priest waved him on, where he folded to the ground, trying to hide the grimace of pain from his nephew. He managed to summon a grin as he reached for his sandal, tied it quickly, then looked up at Arimnestos and said, "I am hungry."

Koinos grabbed his brother under each arm and hoisted him to his feet. "You need to rest that." Belos wobbled down the hill, his brother on one side and his nephew on the other, each trying to help, but he swatted away any kind hand or comment, refusing to admit that his injury was anything more than a nuisance.

While still on the hill they could see into the sacred precincts of the temple of Demeter, to the Telestrion and just outside of it the Well of Maidens. Before Arimnestos could ask the question his uncle piped up, "yes, my boy, that is where the goddess spoke to the grand-daughters of Eleusis."

With each step in their descent Arimnestos kept his eyes locked on the well, hoping to see her, sacred Demeter, certain that he would see something holy, something precious, something that anyone could see if they only kept their eyes to it. Soon the rising wall of the temple swallowed up his vision. Now all he could think of was his supper. It had been a grand day, full of new sights. But tomorrow would prove grander indeed. Tomorrow they would be in Athens.

✳✳✳✳✳

Arimnestos staggered from the inn into the stable yard rubbing the sleep from his eyes. There his father tugged one of the donkeys toward the wagon, while his uncle worked on the grass ropes that secured the bales of wool. He studied his uncle—each step, each shuffle, each stride—to see if the charmed fleece had done its work. Belos hardly limped. He ran over to his uncle. "The fleece!" he shouted, pronouncing the miracle.

Belos fumbled with the knot, his thick fingers not suited to disentangling the twisted rope. "That, plus a tight bandage and a smudge of myrrh."

Now Arimnestos could see clearly what his uncle spoke of. His leg, from knee to ankle, was wrapped in linen. A foreign smell, like pine needles but different somehow, hung about him, overpowering even the dung of the animals. His nostrils flared at the strange scent.

Arimnestos climbed up into the wagon, wriggled in between the bales where he waited for his father and uncle to return from the morning sacrifice. They had little money, so they cut some wool from a bale and took it to the altar. Koinos tossed it onto the flames sending their prayer to Demeter skyward, while Belos poured the small portion of wine into the earth at the foot of the altar, their gift to Hermes. Now Koinos looked to graying the sky. The sun had just pierced the horizon and he spotted only a few wispy clouds. "Thank you." Soon they had rolled onto the Sacred Way, the processional route of the Athenians through the Thriasian Plain to the city.

As Helios arced high in the iron gray sky, a tall hill, crowned with painted buildings—temples for certain—came into view. "That, my boy, is Athens!" declared his uncle.

More and more the road grew crowded. Up ahead, low hills spread out from the brick and stone walls of the city, and amongst these sprouted stone pillars, sculpted slabs, and blocks of dazzling marble. The road brought them between these gentle slopes, and here the stones revealed their true nature. Arimnestos, still unable to read, could not decipher the carvings, but he knew men had made them. His father pointed to a stumpy column and read from its inscription, "Aktion, son of Thrasylos."

"What is it," asked Arimnestos.

"A stone for the dead. We are in the field of graves. Whisper, and do not cause them to stir."

His father's words fell on him like a cold hand. He shivered. Now he ceased looking at the stones at all, but kept his eyes on the twin towers that flanked the double gate marking the end of the road. To him it seemed every man and woman alive must be streaming to these open gates and into the great city of Athens. More people had passed by them here in a short hour than he had seen in his entire young life in tiny Plataia. Now he stared up at the huge cross beams that spanned the opening as they passed beneath. His eyes moved to the great hinge pins on the top of both gates, each slick and shiny with olive oil, which had streaked the bronze skin that sheathed the gate's wooden core. Once through and inside they found themselves amongst ramshackle shops, smoky manufactories and open sided potters' sheds. Still the crowd, which they now had become part of, surged forward. Ahead of them the stream of people began to part. A man ran amongst them screaming, his words swallowed by the chatter of the mob. Finally one single word shot through the air—"Spartans!"

Arimnestos' uncle shouldered his way through the swirling crowd to the man. Both he and his father watched as his uncle grabbed him by his shoulders, forcing him to stop, look, and finally speak Arimnestos nor his father could discern a single word over the roar of the crowd, and only watched as the man gestured wildly at Belos.

"There may be other things on people's minds than wool," quipped his uncle as he moved in next to the wagon. "The Spartan king Kleomenes is in the city with his army."

Suddenly the crowd began to shout, not in terror as the Plataians had expected, but seemingly in joy. A boy jumped into the bed of an empty wagon, flute in hand, and began to belt out a tune that others added words. Soon hundreds around them danced about in wild celebration. Arimnestos' father tugged on the arm of a passer-by. "What about the Spartans?" he asked.

The man, red-faced from screaming lyrics, returned the question, "What about the Spartans?"

"You dance about and your enemy is in the city. Have you all gone mad?" Arimnestos' father waved his hands in the air in disgust while Arimnestos himself slid across the wagon, then leaned out, almost into the stranger's face, awaiting his response.

With a huge grin the man said, "Kleomenes and his Spartans are our liberators. They freed us from Hippias."

"The tyrant?" shouted his uncle, trying to be heard above the boisterous mob.

"Hippias, his wife, sons and daughters. The whole lot of them sent packing by Kleomenes." Finished, the man threw his arms up and joined in with the raucous dance. Over and over the words burst from the tumult—"Hippias is gone! Hippias is gone!"

Arimnestos, overcome, looked at the riotous celebration, people abandoning reason, he thought, shouting, leaping, singing—all because of the departure of a single man. "Hippias," he mumbled as he watched it all. "They must despise him."

Chapter 3

Susa, court of King Darios—509 BC

Darios reposed above them all on a tall throne fashioned for a tall man and both made taller by the tiers of marble stacked beneath. Two slaves stood behind him, gently moving the air with floppy, scallop-shaped fans, while Bupares, his horsetail whisk in hand, snapped at any fly that would dare approach the Royal Presence. The eunuch hovered near Darios, looking down his tapering, pointed nose at each solicitant, his wispy, adolescent-like beard a contradiction to his age. Courtier after courtier, petitioner after petitioner held brief audience. The king discharged his duties perfunctorily, listening without expression then whispering to Bupares, who, in turn, relayed Darios' words to a gaggle of scribes: two wrote in Elamite, two in Aramaic, at least three in Persian, and finally one each scribbled in Egyptian and Ionian Greek. There was a certain order to it all, a hierarchy of petition. Foremost and first in precedence were complaints of a religious nature, the desecration of shrines, pilfering of thank offerings to Ahura Mazda, or any other god that the vast and varied population of the Persian Empire worshipped. Secondly, complaints of abuse by his majesty's officials were entertained. If Bupares knew the culprit and disliked him he most assuredly supplemented any evidence against him, embellishing the testimony as recorded by the Royal secretaries. On it went, from mid-morning until late afternoon, until finally the appointed time of the ambassadors arrived. Once the internal affairs of the empire were dealt with, the king felt at ease with discussions of foreign nations, ambassadors, and the ever-present influx of the disenfranchised or exiled, men who would provide insight, albeit with their own motives, to their native land—land that might soon fall under the reign of the Great King Darios.

Gobryas entered the immense throne room, marching confidently at the head a small procession of foreigners. He approached Darios solemnly. Upon reaching the stairs leading up to the throne he knelt, bending forward while spreading his arms, his face almost scraping the thick carpet stretched out before him. The foreigners behind him looked at each other somewhat puzzled. The courtiers in their proximity scowled at them. A rumbling of whispers percolated through the great hall.

Gobryas drew himself up. "Your majesty, forgive our guests. They are strangers to our land and unaccustomed to convention."

Darios, for the first time all day, summoned expression. He grinned then laughed. "They are Greeks. That is excuse enough for this rude behavior."

Gobryas turned to face the small party and stated quietly, "Great Darios will grant your favors, but he will require something in return. You must pledge fealty."

"Father, I refuse to bow to any man. He is not a god, nor a hero," growled Thessalos, Hippias' son, as his face flushed with rage. He fought to keep his words quiet.

Hippias stepped forward. He did not kneel, but simply bowed his head while touching his brow.

"That is a start," said Darios as he waved him forward.

Gobryas moved with Hippias, all the while staring at Bupares, who nervously flicked his flywhisk to and fro. "Your majesty, this is the man I told you of, the Athenian Hippias."

"Ah, Hippias," said Darios as he fingered the curls in his beard. He reached into the cavernous sleeve of his robe and pulled out a perfumed scarf, quickly burying his nose in it. "And what favors do you seek from us?"

Hippias shuffled forward, adjusting the folds of his himation cloak on his left arm. "Great King, I come to you as a suppliant, seeking your protection." Gobryas, acting as interpreter, conveyed these words, and more, to Darios

"The Great King grants you his protection," said Darios as he sniffed through his handkerchief. He arched his eyebrows, awaiting an answer. Gobryas repeated Darios' words in Greek adding, "and you must, by custom, offer something in return."

Hippias said only one word—"Athens!"

There was no need to interpret. Darios' lips turned up ever so slightly, part grin, part smirk. He called Gobryas closer and whispered to him.

"Hippias, the Great King Darios says you are welcome in his land, and shall be attended to by a Persian of noble birth, to instruct you in our language and customs. When you have learned all of this, return here and speak with him directly." Gobryas' eyes scoured the great hall, or apandana as the Persians call it, until they found Datis. He waved him forward. "Datis, a nobleman of Persia and captain of Immortals shall supervise your instruction." Datis dipped his head, acknowledging his charge, while at the same time barely glancing at Hippias and the other Greeks. Hippias, following Datis' lead, backed away slowly from the throne, turning away only when the customary steps had been taken.

Gobryas hurried after them, catching up outside the apandana and on the sun-soaked marble stairs that spilled down toward the Gate Road. "Do not worry, my friend. You will have scribes to assist you, and a Lydian slave who speaks both Greek and Persian. Your task is to find out what this Greek truly knows." Gobryas turned toward Hippias' son, who he caught staring at him. "What is it? Are you afraid that someday you will dress, talk, and even think like us?" He stroked his beard confidently. "Do not worry Greek, for I think we may never civilize you."

✱✱✱✱✱

Datis and Hippias did not linger overmuch in Susa. The high heat of summer sent the Royal court north to the cool mountains and the summer palace of Ekbatana, while they traveled west along the Royal Road. The journey spanned almost three months, but proved tolerable due in no small part to the excellent Persian roads. Even so, Hippias and the other Greeks with him exhibited nothing less than awe at the meaning of this excursion— three months from Susa to the sea, three months across lands that composed only a fraction of Darios' empire.

But the Persians, a people obsessed with order, insisted upon a most orderly road system. Almost magically to Hippias, at the end of each day's trek their caravan would come to another pirradazis or postal station, a place where imperial couriers would pass on, in relay, official correspondence. As the Persians say, the arm of the king is long and it stretches to the limits of his empire by these roads. Each pirradazis was sumptuously stocked; maza barley cakes, cardamum, boiled meat, various types of citrus, and date wine comprised the typical fare. They journeyed without much discomfort, three months and more passing quickly on the road flowing with trade, talk, and a constant parade of bizarre animals tended by even more bizarre men.

Hippias was installed as master of Sigeion, a town not distant from ancient and hallowed Troy. But in truth Datis commanded, while educating Hippias and his family to Persian custom. The Athenian proved slow to learn his lessons, while on the other hand Datis mastered Greek quickly both in the spoken and written word, learning idiom and expression, so that all were impressed with his progress. In five short months he had become fluent in Attic Greek. Here at Sigeion a caravan passing from the coast on the way to the heart of the empire stopped. Here Datis became reacquainted with another Greek. Histiaios, guardian of the bridge over the river Ister, had unfortunately gathered the attention of one Megabazos, general to Darios, and his commander in Thrake. Histiaios had collected his reward from Darios—rule over the city of Myrkinos, but at the same time proved so competent at supervising its defense and so expert at extending his influence far beyond its boundaries that Megabazos grew worried. Megabazos also conveyed his concern to Darios. By all honor Darios could not bring down such a man, one who had at least outwardly displayed unwavering loyalty, so instead of banishment or death he summoned Histiaios to court, to enter his circle of close and trusted advisors. Here Darios could keep more than one eye on this ambitious Greek. Datis, innocently enough, arranged the meeting of the two, a good deed to friends of the Great King and a chance for him to test his Greek.

The acropolis, modest in height and not much taller than the grain tower of a farmhouse, nudged the west wall of the town, itself wrapped in another wall of mud brick piled on stone. From here Hippias took his abode, preferring to sleep safely above his adopted subjects. Here also the symposion of the two Persian guest-friends met.

Hippias, along with Datis, insisted that the furnishings reflect those of Miletos, Histiaios' former city. The dining couches had few pillows, and the serving ware was from Lesbos, red figures painted and incised upon an indigo baked clay surface. Only themes of festival cavorted upon them—no Akhilles nor Hektor, no Ares nor Apollo, not a hint of struggle, for Dionysos, god of wine and madness, adorned every pitcher, kylix and serving platter, surrounded on each scene by thyrsos-bearers and bountiful vines. Although Datis retained his Persian dress of trousers and sleeved cloak, in all other things he imitated the two Greeks. He had allowed himself to be crowned with a garland of hyacinth, held his bread with the left hand, reserving the right for food picked from the amply stocked platters, and drank not from deep golden goblets but sipped his wine from a saucer-like kylix.

Histiaios stared long at Datis, impressed with his manner, but also by something else. "Lord Datis," he said, still studying him, "have we met before?"

Datis nodded. "We have, in a time gone by, been together in the same place, in the company of the same king, while confronting the very same foe, but we did not meet."

An aspect of recognition transformed Histiaios' face. He pointed at Datis with his kylix. "The Ister! You were an officer in the guard of Immortals."

"You flatter me with your recollection, sir. The only Greek that I can put name to face is the one called Miltiades."

Histiaios smirked. "It is strange that of all of us you would remember the one singularly disposed to do you the most harm."

Datis did not answer him straight away, but tipped his empty kylix over and began to study the bottom of the stem. "You Greeks if anything are extraordinary, for who else but a Greek would carve such a thing own his own cup?" Now he held up the kylix for all to see, but without close examination the words remained obscure to them all. "The inscription reads, 'Made by Euphronios, one that Pheidon could not manage.'" He tossed the cup to Hippias. "Who but a Greek? I think it is something that Miltiades would write, not upon a cup, but upon his deeds."

Hippias smiled politely. "He should concern you no more. He is in no position to help Athens, or himself for that matter. The Skythians hardly forget an ally and most assuredly never forget an enemy. Skopasis will remember Miltiades."

"You Greeks are so quick to turn on each other, my friend Hippias," said Datis. "Your only hope as a people is for Persia to unite you."

Histiaios laughed. "I think in the end you will unite us, but not in the manner that you think. Nor by the deed you have in mind."

"Oh come now. The Great King rules over Ionia and all the Greek therein. I do not see your brothers from the mainland rallying to liberate you. My good fellow Histiaios, you would tremble at this emancipation of your countrymen, would you not? For why else did you hold the bridge over the Ister?"

"You, sir have conjured your answer to that and there is nothing I could say to induce you to reconsider. Eventually the Greeks will take arms against you because they like to fight. It is as simple as that."

Datis rose from his couch, simultaneously his servants scurried into position: one for his wine cup; another for his cloak; still another clutching his peaked cap. "I am going to afford myself the luxury of a stroll through the paradeisos. The gardens are lovely during a full moon. I invite you to join me. Or if you prefer stay here and talk to each other about the barbarian Persian."

Datis slipped into his embroidered cloak then strode through the doorway, his parade of servant hustling after him.

Histiaios got up slowly meandering toward Hippias' couch, pausing to inspect the food on one table or pretending interest in the amount of wine in the cup on another, tossing a clever comment to each one he passed by. He sat opposite, leaning forward to speak. "Neither of us wants to remain in Persia as part of Darios' menagerie."

Hippias looked around, his eyes locking on the two guards at the doorway. He knew they spoke Greek, for a few days past he tossed them a mouthful of insults; they, in murmurs, returned them. "Believe me; I more than suggested to Darios the trouble the Greeks would pose to him if they remained independent. He laughed and told me, 'with every campaign there is a cost and a benefit. My cost, as always, would be the lives of my subjects. There is only one benefit in conquering Hellas—and I do not fancy olives.'"

Chapter 4

509 BC—Elaios, on the Peninsula

Early in the morning, while the sky was still dark and drained of color, before Helios rises and the mists have seeped ashore from the Hellespont, Miltiades had departed to inspect the new warehouse at the great dock of Elaios. As he left his grand house in the city, others rushed past him into the courtyard where the omphalotomos, or mid-wife, waved at them, chattering, "Which room?" One of the servants bounded up the stairs then swung open a door at the top. The mid-wife stopped to inspect the doorposts and lintels. "More pitch! Or do you intend to fill the house with evil daimons?"

Illyrios snapped up the cauldron of pitch and began swabbing the wooden framework. The pungent, resinous aroma drifted to Miltiades, filling his nostrils, and staying with him long after he had swung the courtyard gate shut. His wife Hegesipyle had gone into labor not but an hour earlier. Miltiades had to plan his day, keep it full, being sure not to return until the child had been born.

Now the problem rose up from the depths of his thoughts to unsettle him. If a girl it would be a small concern, for he could call for ekthesis, or exposure of the infant as was his right as father and head of the household, but if it a boy, how would he bring him to Athens to be acknowledged by his tribe. Without this he would be no citizen. Then he remembered the rumors. Hippias, his enemy, had been banished from Athens. He could go home, he reasoned, but here at the Hellespont he was master of a city and lord of all the Dolonki tribes; in Athens he would be one of many, with sway over his house and family only. He knew his countrymen, and he knew they would never again submit to rule by a single man.

Near the stables a groom stood, gripping the bridle as he stroked the horse reassuringly. Another servant presented his hands, eight fingers weaved, as a step for Miltiades. Around them, five mounted and armed horsemen, part of Miltiades' personal guard, pulled tightly on their reins, exerting their wills over the skittish horses that struggled to prance, to trot, to gallop—anything but to remain penned in the stable-yard. Propelled upon his mount by the servant's two-handed boost, he wriggled into position and opened his mouth to give the order to ride.

"Father!" The gate exploded open, and in the portal stood his eldest, Metiokhos, clutching the silver bridle Miltiades had given him upon his tenth birthday. "May I ride with you?"

Miltiades nodded. "Hurry, though, for we cannot wait." He rapped his heels into the bulging sides of his horse, sending it into a brisk canter, out of the stable-yard and onto the main road of Elaios. His bodyguard poured out through the gate, being sure to keep close, the measured gait of their horses and the even intervals providing an air of procession. They all wore armor, shining bronze breast-plates that were formed to fit a seated man, kopis swords clanging at their sides, while bundles of cavalry javelins rustled in quivers slung behind them. Quickly, they scattered, as Metiokhos whipped his horse to a gallop, trying to catch his father. Miltiades turned as his son pulled up beside him. "You may ride with me, but you must follow behind, a guard in front and a guard behind." Metiokhos' grin reversed to a scowl.

As Miltiades rode through the streets, the locals dipped their heads in respect, some jumping out of the way in exaggerated fashion to exhibit to their master extreme deference as he passed. But with the Athenian colonists it was different. Some looked at him, but with hardly a visage of respect. Others looked through him, as though he was a mist, vapor or other formless apparition. No, for now he would remain in Elaios. The few Athenians he encountered reminded him of what power he would forfeit on returning to his home city. Here he was a virtual king, accountable to no one but himself. In Athens he would be just a man contending with others, and there were the rumors of more Athenians, men of lower station, clamoring for a voice, a say, a bit of control in their lives and the life of their city. He rode on.

The work on the warehouse was hardly complete, so there was less to inspect than he would have liked, and his discussion with the master carpenter consisted of more bowing by the man than any expressed words; he should have come without his bodyguard, but this was Elaios and not Athens, a wild place surrounded by wild men, where might stood surrogate for law.

For a moment, and only a moment, he longed for a sharp-tongued Athenian riposte.

Mercifully, his inspection of the docks had exhausted the morning, and he knew that several hours could be spent circling the city's walls, so he took the road away from the waterfront and back into the heart of the city, to the agora, and beyond to the north towers. Here farmers ambled in through the yawning gates, choking on the dust of teamster driven wagons of timber. A band of spear-clenching mercenaries skulked alongside a cart of gold from the Peninsula mines, causing each man in Miltiades' escort to calmly slide a hand from reins to sword-grip. Hurrying by them all, a goatherd snapped a thumb stick to persuade his moiling herd.

After exiting, he turned around to gather in the gatehouse. Yes, the flanking towers stood tall, nearly 24 cubits, or the height of four men, but the walls hardly seemed formidable. He yanked gently on the reins, veering right. While circling the city, he noticed here and there fissures in the rocky foundations, and the dust of crumbling mud-brick that capped the walls. "It will keep out bandits at least," he mumbled as he reached forward to rub the neck of his horse. By the time he had finished his circuit, the sun barely hung above the low hills to the west, and the forest beyond had swelled with shadows. "Time to get you home, Metiokhos."

With the onset of dusk one of the twin gates had been swung shut, and in the towers flickered a pair of torches each. The traffic to the agora had dwindled to nothing, while here and there the sound of shutters slamming closed announced the end of business for another day. *It must be over*, he thought. But even still he kept his horse to the slowest canter, making way for anyone that crossed his path, until inevitably he came to the gate of his courtyard. His heart began to race at the sight; there, in plain view and for all to see, dangled a token of wild olive, a huge branch in fact. "Look father! It is a boy!" yelled Metiokhos, pointing to the branch.

Illyrios stood at the foot of the stairway, silent, arms crossed, guarding the cauldron of pitch. As Miltiades entered, the slave bent to snatch the container of resin. "Enough. You have done more than a good job." Miltiades grinned. "No spirit could get past all of that." He swept his hand around the entire courtyard, acknowledging the oozing pine pitch that coated every lintel and frame in the house. From the closed door of the women's quarters he heard the shivering wail of a newborn. Before he could make the landing all was quiet. He nudged the door open, only enough to poke his head in. His eyes were first drawn to the figure of Hegesipyle, her rusty hair spilling freely about her shoulders, as she lay propped upon the sleeping pallet by a bundle of Carthaginian pillows. Miltiades winced. They had cost him more than a few amphorai of oil, these pillows. His wife smiled at him as he entered, directing him with her eyes to the slave-nurse sitting upon the stool near the window. She cradled what looked like a bundle of linen, only the reddened face of the infant visible through the swaddling cloths. He lifted a small oil lamp from the table near his wife and crept toward the slave-nurse. She rocked the baby gently, murmuring softly some Thrakian lullaby. The infant slept soundly now, its mouth puckering instinctively as though it was nursing. He smiled, more than he would like anyone to see then whispered, "Kimon." In the doorway and not daring to enter hovered Metiokhos, swaying on tiptoes to catch a peek of the baby.

✳✳✳✳✳

"A day and not more!" The messenger from the frontier gulped for breath, his chest heaving, his hands shaking on the reins.

Miltiades raised his hand, still clutching his riding whip, the rings on each finger flashing wildly in the midday sun. The news had caught him unaware, extinguishing what little patience he possessed toward his inferiors. "I need facts, not hysterical rumor!" He lashed the courier once and once only, before reason compelled his to stop.

"Hit me all you please, but that will not change what is riding down upon you." The man swiped away the trickle of blood from the corner of his mouth.

Miltiades' bodyguard squeezed around him, each one of them anxious to hear all. He lowered the whip. "Are you certain they are Skythians? Not, Persians, perhaps?"

The messenger eyes widened. "By the gods, I can tell a Skythian from a Persian. They all wore pointed caps and had leather trousers. And their horses were half again larger than any Persian breed."

Immediately he ordered his cavalry to ride out into the countryside, sound the larum to all the settlers, while another contingent galloped off to the nearest village of the Dolonki. They still had time to get most of them behind the walls.

Late afternoon, and by now Miltiades stalked the gate-tower, searching the northern road, checking the rabble that streamed in from the outlying farmsteads, every so often gazing north to the horizon. He imagined dust and the sound of approaching riders, but still nothing. Suddenly, where the forest parted and the road snaked into open fields, he spotted a single blue-cloaked rider tearing toward the city. Within a few moments a troop of horsemen thundered from the trees, their horses churning a storm of dust as they charged in pursuit. At fifty meters and while still at a full gallop, the lead riders notched arrows, drew and launched them. Five shafts sprung from the blue cloak, tumbling the hapless rider into the dust-choked roadway.

"Close the gate!" Miltiades screamed the order. The farmers, vintners, husbandmen and their families, the ones that heard the order, abandoned hand carried bundles, the tethers of the draught animals, and the remnants of their herds as they ran for the fast closing gate. Two guards flanked the quickly diminishing entranceway, waving and shouting for the rest to hurry, shoving them through and into the safety of walled Elaios. In the fields, the rampaging horsemen overtook a family. First they circled the cart until the donkey bucked and kicked to a halt. Mercilessly one of the Skythians drew his bow and before he could even acknowledge the screaming pleas of a women in the bed of the cart he loosed an arrow, its impact from so close range lifted the man out of the cart and into the field. A boy jumped and began sprinting across the field, not toward the gate but directly away, for the trees stood less than fifty meters distance. While several of the Skythians yanked the woman from the cart and began to rip away her cloak and chiton, a lone rider sat atop his horse inspecting the arrows in his quiver with deliberation and coolness, until satisfied with one, withdrew it. He wriggled a bit, whether to increase his comfort or aim one could not tell, then slipped the shaft atop his cradled bow, lifted it, drawing the bow-string back till it buried in his cheek. The boy tumbled, a single arrow piercing his throat, not but a meter from the forest.

Now a cleft in the trees unleashed a flood of cavalry, horses trotting in a brazen gait, the invaders fanning out to engulf the empty fields. Miltiades could see them clearly now, warriors appareled in glittering fish-scale armor that covered body, arms and legs. Even the horses were afforded this lavish protection. From the center of this swell of horseman emerged eight riders; they galloped up onto the main road toward the town walls and halted before the gate.

"Where is the master of this town?" the tallest rider shouted in perfect Greek. "Where is Miltiades?"

Miltiades hesitated for only a moment then leaned out of the tower. Skopasis! Without a doubt it was the very same Skythian he had parleyed with three years past. Before he could speak, Skopasis yelled to him,

"Athenian! As you can see, no river separates us today. Tonight my army will dine out here amongst your orchards, vines and fields. Tomorrow we feast in your town." Skopasis wheeled his horse around and galloped off to the forest beyond.

Philomarkhos, the xenagos, or captain of his mercenaries, bounded up the stairs and into the tower room. "Here it is." Miltiades snatched the wooden tablets and began counting. "Three thousand," said Philomarkhos before Miltiades could finish tallying the names on the katalogos.

Miltiades gazed out into the fields. The distance between the walls and streams he calculated to be four stadia—nearly 800 meters. He would need enough men to cover this ground. Here and only here his flanks would be protected, but he could deploy his phalanx no deeper than four men or half its normal depth. He had not realized it until now, but he had been rolling Xenias' knuckle-bones around in his hand, the clicking sound only now audible in the quiet of the tower. He knelt and began to toss them, but stopped himself. "No, not today," he said. "I'll save this throw for tomorrow."

*****

Miltiades felt confident that his flanks were well protected. On the right, in the place of honor, he along with his five hundred mercenaries, all exquisitely equipped, anchored the line. Assembled on the far left were the Athenian colonists, most geared as hoplite heavy infantry with huge round shield, bronze helmet, breastplate and eight-foot spear. By necessity the Thrakians—fierce warriors, but equipped only with leather armor, crescent hide shields and javelins—comprised the center.

"If they attack us, as the Persians do, Skopasis will be at the center." Miltiades poked the air with his spear, directing the gaze of Philomarkhos to the slight dip of ground before them. "Our Thrakians will be hard pressed." Miltiades handed his shield and spear to Illyrios then followed the mantis out into the field before his army, where all could witness the sacrifice. Quickly Miltiades dispatched the goat, leaving its lifeless carcass to the mantis, who worked upon it; he stood, the beaming smile upon his face betraying the omen before he could speak.

"Artemis is with us!" bellowed Miltiades.

From the woods beyond, the rumble started, faintly at first, like a far off mountain storm clinging to the peaks. Suddenly the trees seemed to exhale cavalry, as several thousand Skythians thundered into the fields. Behind them marched and equal number of infantry. The sight of the Greek army arrayed before them gave them pause. They seemed a bit confused at the sight, expecting no one to be outside the high walls of Elaios. Two riders exploded from the center of the massing enemy cavalry, each galloping parallel to the coalescing front lines, waving and shouting orders. Sunlight glinted off their armor and the conspicuous golden stag ensigns on their shields, as they jostled into formation, fashioning what seemed like three huge blocks of men and beasts, all the while shouting their war-cries.

Miltiades extended his left arm, accepting his dish-shaped aspis shield from Illyrios. After pulling his crested helmet down to cover his face, he snatched up his spear. Exterior sound became instantly muffled, sight confined to a pair of narrow slits; the pounding of his heart and the rasp of his breath became amplified within the bronze.

High above in the gate tower and aided by a small stool, Metiokhos peered out at the gathering spectacle. He saw the slightly undulating line of hoplites spanning the open field between the walls and the stream, and beyond the boiling rectangles of Skythian cavalry with their infantry filtering out of the trees behind. Quickly he spotted his father on the right, not far from the tower; he watched as Miltiades paced before the lines, waving his spear while haranguing his men. A single man began to jog out from the Greek lines holding a herald's kerykeion staff, its twisting, twin snakeheads forming an open-ended circle at the top. He extended the kerykeion before him as though it was a shield against arrows or an amulet to ward off evil. A solitary rider galloped out from the Skythians to intercept the herald. The two spoke, waving their hands wildly, pointing this way and that until exhausted by talk they separated. The herald ran directly to Miltiades: after a short talk he raced from the phalanx, squeezing through tight ranks of mercenary hoplites and into the narrow gap of the partially closed gate, safe at least for now behind the walls of Elaios.

One of the tower guards, an old man with an unkempt gray beard and a body that refused to fill his tunic, edged next to Metiokhos. "If our men stay tight and fill the front quickly, we'll hold 'em."

Metiokhos turned to the ancient guard. "What do you mean, fill the front?"

The guards traced the fore ranks of the phalanx with his finger. "Their arrows will bring down many in our front ranks. The ones in the middle must move up quickly to fill the gaps." Realizing what he had said, he looked directly at Metiokhos. "But your father is on the right, amongst his chosen men. He would, I think, be safer than most."

The unexpected blast of a salphinx trumpet shook Metiokhos. He spun around and leaned out of the tower window to watch the phalanx roll forward. From here he could see every gap, each waver and every discordant shiver of movement as the Greek formation advanced. By accident or design the right wing, his father's wing, began to outpace the center and left, tilting the phalanx toward the enemy's left.

From across the battlefield the war cries of individual Skythians exploded randomly; the Greeks, in unison, began to yell, "Ala, la, aleu," over and over so rapidly it melded into an indiscernible, shrill melody. The Skythian cavalry seethed forward then suddenly reined up little more than two hundred meters from the advancing Greeks. Even above the singing of the Greeks and the piercing war hoots of the Skythians, the unmistakable rustle of arrow being fitted to bow multiplied several thousand fold drew Metiokhos' attention. Suddenly the very air shivered as myriads of iron-tipped shafts exploded from the Skythian lines, hardly arcing, but drilling straight, fast and with a trajectory as flat as the fields beneath them. It sounded like hail! The arrows struck so quickly, and in such numbers, their impact mimicked a deluge of hail upon the hard roof tiles of a town. Wounded Greeks and Thrakians stumbled and fell. Metiokhos remembered the old guardsman's words as he watched gaps open up, but quickly—thankfully—middle-rankers unhesitatingly moved in to fill these. The phalanx maintained its measured pace, each man clearly understanding his place in the line, and the importance of presenting an unbroken wall of shields. Still, the interval between the Skythian archers and hoplites diminished ever so slowly, allowing volley upon volley to be launched and Greek upon Greek to fall. The center had been thinned to half its original depth, while the wings too had been attenuated, both right and left tapering to finally blend with the precarious middle. Over 150 meters till they would hit the Skythians. By then their phalanx would be only a whisper of the original.

Suddenly the core of the Skythian cavalry burst forward, slinging their bows, exchanging them for sword, battle-ax and mace. Like a storm wave they inundated the center of the phalanx, the Thrakian infantry virtually evaporating beneath the charge.

"They only need slow them!" shouted the old guardsman. "Look!" He directed Metiokhos' gaze to his father's wing. The center of the phalanx had bowed back as the Thrakians perished under the onslaught; while more Skythians charged forward, funneled into the cavity in the Greek phalanx, giving Miltiades and his mercenaries their chance; they tried to wheel left, to bring their shields to bear on the center, and shove their way into the whirling Skythian cavalry but the ranks of enemy infantry thickened as reinforcements poured from the forest. Greek after Greek became swallowed up by the burgeoning horde of Skythians: the center—the long section of Thrakians—stretched so thin it almost dissolved; the right flank held its ground, but its ranks, too, eroded; the far left had become obliterated by the dust of combat.

Suddenly, like an ebbing wave on a steep shoreline, the Skythian center retreated. Now, as the withdrawal bled away Skythians from the right flank, Miltiades waved his men left to the relief of his battered Thrakians

Metiokhos tugged on the guard's cloak. "Why did they retreat?"

"Who knows? That infernal dust keeps all from our sight now."

What was once an ordered phalanx dispersed into a swarm, some Greeks chasing after unhorsed Skythians, while others ravaged the dead, stripping off armor, gold and other loot. In the middle of the field, where the bodies lay thickest, Metiokhos watched where his father motioned frantically, trying to reform his men. He stared out at the battlefield in silence. Written upon it, as clear as any words, was the pattern of combat. Corpses of Thrakian and Greeks were scattered thinly where the first arrows had struck, arrows that sprouted from the torn earth like a blighted crop. Where the arrows ceased to grow, the field was at its thickest with the dead-horses, Skythians, Thrakians and Greeks, their bodies twisted and crammed together and amongst them stalked small bands of hoplites, poking and prodding at random with their bronze spear butt-spikes. The trail of dead faded toward the forest and the still assembled Skythian infantry.

"We have won!" shouted Metiokhos.

"The old guardsman shook his head. "We have merely survived. Look again, lad. There are far fewer dead Skythians than Greeks out there. Our enemy has decided, for today at least, that the price of victory is too high."

Indeed the old man was proved correct. The next day, after the dead were collected, a great funeral pyre was constructed outside the town—a huge mountain of criss-crossed timbers large enough to incinerate four hundred townsmen. The Skythian count stood at less than a hundred, amongst them their leader Skopasis. Miltiades stood over his dead adversary, staring at the waxen face and lifeless, crystal blue eyes that looked to the sky.

Philomarkhos, keeping his horse to a deliberate canter, reined up beside Miltiades. "Who is that one you seem so interested in?"

"A man I met years before. A man who wrought destruction on the Great King Darios, and yesterday, upon his own army."

Chapter 5

Susa—507 BC

The searing wind off the desert whipped the scores of pennants that streamed above the Royal pavilion. Every color known to man and nature swirled and snapped on high poles above the billowing canopies; the Royal court beneath, shaded from the unrelenting sun, waited with anticipation for the procession to commence. Bupares hovered near Darios, fending off gnats with his flywhisk, while the king himself sat almost motionless upon his gleaming marble throne, holding his chin with his right hand, imparting an aspect of regal deliberation. Through the open gates of the city a company of drummers marched in, pounding out a thunderous rhythm that shook the gilded cups and dining platters upon each table in the pavilion, and elevated whispered conversations to shouts. A mild grin crept upon Darios' face; Bupares tilted his head back, seemingly to study the rippling canopy overhead, his flicking flywhisk purposely out of synch with the drumming.

First a cavalcade of Nisaean horses—all led and not ridden, for they were bred exclusively for the Great King and would fill his stables—trotted into Susa and by the pavilion of Darios. A small band of musicians followed: some with hands furiously wrapping cymbals while others, cheeks swelling red and round as pomegranates as they blew into their flutes. Next the grind and groan of wagon and cartwheels replaced the music as cages, pulled by oxen, rumbled forward.

"What manner of beast is that?" asked Hippias. "They appear to be lions, but with such strange orange and black fur."

Datis pointed to the first rank of cages, three abreast, an attendant walking beside each with a long pole and whip, poking the beasts as they passed before Darios, to animate them. "Tigers! That is what they are called. From the eastern satrapies of India. Wonderful pelts. I must have a cloak fashioned from one. Such exquisite colors."

The train of cages continued far out of the gates, and separated into groups of thirty, the most uncommon and fearsome beasts making up the front of the parade, tigers first, followed by lions, leopards and finally pens crammed with what looked like huge, fur covered men, but with the snouts of dogs. "Those are from the land of the Skythians," said Datis. "As I recall, the Greek name for such a beast is arktos, is it not?" Histiaios nodded in affirmation.

And the grand procession rolled on. Jackals and hyenas from Libya, hooting monkeys from Ethiopia, even carts full of peacocks, storks, cranes, and twisted neck flamingoes. Still more, with smaller cages within larger ones, held black partridges, owls, sand grouses, reedbirds, snipes, belderjin and quail. And punctuating the contingent of fowl, three score of ostriches, each leashed by an attendant, their feet loosely bound to abbreviate their gate. Now instead of musicians, a company of dancers entered next, each one holding a long pole with streamers of ribbons whipping in the breeze like tethered smoke.

From outside the walls what sounded like trumpets blasted over the noise of the crowd, then the gateway filled with the forms of immense beasts sporting snouts that looked like tails and tails shorter than snouts, each one ridden by a spindly youth wielding a hooked stick. Hippias felt the very platform that he stood on shiver as they rumbled closer. Grooms and riders struggled to keep their horses to station as the scent of the animals wafted over them. Anxiety and awe gripped everyone and everything.

"Elephants!" the word popped here and there from the crowded pavilion, answering the Greeks' question before it was ever posed. The people tossed garlands and blossoms at the feet of these ponderous brutes; most were ignored, but once in a while, and impelled by curiosity, an elephant delicately plucked one up from the dust and curled it back with its trunk into its mouth.

Men with open carts, spades and pitching forks scurried along behind, clearing the inevitable refuse deposited by this cortege of fauna. During this lull, servants rushed forward with their platters of fruit and pitchers of date wine to replenish empty bowls and cups. Bupares waved off the goblet as he looked down his noise at the handsome boy that presented it to him.

Gobryas leaned toward Darios. "Great King, I think you will be pleased with what comes next." He pointed to the yawning gateway.

Histiaios, Hippias and the other Greeks did not sit but flocked together near Datis' chair, surrounding the Persian, chattering amongst themselves and intermittently with Datis. They continued to talk as a regiment of Immortals marched in, resplendent in sleeved cloaks embroidered with scores of eight pointed sun emblems, the mark of Ahura Mazda, the golden apple shaped butt-spikes on their spears gleaming in the midday sun. But all chatting ceased on the sight that followed. Columns of prisoners shuffled into the city through the gatehouse, some with loincloths, and many naked. Hippias bent to whisper in Datis' ear. "Who are they?"

Datis sipped from his goblet, then answered casually, "The first you see are Egyptians rebels." He leaned back into his chair and waved the steward over. "More date wine."

For over an hour the sad procession of Egyptians hobbled by, the noses and ears loped off, each bound to a wooden yoke that bent their backs and stretched their battered and bleeding arms. Every so often one would stumble to the dust, whereupon the townsfolk that lined the avenue spat upon them, hurled rocks, or kicked dirt into their faces while cursing unabatedly. Behind the Egyptians cantered a squadron of Sakai heavy cavalry, their chain mail armor sparkling, their horses snorting confidently, as they poured through the gate to the cheers of crowd and the acknowledgment of Darios.

With the cavalry long passed, a new contingent of prisoners staggered forward, all naked, their backs striped from the lash, the entire column of over four-thousand all strung together with rope leashes about their necks. This throng halted in front of the Royal pavilion, and one prisoner was cut free from the rest and tossed to his belly before Darios. Gobryas, fingers intertwined, pushed his gauntlets tight to his hands then yanked on the man's hair to present his face to the Great King. Darios looked at him for only a moment and nodded. A pair of huge Baktrian guards heaved the prisoner up and dragged him to a large board. There was not much fight left in him, but still he squirmed and twisted as the burly guards stretched him out across the board, till his arms and legs spread wide, and lashed him to it. One knelt upon a shoulder, pressing down an arm while the other poked a long spike into writhing flesh, whacking it through his arm and into the board with one powerful swing. The captive wailed, his voice hardly recognizable as that of a man, but more like that of a wounded beast that had been snared, struck, and dealt its deathblow by the pitiless hunter. With both arms and legs spiked securely, they propped the board up to display their work to the Great King. Darios, without a trace of compassion, looked upon him as though he were studying a bolt of cloth, a measure of grain, or some other commodity, before disdainfully returning his glance the procession.

Before Hippias could ask the question, Datis spoke, "—the leader of the rebels. The Great King has shown his mercy in letting the other men live."

Hippias, upon hearing these words, finally realized what Datis meant. Every prisoner that had been paraded before Darios was a man. Not a single women or child had come through the gates the entire day. "What about the women?"

"Most, I would say, are dead. Sport for our men upon their victory." Datis emptied another cup of date-wine with a long gulp.

Histiaios' eyes widened with alarm. "And the children?"

Gobryas, hearing the question, interposed, "Dispatched, no doubt. Far better off that way, don't you think? Only the most handsome boys we kept, after we castrated them, of course." He stared at Bupares, smirking before turning to one of the Baktrians. "Don't let our friend doze off now." The Baktrian snatched up a skin of water and lumbered over to the prisoner staked to the board. He bent low, placing an ear near the man's mouth. "He is dead, Lord Gobryas."

Gobryas, not happy with this report, rose slowly from his cushioned chair and strode toward the impaled captive while withdrawing his akinakes sword from its scabbard. He plunged it beneath the ribs. The man's eyes opened wide, his mouth opened too, but only red foam spewed out. Gobryas twisted the blade to free it quickly. "I told you he was only sleeping." He tossed the bloodied weapon to a servant, who briskly swabbed it dry, while moving to join Datis and the Greeks. "I have news from Athens, my friends."

Histiaios turned a casual glance, but Hippias faced Gobryas directly and asked, "What sort of news?"

"Your countrymen grow restless. Seems they have dispensed with another ruler. They tell me his name is Isagoras, Do you know him?" Hippias nodded. Gobryas perceived a glint of optimism upon Hippias' face, which he promptly worked to dispatch. "No Hippias, they are not crying out for your return. Far from it. They want you and your sort to remain here as our guests in Persia."

"And how do you know this?"

Gobryas smiled broadly. "Because we have concluded an agreement with the Athenians. They are now allies of the Great King."

Hippias clenched his jaw. This news caught him off guard, but it took him little time to deduce the reason. Sparta posed more a threat to Athens than

Persia. With Persia as an ally, Athens would be secure from Spartan interference. This new way of governing that the Athenians had concocted, not the tried and true method of rule by the best, but now rule by the *hoi polloi*—the many—would threaten the very order of life in Hellas, and the Athenians did what they must do in order to defend it.

Now raucous cheering compelled Hippias to look once again upon the grand parade. Neither prisoners, nor exotic beasts entered Susa, but the troops of the Great King. "Gobryas, is that not your son at the head of the army?" Datis could not mask his scowl, which Hippias noticed. Gobryas, on the other hand, could hardly contain his pride, and this too Hippias saw, providing his only real amusement so far this day.

Indeed it was Mardonios leading the main portion of the army before the Great King, his golden, fish-scale armor glittering wildly in the hot sun, his horse cantering with proud exuberance. Behind him, for hour upon hour, rank upon rank, followed what seemed to Hippias the entire population of the earth: First a baivarabam, or division of 10,000 Persian cavalry, all with brilliant saffron tunics and intricately embroidered trousers of leather. The remainder of the Immortals trailed the cavalry, then full divisions of Medes, Kissians, Hyrkanians, Assyrians, Chaldeans, Baktrians, Egyptians, Parthians, Arabians, Sarangians, Ethiopians, and so many more that Hippias lost all command of numbers to tally them. Dusk, with its cool breezes, began to fall, but the display of arms continued. Still with no end in sight Hippias leaned close to Histiaios and whispered, "This army was defeated by the Skythians?"

Histiaios shook his head. "The one I saw near the Ister was like the water in a bowl. This one, the army that marches before us now, is like the ocean— vast, relentless and indomitable."

Chapter 6

505 BC—Plataia

The plowshare carved only a few feet of earth before striking another boulder. Arimnestos stumbled to the side, trying with wobbling arms to keep the plow upright as the pair of oxen mindlessly plodded along. "Hold!" The team loped to a stop, their tails flicking back and forth while mouths chewed upon imaginary fodder. Arimnestos dropped to his knees and began to scour the dirt from around the large stone.

"Not another one!" yelled his father as he heaved a rock into the bed of the cart. Even the thick calluses on his hands could not protect him from the sharp edged rocks; he spit into his palms, then rubbed them together, hoping to stanch the bleeding. In a fit of disgust he yanked the spade from the cart and lumbered over to Arimnestos. "Watch it." As soon as the boy withdrew his hands from the hole, his father plunged the spade then worked it deeper. The boulder rocked a bit as he leaned on the handle. "Get that." He flicked his head toward the cart. Arimnestos hustled over to it and pulled out a branch of olive wood that his father smoothed into long tapering pole. "As hard as iron. That'll move it." Arimnestos drove the pole beneath the boulder, the pair working their levers, finally prying it free of the earth. "I'll take care of this. You keep to the plow."

The boy lifted the plow handles, and slid between them, plunging the share into the interrupted furrow, and then barked at the oxen to move. His arms shivered as he fought to keep the plow deep and the furrow straight and true. Though autumn, the sun wore on him and the oxen too, but he kept to his task until near mid afternoon, when his father returned to the field with the cart empty.

"Enough for today, my boy."

He did not have to hear that twice, letting the plow slip from his hands, as he ran to grab hold of the oxen. "Stop you two. I'll take you home to feed you now," he said, slapping one on its broad back affectionately. They both snorted at him, seemingly acknowledging his words and the reward to come. He untied the plow from the harness, his father helping him toss it into the bed of the cart, grabbed the tether of the yoke before leading the oxen toward the stable. Their farm was not a large one, but it was close to the Asopos River and this meant it was well watered, and proved productive for its size. Part of their family's land included Tower Hill—from here Arimnestos would scout the river and the broad plain beyond, looking north toward Thebes, imagining the hated Thebans on the march to challenge them. Now it struck him why his father stopped their work. Tomorrow was an important day. Tomorrow the militia would gather in the plain between the town and the river, all one thousand, sacrifice to the hero and the goddess, after which they would commence their annual hoplite drill. The prospect energized him. He wrapped the oxen with his thumb-stick. "Let's go."

Almost an hour had passed by the time he reached the stable, for the beasts meandered about, barely heeding Arimnestos, especially when they tromped into the low water of the Asopos. His uncle Belos greeted them both, swinging the squealing door open and guiding the team in, where both he and Arimnestos unfastened the yoke and harness. Arimnestos led the oxen to the trough, talking to them all the while, thanking them for their day's work and encouraging them now to rest. His father wrestled the plow from the bed of the cart, placed it right side down and eyed the share, while running his thumb along it to test the edge. "I think that last rock did it." He shook his head. The smith will have to pound that out for us." He straightened up and sighed. "You mother will be cross if we are late."

The main room of the farmhouse had barely enough space for them all to sit around the cramped table, so his mother hovered near the hearth, waving them all to take a place. "How can I feed you if you are stumbling about?" she admonished, She wrapped her hands in her chiton, enabling her to heave the sizzling cauldron from the coals, plopping it upon the center of the table. Whether by accident or design, the heavy cook-pot landed hard, sending a small shower of broth onto Arimnestos' face. "Hmm, it is tasty," he said, smiling as he sampled the drops that he wiped from his cheeks with his finger.

His mother cuffed him then bent over to kiss his forehead. She smacked her lips. "It is good," she confirmed with a grin. Now she brushed the curls away from his brow. "Looking more like your father with each day gone by," she remarked. Intended as a compliment, her words also reminded her how quickly he was changing: his golden hair—the very shade of hers—had darkened to the color of weathered bronze; his once crystal-blue eyes glistened now like polished iron. Still she smiled.

His father and uncle laughed while reaching for their bread and kept to it until their mouths were finally stuffed to silence. Arimnestos lunged at this opportunity to speak. "Father, tomorrow may I go with you and uncle?" He caught sight of his mother passing a signaled grin.

"Of course you can come with us. Who else would carry my armor?" His father watched the ladle pass from cauldron to his bowl, then back again, and only nodded to his wife when it was brim-full. She exchanged another glance with him. "You know it will be eight more years till you can take up arms," he said just before spooning the broth into his anxious mouth.

"Do not rush to the inevitable," cautioned his uncle. "You will indeed get your chance to fight. The villages of Skolos or Hysiai may be content with their borders now, but one drought, or storm, or any other whim of the gods, and they may covet what we now own. And do not forget Thebes."

Arimnestos dipped his head low till his lips touched his bowl. His mother moved behind him and rubbed his shoulders with both hands. "Why do you men rush to die?

"Because," piped up his father, "we have tasted your broth. It would do in a Spartan!"

His mother swooped around the small table, Arimnestos, his uncle and his sister all ducking as she passed. She clubbed her husband twice with a clenched fist, then fell into his lap and kissed him. "You are lucky I appreciate your humor." Everyone burst out in laughter except his sister. She scowled at them all. "Come, come dear, that is your father's way," said his mother, trying to console her daughter.

"Little Artemis," mocked Arimnestos, this nick-name of the virgin goddess he thought befitting of so belligerent a female, although unlike the goddess he did wish her to marry some day, if only to introduce another male as a target for her scorn.

His sister reeled back and swung, landing a blow to the back of his head that sent his face into the broth. He tried to spring to his feet, but his uncle grabbed his arm. Kyra threw the kitchen door open, slamming it against the outside wall as she stormed out. Arimnestos accepted the linen rag from his mother and began swabbing his face. In the meantime his father and uncle, faces down, restrained their laughter.

Arimnestos wanted to be angry. In fact for a short moment he was, but he loved his sister, and realized at a young age that the people he could rely on were the people he sat down to dinner with every night. "I think I have had enough broth," he said as he rose to take leave of them. He left the kitchen, and walked out toward the grain tower. As he passed by the stable he heard sobbing from within, so he carefully nudged open the door, just enough for him to squeeze through.

"Get out!" His sister sat cross-legged just inside the doorway, her face buried in her arms. She looked up. "I said get out!" Her face was streaked with tears, her cheeks flushed.

Slowly he lowered himself into a crouch in front of her, ready to flick an arm out to fend off any blow. He did not speak, but just stared at her.

"What!" she barked between sniffles.

"I came to apologize," he said.

She looked into eyes that were disarmingly gentle. Her sniffles faded. Her chest heaved only once or twice, but she cried no more. "You apologize to me?"

He reached out to her, slipping both her hands into his. "I should not tease you so." He stood and pulled her up with him. Gently, he wiped the tears from her cheeks with the back of his hand and brushed back the hair from her face. "I tease because I admire you."

"Me?" she squeaked, craning her neck to look into his face.

"Yes you, my sister. You retreat from no one. I, for one, would not want to be your enemy." He wrapped his arm around her shoulder and led her toward the doorway. "Not too very long from now, you will marry and I will be taking my place among the men, and I will be separated from my dearest friend."

They walked out into the stable yard. Suddenly she pushed him away. "I will not let them see me being soft on you." She bolted across the yard and into the shuttered farmhouse.

✻✻✻✻✻

His uncle Belos sat near the hearth, tilting the blade of the sword as though it had words etched upon it that he strained to read. He rubbed it with the tips of his fingers before grinding the stone along its edge. This he repeated again and again. Arimnestos had his father's bronze corselet wedged between his knees and stroked the bell-shaped armor with an oily rag. His sister sat next to him, brushing out the tall horsehair crest upon his father's kranos helmet, humming a comfortably circular melody, seemingly pleased with her task.

The door creaked open and in waddled his father, a great, round aspis shield on each arm. Arimnestos bolted up from his seat to relieve his father of one of the shields; he lowered it gently, almost solemnly to the dirt floor, tilting it upright against the table, then knelt, dragging an open palm across the scarred and battered leather facing. "If I had the money, I'd have it repainted," commented his father. Poor Medusa has faded into one huge smudge."

Now Arimnestos began to trace the outline of the grim emblem with a finger, starting at her fanged mouth and continuing around her writhing, serpentine hair. "I could do it. A potter's brush and some lampblack, and I could bring her back to life."

His father shook his head. "Must be done proper, or the image will not do its work. On our next trip to Athens, perhaps."

Arimnestos left the shield, returning to corselet and rag. By now his sister had finished with the helmet and was helping her mother distribute bowls and cups to the men. The wine was warm, the bread hard and cold, but it was savored nonetheless, for it would be their only food till this evening's feast. Arimnestos finished polishing the corselet. He held it up now for his father's fitting. He cinched the straps tight then slipped in the hinge pins to secure the armor. His uncle's body armor was not thick bronze, but was constructed of glued linen, many layers thick, and painted gleaming white. Both men, helmets and shields in hand, stepped out into the early morning chill with Arimnestos following, clutching a pair of eight-foot spears, earthenware canteens clanging at his side. From here they could see dancing torches near the shrine of Androkrates—others had begun to gather. The three started their trek down the gentle slope at the foot of Tower Hill toward the fluttering lights, careful not to trip over the scarred and pot-holed earth that surrounded the cultivated fields. The stars above began to fade as the first hint of day tinged the eastern sky. Slowly the gray veil of night receded; first the red-orange roof tiles of the shrine cut through the gloom, then as they drew closer, the flamboyant helmet crests of the hoplites, shuddering in the breeze, set colors dancing: scarlet, blue, saffron and more blossomed near the shrine. Men talked together in small groups, nodded "good morning" as neighbors passed by while monitoring the sky. The blast from a lone salphinx trumpet commanded silence.

Polyandros, the commander of their militia and battle-priest, climbed the few steps of the shrine. "Men of Plataia!" he shouted. "We gather to honor the hero Androkrates, protector of our city, and patron of warriors." The crowd, numbering nearly one thousand, edged closer, the rustle of weapons and the clatter of armor the only sound, for all voices but Polyandros' went silent. At the altar, placed just before the steps and aligned with the path of the anticipated sun, stood four men and a great black bull. At the foot of the stairs clustered more bulls tethered to men; a single bull might satisfy the appetite of a single god, but here an entire town must be fed. One man heaved up a double-headed ax from its resting place against his leg; it swung high over head, crashing down upon the unsuspecting victim. The bull's head slammed into the earth at the base of the altar, neck twisting awkwardly to reveal a gaping wound. Polyandros descended the stairs, to kneel with a golden bowl near the fallen bull. In a moment he stood upright, arms stretched out, presenting the blood filled vessel to the army, and once satisfied they were all witness to the sacrifice, walked to the altar where he slowly emptied the bowl, glistening, steamy scarlet spilling over the white marble that had been stained dark from countless other victims. As if on cue the first band of golden light cut across the horizon to the east—every head turned. Kithairon's summit burned in the dawn. Its slopes soon took on life, the green of plane, olive, pine and oak revealed, while hawks began to patrol high above. The clouds, now drained of their gloom, burned too, their bellies flaming red as they scudded across the sky on the breath of gods.

"Those bulls will make for a splendid feast tonight," said Arimnestos, to his father. He could still taste the meager portion of wine-dipped bread. The once silent assembly of militia erupted into a cacophony of boisterous exchanges mingled with the clatter of arms. Men swirled this way and that, shouldering into ill-defined files and staggered ranks. Arimnestos handed the spears to his uncle and father before jogging off to the slope of the Asopos ridge where he would watch along with the other sons and servants who had come as armor bearers. Now, as the sun crept higher, more townsfolk ambled up to the ridge, swelling the crowd of spectators.

Arimnestos gazed keenly at collecting phalanx, spotting his father easily, for he was a front ranker in his tribe. It was difficult to make out, but after watching how far each phylarkhos, or tribal commander, paced in front of the first rank he could mark out the four tribes and their companies. In most places the phalanx stretched to a depth of eight men, but in other spots it was four only. It took the better part of an hour to finally get all the men in their places.

"Arimnestos!"

He turned to see his friend Lampon scrambling down from the crest of the ridge, who quickly skidded to a seat next to him. "Is your sister coming?"

Arimnestos laughed a bit. He squinted at his friend as though he were trying to find some hidden thing upon his face. "It looks as though your nose has healed. Why would you want to break it again?"

"Oh, stop it. She didn't mean to hit me, did she?" He rubbed his nose. "I think that pot was meant for you," said Lampon. "Did you see who is here?" Lampon stared back over his shoulder at the crest of the ridge. Several men, all in armor, hung together there, seemingly inspecting the militia in the plain below.

"I see Aristokrates, but the others I do not recognize."

"They are Athenian generals. See the tall one in the middle." Lampon pointed discreetly at the most prominent in the group, a man in gleaming bronze armor with a triple crest upon his helmet that bobbed magnificently in the breeze. "That one is Kleisthenes, the prostates of Athens."

"The first man of their city. That is an honor indeed. But why is he here?"

"For our feast of course. And to take stock of his closest ally." Lampon spun back to face Arimnestos. "Is she coming?"

It took a moment for the question to register with him. "I really don't know?"

"Does she like me? I mean does she talk about me at all?" Lampon's words became hurried now. He wanted the answers, but without the pain of asking the questions. He plucked up a handful of grass and began tearing it.

"I'll ask her. There she is. Coming this way with mother." Arimnestos grinned as he nudged his friend.

"Hmm, I forgot. My father left his water flask at home; I must fetch it for him." Lampon sprang to his feet. "I'll see you tonight at the feast." He raced down the slope and disappeared into a grove of olive trees.

"Where did Lampon run off to?" His mother knelt beside him. Kyra stood, staring out into the plain at the phalanx.

"An errand," said Arimnestos, as he shrugged his shoulders.

Out in the field the four companies of hoplites surged and swayed as they traversed the simulated battlefield, any change in direction or speed compressing then stretching the files. Spears wavered like wheat in the wind. Helmet crests spun right, left, and right again as each man checked his neighbor, tentatively measuring pace and interval, struggling to keep the phalanx intact.

Kyra mumbled beneath her breath.

"Did you say something?" asked her smiling mother.

"I said they looked clumsy. They move like lame, drunken dancers." Kyra stood straight as one of the columns of the shrine, her hands clenched. Unlike the others gathered on the ridge, the spectacle hardly entertained, but seemed to upset her.

"Our men are farmers first, not soldiers," reminded her mother. "But they are brave, and will do what they must to defend us."

Now Kyra stared up at the Athenians, searching their faces for any clue, any confirmation of her assessment of the mock battle, but nothing was revealed. Every so often one would turn to another, a few words would be exchanged before their eyes inevitably falling back upon the Plataians. The men in the field continued on, charging imaginary enemies, bellowing the war cry, "Ala, la, aleu," rattling their spears menacingly above their heads, trying with all their might to prove fiercesome and courageous. With every counterfeit charge more than a few would stumble and fall, sending some townsfolk into fits of laughter—and their relatives cowering in shame. As the hours passed, each subsequent rumble forward slowed, each war cry sputtered, each spear lowered until most dragged across the pot-holed fields of Plataia. At day's end the sun slipped behind the mountains, the phalanx disintegrated, some men falling to their knees, some rolling onto their backs, while the rest trudged off toward the ridge and their waiting relatives.

"Here comes your father." Arimnestos' mother pointed to her husband as he lumbered up the slope. "Help him, will you."

Arimnestos snapped to his feet, embarrassed he had to be reminded of his duty and ran to relieve his father of the heavy aspis shield and spear. "Any water?" his father asked, as he pushed his helmet clear of his face. Now he fumbled with the baked-clay canteen he had slung from his neck, finally managing to slip it free and hand it to his father. After chugging the canteen empty, he swiped his beard with the back of his hand, while sniffing the air. The aroma of roasting meat, the sacrifice of early morning, had wafted its way from the town gate down the gentle slope and onto the plain. Most of the men paused only briefly upon the ridge, to surrender some of their panoply before making off for their anticipated feast.

"Koinos, my dear, our daughter was truly upset today." Arimnestos' mother glanced to their daughter. Kyra said nothing as she took her father's helmet from him and cradled it in her arms.

Koinos knelt before his daughter, a hand on each of her shoulders and asked, "Are we that bad?"

Kyra stared at her father in silence, her eyes welling with tears.

"Do not worry, Kyra. This is more play than work for most of them, but when the real fight comes they will do what must be done."

With an air of pomp Arimnestos strode up beside his father and sister, shield gripped high upon his shoulder and spear stiff and upright. "Orders, general Kyra?"

She raised her hand to strike, but Arimnestos, in anticipation, lifted the shield to fend off any blow to his head or body. With a feint Kyra made him raise it further, then swung her foot beneath its rim, kicking her brother right off his feet. Now she jumped on him, fists flaying wildly, until Koinos pulled her free. "Enough! Kyra, go ahead with your mother." Now he bent over his son, a scowl simmering on his tired face. "You and I will stay here awhile." Koinos lowered himself to a seat on the ridge next to Arimnestos. "You must learn to keep that tongue in your head."

"She must learn to smile," countered Arimnestos. "Or you will never get her out of your house. She would chase even doting Lampon away."

Kyra and her mother moved along with the crowd toward the north gate of the town, drawn by the smoky scent of meat roasting and mesmerizing light of cook-fires. One man, the carver, plunged a long bladed knife into the flank of meat that still hung on a spit. Steam spiraled out of the wide slice and succulent juices rained down upon the flames as he worked the blade back and forth until the portion plopped onto a wooden tray held by another cook. With several more passes a mountain of steaming flesh filled the tray, and this was brought to a table where more carvers worked on it, cutting large pieces into smaller ones; attendants filled the bowls of the townsfolk as they filed by. Rows of amphorai leaned against the town wall and near these servants poured wine and water into huge mixing bowls that stood like sentinels protecting the road. On the battlements above, torches sputtered and little boys scurried about pretending to guard their town with unflinching valor against an overwhelming foe. Near the gate a band of musicians, hardly accomplished, struck up a tune that set some to dancing, while others joined in with wine enhanced voice, bellowing out the simple lyrics with brazen confidence.

Kyra moved along in the queue, a wooden bowl in one hand and a small earthenware cup in the other, lost in the noise and prancing shadows. Behind her, her mother glanced here and there, acknowledging neighbors and relatives with a smile, a nod, or a brief chat. Kyra hardly noticed the cook as he dropped the portion of meat into her bowl. She shuffled along to the mixing bowls, dipped her empty cup, scooping it full and moved away. The wine, even watered down as it was, stung the cuts on her knuckles, reminding her quickly of her brother, and reminding her also that the grudge lived and payment was still due. As she walked along, eyes down, she noticed a pair of sandaled feet blocking her path.

"Kyra, w-would you like to sit with me, over there?" Lampon fumbled a bit with the request, as he motioned to the array of stools near an inconsiderable fire. She recognized Lampon's family, with two conspicuously empty seats near his mother and father. She paused for a moment, looking back, spotting Arimnestos at the carver's table with her father. She nodded once and followed Lampon.

Chapter 7

500 BC—Persepolis

The Persians called places like this a paradise—to Histiaios and Hippias it was a garden, but aggrandized to encompass the land of many Greek farms. Groomed lawns and beds of poppies filled the intervals between stands of perfectly trimmed, plum, mulberry and almond trees. The sweet scent of citrus hung in the moist air, while the only sound audible was the anesthetic gurgle of water upon stone from the score of handsomely carved marble fountains acting as hubs to the network of tidy paths. Several iridescent-feathered peacocks strutted about, secure from any predator. The slave approached, his head bound in cloth; he knelt before them both. Histiaios carefully scanned their surroundings, looking for a Persian spy or a curious passer-by, before he began to unwind the wrapping from the slave's head. With the last of the cloth peeled away the writing was revealed.

"This is the only secure way to get the message to Aristagoras." Across the man's scalp ran rows of letters, incised into the skin with ink, the scabby words still hard to read and would be for some days until the cuts and pin-pricks began to heal. Until his hair re-grew, they—Histiaios and Hippias—were in peril. "Cover it." At his master's words the slave spun the long strip of cloth around his head.

"Are you certain about this?" asked Hippias.

"That the message will reach Aristagoras?" Histiaios tugged on the wrappings, making certain they would not come undone.

"No! That your revolt will get us out of Darios' court." Hippias winced, knowing his words might have carried.

"Not only will we be free of the Great King's smothering hospitality, but if things proceed as I know they can, we will both be at home, virtual kings ourselves." Now Histiaios gestured for the slave to stand. "Krios, you are to remain in my quarters. And do not leave unless I, by my own words, allow it."

The slave nodded before turning to depart, his sudden movements scattering the gaggle of peacocks. Voices, faint at first, grew louder, laughter mixing with words until the two Greeks caught sight of the approaching Persians. Everything about them was loud: the clinking of gold announcing their wealth; flamboyantly colored trousers and cloaks screaming for attention; their talk amplified for all to hear.

"I feel like one of them," said Hippias, as he glanced at the retreating peacocks. "Pampered, protected and unable to fly."

Histiaios grinned. "In a while, my friend, we may both have wings."

✳✳✳✳✳

Each day passed with excruciating slowness, certainly for Hippias and Histiaios, but more so for Krios. In the morning, before the lamps were lit and the sun cut the horizon, he would unwrap his bandage and skim his hand across his head, measuring, at first only stubble. After several weeks he had to push his fingers hard to feel the scarring letters through his thickening hair. After a month he was summoned by Histiaios to unwrap the bandage.

"Krios, come closer," he commanded. His slave stepped before, dropping to his knees. Histiaios took a lamp from the adjacent table and began to pore over the man's head as he would a writing tablet. Thankfully there were no words to read. "Come!" Now he walked out to the balcony of his room, catching the eye of the Immortals who stood guard in the courtyard below. Far off, framing the horizon, stony cliffs climbed quickly from the flat plain surrounding Persepolis. Above, an unblemished sky beamed brightly. Now Histiaios studied Krios' head more closely, fingering his hair, pushing it, pulling on it, squinting as he strained to catch sight of the slightest hint of a mark upon his scalp. He smiled.

"Tomorrow you depart. This is the message you will carry, the one for all to see." He handed Krios a roll of papyrus. "That is a birthday greeting for Aristagoras." Now he plucked up a small, jeweled casket, one not much longer than his forearm. He carefully pried open the lid. It was filled with a fragrant ochre powder. "That incense is worth more than gold. It is our offering to the gods, an offering that will ensure success."

The slave now traded his bandage for a broad-brimmed felt hat, a petasos, headgear familiar and to him indeed more comfortable. In addition to the casket of incense, which he now slid into a hide bag, he carried a bedroll slung across his back and a small basket tied to a short pole that he balanced on his shoulder with the aid of a hand. He walked out of Histiaios' room, past the two Median guards, down the echoing corridor and out into the blinding light of mid morning. Krios instinctively pulled down the brim of his petasos to cover his eyes; it took long moments before his vision adjusted. In front of him, and flanked by two Immortals, stood the Persian Datis.

"Traveling to the coast, I understand?" Datis, feet spread, hands on hips, looked the slave up and down. "Strip him!"

The two Immortals moved to either side of the slave; one snatched his hat and glanced at it perfunctorily, before handing it to Datis, while the other grabbed the hide satchel, mugging it rather violently. Krios' eyes, even in the stark sunlight, widened with concern.

"Something important?" growled Datis as he read the slave's face. Krios said nothing. Datis pulled the jeweled casket free of the satchel. He studied it briefly before removing his gauntlets so he could work the delicate latch. He flipped the lid open, eyeing the contents a bit before dragging a finger through the powder. "Incense!" he declared, with a bit of disappointment. Before he could drop the casket to the ground Krios stepped forward and slid his hands beneath it, gently placing it at his feet. The two Immortals unfurled his bedroll. One barked at him to strip out of his chiton. Now they spilled his basket empty, and cut the seal on the papyrus roll. Datis scooped it up and read it summarily, then withdrew his akinakes sword and commenced to poke and prod the meager contents of the basket that were scattered atop the glazed brick courtyard floor: a water flask, two loaves of flat breads and a talisman of Egyptian blue-glass resembling a human eye. He spun away, slipping the akinakes back into its gilded scabbard. "He may go."

✳✳✳✳✳

Krios fell in with a caravan heading for Nineveh, spice merchants on their way to bargain for Arabian incense. After a significant mark up, they would peddle it to temple priests and others along the coast of Ionia: piety had its price and many were willing to pay it. Every day, just as this procession of mules, carts and camels trudged to the fading light of dusk, another Royal way station would rise from the stark landscape to greet them. Here they would pitch their broad canopies, tether their animals and prepare their humble fare. Nabusera, the servant of a trader from Persepolis, befriended Krios. At every stop he would seek out the Greek, and badger him with questions of his master, their home and his task.

"Gifts for my master's friend. The same answer to the same question every day you ask it." Krios hustled away from Nabusera, finding a sheltered nook in the station wall, which kept him out of the gritty desert wind, a place too confined for a companion to join him.

Nabusera wriggled in next to him, pushing the last piece of onion into his remarkably quiet mouth. He chewed slowly, like a cow would on succulent grasses, nodding his head to an unheard rhythm. "And why do you always wear that hat?" He reached to lift the wide brimmed petasos from the slave's head. Krios jerked away instinctively. "Truly, I only mean to look at it."

Krios plucked the hat from his head and handed it to the inquisitive Persian, being certain not to lean forward, even though his scalp lie buried beneath several inches of hair. He tried his best to look unconcerned, but still he fingered the blue glass charm hanging from his neck. He leaned back against the wall, staring up at the stars that began to poke through the receding haze of dust stirred up by the late afternoon winds. For a moment he traveled back to Miletos, but the stench of the tethered camels broke the trance of his brief dream.

"This won't stay on your head in a storm," said Nabusera as he fitted the petasos. "Here." He tossed it back to Krios. "I, on the other hand, prefer a real hat." He pulled out his pointed cap from beneath his yellow and crimson striped tunic and pulled it tight to his head by the long flaps that covered his ears. "No wind will steal away this," he said smiling as he tied the flaps together beneath his chin. Your hat is for a more dainty clime."

Krios quickly covered his head with the petasos. "Are you not missed by your companions?"

"Me?" Nabusera said, with a bit of pretentiousness. "Truly I am missed, and if you continue to avoid conversation, you too will be missing Nabusera."

Krios clamped his lips and grinned.

"Fine Greek. If you do not want to talk, I will leave you to your thoughts, and your silly round hat." He unfolded from his tight crouch and rolled his eyes as he strode off.

Krios lifted his hat, just enough to slide a hand atop his head. He fingered his scalp, searching out with touch any remnant scab or scar of the covert missive. It felt to him as though every letter was boldly embossed upon his skin. He was much too young to be balding, yet the prospect of this frightened him. He measured every hair with his fingertips, trying to chase away the anxiety that clung to him like a wet cloak. He thought he heard the rumblings of a far off storm, distant thunder, so he scanned the star flushed night sky.

Not a cloud. But the rumble grew louder until he could distinguish the gallop of horses and the jingling of war-bits and reins. A squadron of Baktrian cavalry streamed off the Royal Road and poured around the way station, upsetting the mules and inciting pandemonium amongst the camels.

"Search them all!" shouted the captain of horse as swung off his mount. He smacked the dust off his saffron tunic, clanging the scale armor underneath, while looking around before marching through the open door of the station. He quickly disappeared into the light within.

Krios wrapped himself in his cloak, burying his face in it as he feigned sleep. With his eyes closed he heard the ruckus of the merchants and their servants being roused from sleep or pulled away from drink and conversation. They protested, but only meekly at this treatment. He heard one of them shout, "Over there." He knew they came his way now, the rustle of their leather trousers and their ribald laughter growing louder with each step. One of them barked out a command in Persian, which he gathered a rough meaning, but instead of rising, he clutched the edges of his cloak tightly, ignoring the gang of cavalrymen that approached. A booted foot kicked the air out his lungs as he tumbled sideways. He needed no interpreter for the flood of curses that followed, so he reluctantly peeled away his cloak and stood, doing his very best to appear bleary-eyed.

Two jabbered away in Persian, Baktrian or some other tongue incomprehensible to him. They struck him only once with a riding whip until finally the captain emerged from the brightly lit doorway of the way station. "You imbeciles!" barked the captain. "He can't understand you." The captain strode over to Krios, inspecting him as he approached. "Greek?"

Krios knew this word and responded with a nod.

The captain snatched a sputtering torch from the hands of one of his men and waved it slowly in front of Krios' face, tilting his head slightly as he inspected the Greek. "Search him!"

Immediately a pair of Baktrians grabbed Krios. He resisted, but only for a moment. He did not want them to tear the chiton from his back so he quickly pulled it overhead and handed it to one of them. The two laughed as he shivered, wrapping his chest with folded arms to fend off the cold night air. The captain circled him, moving the torch up and down, examining every inch of his bare skin. Krios shook now, not from cold but fear as he looked at his petasos hat on the ground before him. It seemed to him that his knees wobbled frantically, and hoped the Baktrian would attribute it to nothing more than cold. He prayed to Hermes for protection, and petitioned in silence every deity his fear-wracked mind could recall. The torch hovered now but a few inches from his face.

"Not a mark on him!" snapped the captain, his voice laced with disappointment. "Bah! Let him go." He tossed the torch to one of his escort, laughing a bit as the man scorched himself with a poor catch then walked amongst the others of the caravan, poking some with the handle of his whip, kicking others that slept and did not see him approach. At the corner of the station wall the captain met with Nabusera. Krios watched through one eye, feigning sleep, as the two conversed for several minutes. They turned his way once, both nodding, and continued on with their talk. Krios was hardly the brightest of men, but it did not take him long to put it all together. Someone knew about the message. Tired as he was, he drifted in and out of sleep that entire night, not sure if the sounds he heard and the glimpses of men passing by were real or imagined. His eyes blinked open. Two sandaled feet stood before him. He scanned upward, following the yellow and crimson-banded tunic until he came to its owner's face. Nabusera loomed over him, staring at his head.

"Don't move," whispered Nabusera as he lowered himself to a crouch, his eyes widened, his hands moving slowly toward Krios' head. Suddenly the Persian shot out a hand so quickly Krios did not have time to duck. "Look!" Nabusera pointed to the earth a few feet from Krios. There a scorpion wriggled upon its back, righted itself, then scampered off to a crevice in the wall. "Those won't kill you, but you would be sick for days."

In a snap Krios jumped to his feet, no prodding needed this morning to get him moving. He pushed his petasos hat down upon his head and wrapped his himation cloak around his shoulders before heading off for the bread vendor and his meager breakfast.

As with every morning the caravan awoke, fed itself, and moved northwest, following the Royal Road. In less than a month they maundered into the outskirts of the once great city of Nineveh. Here the spice merchants met their suppliers. Here they negotiated their deals. And from here on, they grew anxious, sleeping with one eye open, even on the protected Royal Road. On this leg of the journey, they had been stopped and searched no less than fifteen times by patrolling squadrons of cavalry. But with each passing day Krios felt a bit calmer, secure in the knowledge that his hair grew thick, and secure also that although the Persians may know of a message inked on the body of a traveler, it was proved fifteen times that they did not know precisely where that message hid.

By the time the caravan had reached Sardis, Krios managed to converse in Persian, but his accent and his clothing still marked him as a foreigner. Nabusera seemed to lose interest in him as their journey neared its end, and on its final day he did not lay eyes upon the Persian at all, that is until they entered the gates of Sardis. There sitting upon a lion skin caparisoned warhorse sat Nabusera, his scale armor glittering. Krios stared at him, mouth wide open. Nabusera grinned back.

* * * * *

"Master Aristagoras, only you are to look upon the message," warned Krios as he stared at the gaggle of servants in the andreion.

"Out! All of you out!" Aristagoras barked at them, sending them scurrying for the door and in such a hurry that none dared look back, pause or question the order. The cloak he wore, the one of cloth at least, was of rich embroidered linen, but the mantle of authority that he donned everyday here at Miletos was woven of heavier stuff—a garment not seen, but as substantial as any other. It demanded attention. He circled Krios, peering down his long, meandering nose at the slave's thick scalp. "You expect me to shave you?"

Krios plucked the bronze razor from the black lacquered table, but left the mirror. With a snap of his wrist he dunked the gleaming blade in the bowl of water, tugged his hair back away from his forehead, then in short, grinding strokes began shaving. A few passes, a dunk in the bowl, the swirling strands of shorn hair floated atop the water, and clung to his wet fingers.

All the while Aristagoras paced around, leaning closer now and again to try to glean a word, even a trace of a letter. Before Krios could finish, he grabbed a swatch of linen and commenced to scour the slave's head clean of the remnants of cut hair. He squinted. Finally he snatched up an oil lamp to aid his aging eyes. "Come to the window." Without thinking he almost pulled the slave up by his ragged chiton, but caught himself before he soiled his fingers. Krios obliged, leaning into the light of early morning that poured through the east-facing window. Aristagoras stared. From beneath the stubble and streaks of blood the words formed: **Now is the time. Seek the Spartans.** A grin of satisfaction stretched across his face now. The message was clear. His mission was clear. Now his heart drummed wildly as he looked back at the bald slave, back into the eyes of a man unaware of his predicament, innocent and trusting. Aristagoras calmly walked to the black lacquered table. He looked at the razor for only a moment before he picked it up. "Lean forward, will you. There is a bit more hair to go." With one deep, swift draw of the blade he opened the slave's throat. Aristagoras staggered back, staring down at his blood-splattered chiton, not seeing Krios clutch the gaping wound, not seeing the slave's eyes searching out Aristagoras in disbelief.

Krios folded to his knees, blood coursing through desperate fingers as he clamped down on his throat. He turned to face his murderer. "Why?" The word gurgled out of his mouth along with his last breath.

Aristagoras tossed the bloody razor onto the azure tiled floor. "Pah!" he answered as he daintily sidestepped the pooling blood on his way out. "Why not?"

Chapter 8

Port of Gytheion—499 BC

Aristagoras leaned over the bow of the penteconter savoring the salty breeze and the prospects of a successful visit. Unlike the cities along the Asian coast whose harbors melded into the towns, Sparta lie a day's ride inland, and he knew no special attentions would be afforded him, no greeting royal or otherwise would await in the small port of Gytheion. The port lies in a curving, quiet bay where the hills tumble steeply to the water's edge like the seats of a great amphitheater. They glided slowly by the island of Kranai, the place where Paris left for Troy with his abducted Queen Helen, heading for an empty berth.

Once in Sparta he would petition the ephors or city magistrates, make an official request for aid against the Persian foe, but then meet with the real power. Sparta had two kings, but in truth one real leader and it was Kleomenes—and Kleomenes hated the Persians. He had fought other Greeks who he suspected of entertaining alliances with the Great King. He would indeed fight alongside Greeks in defiance of these masters of Asia.

His grin drew stares from deck crew as they hustled about, some to the rail with lines in hand, others to the rigging that stretched from the single mast. The kaleustes barked out his orders. Oars, which until now had dipped shallowly into the swells of the harbor, abruptly plunged deep, the rowers arms locked and shivered as they fought to brake the momentum of the fifty-oar warship. Water foamed and swirled. The vessel slowed. Another shout from the kaleustes and the rowers tugged their oars inboard as the ship slipped smoothly along the quay. At the command of the pilot, two men leapt to the dock, trailing thick lines of rope, and deftly threaded them through huge bronze rings; they yanked hard, drawing the penteconter tight to the quay.

Aristagoras' legs wobbled a bit, unprepared as he was for the loss of movement and the sudden steadiness beneath him. Instinctively he slid his hand along the rail, bracing himself until he shuffled down the brow and onto the dock. His three slaves hustled after him. No one else from Miletos accompanied him. No other freeman, soldier, merchant or aristocrat. He would not speak of this mission to Sparta, and he was certain the Spartans would not either. His horses were unloaded thereafter. Next his mules. Finally two carts. Four men only, but they formed a more than noticeable caravan as they departed Gytheion onto the road north towards Sparta.

It irked him a bit that he had no one to converse with. The three slaves that attended him had the vocabulary of infants, at least that is what he thought as he listened to them each night preparing the evening meal. "Bread!" one would say pointing to a basket. "Huh?" a second would answer. The third would barely manage a nod. *Well*, he thought, *the Spartans shall appear almost eloquent by the time I reach their city.* He turned to look at the three slaves. Their heads bobbed up and down with each step of their horses, eyes closed, one even snoring loudly.

His pace was unhurried, a strange thing for someone on so vital a mission, but he would hardly appear anxious to the Spartans. No, in fact he would be reluctant to accept their help. Even better, they were simple sorts and he would have them begging to come to his aid. It would be to their benefit to fight the Persians. Their reputation would grow. And their influence. No one would challenge their mastery over the mainland if they vanquished the Persians. Yes, his grin returned.

Once over the coastal hills the road plummeted to the level plain of the Eurotas, the massive stone curtain of the Taygetos Mountains to his left and the heights of Mount Parnes far off to his right. The valley was formed like a great funnel, leading them to its neck to the north—Sparta.

They rode for hours, from early morning right after their landing, into mid-afternoon without spelling the horses or themselves. Although an accomplished horseman, Aristagoras' thighs cramped now from pressing hard to his mount's side, his legs chaffed by the hours of riding without boots, and he would have stopped sooner but there was nothing along this road. In the shade of a grove of olive trees he spotted a small columned building, not large enough to be called a house, but more likely a shrine. He slid free from his horse, handed the reins to a trailing slave and walked slowly down the groomed path to the shrine. Two columns flanked a small portal; adjacent to the door and upon vine-like legs stood a tripod, its inner bowl scorched black from offerings. The hinge pins squealed as he pushed open the heavy, oaken door. Inside four oil lamps hung from the low ceiling, a pair on each side of the figure of Ares-Enyalios. The floor beneath the statue of the Spartan war-god was littered with leaden figurines of warriors and diminutive jars containing small leaden rolls of prayers, all votives from pilgrims. *It must have taken many years for these to accumulate,* he thought, looking at the twisted heaps of figures and tumbled pottery. Suddenly he felt the hair on his flesh rise, for he heard singing mingled with what sounded like far off thunder. He fells to his knees, imploring the god that his intentions were indeed pious, and that he would instigate no war that was unjust. The singing grew louder, and now the distinctive peal of Lakonian flutes wove within the crescendo of voices. The thunder transformed somehow to the tromp of feet. Straightway, the humble shrine became enveloped by the sounds. He rose respectfully from his knees, backing away from the statue of Enyalios until he emerged into daylight. All around him stood rank upon rank of scarlet clad hoplites, brazen shields gleaming in the late afternoon sun.

One of the infantrymen approached him, pried his tight-fitting kranos helmet from his head and smiled. "Did we frighten you, Stranger?" the warrior pushed away his sweaty locks, and stroked his trim beard. "My men cannot help but sing when they march."

Aristagoras cleared his throat. He tried to wet his tongue, but his mouth had gone dry. He coughed. Finally words began to emerge. "Oh no, I was paying my respects to the god."

"But, I would venture that is not why you are here in Lakedaimon." The soldier handed his shield to a Helot servant. "Tell me where you are going, and perhaps I can speed you on your journey."

"I have traveled from Miletos to take counsel with King Kleomenes," answered Aristagoras with an air of authority. Behind them several Spartan hoplites circled the three slaves, grinning. One shook his head. Another peeled back the hide covering of the huge bronze map that Aristagoras brought with him to instruct the Spartans on the geography of the Persian Empire

"The gods must have answered your prayers Stranger, for I am on the way to see him myself, along with my company of infantry." Now the Spartan began to walk toward the road. "Ride along side us, and you will see Kleomenes all the quicker."

Aristagoras followed the Spartan. "I do not wish to doubt you, but why are you so certain that you can arrange this meeting. I was told that I might, in fact, wait days to see him."

"Oh, he will see you, for I think I know the ways of my own brother—and may have just a bit of influence with him," added the Spartan with a chuckle.

Now Aristagoras felt even more unsettled then he did within the shrine. "Please pardon my lack of manners, sir. My name is Aristagoras of Miletos."

The Spartan smiled genuinely. "And I am Leonidas of Sparta."

✳✳✳✳✳

The house was not large by his standards. Aristagoras hesitated momentarily before rapping upon the gate to the courtyard. He waited. *That soldier must be wrong*, he thought, as he looked the place up and down. *Not a king's abode. No, an oil merchant would live more richly, even in Miletos.* In a fit of impatience he pounded his fist upon the polished oaken gate. Finally he heard someone walking, announced by the sound of gravel crunching, and the shuffle of feet close to the gate. There was no peephole, no shuttered window, no way to verify what person approached. The gate swung slowly but unhesitatingly open to reveal a young man in a scarlet chiton on the opposite side of the threshold, his fingers lightly furled around the gate-ring. "Kleomenes bids you enter," is all he said as he dipped his head, before turning to lead them in.

"Your master would be disappointed in your lethargy," said Aristagoras as he strode into the courtyard, carrying as much confidence as he could muster.

The young man turned, eyes looking to the earth. "He is not my master sir, but my king." He led on.

Aristagoras sped up his gait, anxious to catch up to the young, impertinent servant, wanting to impart some manners and urgency in the execution of his duties, but before the words could escape his mouth the unmistakable clang of metal striking stone arrested them. He spun around to catch sight of his three servants fumbling with the heavy bronze map, its edge slicing through the hide covering, gleaming brightly and notched into a gouge taken from the marble threshold of the gateway. Aristagoras' face drained. The young Spartan grinned covertly.

The interior of the courtyard exhibited nothing elaborate: a single plane tree grew centered in it; behind this a blue-tiled fountain shimmered; nestled in the columns a olive-wood statue of Athena stood as mute sentinel, her face smiling knowingly at everyone who entered. Aristagoras passed it all without taking notice, stepping into the andreion, his eyes adjusting slowly to the darkness within. A broad-shouldered man, comfortably settled in middle age,

80

rose from a dining couch and extended a welcoming hand. "We have been expecting you," he announced. "Wine for the Stranger."

A servant clad in a tattered gray chiton scurried to the mixing table, quickly plunged a kothon into the krater of wine and handed it to Aristagoras. His arm dipped under the weight of the filled tankard. He nodded politely and sipped, supporting his cup with both hands. Over the rim he could see the Spartan grin a bit as he watched him drink. He cleared his throat of the wine. "I am..."

"...Aristagoras of Miletos," said the Spartan, completing his sentence. "My brother sent word of you."

Aristagoras puzzled look obliged Kleomenes to continue. "Our messengers are very fast, even faster than our soldiers. He was here hours before both you and Leonidas."

Aristagoras paused a bit then spoke. "King Kleomenes, I have traveled far to speak with you, your magistrates and your assembly. I have a proposition that will benefit us both." Kleomenes sank back into his dining couch, while the three servants lugged the bronze map forward. Aristagoras hustled to fetch an oil lamp, and hovered with it over the map. "This is the world. Here are the Pillars of Herakles," instructed Aristagoras as he pointed to the end of the bronze sheet. "Here we are in Sparta." his finger wobbled over what seemed like an insignificant speck near the center of the map. Now he swept his arm past Attika, over the Sea of the Hellenes, across the places marked for Kilikia, Phrygia, Kappadokia, Armenia, Paphylagonia, Babylon, Media, Persia and beyond. "That, good king, is the empire of the Medes. The Great King Darios holds possession of these lands." He drew his finger along the Asian coast. "And many a Greek that call Ionia home toils under this same yoke."

Kleomenes said nothing. He eyes took it all in, every line, each letter, no detail slipping by the canny Spartan. Suddenly the slap of bare feet echoed on the hard marble floor of the corridor outside. A young girl, hardly aged ten, burst into the room at a full sprint, her chiton tugged up by a free hand to clear her thighs. She skidded to a stop before Kleomenes, glanced furtively at Aristagoras, then squeezed her hips with her hands and she bent over, chest heaving as she caught her breath. While gulping for air she looked up at the king. "Who is the Stranger?" she whispered. Now she swept her long hair clear of her face, revealing sparkling azure eyes that seemed to catch every bit of light in the room and intensify it somehow. The sight of her brought a smile to Kleomenes. Aristagoras hung over his map, stunned.

"Gorgo, this is Aristagoras. He has come to Sparta from a far off island." Kleomenes tone was decidedly patronizing.

The young girl resented it. She scowled at her father. "Why is he here?"

"To speak with a king." Kleomenes eyes conveyed his thoughts to his daughter. "Now go." Before he could finish she had bolted out of the andreion. In the courtyard the crash of pottery broke the silence. "She is of a spirited sort." Kleomenes waved his hand. "Continue."

Aristagoras carried his lesson of geography deep into the night, enhancing his tale with descriptions of the vast wealth of the Persian Empire and its subject nations. He had manufactured a grandiose image. "Now Kleomenes, with all I have told you, of the many nations, their wealth and the tribute paid to Darios, would you not agree that this is a prize worth contending for? Together we Ionians and you Spartans could lay claim to it all." Now he left his map and reclined into his divan, plucking up a fig, which he nibbled on between words. "As formidable as this empire may appear, it is defended by lesser men than you have vanquished already." Kleomenes expression, for the first time all evening, transformed and Aristagoras gleaned the change. "Why do you contend with Messenians, men who even as slaves exhibit far more valor than the Persians? You are the very best warriors on earth. What could stop you from laying claim to what your virtue can deliver?" Aristagoras ceased his harangue, tired no doubt from his journey and his one-sided discourse of this evening.

The inscrutable Kleomenes yawned then carefully slid his empty kothon upon an adjacent table. "Aristagoras of Miletos, I will consider everything you have said here tonight. For two days you will be our guest here in Sparta. On the third you will have my answer. Until then I will assign a young man to act as your guide."

Aristagoras did not, at first, know how to accept this answer. He was sure that no man could resist such an offer. Certainly a king even as modestly appointed as Kleomenes could envision the wealth that awaited him, if he allied himself with the Ionians. He nodded. "Thank you King Kleomenes for your hospitality. As far as your servants are concerned I could not in good conscience let my encounter with yours go without a word of concern. The one that admitted me today, well, he is less than enthusiastic in his work."

Kleomenes laughed a bit. "The young man at the gate was no servant, but one of the Hippieis or Knights. His name is Amompharetos. A bit of advice while you are here, friend—do not assume that a man possessed of plain attire or reserved manner is without accomplishment. Loud clothes and a loud mouth count for nothing here in Sparta. Valor is the measure of our men and *our women."*

$$*****$$

That evening Aristagoras dined at the Ephorion, the building where the five principle Spartan magistrates counseled, deliberated, and ate each day. They were quite cordial, and partook of both wine and conversation abstemiously. At first he thought them simple, incapable of coherent speech, much less eloquence, but after he carried much of the talk single-handedly, he began to realize that he told them much while they revealed nothing.

"My gracious Spartan hosts, I thank you much for your hospitality. Your food, though not elaborate," he said unfurling his hand over the platter of barley bread and bowls of black zomos broth, "is more than hearty. I would dare say that no guest leaves a Spartan dining hall still hungry."

Each of the five nodded, acknowledging the compliment. The ephor named Astros rose. "Milesian, my son Ankhimolios answered the pleas of Strangers to deliver them from their enemies and now lies buried in a foreign land. Tell me—what am I to say to him when we meet in Hades Hall? What will we say to our sons and brothers who will lie buried in your land?"

Aristagoras mouth opened but not a word slipped out. He felt his belly collapse as though he had been kicked there.

"Aristagoras," interjected the ephor Perkalos, "be not compelled to answer tonight. But be assured that when you meet with Kleomenes two days hence, he will ask you the same question."

$$*****$$

For two days Aristagoras toured the five villages that comprised Sparta, guided by the knight Amompharetos. Large buildings were few here, the Skias being the most pronounced, for it was the place of assembly for the Apella. The acropolis was a less than ordinary hill, and did not possess the steep walls and high vantage that the citadels of most other cities. A small collection of civic buildings clustered to the southeast of the acropolis, meeting places for the ephors, magistrate of games, and other important officials of the State. The agora itself proved to be something of a novelty for him, once that is, he took the time to examine it and its attendees. Amongst the stalls of wine merchants, potters, fishmongers and olive growers he saw mostly women—an utter contradiction to the rest of Hellas—each adorned in a simple peplos gown and hair close cropped, almost like a boy's. These he soon found out, were the wives of Spartiates, or full citizens, men who were called Equals. Here and there he spotted a young girl poking at the wares in a stall and chatting with one of the older women. "Where are all the men?" he asked.

"At the practice fields or the gymnasion. Some on campaign to the north," replied Amompharetos without looking up, for manners here dictated that all youths keep their eyes downcast out of respect.

"And the boys?"

"Why sir, they attend the Upbringing." His face conveyed his puzzlement at this question. *Even Strangers must know of the Agoge*, he thought.

"You mean they are being tutored at their homes?" Aristagoras prided himself on being well traveled and of considerable experience, so he responded quickly, and expected an equally quick confirmation.

Again, the youth's face betrayed his thoughts. His brow wrinkled. His lips puckered as though he swallowed a dose of vinegar. "Why no, sir. All boys leave their homes at aged seven, to live in the barracks and learn from our superiors."

Aristagoras could not help but pursue this further. "Learn what? Verses of the Poet? Numbers for economics?"

This time Amompharetos exhibited better control. "Why, to be a citizen, of course." Now the youth motioned for Aristagoras to follow. They walked through the agora, keeping the low hill of the acropolis to their left, going beyond the last stall, the final building and onto a narrow road that dipped into a shallow ravine as it approached the Eurotas River.

The two walked for the better part of an hour. Finally Aristagoras put a halt to the excursion. "Where are you taking me? There is nothing here but trees and the sound of the Eurotas."

"I am taking you to where we Spartans learn." At the bank of the river he stopped. "Out there, sir, is our school. The cold waters of the river. The snow capped peaks of Taygetos. The dark woods and the rocky cliffs. That is where we learn. But if you follow me further I will show you where we are tested."

Aristagoras whipped the end of his himation cloak around his left arm adroitly and bounded after the youth. They traced the southwards course of the river now. Above the sound of the wind tossing tree-bound branches they could clearly hear shouting intermingled with cheers. They walked on. As they threaded their way through the tightly packed brambles and reed-choked bank, they suddenly emerged into a clearing filled on its sloping flanks with men. In the center stood neat files of boys, and at the far end of the clearing rose a wooden statue of a goddess that watched over a meter high altar of gleaming white marble. "Which goddess is honored here?" he asked, almost in a whisper.

"That is the Upright goddess Artemis. She is the protector of all who attend the Upbringing." Two men, slaves no doubt, by the look of their tattered chitons and dog skin caps, approached the goddess with plain, woven grass baskets. They stopped before the altar and began to empty the contents, one handful at a time, upon its glistening top. Soon it was covered in small linen wrapped bundles no bigger than a grown man's clenched fist. Now one file of boys edged forward, fifteen in number, each snatching up a long switch of ash from a neat pile in the center of the clearing. Another file of fifteen stepped up and took a switch each; one file faced the other in perfect parallel, not a meter separating them.

"Are they going to fight?" said Aristagoras, his eyes wide and his face thrust forward in anticipation.

"Why of course not," replied Amompharetos. "Watch."

"What is on the altar?"

The youth replied, "Only cheese."

He had not noticed this before, but as he and his guide moved closer to the center-line of the clearing, he could see that the two files of boys did not form battle lines but instead a corridor that led directly to the altar. The last group of boys in the clearing shuffled toward this corridor, stopping at the out stretched arm of a graying man in a crimson chiton. He held a long T-shaped walking staff that he now employed as a barrier. The boys pushed forward against the staff. The old man looked at them then glanced at the thirty youths armed with ash saplings. Aristagoras now knew that they were guards, and the prize they protected lay scattered before the goddess.

"Off!" shouted the old man as he swung his staff aside, the small herd of boys charging without hesitation at their release. The first one burst between the lines of defenders, not even bothering to shield his head and face with his arms. The snap of green wood striking bare flesh was the only sound emanating from the fracas. No one cried out, no, no one even shouted with bravado. Not even the false courage summoned by a rage-induced battle cry protected a single one of them. After an excruciatingly long stretch, the last boys stumbled through the gauntlet and towards the altar. Here some greedily scooped armfuls of the cheese, while others took only what they could secure in clenched hands; they raced back through the line of defenders. Four stumbled out the far end, each still with at least one prize of cheese in hand.

The fifth boy though, had tripped midway through, and there at the feet of his tormentors he collapsed under the barrage of whips. So intense was the beating that in their zeal the defenders had opened deep wounds on each other as they lashed at the boy at their feet and the others that had piled up behind him. It was only when three of the cheese-stealers dropped their loot and dragged and pushed their injured companion forward and beyond the whips did the spectacle finally cease.

Aristagoras said nothing. He watched as slaves worked on the one boy who had fallen under the whips. They cradled his limp body into a sitting position, and began daubing his bloody cheeks with a water soaked cloth. Others knelt, the dust clinging to their naked, bleeding bodies while only a very few retained the energy to stand. Now each took a quick survey of his own body before slowly walking toward a group of seated Spartiates on the flank of the clearing. Not one paused to look at their fallen comrade, not a hint of hesitation as each passed by. Aristagoras thought this cruel. "Why don't they help him?"

"Why sir, they did. Most lost their prizes to deliver him from the whips. But now he is in the hands of the iatros, and the goddess. There is nothing more any of them can do for him."

Aristagoras, once he had realized the logic of the explanation, moved out of the sanctuary of the goddess along with the departing crowd. He reasoned these actions sensible, but his gut tightened at the cool logic of it all. Suddenly he felt a tug on his cloak.

"Sir, it is time. I am to bring you to Kleomenes."

The walk back through the agora and along the Aphetaid Road proved a quiet, almost restful one. They had encountered no one on its course until they approached the house of Kleomenes and neither spoke of the contest at the sanctuary of the Upright goddess. Amompharetos rapped on the gate, and did not wait for someone to answer, but pushed it open, allowing Aristagoras to enter before him. "You know the way from here, do you not?" He turned and left, not waiting for, or expecting a response. Aristagoras hurried across the courtyard, and halted just before the threshold to the andreion, collecting himself for he did not wish to appear too eager.

"Welcome Aristagoras. Please enter and be seated." There sat Kleomenes upon a stubby, three-legged stool, his daughter on his knee. The girl studied Aristagoras as he made his way to an adjacent couch. Propped against a plain square oaken table was his bronze map. Kleomenes gently whisked his daughter off his knee, quickly rising. He pointed. "How long a journey is it from the Sea of the Hellenes to Susa?"

Aristagoras crouched over his map. "Three months time." He was sure his answer would do nothing but impress the Spartan, considering it would take less than a day to reach the sea from Sparta.

Kleomenes' daughter grinned and shook her head. She stared at Aristagoras now. The steady gaze of her azure eyes unsettled him.

"Must the child remain during discussions meant for men?" Aristagoras flashed a look of contempt her way.

"She is but a tiny girl. No harm to you, but a comfort to her father. I have no cause to send her away." Kleomenes moved to a dining couch, snapped up a kothon of wine and leaned back. "You sir, are to depart Lakedaimon today."

Aristagoras was stunned by the edict. He had expected discussion, debate, even argument—anything but a terse rebuff. "What have I done to offend you?"

"You insult my intelligence Aristagoras. Three months' march from the sea! Either you exaggerate to impress me or you think me mad that I would entertain such a ludicrous proposal. Three months from the sea!"

"King Kleomenes, I neither exaggerate nor insult, but offer you the truth. A truth not couched in qualifications, nor embellishments, but delivered to you without manipulation." Aristagoras winced at Gorgo's constant gaze as though she worked the eye curse upon him. He slipped the blue-glass charm from beneath his chiton and rubbed it between his finger and thumb. *It did Krios little good*, he thought as he worked to conjure its magic. "If the prospect of wealth does not induce you to join us, perhaps the realization of it might. I have brought with me half a talent in gold. That is to be my gift to you if you join us. And when we reach my island, two talents more will be waiting for you."

Kleomenes tried to bring his cup to his lips, but Gorgo pulled it away. "Father, send this man away now, or he will surely corrupt you." Her eyes drilled Aristagoras.

Kleomenes rose. "You, Stranger, will depart for Gytheion now."

Chapter 9

Athens—499 BC

Aristagoras descended from the bema exhausted. He had promised the Athenians the very same things as the Spartans—and more. He and his sponsor, the Athenian Melanthios, shouldered their way through the crowd toward the exit of the Pynx. As he departed, he caught sight of the templed Acropolis gleaming in the pure light of an Attic summer morning. He shuffled down the steps and onto the pathway that would lead him to the Agora.

Behind him he heard shouts—arguments, no doubt, before the vote would be taken. Unlike Sparta, Athens Agora teemed with commerce, peddlers barking at passers-by, extolling the quality of their wares. The men here were metics, foreigners now residing in Athens, slaves or women, for the male citizens had been herded up to the Pynx by slaves, who whipped any lolly-gaggers with rope dipped in ochre paint to mark them out as being less than enthusiastic at fulfilling their civic duties. Here casting the vote proved as important as casting a spear in Sparta. In neither place could one neglect his duty.

"Come, let us find a shady place and a drink of wine," said Melanthios. They strolled through the Agora, passed the statues of the Heroes, the Fountain House and toward the Kerameikos. "In here." Melanthios tugged Aristagoras' arm. They both ducked as they entered the dark, cool kapeleion, an empty place except for a single slave who tended to it while his master was at the Assembly. He asked for a pitcher of both water and another of akratos wine, having the slave mix the two in a coarsely fashioned bowl. They each dunked a cup into the bowl then sipped. Melanthios' eye's watered. He spit.

"Is this from the top or the bottom," he bellowed as he tossed the cup at the slave.

"Sir, this is fresh from Khios yesterday. I just opened the amphora this morning."

Melanthios shook his head. "Something different. That is more resin than wine. It tastes like tree sap!"

The door of the wine shop flew open. "Master!" A young boy stood in the doorway struggling to catch his breath.

Aristagoras' heart drummed in his chest. He knew why the boy was here, and he almost wished he would not tell them. The vote, he was sure, would not be in his favor. Melanthios got up from his stool and strode to the panting youth. They exchanged words, but Aristagoras could not hear them.

Melanthios turned from the doorway, a huge grin upon his face. "I think it easier to convince thirty thousand Athenians than a single Spartan. You have been promised twenty warships and I, my friend, will command them."

*****

His penteconter slipped out from the harbor at Phaleron, just as it had slipped out of the Spartan harbor at Gytheion, but this time he departed with a full load of cargo, not of grain, nor wine, nor olives, but of possibilities. Not only had Athens promised aid in his war with Persia, but Eretria too was sending a contingent—only five triremes, but it was help all the same. He smiled while rubbing his natty beard. *That little Spartan brat had more sense than the whole of Athens*, he mused.

By midday they had turned cape Sounion, skirting the high-cliffed shoreline as they steered due east, their course set for the island of Andros.

He had hoped to make land fall by dark, but day light fled along with the late afternoon breeze and the sky ahead to the east began to reveal the flicker here and there of stars, while in their wake the last hint of day tinged the sky deep red. Now even the stars blinked out, swathed in the thickening night mists upon the flat-calm sea. Aristagoras kept his eyes locked ahead, straining to pick out the telltale crease of black that would disclose their destination. It seemed as though the oarsmen rowed in slumber, no conversation, not a single word floated up from the sub-deck benches, only the slap and slice of oars followed by a gentle gurgle as they penetrated the quiescent water. With each draw they were propelled forward. Suddenly a star shimmered, followed by another and another, oddly forming a straight line low on the horizon.

The captain strode by him on his way to the bow. "That be Andros." He kept on till he clutched the rail, leaning out over the bow like a figurehead. "I can smell land before most can see it."

Sure enough the line of stars swelled into the sputtering flames of torches that lit the quays of Andros. Silently the penteconter sliced through the harbor as the pilot leaned hard on the tillers to bring them parallel to the tongues of planks that formed the quay. All along the dock figures seemed to ooze from the mist, until the vessel slipped by them only feet away. The kaleustes yelled. Oars dipped and shuddered, easing them to their berth as crewman scrambled over the rails, working the lines to secure their ship. Aristagoras and his servants made their way off the ship on wobbly legs, to be greeted by the harbormaster and his two sons.

"Safe and sound are you. Safe and sound," repeated the harbormaster. "I have ordered a fine deipnon meal prepared for us." His two sons, both of less than ten years, pushed and poked at each other as their father tried to converse with Aristagoras. "Come. We must hurry before they can do real damage to each other." He tugged on Aristagoras' arm, leading him away from the docks and toward a small hillock that dominated the harbor. "It's not far." He looked up for a moment to the house and tower upon the hill. The party quickly made their way through the alleyways and beyond the smell of spoiling fish to the path that lead up and to their waiting supper.

And so the same scene repeated itself the next evening at Tenos, then Ikaria, until finally they arrived at Miletos on the shore of Asia.

"This is the beginning of great things," declared Aristagoras as he strode into his courtyard and the embrace of his brother Kharopinos.

Chapter 10

Koresos, Port of Ephesos—498 BC

Kharopinos nodded with satisfaction as he surveyed the arrival of the fleet. Even the gulls swirling overhead seemed in awe—the entire harbor was crammed with war-ships, the docks swarming with men, and the very air shuddered with the cacophony of frenzied activity. Of course he expected the Ionian Greeks—the very ones who for years bent under the Persian yoke—to dispatch contingents, but it was the sight of twenty vessels from Athens and five more from Eretria that roused his spirits and confirmed his brother Aristagoras' promise. But upon the docks and in the narrow streets it hardly looked like an invasion. Troop ships unloaded their cargo of heavy infantry with the casualness of freighters dealing grain. Servants paid more attention to arms and armor than did their masters, who toured the harbor town like gawking merchants, stroking bolts of fine eastern cloth, sipping date-wine, and tilting delicately etched bronze pots to catch the golden light of late afternoon.

"Kharopinos, when do we march inland?" Melanthios, the Athenian, stood poised on the brow-plank, his very presence beckoning Kharopinos to disembark.

"First light. It will take us till then to organize it all." He swept his open hand across the scene of the gaping harbor—a scene of tumult and optimism. Now he spun around and pointed to a distant peak to the east. "That is where we march to." He bounded down the bowing brow-plank, halting to embrace Melanthios. "With your help we will free all the Greeks of Ionia." He squeezed the shoulders of Melanthios, more to assure himself that this man was no phantom, no hollow promise, but flesh, blood, and the true substance of an ally. "Come. I have secured a house, a place for all the strategoi to meet before we embark on our great enterprise." He hastened them along the bustling Harbor Road quickly departing Koresos, his eye drawn down the unbending thoroughfare to the agora of Ephesos.

As they passed the marketplace the road angled sharply to the right onto the Marmaro Dromos. Here, amongst the tightly packed houses, he saw lamps flicker on through open windows. Soon young women with painted faces leaned out. They shouted their prices while directing the interested to the proper doorway. The men in the streets glanced up, some laughed, while others counted the coin in their purses. Only a few slipped inside.

"Pornes," said Kharopinos with disgust. "Why waste your money on them? They cannot sing, nor play the flute. And as for conversation, you can expect none. They spread their legs and open their hand."

Melanthios thought, *sometimes that is all a man requires*.

Kharopinos tugged on his arm. "But when we take Sardis—." He grinned. "There are women who know how to please, and you will not have to pay an obol for one."

After they passed through the Gates of Herakles, and by the Fountain House, the neighborhood thinned as they wended their way further inland, away from the noise of temples, shops and manufactories and toward the open meadows and fields that flanked the river Kaytros. One large house, its windows spilling light, commanded the roadway. "Here, my friend," Kharopinos announced as he turned down the path toward the sprawling estate. His stride lengthened with anticipation as he swung the courtyard gate open. Inside several servants stood in a row, crowns of garland in their hands. Kharopinos plucked one up and handed it to Melanthios while placing another upon his own head before entering the spacious andreion. Inside more than a dozen couches lined the walls, ornate lamps hung from chains in the ceiling while a crazed scene of the god Dionysos leading the Mainads embellished the brightly tiled floor. In the center and flanked by two slaves stood a huge krater, or mixing vessel for wine. Five men already inclined upon sumptuous couches. Kharopinos walked directly toward one of them, latching onto Melanthios' arm to be certain he still followed. "Eualkidas of Eretria, this is Melanthios the Athenian."

The Eretrian smiled congenially. "Please gentlemen, you must assist me with the wine. I have tried, but no matter how much I drink I cannot seem to empty that." He jabbed his finger to the immense krater in the center of the andreion. Kharopinos bellowed with laughter. Melanthios forced a smile.

In not much time the andreion had filled, commanders from each of the Ionian cities joining the symposion, all wanting to understand the strategy of Aristagoras through the words of his brother. The obvious was restated. They would, in the morning, march on the great city of Sardis, jewel in the crown of the western satrapies of King Darios. But then what? At least that is the question that swirled in the mind of Melanthios. Aristagoras has no aim, no goal, no solution to the Persian occupation. Athens sent only twenty warships, a small force in the scheme of things. But the implications were large indeed. Once they marched, the only alternative to victory over the Persians would be defeat at their hands. He strained to imagine it, but his mind could not conjure such a victory.

*****

The army lumbered out of Ephesos, using the open banks of the river Kaytros as its roadway inland. All around them cultivated fields stretched out towards the mountains, their stalks of grain bristling skyward, rippling in the breeze, here and there the head of a farmer poking above the crops, staring in amusement at the great army. For two days the march tracked the river through this abundant land, keeping to a level, and easy grade. On the third they began their ascent of Mount Tmolos. Although more taxing than the banks of the Kaytros, Tmolos proved an easier climb to him than any of the peaks that surrounded Athens. Melanthios gauged the height by the effort to ascend it. *Maybe the height of Aigilaos,* he mused, *but certainly not as tall as Pentelikos.* At the modest summit he felt the wind change, sweeping up from the plain. Wood-smoke filled his nostrils, mixing with the scent of bread baking, wafting up from the city below. The walls appeared unimposing to him, but beyond them and cut into a tall, ragged hill loomed the terraced citadel, its stone-work gazing blankly back at him in defiance. He traced the road down the slope of Tmolos to the open, imploring gates of Sardis. Like ants, he watched tiny figures swarming into the city, pouring in from the fields and the tiny clusters of farmsteads and outbuildings that lucklessly stood beyond the protection of the walls. Now the alarm horns echoed up from Sardis, while a squadron of cavalry streamed out from the gates. This troop of horsemen, numbering no more than a hundred, reined up bisecting the road. He knew they returned his long stares. He also knew that a mere one hundred stood little chance against them.

Kharopinos, surrounded by the other strategoi, called to Melanthios. "Have your Athenians assemble down there, where the river Paktolos cuts through that grove of olive."

Melanthios' eye picked it out at once, a fine and proper spot for assembly, so he waved his men and their train of baggage forward and down the snaking path toward the plain below. With each step in their descent the heat rose up to meet them, until the breeze fled entirely and the sun drilled down unabated. Men emptied their flasks, and yelled to slaves to refill them, but these poor souls toiled under the weight of their masters' armor and kit, for few led mules and fewer had horses to relieve them of the burden, freeing them to fetch water. As the Athenians fanned out at the foot of Tmolos, they began to surround each tree trunk, collecting under the sparse foliage to acquire any wisp of shade and bit of shadow, knowing that as uncomfortable as the heat had been, it would soon become intolerable here on the searing, breezeless plain. They reluctantly commenced to gear up. Some men squeezed between halves of hammered bronze chest plates while others wrestled with linen and leather corselets, prying down the stiffened shoulder-flaps before lacing them to their chests. Melanthios pushed the bronze pins that held the halves of his armor cuirass together, enclosing his chest and belly in protective, thick bronze. A servant handed him his kranos helmet. He stroked its horsehair crest as though it were the locks of a beautiful woman—gently, with almost a caress, and an admiring glance. His smile left him as he looked to the sky. He would not don it yet, not in the heat of this sun. It would cook him.

His Athenians formed their lokhos or unit, the Eretrians to the left and the Paktolos River to his right. Several hundred meters away, across the shimmering plain, the Persian cavalry pranced about anxiously, cutting the road leading to Sardis. More Greeks poured down the mountain and spilled into phalanx order. With each passing moment the formation swelled. Now a single rider tore down the road from above, dust billowing behind as he reined up before Melanthios. "Kharopinos says all the Ionians are in rank and file. Advance at the signal."

Melanthios grabbed the bridle of the horse, inducing the beast to snort in defiance. ""What of the sphagia? How can we do battle without sacrifice to Artemis?"

The messenger shrugged his shoulders. "Kharopinos says there will be no battle." Without another word he spun his horse around and galloped back along the restless phalanx. Now a single blast from a salphinx trumpet tore through the stifling air. Melanthios looked to his left. First one hoplite, then a few more stepped off, until at last the entire front rank strode forward in a clumsy surge. Spears rattled and shields clanged as the Greeks lumbered toward the Persian horsemen and Sardis. The distance compressed, but still the enemy clung to the road. At two hundred meters Melanthios watched as the Persians notched arrows and drew their bowstrings back, burying them in their faces. Suddenly the air hummed and whistled with bronze headed shafts swirling down on them. Not a single arrow hit its mark, most drilling harmlessly into the dust of the plain while a few rattled and pinged off the bronze shields and helmets of the Greeks. This feeble display encouraged the Athenians, accelerating the measured left-right pace of the phalanx to an uncoordinated jog. Suddenly the defenders of Sardis wheeled about and retreated for the open gates, causing the Greek army to explode into cheers, some brandishing spears over head while other thumped them brazenly on their shields, all yelling obscene taunts at the fleeing cavalry. Now the phalanx disintegrated into a boiling mob. Melanthios shouted out the order for his lokhos to halt. Most did. Only a very few mindlessly trailed behind the other disordered contingents.

"Halt! Stop here!" We need the engines." Melanthios shaded his eyes, peering up the slope of Tmolos, picking out plumes of dust that indicated fast movement of men and horse. A band of riders galloped down the road that mirrored the river Paktolos, shouting at groups of hoplites along their way until reining up near the Athenians and Melanthios.

"Kharopinos orders an advance to the walls. It will be some time before the rams can be brought forward." The rider pointed back, over his shoulder toward the ascending road and Tmolos.

Melanthios faced his men. "In column of march," he shouted. They reformed, eight men across and fifty deep, stepping off down the road. By now he had pushed his kranos helmet free of his face, gulping fresh air like cool wine. His hair was slick with sweat, his black beard glistened as the heavy armor and afternoon heat depleted him of what energy he had remaining after the fever of battle had subsided. The pace slowed. Men dragged their spear tips through the dust as their arms dangled. Some stopped to sling their heavy aspides upon their backs like tortoise shells, alleviating their left arms of twenty pounds of bronze and oak.

As they staggered forward Melanthios searched out the walls and towers for movement, defenders rallying, archers taking aim, pitch-men lighting cauldrons, but the parapets and crenellations stared back in stony silence. *Kharopinos was right*, he thought, *there will be no battle.* The gates before him stretched upwards over ten meters in height, the flanking towers another ten, but still a daring hoplite who had stripped from his armor began to clamber up the gate, using the huge bronze reinforcing straps as footholds until he reached the top. Once there he swung a leg onto the sill of the gate-house window then rolled inside, disappearing for a moment before standing tall in the opening, waving for all to see.

"Welcome to Sardis," bellowed Melanthios as he began to break into a trot.

At first it moved ever so slightly, a shadow cutting a deep line between the two gates, while the hinge pins squealed and groaned. Men tossed away their spears and shields, rushing to shoulder the gate full open. The Greeks streamed in.

*****

Artaphernes, son of the elder Artaphernes, gazed out from the terraced fortress of the citadel. Sent here as a favor to his father by Darios, he was posted to Sardis as an extension of the Six—the men of the Great King's inner circle—to report full truth about the gossip of revolt. He could hardly have expected an attack. From here he could clearly see Greeks from beyond the walls swarming toward the Smyrna Gate. He watched as men in the gatehouse tower signaled out to the plain beyond. Now he scanned down to the marketplace in the center of the city and to the remnants of his garrison troops as they mustered, a pitifully small force of Lydian dismounted cavalry, Paphalagonian javelineers and Lykian sickle-men. They had been caught unawares and almost defenseless, the bulk of his troops departed to rendezvous with the army of Datis. He knew the city now belonged to the Greeks. But the citadel—that was a different matter.

The captain of archers shouldered his way through the crowded battlement. "We are holding the market—."

Before he could continue Artaphernes cut him off, "Withdraw to the citadel."

The archer opened his mouth, but spoke not a word, at once wanting to protest the order for this withdrawal, but at the same time embracing it—and life. He paused for a moment before touching his brow with the clustered fingers of his right hand, while backing away for several steps until the press of soldiers forced him to turn. Artaphernes returned to his vigil, keeping watch on the marauding Greeks in the city below, shouts of drunken men, screams of women—the uproar of havoc—overwhelming all other sounds. Evening light withered but the cry of a dying city swelled along with the descent of night. A whiff of burning wood shook him from his unfocused gaze. He scoured the city intently, looking for a flame, a spray of embers, a telltale spiral of smoke, then suddenly a monstrous crackle echoed across the chaos. Not far from the Smyrna Gate the roof of a nondescript building split, releasing a column of sparks that lit the night sky like an immense torch. Embers showered down upon the roofs of the houses and shops where they buried deep into the reed thatching, multiplying the destruction in moments. Gusts of wind swept down from Tmolos, stoking combustion on a grand scale.

Artaphernes stared out at the King's city, watching it as the flames gorged on every structure in sight, the roar of turbulent fire replacing the human cries of terror. He knew he was safe, here upon the terraced hill, behind the thick stonework of the citadel. He drew scant satisfaction from the fact that the Greeks had foolishly destroyed the wealth of the very city they had come to plunder. "They will not get far," he whispered to himself.

$$* * * * *$$

Datis kept his horse to a slow canter. It was finished. The haze that hung like a veil beneath the midday sun was no fog gathered by mountains, no mist conjured by a warm sea, but the result of destruction. Carcasses of burnt oxen, sheep and goats mingled with charred corpses of men, and around him, as his column advanced past the foundations of the tower, mounds of smoldering rubble pressed from all sides. None of his men spoke. Only hoof beats of his cavalry echoed amongst the silent devastation. Far off, a dog barked. As they rode deeper into the ruins of the city a gentle breeze began to whisk away the smoke, revealing with stark honesty, the handiwork of the Greeks. Fire had ravaged it all, reed-built houses making for fine tinder. He shook his head in disbelief. He had been part of besieging armies, a conqueror marching into fallen towns and villages before, but never had he witnessed such perfect destruction. In the past he had marveled at the sight of scavenging dogs patrolling the debris, carrion crows swirling above many scenes of pillage and even beggars and thieves foraging amongst the dead, but here nothing moved. Here nothing lived. As his column trotted into the marketplace, they had to thread their way through the clusters of bodies, huddles of flesh that squeezed into the last place of refuge in the inferno that had been Sardis. Only the sight of the stepped walls of the citadel brought any order to the scene around him and any hope that some had survived. Atop the battlements figures stirred. Now for sure he knew some had lived.

"Quickly on," he shouted, kicking his heels hard into the ribs of his horse. Now the only things that filled his vision were the immense hewn stones of the fortress. A horn sputtered out its alarm from the citadel; men oozed into every open space upon its walls and towers. He waved his messenger on. The rider burst by him, galloping at full sprint toward the huge bronze sheathed doors. On the wall a signaler excitedly swirled his pennant overhead.

*****

"They are coming! Persians!" The kataskopos shouted the warning as he sped down the fractured column of Greek infantry, imparting the dread he felt at the sight of their pursuers.

Melanthios turned to his servant. "Give me the wine," he commanded as he planted his eight-foot long spear into the tilled soil of the plain. "I'll drink it before they do." He snapped a glance off toward the horizon to the east, and the growing rumble of charging horsemen. "Have the men form up."

A blast from the salphinx transmitted his order, inciting the Athenians to collect into the rank and file of the phalanx. Some of the Ionians stopped and geared up, joining Melanthios and his lokhos of hoplites as they evolved from open order to close, shields overlapping, their front ranks bristling with a hedge of iron-tipped spears. The Eretrians, too, bravely halted their flight. Still, the larger portion of their army raced headlong towards Ephesos.

At first it resembled wind raking through the trees, then the sound deepened, as though the entire horizon growled. To the east clouds drifted from the plain upward, the signature of men and beasts on the move. As they grew nearer he felt the very ground shiver as flecks of light flashed from within the advancing clouds, the metal of weapons and armor catching the hot light of the summer sun. "Not more than a mile," he said turning to the warrior to his left. The man stared straight ahead, merely nodding. He glanced to his right, to the shallow Kaystor and its negligible protection. Maybe they will avoid it, he thought as he re-hefted his aspis, letting its concave surface smother his left shoulder. The dust cloud swelled, suddenly disgorging thousands of horsemen onto the plain less than a thousand meters away. Alien horns wailed from deep within the advancing enemy ranks. The Persian force veered left, away from the river and toward the flanking high ground. "They are by-passing us," he shouted above the roar of the cavalry. Suddenly a squadron of mounted archers peeled away from the main body and swept down upon the left flank and the Eretrians. The wing of hoplites compressed and curled back, instinctively presenting their shields head on, while unwittingly bending the left flank back at a wobbly right angle to the phalanx. By chance the Eretrians had saved them all from annihilation. The Persians, seeing the once inviting flank sealed, launched a volley of arrows into them before tearing up the ridge to rejoin the main body.

"Wheel left!" Melanthios thrust his spear high in the air as he jogged along with his entire right wing to keep pace with the phalanx as it spun in an undulating arc to face the Persians. What they lacked in discipline they made up for in energy, running through the fields of tall grain under the weight of their panoplies, forming, moving and reforming many times over until the Athenians had swung over two hundred meters before regrouping and realigning their front ranks and trailing files, disorder finally jostled out of the phalanx entirely. The Kaystor, once to his right was behind them now. They did not advance. They stood, shields up and in silence, as thousands of Persian, Karian and Lydian troops poured by them in pursuit of the retreating Ionians. For the moment, at least, they were safe.

Melanthios pried his kranos helmet off his head by the crest, and shouted for his servant Telos. "Wine!" From behind the last rank a wine flask seemingly rose up above the helmeted heads of the Athenians, a man scrambling between the files holding it high as he shouldered his way forward. Melanthios unplugged the flask and licked his dry lips before emptying it in one abbreviated gulp, an escaping trickle glistening on his beard. "You had some, didn't you," he barked at the slave as he tossed the empty flask his way.

Meekly Telos nodded. "Master, like you I worried that the Persians might take it."

For hours they remained in loose formation, armor and weapons partially discarded, eating and drinking away what little they had carried along with them, all the while looking west toward the ridge-line that separated them from Ephesos, their ships, and the safety of home. At any moment they expected to see the smoke rise as the Persians set their fleet alight. Darkness began to settle in around them, the full moon rose, casting eerie shadows amongst the slumping forms of hoplites. To the west, toward Ephesos, every man kept watch, for the returning Persian army for sure, but hoping against all, that the horizon would stay dark, and the sky above it clear, free of the glow of fire and the gloom of smoke.

"Master, wake up." Telos peeled back the himation cloak that Melanthios had pulled up over his head while asleep. He rubbed his eyes as the slave repeated his words while staring to the horizon. Above the hills the sky glowed red. His heart plummeted. He swallowed hard letting his head fall as he slumped forward in despair. "The ships. The ships are lost," he whispered, but still Telos heard him.

"Why no master. That is east. That is the sun."

Melanthios turned quickly around. Stars flickered in the still dark western sky. "Up," he shouted as he sprang to his feet while rubbing the stiffness from his aching left arm. He dreaded heaving his shield again. It would be hours before they reached Ephesos. All across the makeshift Greek encampment, armor clanged and clattered amongst the murmurs of excited conversation while the Athenians, Eretrians, and remnant Ionians readied themselves for the march. As the sun broke over the hills to the east and the sky brightened, the unmistakable sight of carrion birds circling to the west drew all their attention. The ridge was not far off now. Soon they would see what drew the flocks of vultures and crows. But Melanthios already knew. So did most. Ahead of him the first men to reach the crest of the ridge halted and unslung their shields and planted their spears. As more spilled up on to the ridge more stopped advancing. Melanthios had to squeeze through the press of men. All around him they stood in silence. On the plain below, scattered like the bright leaves of a storm struck tree lie the Ionian Greeks. Melanthios squinted, straining to catch sight of any movement, any sign that some, even one, still lived. Vultures hopped amongst the corpses searching out meals, tussling with one another over strands of flesh, tearing away at the mounds of bodies.

His heart raced as he realized what all had forgotten. "The Persians!" He pushed men aside to get to the very front of the crowded ridge, looking right, left, north, then south. For as far as he could see and in every direction, there was no sign of their enemy.

Chapter 11

Ekbatana, Summer Palace of Darios—498 BC

The eunuch Bupares pinched some incense from a small gilded casket and sprinkled it atop the hissing embers of the burner, hardly noticing the gray cloud that issued up on its way to Ahura Mazda. He performed the duty perfunctorily, with hardly the reverence that his god demanded. The pungent smoke drifted toward the throne of Darios, only to be chased away by the long, slow sweep of the fan overhead. The slave seemed to be asleep, but still he kept the rhythm steady and the Great King cooled. Darios waved the messenger forward. The man staggered up the platform to the foot of the throne, his hand trembling with both fatigue and terror. The message had made its way via the pirradazis or Persian post stations that punctuated a full day's ride all along the Royal Road. Remarkably, in only seven days, Datis' message had traversed the distance from Sardis to Ekbatana, a journey usually comprised of months.

"To me," said Bupares as he snorted the fragrant air of the great hall. He snatched the curled parchment from the messenger then waved him off with a flutter of his left hand. He snapped the scroll open and scanned it deliberately. As he read his eyes grew wider.

"Well!" shouted Darios.

"Great King, Datis and Artaphernes the Younger send this message," he cleared his throat as he prepared to recite. "King Darios—Sardis, capital city of the satrapy of Lydia, has been sacked by the barbarous Greeks. The treasury was well defended, and is still in your possession. The Western Army, under the command of your servant Datis, has indeed delivered your full wrath to the fleeing Greeks…"

Darios bolted up from his throne, snatching the missive from Bupares slender, trembling fingers. "What Greeks?" he barked as he began to read. Furious, he tossed the scroll onto the multi-carpeted floor of the apandana. "Bring Histiaios to me. Bring him now!"

Two of the Immortals burst from their station near the great door of the hall and ran out. Darios began to pace in front of his marble throne. "These Ionians! I know them and I know we shall deal with them in our own time. But these others—Greeks from across the sea. Greeks from Europe," snapped Darios as his bejeweled hand shivered at the discarded scroll.

Mardonios knelt slowly then uncurled the parchment, reading slowly. "They are Athenians, Great King. The countrymen of Hippias."

"Where is Histiaios!" Darios strode the length of the apandana, causing the stewards to hurry, barely swinging open the immense cedar doors before Darios burst by and through. His courtiers scurried after him like chicks after a hen. Following them all in no great hurry was the eunuch Bupares, ever flicking his flyswatter in time with his steps. Darios, as he emerged into the light of mid morning, turned and grabbed a bow from one of the Immortals that flanked the entrance to the great hall. He notched a shaft quickly— expertly, for every Persian noble, from his earliest days, was taught to master the bow—and launched the arrow skyward. "Grant, Ahura-Mazda, that I may punish these Athenians." He threw the empty bow into the dust at the base of the wide stairway. From across the expanse of the palace grounds he caught sight of the two Immortals dispatched to fetch Histiaios, their task in hand.

The guards, one on either side of the Greek, dipped into an exaggerated bow then backed away. Histiaios mustered what little reverence he could for another man and merely touched his brow with the fingers of his right hand. In stammering Persian he asked," What service may I be to you, Great King Darios?" Histiaios knew exactly why he had been summoned. He dredged up every bit of self-control to appear surprised at the words that would follow.

Darios continued to pace, but somehow the slave holding the huge linen parasol managed to keep him in the shade—most of the time—struggling to arrest its wild tilt each time the king abruptly stopped and changed course. Mardonios had to fight back the grin that threatened to burst across his face. Darios spun to face Histiaios. "It seems that the very man who you left in charge of the city of Miletos has instigated a revolt against us. How could this have happened without your knowledge?"

Histiaios forced open his eyes wide, feigning astonishment. "My lord, how can you say such a thing? Does it seem likely to you that I would do anything to injure my greatest benefactor? Is not what is yours, mine? If Aristagoras is for certain guilty of this deed, you may without doubt, know that he acted by his own counsel and not with mine." Histiaios dropped to sit on the polished marble stairs. Holding his head in his hands, he drew deep, exaggerated breaths.

Bupares hustled over to the Greek. "How dare you sit in the presence of the King!"

Darios interrupted, "Allow him this discourtesy, if only for a moment." Now he approached the Greek. "What are we to do with your countrymen?"

Histiaios peeked up from his counterfeit despair. "Great Darios, I cannot believe that Aristagoras and the Milesians are acting against you, unless they have totally deceived me also, and waited until I was far from Miletos. Here at your court, I have little influence over them." Now he bounded up from his seat, almost teary-eyed with rage. "Grant me your leave, Great King, and I will go to the coast and put everything right for you. I swear I will deliver unto you any man who has raised his hand against you, most of all Aristagoras, if he indeed be a part of it."

*****

Histiaios stared out from the terrace wall toward the summit of the hill that the city of Ekbatana surrounded. From here he could see the gilded battlements of the Royal Treasury and Palace both ablaze with sunlight intensified by the opulent gold plating that overlaid the brickwork. Ekbatana, originally the capital of the Median empire, was now the summer home to Persian royalty, a place to escape the searing winds that raked the more southerly capital of Susa during the long days of summer. The walls of the city were built in concentric circles, each squeezing tighter as it approached the hilltop and the Royal Palace. The fortified tops of the walls were adorned each in differing brilliant colors, white the outermost, followed by black, crimson, azure blue, then orange, with the innermost two concentric walls being covered not in paint but in the precious metals of silver and finally gold. No commoners dwelt within these walls—this city was built to protect the Royal Family and its treasure. If ever attacked, the most ordinary inhabitants would perish, for they dwelled beyond the walls and upon the indefensible plain.

He smiled more than he had in years. Soon he would be back in his home city of Miletos. As he turned to re-enter the cool darkness of his quarters he studied the stiff, lifeless sculptures of winged lions and gryphons with flying gods hovering above them. It was an alien world and one that would be rid of him.

"Is this the last of it?" Histiaios' words echoed off the bare walls of the all but empty chamber. Only a single lamp hanging above the doorway remained. His servants had packed up everything else: four small lacquered tables, the two fine-crafted footstools that the Great King himself had bestowed upon him, all the bed linens, chests of clothes, caskets of incense, and even his paltry collection of scrolls with the stories of the Poet inked upon them—these had all been loaded onto carts for the journey to Sardis. Two slaves wrestled the last chest out of the room and into the corridor beyond, where they began insulting each other as they continued to fumble it. "I'll take out the damage on your hide!" bellowed Histiaios. Footfalls sped up. The corridor fell into silence.

Finally he emerged from his quarters into a bright afternoon, the expansive courtyard crammed with a half score of fully laden black mules and seven wagons bursting with goods. A slave knelt before his horse, acting as a step stool; Histiaios planted one foot upon his back, and nervously sprang up onto the skittish mare, then led his inconsiderable caravan out onto the main thoroughfare of Ekbatana, where a dathabam of ten Royal cavalrymen waited as escort.

The captain of the Persian horsemen reined up next to Histiaios. "We will be taking a northern road from here to Nineveh, almost a month's time until we join the Royal Road there."

"Is there no faster way?" Histiaios caught himself. "I am an agent of the Great King and have urgent business in Sardis."

The Persian shook his head. "There is no shorter route. Besides, if we were to arrive there today we would have to wait for the flood to recede. The road is not passable in early summer. "He tugged on his horse's reins and spun the animal away, cantering up to the head of the caravan where he talked with others of his dathabam. Soon they all burst out laughing as they glanced back to the Greek.

The horses snorted and mules brayed as they moved off, the groaning of wagon wheels adding to the sounds of the caravan in motion. From windows high above the road, people looked down upon them as they passed. Through one gate, past another they rode, moving through each layer of the city until emerging outside the white painted walls of Ekbatana. Here ragged peasants lined the road gawking at them, and just behind this line of spectators young boys ran, then stopped to view the caravan. This they repeated, over and over, keeping up with them for almost a mile until they crossed a frigid mountain stream that seemingly marked the frontier of the boys' adventures.

The days blended together as they rode, encountering few others on their journey toward the sea. Almost a month out of Ekbatana they passed a slow-moving caravan of copper merchants, men on their way north to Lake Van and trading sessions with the Hurrians. Histiaios talked with them over a dinner of salted mutton and maza cakes. They had no wine, but here in the northern reaches of the Empire they obtained a type of beer from the locals, thick and dark with the substance of a stew. He grew amazed at their tales of this long journey to deal away their copper, but was assured that the Hurrian breed of horses was worth this extraordinary effort. He was sad to see them part ways, for his Persian escort hardly talked with him, nor would he stoop to conversation with his servants or his Persian wife. He almost wished old Krios was here.

As they moved west, the terrain became devoid of cultivated land, but enough scrubby vegetation grew to satisfy the needs of the horses and mules. Here upon the plateau the nights, even in summer, were icy, but the sun proved exceedingly warm and the infrequent breezes that swept the highlands were welcomed by all. Just as predicted by the captain of horse, and almost one month to the day, they sighted Nineveh, the ruined capitol of the extinct Assyrian Empire. The site, long deserted, offered nothing to them, so they stopped at the small village named Camel's House. Here they encountered the plentiful water of the Tigris River, and the Royal Road. Activity increased. Not only did they come across merchants and traders, but villages occurred more often along the route, and where they did not, the welcome sight of a pirradazis post station afforded them with food, news, and refuge from the elements. At one such station, a few days' journey from the city of Amida, Histiaios came across a heavily guarded transport party, men who delivered the precious finds of iron to the Persian capital.

Amongst the transport there were several Greek poppy merchants who had tagged along for protection. Their own caravan guard had abandoned them at Mazaka. Their very profitable merchandise was easily concealed, being only the brown cakes of sap drawn from poppies and sold as medicine deep in the interior of the Empire. One of them approached Histiaios, who he immediately recognized as a fellow Greek. "Do you travel to the coast?" he asked, as he nibbled away at a fig.

Histiaios grinned. "Yes. I have been at Ekbatana, and Susa. Finally I am returning home."

The poppy merchant nodded. "And where is home?"

"Miletos," said Histiaios, repeating it again under his breath for only him to hear.

"Have you not heard?"

Histiaios did not answer with words, his blank expression conveying his response.

The trader leaned over to him, and shielded his mouth from the milling Persian horsemen. "The whole of the coast is in revolt. The province of Karia has broken away from the Great King. And Byzantion. Kypros too. And many more of the island cities. They say Miletos leads this rebellion."

Histiaios could not have hoped for better news. The western satrapies of the Empire were in turmoil. He remembered what harm the Skythians had inflicted upon the Persians, and Darios could do nothing. To his mind the Greeks were much more formidable. Soon he and the other Ionians would be free of their Persian masters.

Chapter 12

The Citadel of Sardis—Winter 497 BC

Artaphernes had conscripted thousands for the rebuilding effort and hired more above these, some from the very islands that had sent men to burn the city. But he was, if anything a practical man, and the talents of these troublesome Greeks for now would serve him. It rained most days, but the work went on, for instead of the sun, bricks were dried in kilns, making them quickly usable and decidedly more durable. He instructed the workmen, where possible, not to rebuild using reed thatching—the very material that rendered Sardis so vulnerable to the torch during the attack of the Greeks. But unlike before the sacking, the streets teemed with troops of the Empire, dathaba of Medes, Lykians and Persians patrolled relentlessly, interrogating any travelers, especially Greeks that entered. Histiaios avoided such attention, due in no small part to his Persian escort that delivered him to the very gates of the citadel.

"I thank you for an uneventful journey," said Histiaios in his parting words to the Persian cavalry commander. The man said nothing in return. Artaphernes secretary, a Tyrian, greeted him with a nod and no words before leading the way through the gates and up to a tunnel in the first terrace. The ceiling was barely high enough for a man to walk upright and only small lamps burned away in niches carved into the flame licked stone blocks. The tunnel burrowed half a stadion into the fortress and hillside finally emerging into the evening light, bringing them to a wide courtyard bracketed by imposing walls. Armed men looked down upon them as they passed to another tunnel, but this one angled upwards steeply. Histiaios sucked the damp air, trying to catch his breath lost in this strenuous climb. He could see the inviting, bright exit ahead and forced himself to keep up with the Tyrian. In the next courtyard soldiers milled about in small groups, chatting away, waiting for the evening meal to be served in their barracks. It struck him. Never had he seen so many of the King's soldiers outside of the Persian capital. And these he knew, were only a garrison. Battle troops would be afield.

"Ah, Histiaios." Artaphernes said through a manufactured smile of a greeting. "The King has sent word ahead of you. You are to aid us in suppressing this rebellion?"

"Without a doubt I am here to provide what service I can to Darios, and to you also, my friend Artaphernes." Histiaios followed his host into the great hall of the citadel. Two huge maps embroidered on richly dyed linen hung on the far wall as he entered, and both were surrounded by Persian officers who pointed and talked amongst themselves as they studied them. He could see all the cities of coast from Byzantion in the north to Tyre in the south marked out on one of the maps. His Persian was good enough for him to pick out words from the various conversations that buzzed around him. He knew the word hazarabam meant a Persian contingent of one thousand, and he also heard that each one of these Persian officers commanded such a unit. At least fifty officers huddled here and there in the hall.

The Persian waved Histiaios on, past the war-council and to an arrangement of couches and tables placed away from the maps. Artaphernes eased into the cushions of his divan. Histiaios finally sat upon his couch just as another Persian joined them. "This is general Otanes," he announced. The thick-necked Persian took a couch adjacent to Histiaios. He did not carry himself like Artaphernes or the other Persians of high rank, rather he appeared exceedingly less refined, chiseled and square like the stonework of a fortress with a face that seemed incapable of either a smile or a frown.

The Tyrian, who himself did not choose to recline upon a couch but remained standing near Artaphernes, clapped his hands twice, signaling the steward to commence the apportioning of the wine and the serving of the first platters of food. Two muscular slaves, their arms banded in gold, carried in a small litter with the steaming carcass of a roasted goat upon it. They settled it atop a low table where another slave, the appointed carver, began to slice off hand-sized slabs of meat onto a golden handled tray. Other slaves entered the hall bearing plates of figs, white mulberries, plums, quince, and pears.

Once the food had been distributed and the wine cups drained at least several times, Artaphernes addressed them all. "As you can see, the attack of the Greeks has been but a mere inconvenience, suffered by me in a most personal matter." His face grew dark and stern, causing all the diners to drop their cups from their lips and attend to him. "I had to endure almost three days without these." He plucked a fig from his bowl and dropped it into his mouth, smiling. The others began laugh, but not Otanes. "This revolt shall be crushed. In this I have no doubt, for a fraction of the Great King's army numbers more than all the inhabitants of Ionia. But it will cost us much, and with meager profit, for what do you Greeks have of value?" His glance now turned to Histiaios. "Your countrymen have sown a most sorrowful crop. General Otanes here, along with others, will ensure that they take in the harvest." Artaphernes rose from his couch, and now directed his words at Histiaios. "The King's arm is long, and will reach to the ends of the world to exact vengeance." Now he stepped over to Histiaios, sitting uncomfortably close to the Greek, leaning close so only he could hear. "You, Histiaios, have stitched this shoe, and it is now time to put it on."

Inexplicably Histiaios thought not of the Persian's word, not of his home, Aristagoras nor the unraveling of his plans, but of the day many years ago, when he stood on a bridge with the Athenian Miltiades. *He was right*, he thought to himself. *We should have cut that bridge.*

✵✵✵✵✵

The next day Histiaios set off with Otanes and his army toward the coastal port of Smyrna. The imposing columns of Persian and Median infantry marched with slow and deliberate confidence along the fine Royal Road, lengthening the passage to almost three full days. The anticipation proved excruciating for him. Histiaios, on the third day, could smell it—the salty air of freedom. But during the trek, Artaphernes words spun in his head persistently. He was certain that the Persian could peer into his very soul, but he soothed his whirling thoughts with the prospect of seeing his home again and this salve helped him through the remainder of the journey.

Late afternoon and the fishing boats of Smyrna, low in the water with their catches, docked. Otanes had continued onto to the citadel, but Histiaios lingered near the waterfront. "You must understand," he lectured to the Persian, "that to a Greek the sea is everything."

"Like the mountains are to me," replied Otanes. "Artaphernes insisted that we dine together this evening. I will send someone to collect you." The Persian and his entourage moved on, their horses prancing nervously amongst the crowded docks and narrow streets until they were out of sight.

Again Histiaios breathed in the salty ocean breeze, an antidote to the dust and sand of the Persian Empire. He swore to himself and Zeus above that he would never set his gaze upon Susa or Ekbatana again. Swiftly in his mind, he calculated an inventory of his gold and what could be smuggled unnoticed by his slave, and whether this amount would fund the inevitable bribe that would be required. First his guards. They could easily be sent along to a wine-shop or brothel with a token gift. But the ship and its captain—that would cost him.

That evening he followed Otanes' escort to the citadel and endured what he hoped would be the final dinner amongst these barbarians. No matter what the conversation, his mind conjured up the image of Artaphernes and his warning. The second night in Smyrna, his nerve and patience forfeit, he fled, paying much more than he needed to gain passage on a fast ship that smuggled copper to the island of Khios.

Chapter 13

The Bay of Lade, off Miletos—494 BC

Datis stood at the bow of his trireme—a Tyrian warship—assessing the battle-line of the enemy arrayed before him. It had been over four years since the Ionians instigated the revolt. He relished this moment. By afternoon it would all be over: the last remnant crushed; the authority of Persia re-established; the Great King once more lord of all. With the wind down, the swells of mid morning proved tranquil, glimmering like molten silver under a sweltering sun. He did not need to count the enemy, for his spies had already done that for him days before. 353 warships of the Ionians, mostly triremes, faced his 600 vessels of Phoenicians, Rhodians, Kyprians and Egyptians. He outnumbered the foe, but that fact provided scant comfort, so days beforehand he had dispatched spies, along with the deposed tyrants of the Ionian cities, men that Aristagoras had expelled during the course of his inspired revolt, to talk sense to their former countrymen. And if these men failed to persuade them, the bulging purses of gold that he offered would certainly do no harm. Opposing his right wing were the ships of Samos and opposite his own left wing of Egyptians, the Milesians formed up almost directly in front of their home city. The Greeks between hailed from various cities along the coast, but it was the Khians who concerned him the most.

He pushed his calfskin gauntlets tightly to his hands with criss-crossed fingers, and slowly drew his akinakes sword from its gilded scabbard and swung its overhead. The horns blared. The bowman turned and shouted the order, while the row-master stalked the deck between the oarsmen, urging them on. His trireme lurched forward as the rowers dug deep into the swells. The enemy line appeared no more than black smudges, blending into the shoreline behind and the bright seas beneath. Now from across the calm waters he heard the flutes of the Greeks marking time for their oarsmen. Slowly, the distant line of specks grew, taking on the form of individual ships, the oars dipping then rising, glistening with seawater after each stroke. His marines edged forward, almost surrounding him as stood at the bow, the look of bridled fear upon the faces of most, for the Persians were men of the highlands and most disliked the sea. Suddenly his vessel dipped, struck by a single rogue wave, spilling his men to one side. A young archer, trying to regain balance, grabbed at the rail but his bow went skidding across the wet deck, where his deputy Nabusera snatched it up just before it shot off into the sea. Smiling he handed it back to the archer, who repaid him with an explosion of vomit. Datis grinned. Nabusera snarled. The young archer pushed his way toward the stern and out of sight.

Even with the relatively calm seas the trireme dipped and rose more violently now, for the meek swells became magnified as their speed increased. The sea sprayed upon them, propelled up by the slicing prow and the huge triple-prowed bronze ram that pulverized the water before them. Nabusera swiped the seawater from his beard. "This is surely testing my loyalty to you, Lord Datis," he shouted. He fought to stand upright, but the swaying deck forced him to his knees.

"Now you see why the Greeks practice tossing their javelins while sitting," barked Datis. "And why my archers have done the same." He pointed with the blade of his akinakes to the rows of bare-chested Cretans sitting with arrows notched and poised to draw. It would take powerful men indeed to discharge their shafts accurately and with distance while employing only half their bodies.

Upon the Ionian ships he began to make out figures, kneeling archers raising bows, epibates or marines jostling about, their brazen shields flashing brightly. He reached for his own shield—one made of wickerwork and leather—and could not help but compare it with those of the enemy. But if his plan works, he would have little use for it, and that thought brought him comfort. To his far right he could see the Egyptians out-pacing his wing, eager to engage the Milesians, to strike at the instigators of this war and steal away the Great King's favor from Datis and his Phoenicians.

"Pick up the pace," he yelled to the row-master. He poked his finger up and down, indicating a swifter stroke. The metallic clang of hammer on bronze sped up the rhythm of every oar while the row-master screamed both encouragements and threats. The once tight formation of the Greeks began to disintegrate, for the Samians and their entire contingent of sixty triremes executed a furious left turn toward the island of Lade. Once they had initiated this maneuver the Mytilinians too, back-watered hard to port spinning their ships toward the island and away from the advancing fleet of Datis.

But the center of the Greek line, mostly comprised of the one hundred warships from Khios, surged forward while shifting into several columns of ten to twenty ships deep. This was no tactic of retreat, no stratagem to escape. They meant to fight. Datis pushed aside the men surrounding him, desperately trying to make his way back to the stern of his trireme and the pilot. "Faster!"

"And open gaps in the line?" The pilot hugged the tillers, his arms shivering as he fought to keep it steady.

"Can't you see what they are doing?" Datis pointed out across the dwindling interval toward the Khians and their multi-pronged attack formation. "We must turn into their flank."

"Are you daft?" barked the pilot. "Then we will be exposed. Look!" the pilot thrust his arm out, stabbing at the spray-filled air. Truly, the Khians had formed their columns—the tactic of diekplous—but the Milesians continued to advance in a straight line, ready to swoop down upon any Persian vessel that would try to turn into their flank. "The only way to stop them is to form a double line, and it is too late for that."

Datis stormed off, returning to his marines and archers huddled near the bow. The pilot was correct. They had to keep the line intact. The Phoenicians in the middle of their formation would have to deal with the Khians alone until he could bring his greater numbers to bear once the enemy was fully entangled in combat. He reran the calculations in his mind—less than one hundred and fifty Ionian triremes faced his six hundred warships. The time would come. He would strike then and not before.

In a low crouch he stalked the deck, listening to the collective grunts of the oarsmen that mingled with the accelerating cadence of the hammer. His trireme ceased to glide through the swells but heaved and lurched with each desperate draw of the oars. To his right, toward the center of it all, the Khians closed, the lead vessel of each column slowed suddenly, back-watering their oars on one side, executing sharp turns that brought their bronze-beaked rams to the broadside of his Phoenicians. Now a roar of crackling wood rolled over the waves as he watched the oars of his ships snapping, exploding into splinters as the Khian rams scraped them off at the tholepins. Rowers tumbled inboard, holding only the severed portions of their oar-looms, some bleeding from wounds caused by the flying wood. Archers launched arrows as the ships came to close contact, but the marines had no chance to board—the Khians were quick and their seamanship too sharp to be caught foundering and disabled. The ramming vessels skidded by each victim and cut sharp turns, readying another attack from behind the Phoenicians. Trailing Khian vessels finished off the helpless. Their attack had succeeded in inflicting great damage, but it took them far from the very shore they had wished to defend. It was almost as if their entire contingent at a single moment realized their position and how unsuitable it was for defense, for they coalesced into a tight formation and continued rowing through the Phoenicians and toward the shore of Mykale.

Datis turned back to signal the pilot, but before he could, the rhythm of the oarsmen picked up, while the pilot pushed hard with quaking arms into the tillers, veering the ship toward the middle of the battle and the remaining Ionians. His vessel sliced through the dipping swells, its ram crashing into the waves as they sped toward an exposed Erythraian trireme, its oarsmen caught disorganized. Aboard the enemy vessel marines scurried to the immediate balustrade, archers knelt, bracing themselves for better aim and the inevitable collision, while panicked rowers dropped their oars and flung themselves into the sea. At fifty meters arrows arced toward him, but Datis casually flicked his shield over head to deflect them. Now his archers loosed a barrage in return, most arrows finding their mark in the bare flesh of the deserting rowers, while the armored Erythraian marines hunched down behind the bronze sheathed bowls of their shields, all but impervious to the hail of missiles. The pilot yelled. The rowers dug their oars deep. Men's arm shuddered as they fought to slow the trireme. There was a hush, a moment of absolute silence as the men on each warship stared out at their opposites in anticipation of the impending collision.

Suddenly a peal of thunder roared from the bow of his ship as the triple ram struck deep into fir planking of the Erythraian trireme, while a shower of splintered wood and water shot high into the air. Datis was thrown across the deck, as was every one of his marines, so violent the impact and so very sudden the restraint of all momentum. He gathered his feet under him, snatched up his wickerwork shield and heaved toward the impaled Erythraian vessel. His archers had recovered before him and lined the balustrade, launching arrows point-blank into the enemy marines as they prepared to repel his Persians. Now the hostile vessel began to list, their marines and archers slipping across the wet, slick decking, its timbers groaning in protest as the sea twisted and pulled at it.

"Reverse stroke!" yelled the pilot, as he frantically waved at the row-master to strike up the cadence again. The ribbing of the Erythraian wailed as his trireme backed away, withdrawing its lethal ram. A final hideous crackle and they were free. Seawater whooshed into the gaping hole now, causing the Erythraian to roll violently into the waves. He heard the screams of rowers trapped below deck, but only for a brief moment, for it plunged quickly beneath the surface, the water boiling as the last bit of air found its way up along with bodies, shattered planking and rowers' cushions. His men leaned over the railings, some with bows, others with light javelins, and began skewering what survivors attempted to clamber aboard their vessel. They cried out for mercy, even after arrow shafts had thudded deep into flesh, their blood staining the sea red as the life poured out of them before they and their cries slipped beneath the swells to join their sinking trireme.

Datis moved forward. He had not even drawn his sword. He looked out at the sea between the island of Lade and Miletos and saw destruction. Some ships were set alight, the acrid smoke rolling over the waves, momentarily veiling the scene from him, while screams and cries faded, smothered by the sea. His victorious war-ships cruised through the wreckage, steering for the harbor at Miletos.

✵✵✵✵✵

Datis had landed to the west of Miletos to confer with general Otanes, whose five hazarabam had begun the investment of the city even before their sea-borne victory was complete. Carpenters hacked away at timbers, fashioning the components of siege towers and rams. Slaves from the Taurean silver mines now worked as sappers, excavating tunnels under the walls. As dusk began to spread across the peninsula, myriads of Persian campfires swathed the land encircling the city of Miletos.

"We will be dining in Miletos tomorrow, my friend," said Otanes, confidently. "Without their fleet, they are at our mercy."

Datis nodded politely. "I pray you are correct in this." Now he looked out to the darkening sea. Datis lowered himself and knelt beside the fire that crackled on the gravel beach, its flames reflecting wildly upon his scaled silver armor. "I regret I cannot accept your dinner invitation. In the morning I am taking the fleet north, and restore to the Great King all of Ionia—island by island, city by city."

"Then, my friend, I extend the invitation upon your return." Otanes strode away toward his tent leaving Datis to ponder the flames. He turned one final time. "Tomorrow it will be ours." He spun away, his cloak unfurling behind his thickset shoulders as he lumbered off.

Datis' eyes leapt from the flames of the campfire to the flickering tongues of torches that covered the high battlements of Miletos. *If he takes it by winter...*he mulled. Nabusera hovered at the outer limit of the firelight, but still he heard his commander. His mouth widened to a huge grin, teeth gleaming from out of the black of night.

Datis looked over his shoulder at Nabusera, while rising ever so deliberately, brushing his trousers clean with a swipe of his hands. Nabusera hustled after him as he made his way across the beach to where his Phoenician triremes were being dragged ashore to dry. Pilots and shipwrights yelled commands to the men on the lines, running here and there to shoulder a section of rope, or bellow instructions directly into the ear of a negligent or clumsy rower. Once grounded these same men methodically walked the entire length of each vessel, a torch in one hand while fingering the hull with the other, feeling for any gaps or imperfections that eyesight alone might not reveal. Slaves wobbled behind them toting cauldrons of hot pitch mixed with shredded flax. Every so often the shipwrights would halt, pointing out a spot on the hull that the slaves swabbed with a viscous, steaming liquid. Datis kept walking, away from his ships, toward an outcrop of rock that whispered with lapping surf. He didn't bother to keep his calfskin boots dry, stepping further out into the sea. Even the persistent Nabusera knew not to follow. Datis bounded up and onto a boulder as nimbly as if he mounted a war-horse. Beneath him the debris of battle gently advanced and retreated with each stunted wave, a cadence of splintered wood softly thudding in rhythm with the sea. He looked north, to the unseen waters of battle and beyond. There would be little glory in the task ahead. The Ionians' fleet was crushed; their cities defenseless. In the days to come he would murder in the name of the Great King.

✴✴✴✴✴

"Lord Datis."

His hand moved instinctively to the hilt of his akinakes sword. Kneeling beside him was his bodyguard. He did not speak, but tried to gather himself. He certainly was not in his tent. The star-lit sky above revealed itself immediately as he looked up.

"Lord Datis, it is past midnight."

He had fallen asleep, but for only a short while. As late as it was, torchlight still danced amongst the beached triremes, men labored and the incessant sawing and hacking of the siege carpenters kept on. His tent was not far. He ate some maza cakes and washed it down with a ration of beer before calling for the commanders of his triremes to assemble. Outside, slaves ringed the assembly area with torches, guiding drowsy commanders to their meeting.

"Be ready to sail at first light. We are to land on Samos."

And so it began. The Persian fleet under Datis embarked upon its journey of retribution. They would strike at every Ionian city as they sailed north toward Byzantion. He would snuff out the last embers of rebellion.

Chapter 14

Elaios, on the Peninsula—494 BC

Miltiades knew their time was short but he did not wish to incite undue concern, much less panic amongst his family. Four of their five vessels had been fully loaded, emptying out every possession from their estate at Elaios. What towns-folk still remained gawked at them in disbelief. "Hurry! Get the horses on board now." His farriers tugged the reluctant beasts up the gangway and onto the swaying deck. He turned to Metiokhos. "This is your ship." His son understood why they must each command a vessel, along with his mercenaries. Not only was each laden with gold and silver but Darios would reward anyone turning them back and into the arms of their pursuers. Only his most trusted would command a ship today. He looked up studying the sky, feeling the wind upon his face while trying to convince himself that the weather would hold.

A rider galloped hard along the waterfront, scattering the wharf-workers and servants that moved toward the last moored ship, a round-hull freighter with a bright crimson mast and railings. He reined up before Miltiades and slid quickly from the back of the horse. "They are less than a half day out."

"Cast off now son. You must get out of the straits before the Persians seal it off." Miltiades grabbed the cloak of the messenger to hold him still. "What other news."

The man stared directly into Miltiades' eyes, transmitting nothing but gravity. "The Persians are overrunning all the cities from Halikarnossos to here. Who knows where they will stop."

"Metiokhos!" He embraced his son, then quickly shoved him away "You must go."

Instead of obeying, as he was always wont to do, Metiokhos stood frozen upon the quay devoid of both word and motion.

"Go now!" Miltiades barked angrily.

"What about them?" The question erupted from Metiokhos. He swung his head left then right, scanning the pockets of Elaians, poor tradesmen, hardscrabble farmers and even some of Miltiades' very own mercenaries, all collected together with children, wives and slaves, expecting at first, but now desperately hoping that their leader would deliver them from the advancing Persians.

Miltiades, at first looking through the gathering Elaians as though they were a thinning mist, finally focused on them and the question. "Son, a man must first look to himself and his own."

Metiokhos turned away while exhaling a loud sigh, and started to shake his head. He turned back. "But you are not just a man. You are their leader. What good is a leader if he cannot protect the very ones he leads?"

Miltiades clenched his fists. His arms shivered as he fought to apply a measure of self-control. Beside him stood Illyrios and Philomarkhos, his captain of mercenaries. It took him only a moment to decide. He trusted Philomarkhos more. "Toss him aboard. Sit on him if you must, but cast off now!" Philomarkhos, not a particularly large man, but an exceedingly strong one, plunged a shoulder in Metiokhos' belly and lifted him off the quay. In a moment he had scrambled up the brow-plank and onto the freighter. Resigned for the moment to his fate, Metiokhos retreated to the mid-mast and tugged on the brail-lines with the other crewmen, unfurling a large, crimson histion sail. Thankfully it filled with the stiff north breeze, a breeze that would take them away from Elaios and the straits.

Miltiades ran along the quay, keeping pace with his son's ship as it slipped through the water until it finally separated from the dock, the land and him. Metiokhos glared back at him. Miltiades paused only for a moment before jumping into the small skiff that Illyrios managed to keep against the quay by grabbing a dock ring with his paw-like hand. The slave released his grip while snatching up an oar to join the other slave who had already begun to furiously dip and draw his oar. The dock grew smaller with each stroke, the faces of the abandoned dissolving to shadows and their cries melding to an indiscernible murmur. His vessel, a fast penteconter, lay moored in the harbor, already loaded and prepared to make sail, where onboard, he could see his youngest son Kimon shading his eyes from the sun, waiting anxiously for Miltiades to board. Both the tide and the wind were with them, but just barely, for once evening would fall the breeze would quit and the tide would turn, allowing the Persians to row effortlessly northward and up the straits. Still, he was more than certain that his oldest, Metiokhos, would out-distance any pursuit, especially with Philomarkhos on board. And his own penteconter could drop its sail and move under oar. Plus, these waters he knew better than most, and once amongst the islands, his vessel could lose itself, and the Persians. He had repeated his instructions over and over to Metiokhos: "Take the western route past Lemnos," which he now repeated under his breath.

Their skiff thudded against the pitched hull of the penteconter as it slipped along side, sending jittery crewman scrambling to heave Miltiades and Illyrios aboard before shoving the empty skiff away. Kimon, mesmerized, followed the lazy recession of the skiff as the waves coaxed it toward the shore.

"Come on son; let the men do their work." He hustled Kimon along the deck to the stern where they sat cross-legged near the pilot. Amidships, the kaleustes bellowed at the sail crew to hoist the mast, while the oarsmen bent into each stroke, working to clear them of the wind shadow created by the land of the harbor neck. Quickly the mast was up and the square histion sail extended across the sailyard. In moments it became gorged on the stiff breeze, inciting the lines to creak as the penteconter sliced south through the choppy swells. They would make for Imbros, the first island out of the straits, and beach for the night. Miltiades knew this island well—he had attacked and occupied it ostensibly at the order of his city Athens, which had been inspired by the oracle at Delphi, but he also sailed against the island for his own profit and to secure his southern flank on the Peninsula. While there he surveyed its coast and found several places where a vessel, under an expert pilot, could land unseen and remain so from both land and sea. Here he would wait, and watch, being sure the Persian fleet was well up the straits, and Metiokhos and the other three ships were safely on their way to Athens, for the value of their cargo would secure his position and his family's for generations to come. He would not cast away a lifetime's pursuit in a moment of panic. What looked like nothing more than a shadow in a cliff drew his attention. He directed the pilot to steer for it, while passing his orders to the kaleustes to have the rowers slow, allowing them to coast just off shore. Soon the penteconter was dipping and rising in the swells a scant few yards from the rocky coast, gliding slowly.

Miltiades waved his hand. "Hold!"

The rowers plunged their oars into the sea, slowing all forward momentum.

"Can you see it?" Miltiades shouted to the pilot who squinted, trying to see past the light of the setting sun into the dark shadow of the narrow slit of a cove.

The pilot nodded and leaned hard on the tillers, while the kaleustes, or row-master, shouted the order to reverse stroke. In moments the penteconter had slipped into the shadows. Deep into the cove, a slender crescent became visible, just enough to drag a single ship ashore to dry. The waxed keel of the vessel groaned as it buried itself deep into the sand. The entire crew except the pilot, who leaned over the rail at the stern, jumped to shore and picked up the lines. The pilot yelled. The crewmen heaved. In great jerks the ship edged out of the water, until finally satisfied the pilot threw his hand overhead. "Enough!"

Miltiades, along with Kimon, scampered up boulder-strewn beach to a spot where they could look out to the sea towards the east. The swells were flattening as the wind subsided. The sky above faded to violet, only traces of clouds scudded by. *The weather will hold*, he thought. *Poseidon and Zeus are with us.* Weeks of diligent sacrifices by Miltiades to these two gods and others had not gone to waste. "Lord Poseidon, see me safely to Athens and I will sacrifice nothing less than a bull in your honor."

"Father, is anything the matter?" asked Kimon as he stared at Miltiades.

"Why nothing son. Nothing at all. Why do you say such a thing?'

"You are talking to the gods again and squeezing those knucklebones. You only do that when you expect bad things to happen."

Miltiades smiled. "It is time to eat." He clicked the bones one more time before putting them back into the leather pouch.

The pair had made their way back to the covert beach, where most of the crew had begun eating. Illyrios knelt beside a small fire, turning a boarfish he had speared over the flames. He looked up, his ruddy cheeks glowing in the firelight. "This is for you, master Kimon."

The boy moved next to the huge slave, listening to his fish sizzle as the flames gripped it. Illyrios pointed to a capped earthenware bowl. "I have another for you lord Miltiades."

"Ahum," said Miltiades as he lifted the cover, revealing not one but two boarfish, their gills still puckering desperately. "It was kind of you to remember me."

Now Illyrios stammered, "N-no master, I meant no disrespect. I thought the boy would be the hungriest of us all."

Miltiades, in rare good spirits, slapped him on the back. "There is no disrespect in attending to my son."

Illyrios, as mighty a man as he was, almost collapsed. Never had Miltiades ever touched him, in rage or affection, unless of course the lash of a whip counted. The fish slipped from its skewer into the ashes. Without thinking he snatched it up and swiped it clean before impaling it again. Kimon began to laugh.

For most of the evening the trio sat around the fire, a thing that before this night had never happened, for slave and master rarely spoke. Illyrios, most times tight-lipped, now entertained Kimon with stories of his own childhood and of his adventures at the bridge over the Ister, so many years ago. Miltiades listened, but his thoughts were elsewhere. He mulled over his escape from the Peninsula, a land where he was all but a king, but also a land where he could never sit down with his son and just talk. Here too, he saw Illyrios in a different light. A man that had scant obligation to render this trust—but he did and Miltiades had difficulty understanding this. Most of all he realized that the things that he prized most were either here with him or safe on their way to Athens. Now his heart sank. The Athens he was returning to was hardly the one he left those many years past. He looked to his son. Kimon gnawed away on his roasted fish, returning his father's glance with a grin of satisfaction. *It will be difficult for him, most of all*, he thought.

The night deepened, stars flickering on in the dark cloudless sky, while the slap of waves upon the jagged shoreline provided the only sound above conversation. Kimon stared up in long bouts, which he would punctuate with an explosion of questions about the constellations. "Is that the Archer?" or "Is that one the Hydra?" Miltiades would patiently answer. Kimon began another hushed study of the night sky. "Father, tell me about Athens."

The question surprised Miltiades. He would be more comfortable explaining the heavens. But still, he would reply, and maybe both would receive an answer. "Athens is much larger than Elaios, or Sestos, or any other city on the Peninsula."

Kimon stared at him. "Yes Father, I know that. What I meant to ask, well—tell me about the Athenians themselves."

Miltiades laughed out loud. "I am an Athenian."

Kimon wrapped his arms around his knees and hugged his thighs while he unknowingly swayed to the rhythm of the surf. "Are they all as powerful as you?"

Miltiades pondered the question for a moment. Athens, as he had been told, was much changed, but he knew men still craved power. It is, after all, a natural thing. "Son, you know that all great men are powerful men. But to be powerful, others must be without power. One leads many, but many do not lead one. Think upon the heroes—Theseus, Herakles, Akhilles and the rest. They were powerful because they dominated other men."

Kimon peered out of the corner of his eye at Illyrios. He knew Illyrios to be powerful in his own way, but dominated no one. "But Father, if the powerful are intent on dominating others—even men like themselves—how can they be devoted to their city? Illyrios says that the Spartans are subject to no man, but only to their laws. He says that in Athens it is the same."

Again Miltiades laughed. "The gods only reward men who strive to win, to excel. Laws, I regret, are fashioned to protect the weak, the ones who do not excel. Akhilles was most incorrect when he said he was better to serve on earth than to rule in Hades. There is no place, not even Athens, where I would defer to another. Give me Hades, if that is where I can rule." Miltiades, anxious to see his son's reaction, turned toward him. Kimon was lost to slumber. Illyrios spread his hide cloak over the boy before curling up himself on the sand very close to the waning fire.

Miltiades, on the other hand, found it difficult to sleep. He had become accustomed to softer surroundings, and the damp beach sand caused his bones to ache and his mind to stir. To him this night passed slower than a score or more combined. Every so often he would stare to the east, trying—hoping—to pick out the first shimmer of light as day approached.

Even before any hint of dawn revealed itself, Illyrios was up and scouring the beach above the tide-line for driftwood. Shortly, the orange glow of a small fire chased away a small portion of the gloom. Miltiades, his cloak pulled almost entirely overhead, lie there, watching the slave tend to the fire. He had not noticed until now but Illyrios did not stoke the flames for his own warmth, but had placed the campfire adjacent to Kimon, and piled rocks on one side to reflect the heat of the flames toward the boy and away from him. Miltiades looked up. A bank of thin clouds slipped by, their undersides glowing almost imperceptibly. Dawn had arrived.

He tossed his cloak aside and sat up, but his back and knees throbbed with pain in protest of this sudden movement. He rubbed his legs, starting low above his ankles, working his way to his knees until the pain subsided a bit. He moved toward the fire and his son and stood near the flames, letting the heat embrace his bare legs.

Across the small makeshift camp the nautai, or rowers, began to awake; slowly words and movement began to extend over the beach. In their cove they hid in deep shadows while the scrub and small trees on the ridges around them were soon ablaze in golden light. The wind, that until now had been absent, rose coincidentally with the sun. Miltiades did not linger around the beach as the others ate, but took a flap of bread and a bowl of honeyed wine and climbed to a vantage point high above the cove. He sat cross-legged in the warm morning sun, a mild southerly fanning away the flies and mosquitoes, as he stared northeast toward the straits. Almost midday and no sight of a ship, Persian or otherwise. This gladdened him for with each passing moment his own Metiokhos, and his three other ships were further from the Persians. His belly tossed with anxiety though—he wanted to set sail now, and catch up with his son, but knew also that he must wait until the Persian fleet passed by him and into the straits, to the Peninsula and beyond. Then and only then could he be certain of their safety.

He turned, the clatter of stones grabbing his attention. Clambering up the rocky cliff, Illyrios came into view with Kimon trailing him. "Some water for you, master." The slave handed him the uncorked skin. Miltiades gulped away. Stray trickles glistening in his beard. Kimon, upon reaching the pinnacle of rocks that his father sat upon, shaded his eyes with a salute. "Father, look!" He thrust a finger out toward the open sea. Miltiades squinted, the glaring waves and perfect sun forcing his eyes almost closed as he stared out. The southern horizon, once almost melding without a blemish into the bright sky, now seemed flawed, smudges of black growing in the distance. Not one ship, nor a merchant contingent, but a war-fleet grew from the gently rolling sea, and it seemed to be heading directly for them.

"Kimon, run down to the pilot and tell him we have sighted the Persians." Kimon, anxious to carry out his father's command, began to turn away prematurely. Miltiades grabbed him by his chiton. "Tell him to snuff out all the fires."

Illyrios and his master sat atop their perch of stone on the hilltop as the great fleet inexorably closed in on the island. What at first was a cluster of specks swelled to become a mass of triremes spanning the horizon. Miltiades counted up to five hundred rocking masts and quit. This was no patrol. This was a fleet of domination, a fleet they could never hope to out-run. No, they must remain here, hidden amongst the rocky cliffs, until the Persians passed them by. As the ships grew nearer, the peal of hammer on bronze that marked the rowers' time leapt over the waves. Now he could make out individual figures scurrying about on the top decks of the warships. By late afternoon the Phoenician triremes, sailing under command of their masters, the Persians, were only meters off the island, their rowers spelled and their large square main-sails and leading boat-sails catching the potent southerly. This procession continued for more than two hours. Suddenly the rustle of leaves in the wind went silent and the swells off the island flattened. Sail after sail went limp, empty of any breeze.

Now a squadron of ships veered from their northern course directly for Imbros. With evening approaching and no wind to carry them, the ships would need to beach for the night, and with so many of them, Miltiades worried that one would stumble upon their secluded cove. As narrow as it was, they would have no exit if a trireme decided to beach here. To his left, beyond the neck of land that concealed his vessel, Miltiades looked to the long sickle-shaped beach, one that should prove more than inviting to such a large fleet, although it could only manage to accommodate around fifty full size war-triremes. The cliffs plummeted steeply toward this beach, separating them from the disembarking Persians and Phoenicians.

"Illyrios, I will keep watch here. Tell the pilot to post guards along the ridge."

The slave faded into the shadows of dusk as he descended into the trees. On the far beach the triremes ground ashore, torch-bearing crewmen inundating the strand as campfires sprouted in their multitudes amid the clamor. It would be awhile.

Miltiades left his vantage and crept quietly down to the beach where the remaining crew huddled in darkness, whispering, wondering and calculating how they would escape from so large a fleet. If they were discovered here, in their cove, they would have no chance. If sighted on the open sea, they would fare only slightly better, knowing their small penteconter of fifty oarsmen could not outpace a Phoenician trireme with 170 hardened rowers unless the gods intervened with a timely storm or sight-stealing shroud of fog.

He waved to the pilot and kaleustes to gather 'round him. The three knelt in the cool sand while the others stared in silence at them. "We have but one chance, my friends." Out of the corner of his eye he caught sight of his son Kimon curled up in sleep next to Illyrios. "When the Persians are asleep, well into the third watch, we can try to slip out and head for Athos. With first light their scouts will be all over the island, looking for water. We cannot be here when that happens."

The pilot winced, showing his discomfort with such a plan. "How can I steer a course without the sun?"

"The sea is calm, and the moon will be up soon. You can see Lemnos from here. That is all you need to steer by." Miltiades waved them closer. "You must keep the men quiet, but have the ship prepared. I will go back to the hill and keep watch on our neighbors. When the time is right, I will return. It should not be long." He began to walk toward the rocky slope, but stopped, hearing footfalls pursuing him. Illyrios lumbered up to him. Without a word passed between them the two men climbed up and away from the beach, reaching the crest of the hill, quickly and quietly. Below, in the Persian shore camp, activity had become subdued, while at the same time the fires all burned brightly indicating rest but not sleep for the myriads of troops and rowers scattered across the sand. Off shore a sail, illuminated by a fire cauldron onboard, suddenly slipped from the mist. It was another trireme, but this one had a vessel in tow. A horn sounded. Men scampered from the beach and into the gentle surf. First they hauled the trireme up then the tow, a round-hull merchant ship. Miltiades heart drummed. He strained to make out color in the gray of night. The mast and rails could be crimson—or orange, or ochre. He could not be certain. Persian marines disembarked from the merchantman first followed by a parade of tethered captives. Miltiades began to rise. Illyrios, his hand upon a shoulder, arrested him. "There is no way, master."

Miltiades looked toward the slave, but in the dark his face was without features, only a black form. "But that is Metiokhos down there."

The slave tightened his grip on Miltiades. "And there are over a thousand Persians and Phoenicians guarding him."

Miltiades flung the slave's hand off his shoulder while springing to his feet. Illyrios, with the swipe of an arm, brought him back to the rocks. He pressed his forearm across Miltiades' chest. "Do you want to lose them both!" Miltiades fought to rise up, but the slave proved too heavy, too strong—too determined. Finally Miltiades relaxed. Illyrios did too, but only slightly. "Master, think of Kimon." He released his grip.

Miltiades propped himself up on an elbow. "Will you allow me to get up now?" Illyrios moved away. Miltiades rose slowly, turning his glance to the beach below.

✶✶✶✶✶

"You do resemble him." Datis slowly circled the captive, studying him, while Persian marines stood to either side with akinakes swords drawn. He continued to stare at the young Greek; at his curly brown hair covering his head in tight curls; his thick beard, trimmed to a point on his chin.

"Resemble whom?" answered the captive, not the hint of a tremor of fear in his voice.

"A Greek I once met many years ago. His name, as I best recall, was Miltiades." Datis now abandoned his stalking and collapsed into a couch. Still he managed to notice the captive's expression change. "You know this Greek?"

"The man you speak of is my father."

"And your name is?" Datis turned his open palms upward in anticipation. He politely asked the captive's name, feigning interest, for it was Miltiades he wanted.

"Metiokhos."

Now Datis turned toward Philomarkhos. "You, I suppose are what the Greeks call a somatophylax—his body-guard. He is in my charge and no longer in need of you."

Philomarkhos instinctively lurched forward. Two guards braced him, pinning his arms to his side while Nabusera stepped forward with his akinakes drawn. Datis nodded. Nabusera plunged the blade into the Greek's belly. Philomarkhos' twisted right then left but could not break the grip of the two guards. Blood gurgled up into his throat. He sucked his mouth full of phlegm and blood and stared at Nabusera and his smirking face then spit. The Persian recoiled in surprise, letting the grip of his sword dangle from Philomarkhos' abdomen. Before Philomarkhos could draw another mouthful Nabusera grabbed the akinakes and twisted it, enlarging the groaning wound and sending Philomarkhos' eyes back into his head. His body collapsed, wilted and lifeless, allowing the guards to relax their hold. He crumpled to the sand.

"And where is your father?" Datis waved for a servant to offer wine to Metiokhos. "Still on the Peninsula, I hope?"

Without thinking Metiokhos accepted the cup, but all the while staring at the body of Philomarkhos until a pair of slaves dragged it away.

"Drink," insisted Datis. "And tell me, where is Miltiades?"

Slowly he lifted the cup to his lips, trying to keep his hands from shaking. He could gloat and tell the Persian the truth that his father was most likely well south of here rounding the Chalkidike and out of reach of the Persian fleet. But no, he would spin a different tale. "I would have hoped he would be half way to Athens by now, sir." He sipped again. "But my father remains at Elaios. He has much treasure still to load."

"Well Metiokhos, providence will reunite father and son shortly."Datis leaned back in his couch, stretching his arms overhead while yawning.

"On the morrow you will both be my guests."

✳✳✳✳✳

Miltiades awoke from a brief slumber, rubbing his eyes open. Beside him where Kimon should be was a crumpled himation cloak and a fleece blanket. Illyrios, too, was missing. *I'll whip that brute if he is not with him*, he thought, this burst of anger overwhelming any vestige of serenity delivered by sleep. The footprints were easy enough to follow until they ended abruptly at the base of a field of boulders. He clambered up and over the huge stones, coming to trail that amounted to little more than a slit in the low, ubiquitous scrub. Ahead he saw torchlight dancing wildly, illuminating two Persian scouts. They yanked and pulled on another, smaller figure. Suddenly an immense shadow burst from the adjacent thicket, dropping one of the Persians instantly. Before the other could cry out, or draw his weapon a thick arm descended from overhead, burying a javelin deep into the Persian's chest. Miltiades ran forward. There upon the ground between the slain Persians lay Kimon. Illyrios, heaving for breath stood over them all. The slave said nothing as he dragged one of the bodies, then the next to the edge of a ravine, tumbling each far down the cleft of the hill. Meanwhile Kimon and Miltiades snuffed out the torches. The trio made their way back to the camp in silence, a single embrace the only communication between father and son.

✳✳✳✳✳

The oars sliced into the dead-calm water of the cove softly. They drew them silently. The penteconter glided toward the open sea. The pilot was no fool, and apparently had smuggled before, for he knew enough to smother the tholepins and loops in oil—only the sound of water gently parted by the bow could be heard. A light mist clung to the sea, but above the stars shone clear, while the half-moon began to dominate the heavens.

Suddenly a single rower broke into spasms of coughing. The kaleustes hustled over to him, and muffled the man's face in his cloak. An occasional rattle of an oar or a plank squeaking in protest to the grip of the sea emanated from the fleeing penteconter. Miltiades stood behind the pilot who worked the tillers, keeping watch on the torch-speckled beach. The island shrank, along with his fear.

Chapter 15

The Athenian Harbor at Phaleron—494 BC

Like the carcasses of thirty great, black whales, thirty triremes lay beached upon the sand at Phaleron. Merchant ships—grain-lighters, freighters and trollers—occupied the quays, rocking to the pulse of the sea. Miltiades, at the bow of his penteconter, scanned the docks and the shoreline for any sign of the vessels he had dispatched before him, almost hoping to catch sight of the crimson-sailed freighter commanded by Metiokhos. A man on the beach, the harbormaster no doubt, signaled to them a clear spot to land, so the pilot steered his course and the kaleustes kept the rowers to their cadence until with a few meters off shore he yelled to withdraw oars. Miltiades' body swayed long after they had ground to a halt, legs wobbling and balance not quite restored. A crewman slid the brow-plank over the deck until one end burrowed into the wet sand of the beach while he secured the other end to the penteconter by deftly knotting a length of rope to a fairlead on the deck and ladder. Miltiades stepped back to allow others to disembark before him. He pondered his next move.

Kimon, grinning with excitement, called up to him from the beach. "Hurry father. We must see the city."

Miltiades, hesitating at each rung of the brow, finally touched the soil of his homeland again. He stepped, his sandaled foot leaving a deep imprint in the oozing sand, following his son Kimon as he scurried past the tideline and onto the Phaleron Road. Here merchants that could find no room on the quays lined the thoroughfare, bargaining with traders as they sought to unload their cargoes of Euxine grain, Karian wine, and flax, cotton, and ivory from Egypt. A few sought payment in obols or darics, but many preferred to barter for expertly crafted Athenian pottery. When he had departed those many years past, these very roads were quiet, the quays mostly empty. Not today. Athens had changed.

Kimon, impatient at his father's reluctance to share his enthusiasm, grabbed Illyrios by the hand and tugged, trying with all his might to get the huge slave to accompany him with a quicker pace to the city. Feeling helpless, Illyrios turned back toward Miltiades.

"Hold him right there. I'll not lose another son," yelled Miltiades. He said it partly in jest, but Illyrios knew this was a command and not a suggestion.

As soon as he caught up to his son a man approached them. He nodded while twirling the loose end of his himation cloak around his left arm. "I am Kallimakhos of Aphidna, and I would know you to be Miltiades, son of Kimon and brother to Stesagoras." He raised his eyebrows, waiting for a response.

Miltiades cleared his throat nervously. "Sir, how do you know me?"

Kallimakhos laughed a bit. "I am sorry. When your three lead vessels arrived yesterday, they created quite a stir. It is not every day that a Thrakian princess visits Athens. Then to find out that one of our very own is married to her, well. I for one vowed to make certain that someone would be here to greet such a fellow." Kallimakhos' eyes widened as his gaze turned toward Illyrios. "And where did you find such a large one?" He stared up at the slave's bushy red beard and tree-trunk thick neck.

Miltiades did not answer, but continued to gawk at the frenzied activity of the waterfront. He was a man who could appreciate wealth at a glance, even calculate its worth in mere moments, and knew that a great deal of it was flowing through this once docile port.

"By the look on your face, it is you that has questions. Come. I will walk with you. You may ask and I will answer." Kallimakhos shooed the mingling crowd from their path taking Miltiades by the elbow. "I think you will agree that Athens has changed a bit since you were last here."

As they took to their stroll, every so often Miltiades would look up and sight the High City with its gleaming temples that marked the center of Athens. At least that seemed unchanged to him. Hymettos still loomed on one side of the city and Mount Aigilaos on the other and higher still, just beyond the High City he could make out the summit of Lykabettos. The narrow Phaleron Road had barely a twist or turn in it, following the flat plain right up to the western wall of Athens. Along the way they passed several farms, but a singularly expansive one caused Miltiades to stop.

"This land belongs to a good friend of mine," said Kallimakhos. "And someone who I am certain will become a good friend of yours."

Miltiades stared at the endless rows of olive trees that spilled away from the roadside. It had been so many years since he had walked this road; he remembered only small farms. "And who is this good friend. I must have a name so I will not again be at a disadvantage upon our meeting."

"His name is Aristides, son of Lysimakhos and of the deme Alopeke. You two shall meet soon enough." Kallimakhos tugged on Miltiades arm. "Let us keep to the road. We will want to make the gates by sunset."

While Kallimakhos and Miltiades conversed, Kimon tried to occupy himself. A pair of boys darted by—a tall one urging a wooden hoop along with a switch of ash while the other, a bow-legged youth with short-cropped brown hair, pranced all around his companion, kicking up dust and hooting, trying with all his might to coax the hoop to the ground. Kimon stepped in front of them and grabbed it. "That is a fine one you've got." He picked up the nicked and well-worn ring of wood and studied it with admiration. The two boys stood speechless. "Let me see that, will you?" Without waiting for an answer he plucked the switch from the tall boy's hand. "It's my play until it falls, isn't that so?"

The pair nodded. The bow-legged youth laughed. "You won't keep it out of the dust from here to that herm." He pointed to a square column of marble with the head of Hermes upon it, a phallus carved half way up its front. It was only a few meters away. It had been years since he had played this child's game, but he was determined to show them his skill and maybe embarrass his father into hurrying along.

"I'll wager I can keep to it right up to the gates," declared Kimon. He rolled the hoop over the rutted and stony roadbed, slapping it to keep it upright and rambling forward. His new companions commenced a dance of mockery, calling him and the hoop every sort of name while prancing in circles, keeping up with Kimon. They kept at it, well past the herm, past three other farms, until they began to fall behind. Soon Kimon was lost to them, beyond a bend in the road.

"Isn't he a bit too old for that?" asked Kallimakhos.

"I would say so. He mastered that game in his fourth year. Hasn't played it since his fifth. It is just his way of telling me to hustle along." Miltiades picked up his pace, but only slightly. He did not wish to hurry his new companion along too quickly. He had questions. "I have had many visitors from Athens while upon the Peninsula, so I know of the exile of Hippias. I also hear of innovations. New things in how the polis is governed."

"Yes, there are some new ways, but many will be familiar to you. The one thing that has changed is the people's disdain for tyrants," he said this quite innocently, without any hidden meaning, but winced, realizing that in essence he was walking with one such man. "Hippias was not like his father," he added trying to cover over the comment.

Miltiades smiled. "Do not worry. I am not offended at being called a tyrant, if that means bringing good order to a brute region. The Dolonki benefited from my rule, as did many an Athenian colonist. All prospered while I ruled at Elaios."

Kallimakhos stopped and looked directly into Miltiades' eyes with a glare of concern. "There must never be any doubt that Athens is not the Peninsula—in your heart and in the hearts of any others."

"Have I been away so long? Is the rule of a good man so abhorrent?"

Kallimakhos began his walk. "When Hippias was exiled, one man then another tried to take his place, a single ruler for a single city. But, in truth we are not a single city, but a city of many men. Kleisthenes knew this. That is why, when he was arkhon, he refashioned Athens to be governed by many men, and never again to be at the whim of an individual." Presently he smiled at Miltiades. "A tyrant, no matter how benign, is a despised sort of man here now."

"I will tell you what I know of tyrants, "said Miltiades. "If there were no tyrants, then I am sure there would be no Persian threat."

Kallimakhos stopped in his tracks. "I would hardly expect you to say that, a tyrant in all but name and a servant of Darios—at least at one time a servant."

Miltiades could see Kimon leaning against the tower wall, two boys sprawled at his feet, both gulping air in deep breaths. He turned to Kallimakhos. "Oh yes, I was in the service of Darios, but at a time when he threatened no Greeks. He was far from Persia and far from Greece, deep into the land of Skythia and a bridge away from death." Kallimakhos mouth opened as if to speak but before he could ask a question Miltiades yelled to Kimon. "Give them their toy back!"

Unlike Elaios, no guards huddled around the gate and only children played atop the battlements and in the watchtowers. They followed along with the procession of fishmongers, grain carts and timber wagons that trickled into the city from the harbor.

"I should have told you that your cousin Kypselos dispatched me to greet you. He has involved himself in the preparations of your house in the deme of Lakiadai. Your wife, your servants and your considerable treasure wait there for your arrival.

Miltiades nodded. "I thank you, friend Kallimakhos. How can I return such a favor?"

"By attending a symposion in your honor."

Miltiades stared up at the High City and the temple of Athena Polias, Protectoress of Athens that dominated the Akropolis. "This is a small favor to ask in return."

They passed through the Phaleron Road gates. Kimon left his two newfound companions and trailed his father and Kallimakhos. Inside the walls modest houses spread away from the road and toward the steep limestone slopes of the Akropolis, their orange tiled roofs simmering in the late afternoon sun.

"What is that!" Kimon pointed to their right as they entered, to an expanse of stumpy marble columns occupying a vast rectangle of land between the southeastern slope of the Akropolis and the city walls.

"I cannot believe that it is not completed," said Miltiades. Now he turned to Kimon. "That, my son, was to be the great Olympeion, temple to Father Zeus. The younger Pisistratos had begun its construction before I had left Athens." He looked to Kallimakhos. "What has happened?"

A look of concern transformed Kallimakhos' face. "Anything associated with Pisistratos and his family has become a hated thing, even a temple to Zeus himself."

"But Pisistratos was a good man," replied Miltiades.

"He was a tyrant, and that very name is a curse here in Athens."

They continued their stroll toward the Agora, following the road that slipped between the Akropolis and the Areopagos Hill. From here they looked down upon the rest of Athens and the Agora. *Athens has grown,* thought Miltiades. *Athens has grown indeed.*

✳✳✳✳✳

Hegesipyle barely spoke to him. At first, for only a moment, her eyes betrayed a distinct gladness at the sight of Miltiades, a look of joy and relief to see her husband safe. But she quickly buried any such emotions beneath the hate she now felt at being dragged from her homeland to this new place. She had come to land at Phaleron only two days prior to her husband, and his cousin had greeted her and provided escort from the harbor town to her new home in the deme of Lakiadai. In Phaleron she garnered little attention as the place swelled with foreign traders and seamen, but it proved different once in the more insular precincts of Athens. Even Kypselos could not distract Hegesipyle from the strangeness that surrounded her with his silky words and false smiles. The city and its people shocked her. The houses all crowded together, one against another, just like its inhabitants in the Agora. They all stared as she passed, looking upon her as something alien, one different and not of them, and made no attempt to couch their opinions in polite whispers. She understood Greek, but they chattered so quickly, pointing and giggling as they kept to their talk, regarding her as some kind of exhibition. It was a brutally long trip from the harbor to her new home, and she wished never to set foot outside of it again.

Miltiades tried speaking with her, but gave up, finally ordering her slaves to attend to his wife, to keep her busy with readying their new home. Kimon, on the other hand, looked upon their new life as an exciting adventure and began to explore Athens with a sense of exhilaration. Illyrios had become his guardian, or pedagogos, during his explorations, for no youth of a respectable family could run about unattended until he became an adult, and Kimon would have to wait another year until he could be entered into the rolls of his tribe. Then he would begin his training as an ephebos and learn the skills necessary to fight in the phalanx as a hoplite or heavy-infantryman. A year was a long time to wait, especially at his age. Still the pair managed to visit the Agora each morning, strolling the lines of makeshift stalls, pausing under the awnings of the peddlers, as much to study their wares as to escape the unrelenting sun of an Attic summer.

One morning, as they made their daily rounds, they came upon a great argument at the stall of a grain merchant. Three men with short staffs, which they wielded like swords, surrounded the merchant and began pounding his table.

"What is that all about?" asked Kimon of another boy that worked in a cobbler's stall. "Who are they?" he pointed to the men with sticks.

The boy looked up from his crouch. "Metronomoi. They enforce the weights and measures here in the Agora. They know all the tricks." The boy laughed a bit while plucking up a section of ox-hide that he began to pound with a wooden mallet.

One of the metronomoi snatched a bronze measuring cup from the grain merchant's hand. Kimon could see the markings etched on its surface, even from here, but what he could not see was the upward bulge that the slippery merchant had hammered into the base of the cup, reducing its volume. They took the cup and the merchant from his stall, ushering him violently to the small round building at the edge of the Agora. As they pushed the culprit through the crowd some spat while others slapped and punched at him at him, until he stumbled up the steps of the Tholos and out of sight.

Kimon knelt down next to the young cobbler who kept to his pounding upon the hide and wooden anvil. "What will happen to him?"

"He has broken the law. He will have his trial and he will be convicted. A fine perhaps. I think he is a metic, a foreigner, so they may exile him, or sell him as a slave."

"A trial? So he goes before a magistrate?" Kimon placed a hand on the boy's shoulder to gain his attention.

The boy stopped his hammering. "No. It will be a trial before jurors, not a magistrate." The boy resumed his pounding.

"Jurors? Are these special men, appointed by the magistrate?" Kimon knew of magistrates for even Elaios had them, men who would judge crimes and grievances, but he had never heard of a juror before.

"Where are you from? Are you not Athenian?" The boy dropped his hammer and uncoiled from his crouch.

"Yes I am Athenian, but I have been away and have only just returned."

"Jurors are just men, but they are also *polites*—citizens. The people govern here in Athens. The people judge here in Athens. You must have been gone a very long time not to know this." The cobbler boy bent to pick up his mallet then scooped a ladle full of water from a large earthenware jar. He held it out to Kimon. "A drink?"

Kimon took the ladle, nodding a thank you before he sipped. "And what is going on there?" He flicked a glance to a long colonnade where men queued up in its shade.

"The stoa of the king arkhon. More work for more jurors. That is where one man brings suit against another." The boy took the empty ladle from Kimon, dipped it full again and began to drink. "Does he want any?" The boy pointed to Illyrios, who hovered over Kimon like a wall. The slave shook his head. "I have much work to do." The boy hunkered down again over the anvil and hide and commenced to pound away.

Kimon looked around smiling. He thought to himself, *here, in Athens, a man's greatness is only bounded by his talent.* Then he lost his smile. *I won't be a man for another year.*

Illyrios placed his huge hand upon Kimon's shoulder. "Master Kimon, your father commanded that you be home by mid-day."

Kimon had forgotten about his father's edict. A tutor was to visit his house, a man who could teach Kimon more than the Poet's lines, arithmetics or melodies. After his encounter with the cobbler boy, he was anxious to learn more about his home. He hustled through the Agora, toward the Kerameikos, leaving the city behind as they crossed the modest stream of the Kephisos. His father's house was not far. Illyrios could hardly keep up with him, closing the wide-open gate as he followed Kimon into the courtyard. There, in the shade of the columns, he saw his father sitting upon a marble bench, in conversation with a balding little man who was wrapped in a himation cloak. Kimon approached them slowly, trying to gather himself, and his thoughts to prepare his words. Just as his father began to speak, someone rapped upon the gate. Illyrios swung it open allowing a man to enter. He held a wooden tablet covered in wax and asked to see Miltiades, whereupon Illyrios pointed to the men seated on the benches.

Miltiades, somewhat surprised, reached for the wax tablet. He stood up and walked out from the shadows to study the wax-etched letters in better light. It was an invitation to the very symposion that Kallimakhos had mentioned. The guest list was concise. Some names, like Aristides, he had heard mention of while others were new to him. He nodded as he handed the tablet back to the messenger before pulling his son into his conversation with the tutor.

*****

Illyrios attended to Miltiades as he made the walk to the townhouse of Aristides, where they were met by a servant who stood sentinel at the gate to the courtyard. The slave swung it open and Miltiades strode through, his sight falling immediately upon a life-size wooden statue of Zeus Herkaios, and an adjacent one of the goddess Athena, each fronted by a small marble altar covered with offerings of blossoms, diminutive cups, leaden figurines and several burning oil lamps. To the right of the shrine another servant stood by an open doorway. It was late afternoon and the sun still hovered above, so he could not make out the lamplight that spilled from the andreion. Illyrios took a seat outside amongst several other slaves that had accompanied their masters. Athens was not a dangerous place, and these men did not provide protection, but became guides to their drunken owners upon their return trips home, more often than not carrying them when they could not walk by themselves.

Miltiades entered the andreion, his eyes slowly adjusting to its darkened interior, while the resinous fragrance of incense overwhelmed his every breath. There were seven couches lining the walls, raised from the center of the floor by a platform of half a foot in height. Before each couch stood three-legged table and behind, upon pegs on the wall, hung kylikes, or saucer-like drinking cups.

"Come in Miltiades." The words drew his attention to a modestly dressed man sitting upright who waved his hands toward an unoccupied adjacent couch.

Miltiades nodded, and sat. A servant rushed to him and knelt, untying his sandals with the solemnity of a sacred ritual. He hung these upon one of the vacant pegs behind the couch.

"I think you already know my good friend Kallimakhos," said Aristides as he glanced that way. From there he circled the room, pointing to each guest with an empty kylix. "Melanthios, son of Phrynikhos." He moved on to the next couch. "And Kynegeiros, son of Euphorion. Next to him is his brother Aiskhylos. Aiskhylos' great ambition is to line the Street of Tripods with monuments to his plays."

"I do not understand," said Miltiades as he nodded in greeting to Aiskhylos.

"I endeavor to create tragedies to honor the god Dionysos. Perhaps you will attend one during his festival?"

Aristides interrupted, "Let us drink first. My stomach—and my head—require a bit of wine to inure me to the talk of plays."

A slave reached behind Miltiades to lift a kylix from its peg and handed it to him. He studied the scene painted upon its surface, a maiden playing the twin-piped flute while another gazed into a polished bronze mirror. "I see an empty couch. Are you expecting another?" He knew the answer for he had seen the invitation listing the name of each guest.

"Xanthippos will indeed be here shortly. He always has to make a grand entrance," remarked Aiskhylos, with a smirk and a shake of his head.

Aristides called the steward forward, who filled each of the kylikes with uncut wine. He glanced around the room to be certain his guests had their full cups and his full attention. "In honor of Dionysos." He sipped the strong portion of wine, quaffing most of the kylix, then along with the others poured out the remainder as a libation to the god. Now other servants entered, some placing small bowls of flatbread upon each diner's table, while another refilled their cups with a honey-wine potion that would initiate their meal.

Aristides dipped his bread in the concoction and nibbled a bit. "Kallimakhos tells me of your loss, sir."

Miltiades had almost forgotten about Metiokhos. "Yes. My eldest son captained of one of my ships. The Persian fleet captured him one day out of Elaios."

"I regret this news," said Aiskhylos as watched a servant place a bowl of ribbonfish upon his table. "And what do you think will become of him?"

Miltiades slid his empty kylix upon his table and swung his feet to the floor, to sit upright. He squeezed his curly, thick beard between his fingers. "I know something of these Persians."

"Of course you do," bellowed a man as he strode into the andreion, his himation cloak flowing wildly behind him like he was in the midst of a tempest.

Aiskhylos stood and swept his hand toward the new arrival. "As I predicted. The grand entrance of Xanthippos."

Xanthippos fell into the empty couch, one adjacent to Miltiades. "Well?" He snarled at the slave who nervously tried to untie his sandals. "You oaf!" He sent the slave tumbling backwards with a kick then unfastened the sandals himself. Xanthippos chucked the pair, smacking the slave in the cheek. He snorted out a laugh. "Now he will remember to be more courteous to your guests." The servant plucked up the sandals unhurriedly—almost defiantly—his face reddened by either the strike or rage, and hung them carefully upon the wall.

None of the others in the andreion seemed comfortable with Xanthippos' behavior or his remarks, but none would defend a slave either. Aristides tried to shift their attention. "Miltiades has told us of a woeful event. Both he and the rest of his family were fortunate to escape the Persian fleet, but not so his son."

Before Miltiades could continue with his story Xanthippos started up again. "And why would this be a bad thing? I hear you once served Darios and the Persians. Why would your master maltreat the son of such a loyal servant?"

Miltiades felt the blood rising up. He knew nothing of this man before today, and could not guess why he would attack him. But maybe this is a new and novel way to converse, a test of his self-control, to be withdrawn with a laugh and an apology later. He would not retaliate—at least not openly.

"Come now, Xanthippos. You assault my guest as though he were your adversary." Aristides tried to extinguish flames of confrontation before they could fully ignite. His calm demeanor elicited thoughtfulness.

"Why yes," broke in Kynegeiros, "Must you contend with everyone?"

Xanthippos threw his empty hand up in the air, while cradling his wine-cup carefully in the other. "I am curious as to why an agent of Darios has anything to fear from him. "

Miltiades leaned back into the cushions of his couch. "Darios did not send his fleet to Elaios as a gesture of friendship. I did not lose a son to a benefactor. Any man, or city, that has opposed the Great King is now subject to his wrath."

Xanthippos took the dice from the servant and tossed them upon the floor. "You'll be hard pressed to beat that," he said, as the dice tumbled to a halt. "By the way, how did you gain the ire of Darios?"

The servant scooped up the dice and handed them to Miltiades. He let them tumble from his open hand into the center of the room.

Aiskhylos laughed out loud. "Ah, Xanthippos, you have lost. It seems our guest of honor shall be the symposiarkhos." His glance now turned to Miltiades, a huge grin upon his face. "Lord of the banquet, how shall we mix the wine?"

Miltiades reluctantly provided the wine steward with the proportions to mix. A pair of servants waddled in, each gripping the handles of a large krater. They placed it in front of Miltiades, poured water first, then wine, according to his instructions. "It all began at a bridge," Miltiades said, catching them all off guard a bit with his much delayed answer. For the next hour or so he recounted his adventure while guarding the bridge over the Ister, with Xanthippos all the while listening—and calculating—in silence.

"A convenient story." Xanthippos said as he slid his arm from his eyes as he lay staring up at the ceiling. "You are the only one here in Athens that can attest to the truth or falsity of this tale. Very convenient."

Aristides refused to let their gathering become contentious, even at the risk of becoming totally inebriated. "Come gentlemen, a toast. He waited for the servants to refill their kylikes. "An amystis—a breathless drink!" All smiled, except Xanthippos. Miltiades, as symposiarkhos, led them in the toast. They all put cup to lips and began gulping without stopping, not taking a breath or a respite until each kylix was empty. Aristides hoped this would numb their sharp tongues and lead to more congenial talk. It did not.

Even Miltiades, who was accustomed to the stronger wines of Thrake, fell victim to the amystis. "Xanthippos, my friend," he said with a bit of sarcasm, "I hear you have a special interest in the Persians." Miltiades waved the wine-steward over to refill his cup. "My new acquaintances here in Athens tell me that your trading ships would fare much better with the Persians as our friends, maybe even as our masters. In fact, some say you did everything possible to stop Melanthios here from sailing to Ionia to free our fellow Greeks. War with Persia would not be good for business."

Xanthippos stood up, trying desperately not to lose his balance and the command of his tongue. "You have lived with barbarians, and without a doubt, lost your manners amongst them." He snapped up his himation cloak and slung it over his shoulder, swinging its loose end around his left arm. "This one time I will excuse such an affront." With every last bit of self-control he tried to depart the andreion under command, but slid ever so slightly upon a scrap of wet bread just as he stepped over the threshold. Luckily he braced himself quickly against the doorframe. Once outside he commenced to berate his own servant as they exited the courtyard.

"My regrets that the evening has turned out so," said Aristides.

"No sir, it is my doing that one of your guests went away so angry," offered Miltiades. "I must learn to control the wine and not allow the reverse."

"Bad memory makes for good companions," quipped Aiskhylos. "Tomorrow, the words passed tonight will all be forgotten."

Miltiades looked to the wine-steward. "Since I am lord of this banquet, I say set up for kottabos."

Melanthios laughed. "You are an extraordinary man. You call one of the most powerful men in Athens a traitor after which you want to play a game."

The steward dragged a tall, narrow table to the center of the andreion, and placed a small dish atop it. Their cups were filled once more. Kynegeiros, seemingly the most thirsty, emptied his first. He repositioned his left arm upon the cushions to support his head then with a bent right elbow swung his cup towards the dish in the center of the room, launching the dregs of wine. He overshot by a wide margin, for some of the wine splashed across the beard of Miltiades. They all laughed. Aiskhylos threw next, getting a few drops to ping off the dish, followed by his brother, who fared no better. Aristides, with almost perfect technique, sent his dregs to the center of the solitary dish.

"This game is new to me," said Miltiades as he tried to gauge the distance to the saucer. He bent his arm back then released his throw, sending drops of wine in a wide arc across the room. "What a poor throw!" he said in disgust.

They all tried again, and again. Aristides, his constitution seemingly impervious to the volume of wine, won every bout of kottabos. Miltiades slid from his couch to Aristides', ostensibly to offer congratulations for his victories, but in truth to engage in a brief, but private conversation. "One thing you must know—that is my hatred for the Persians. I have lost my land, my home and my son to them. Darios would see me dead." Now he looked into Aristides' eyes, the veil of wine dissolving away for the moment. "His fleet and his army have been unleashed against all enemies, whether they are real or imagined. He counts the Athenians amongst these enemies."

Aristides returned Miltiades' grave look. "I know this, as does any sane man in Athens. The Persians will come, and we will fight. That I am certain of. That is why we need you, Miltiades." He began to lean back in the cushions, but stopped short. "What I do not understand is Xanthippos." He collapsed into the embrace of his couch. *Unless Miltiades is correct*, he thought.

Chapter 16

Plataia—Late Summer 494 BC

Kyra sat motionless at the table, her face veiled and her head crowned with a wreath of plaited blossoms, while her cousin Telesilla took a seat beside her as nympheutria or matron of honor. On all sides were the women-folk of her family.

Her mother leaned over and lifted the veil from Kyra's face. "Come child, this is a day for happiness. It is your wedding day." She studied her daughter's blank expression with concern. The others laughed it off as a case of nerves, but she knew it was more than that. Many years passed she had been forced into an arranged marriage, but in time grew to love her husband Koinos. But unlike her, Kyra knew her husband, and liked him as much as she would allow anyone to know. Love would come easier to them both. At least that is what her mother thought as she slid the veil back in place.

Arimnestos stared across the courtyard from his sister and the table of women. He sat with the men of his family and the family of the groom, but wished he were at the table in his own home, sitting across from Kyra, in more carefree days. Unlike his sister he had grown comfortable with the company of others, but she still preferred less people and much less attention. He felt for her now. In the past she could simply dredge up her anger as a shield against others, especially Arimnestos, but for today anyway, she must behave, and tomorrow obey—two things that did not come naturally to her. He turned to Lampon. "I don't know?"

"What?" Lampon shook his head in bewilderment.

Arimnestos pointed to Kyra, laughing. "You are the groom and she is the bride, and I don't know who looks more sad?"

Arimnestos' young cousin walked amongst the guests with the offering of sesame cakes, handing one to each guest, repeating the words," I have avoided the worse; I have chosen the better." Once each of the wedding guests had received their cake, one by one they approached Kyra to bestow their best wishes and their modest gifts. She nodded politely as she accepted each cup, vial of perfume, or bolt of linen, her mother gently placing each beside Kyra's chair.

The feast occupied the entire afternoon and continued beyond sunset— Kyra sitting like a statue, and Lampon being forced to drink cup after cup of well-watered wine while enduring the jokes of the men. Arimnestos did what he could to settle his friend and brother-in-law, reassuring him that it would all be over soon. It had been less than a year since he himself had wed, and he enjoyed not being the brunt of all this attention.

Now Koinos solemnly approached his daughter and offered a hand to her, helping her to stand. Lampon too stood at his place at the table, while all the other men remained seated. Both Koinos and Kyra walked slowly toward Lampon, father still holding daughter's hand, leading her toward the groom. Lampon could feel his legs wobbling, and hoped no one would notice these obvious tremors. Kyra stopped just inches before him. Koinos grabbed Lampon's hand and placed his daughter's into his, while lifting up her veil. Kyra's eyes welled with tears, but she would not cry, not before so many. Lampon leaned to her and whispered, "Do not worry." He stared at her with the same innocent look that overcame him the first time they met. Koinos ushered them to the open wagon that would carry the newly-weds to Lampon's house. With his hand still wrapped around hers, he helped her into the bed of the wagon then jumped up himself, still holding onto his new bride as if she were a bird, ready to take to flight. Arimnestos vaulted up to the driver's bench, snapping up the reins in his hands. Just as he was about to send the mules off, Mikkos, Arimnestos' little brother, came running from the road that led to the walled section of the town.

"They are filling the road. Coming over the Oaks-Head toward Thebes."

Arimnestos yelled to Mikkos, "What is going on?"

The boy pointed east, toward the Thebes Road. Arimnestos stood tall on the bench of the wagon straining to see. There, in the settling gloom of night he could see a procession of torches, winding their way like a great serpent through the pass and down into the plain.

"Who are they?" snapped Arimnestos.

"Argives!"

143

*****

That evening Arimnestos brought his sister and his friend to their home, and sat outside, singing and shouting along with the others, being certain to generate all the noise they could to keep away any evil daimons, and ensure happiness for the new couple. Eumenidas grabbed the wineskin from Arimnestos, holding a finger before his lips. "Shhh! I thought I heard them talking." He unplugged the skin and gulped till his breath gave out. Wine bubbled out of his mouth and down his wispy, raven beard.

Arimnestos shoved Eumenidas in the back, releasing the wineskin from his friend's grip. "Sing loud! I don't want to hear what they are up to," he barked as he pointed to the window with the skin. "Sappho's song." Arimnestos stood, swaying under a head full of wine. "Oh groom!' he began, "you should be happy because you hold in your arms the woman of your dreams." Now the others joined in, emphasizing the words they remembered, while mumbling the rest, "Aphrodite! Lovely Aphrodite! The goddess honored you more than any other." Arimnestos missed the stool as he lowered himself, rolling into the dirt. He hugged the wineskin affectionately, gave it a mock kiss while looking up at his companions, squinting. "By the goddess, what I am doing here." He rolled up onto his knees and tossed the bag of wine to Eumenidas, then slowly rose, getting his feet under a tottering body. With a manner of misplaced dignity he brushed the dirt from his chiton, and started to walk away.

"Arimnestos, stay awhile longer," pleaded Eumenidas. "These four would hardly help me finish the wine." He let loose a belch. "On second thought go. I seem to have a vacancy in my belly, and will drink it all myself."

"I will leave, but only if you sing." Arimnestos hovered over Eumenidas until wails of indistinguishable words flowed out. He smiled and took off down the narrow alleyway toward the northern gate of Plataia. He needed no torch to light his way, and could afford neither slave nor servant to guide him home, so he shuffled along the road down the slope and away from the walled town toward Tower Hill. In the center of the plain he crossed the Oeroe, splashing through the ankle high waters of the stream. He stopped and squatted down scooping handfuls of its cool waters onto his face and over his pounding head. A crescent moon hung over Kithairon behind him while mist oozed out from the banks of the stream, creeping up toward his farmhouse on Tower Hill. *Not a good night for men,* he thought. He stared at the expanding blanket of fog. *It is a night for daimons only.*

Finally, after trudging up the steep pathway from the Thebes Road, he carefully opened the cottage door, hoping the hinge pins that he had failed to refit and oil for would grant him a favor and not protest this neglect. He pushed the door gently. The hinges wailed, setting his dog to a tirade of barking as he charged toward his master. The barking ceased as the dog poked its head all around Arimnestos, sniffing and snorting, tail flailing with delight. "Go to sleep," he commanded while rubbing the dog's neck. As he passed through the kitchen he bumped the small table while groping for the doorframe that led to the bedroom. In a moment his still wet sandals were off, allowing him to collapse atop the sleeping pallet. Within seconds he snored blissfully. Later, when the wine had worn off, he began to toss; every sound became magnified, even the beating of his very own heart as he fought to regain sleep. For hour after hour he squeezed his eyes shut, soon opening them slowly as he turned to the window in hopes of catching the first glimmer of dawn that would release him. Much deeper into the night a fit of laughing suddenly overcame him, and it was all he could do to contain it. He thought of poor Kyra and Lampon, both too nervous to move, sitting in opposite corners of their bedroom staring out to nothing but darkness. Just as suddenly the thought arrived that he could be so very wrong, and neither would be hiding in a corner. He laughed out loud.

His wife Theolyte pushed against him, her warm, naked flesh inciting him to envelope her. "What is it?" she purred, partly asleep.

"Nothing," he reassured her as he stroked the curve of her back, his hand gently tracing circles over her hip, until finally squeezing between her thighs. He embraced her in her slumber, all the while staring out at the stars. If he fell asleep it was short-lived, for it seemed only moments before dawn revealed herself.

Before he could rise, Theolyte squeezed his arm, arresting him. "What has happened at Argos? "

Arimnestos whispered softly, "The Spartans have defeated the Argives in a great battle." Gray light began to seep into their bedroom now and he could distinguish the concern on Theolyte's face. "There is no need to worry. The Spartans are our friends. And so the Athenians."

"It is not friends that worry me, dear husband. Our enemy, Thebes is very close. I do not want to be fleeing my home in the night like the Argives."

Arimnestos laughed, setting his head to pounding. He rubbed his eyes, trying to suppress the pain of last night's wine. "Thebes can do little harm to us while Athens is our ally. Even without the Athenians we Plataians have strong walls and even stronger men. No Theban dare attack us." *At least not alone.* Now this very thought he so casually plucked from his hazy mind incited a barrage of possibilities, of explanations of what had really occurred at Sepeia. Kleomenes and the Spartans did not fear Athens, or Thebes, or even the Argives. What concerned them most was the threat of the Great King Darios. The Persians would come. In this there was no doubt. The Argives made a pact with Darios, so Kleomenes dealt them such a defeat that they would be scant help to their Persian master. But Thebes—they hated the Athenians more than they hated Persia. Thebes was a different story.

Chapter 17

Sardis—Spring 493 BC

Datis rode alongside Artaphernes the Younger, both leading the half-mile long serpentine column of horseman as they approached the Smyrna Gate of Sardis. The late afternoon sun hung low in the sky, barely clearing the twin towers, causing the walls to appear a little more than deep shadow, devoid of any detail or color.

"It is almost done," said Datis as he bounced gently in rhythm with his horse's canter. "The islands are subject once more to the Great King. "

Artaphernes rubbed the neck of his horse, jingling the golden war-bridle, while nodding in affirmation. "You are right, my friend, but the mainland Greeks are still left to deal with. 'Tis sad that Mardonios will lead the expedition against them and not you." He turned around. There, amidst the heavy Persian cavalry, the faces of the captives glowed in the orange-gold sunlight, their gaunt bodies casting exaggerated shadows upon the muddy road. Every now and then he heard the crack of a whip or the stumble of one of the Ionians as feet tangled in leg-irons. These were the last of them. Rebels, for certain, but men who had fled from one island to another, keeping one step ahead of the fleet and the land army that shadowed it as it marched from Mykale north to Byzantion. These fugitives had finally exhausted all refuge. The yearlong chase had worn them down, leaving them not much more than flesh draped on bones. They would generate scant income at the slave markets. In fact, Artaphernes had worked all his persuasion upon Darios to allow him to execute every last one of them. If he could not recoup the expenses of the campaign from their sale, he would at the very least reduce the costs of their maintenance. But Darios would not hear of it.

Datis reached for the small wineskin that dangled from his shoulder, clearing it from his gyrtos bow case before handing it to Artaphernes. "It is from Thasos, and very good indeed."

Artaphernes pulled the stopper free and commenced to gulp down a portion. "Needs honey, I think." He handed the skin back to Datis. "Come now, it does not unsettle you even a bit that Mardonios has command of the invasion?" Datis continued to ride in silence. Artaphernes could not. "You defeated the Greeks. It was you who took back Samos, Khios, and all the other islands. Only by Darios' command did you stop at the Hellespont."

"Yes it was certainly the King's command that halted me—and the onset of winter. I would not sail that sea against the proper season." Now he waved his arm sending the standard bearer of his hazarabam of cavalry into a gallop, past him and through the gate. "Mardonios will require at least a year to gather it all, men horses, ships, and the provender to sustain them. Much can happen in a year."

He shaded his eyes as they drew nearer to the yawning gateway and gazed up. "Ask our friends up there." Artaphernes chuckled. "Histiaios and his cousin both look much taller than I remember." Now he could clearly hear the thousands of flies that buzzed above the open gate, all drawn to the pair of severed heads that capped two poles of ash wood. Their eyes stared wildly down at them, hair matted with coagulated blood, the soft, bloated flesh of their faces partially consumed by carrion beetles. An incongruent smile spread across one man's face; the other's mouth opened as if to shout—or scream. Nailed beneath them hung a wooden plaque with the words gouged out in Ionian—**The Greeks Histiaios and Aristagoras for treachery**.

Chapter 18

Athens—Early Summer 492 BC

Hegesipyle, by now, had relegated herself to the managing of the household on the outskirts of the village of Lakiadai, with its view of the High City and the walls of Athens. Every time she stepped outside, either in the courtyard or atop the terrace of their house, the strange, gleaming buildings of the city reminded her how very far from Thrake she was. Unlike in her native land, where she enjoyed the privileges of royalty, she could not simply make an excursion to the city. Women, especially of her stature, would dispatch servants to run errands. The city proper, and especially the Agora, belonged to men.

At first Miltiades stayed with her at Lakiadai, helping his wife become acquainted with the Athenian way, but he tired quickly of the huge estate, and most every day rode into the city, enticed by its activity, but mostly by its opportunity for deliberations with other men of leisure. The Agora seethed with activity—the sailing season was well underway and ships from all over the Sea of the Hellenes docked at Phaleron disgorging their cargoes, most of it making its way to the sellers' stalls and ramshackle booths in the Agora. Miltiades followed the narrow pathway that skirted the Council House to eventually climb the stairs toward the temple of Theseus and away from the crowd, passing only a few of the Skythian police-archers that had come down from their huts on the slopes of Areopagos to keep order in the markets.

He turned to make certain Illyrios still followed. For sure his slave strode up the stairs too, only a few paces behind, toting the small reed cage that held a pure white dove captive. "Hand me that will you." Miltiades snatched the caged bird and presented it to the guardian of the temple, along with a prayer wish etched on lead foil and rolled tight. The fire in the bronze cauldron burned hot, illuminating the columned porch of the temple with its flickering orange light, casting fleeting shadows of the attendant, Miltiades, and Illyrios upon the whitewashed walls. A mantis dunked his hands into the water bowl, reached into the cage and grabbed the fluttering dove, quickly pinning its wings back with his thumbs. With a nimble draw of his blade he opened the bird's neck, letting the blood pulse over the already stained altar. Emptied of life, he then handed the dove to the attendant who tossed the carcass into the flames of the holocaust sacrifice.

The doors swung open, but before entering the priest dunked a small hand broom into the bowl of sacred water and began to flick it over and around Miltiades. At last he walked in following the priest. Only narrow shafts of sunlight penetrated the gloom within, entering from the high, square windows of the temple. Around the wooden cult figure of Theseus, dozens of oil lamps threw dim pools of light upon the marble floors. Clouds of incense hung thick in the air. The chatter of the Agora melted away into a soft murmur. He stayed only long enough to watch the mantis place his prayer amongst the other votives before turning to the doorway. The sunlight assaulted him as he stepped from the shadows of the columns.

"Miltiades, son of Kimon," a voice bellowed from the intense light of mid morning.

Miltiades rubbed his eyes. Slowly sight adjusted. Before him stood Xanthippos, along with two men that looked most familiar to him.

"Miltiades," repeated Xanthippos, "You are summoned to appear before the Council."

Now the faces of the other two registered. Colonists from Elaios. Men he had punished. Men with a grudge. "What business does the Council have with me?"

"I charge you with treason," said Xanthippos, as he looked to his companions.

Illyrios stepped shoulder to shoulder with his master. Miltiades eased him back with a hand. "Treason! What a ludicrous charge." He stepped to within an inch of Xanthippos. "What do you speak of?"

Xanthippos retreated by a step or two. "It will be read before the Council five days hence. These men bear witness that you have received this summons."

Miltiades pushed his way past a grinning Xanthippos, who lost his smile as Illyrios lumbered his way, glaring at him. Both quickly descended the temple hill bearing right as he passed the Council House. There, in front of a cobbler's shop, he spotted Kallimakhos, Aristides, and a man he did not know.

Kallimakhos saw him first as he approached, said a few words to his companions then stepped forward to greet Miltiades. "We see you had a conversation with Xanthippos." Before he allowed Miltiades to answer he tugged on the arm of the stranger, pulling him closer to Miltiades. "This is Themistokles, son of Neokles."

Miltiades extended his open hand to Themistokles. Themistokles responded with an exuberant embrace, leaving Miltiades stiff as a statue. He backed up a step from Themistokles.

"Themistokles here is the chief arkhon," said Kallimakhos.

"I count Kallimakhos and Aristides as friends," said Miltiades. "Can I say the same of you, sir?"

Before Themistokles could respond Kallimakhos laughed a bit and interjected, "Themistokles may be your friend, and Aristides may also be called friend. But please, good Miltiades, do not ask them to be friend to each other."

Themistokles nodded. "Aristides and I do not see things in the same way. Still, when my city is in danger, he is a man I can count on, as I hope we all can count on you." He waved with an open hand to a pair of wooden benches in the shade of the cobbler's shop. The four sat, Themistokles and Miltiades on one bench, Kallimakhos and Aristides on the other.

"What danger comes Athens way?" Miltiades mopped the sweat from his brow with the edge of his cloak.

"A captain of a timber ship from Mende brought word of a massive fleet, ships he counted in the thousands. So many that neither beach nor harbor could hold them all." Themistokles bent forward, causing the others to lean inward also. "Only the Council knows this. The Persians have begun their invasion."

Miltiades heart sunk in his chest. He thought of Elaios. He thought also of his son Metiokhos, captured and slain by these barbarians. "Are you certain of this?" He could not fathom that Darios could reach so far.

"Without doubt. The Aiginetans have thrown in with him," Themistokles threw his hands up but caught himself as several men passing by stopped and stared at him. "By the gods, their island is a blight on the gulf." He spoke of the island of Aigina, less than a half a day's sail from Phaleron. An island now in league with Darios and the Persians.

151

Miltiades looked back toward the temple of Theseus, back to his encounter with Xanthippos. "I despise the Persians, as Kallimakhos and Aristides can attest to. But they are not the greatest threat to me, sir."

Themistokles' face grew red. "What greater threat can there be?"

"Xanthippos!" Miltiades poked himself in the chest with his index finger. "He has charged me with treason."

Aristides and Kallimakhos stared wide-eyed at him. Themistokles, his face never betraying his thoughts, looked at him coolly. "This does not surprise me. You return to Athens with considerable wealth and with many close friends that owe you much. You have become a threat to him."

"A year ago I did not even know the man," said Miltiades expelling a deep breath. "Now, I fear, I may know him too well."

"What can you mean by that?" Aristides was an intelligent fellow, but a painfully honest one. He could not pull away the covers of deceit to reveal the full truth.

"Who stands to suffer most by a war with Persia?" Miltiades, throwing all tact away, blurted out the question.

"No, no, I will not believe that even Xanthippos would sell out Athens to Darios," countered Aristides.

"He would sell his own mother, if it suited him." From behind them the cobbler stuck his head out of the open shop window and continued, "I want only money. Give me my daily ration of obols and I am content. Xanthippos, on the other hand, craves power. Money is but the means to accumulate it."

Themistokles glared over his shoulder at the cobbler, finally rising as he motioned for the other three to follow. He led them to the closed doors of the Bouleterion, or Council House, where the attendant, recognizing him, swung the door open enough for them to enter. Inside light spilled from the high windows onto the stepped wooden benches that climbed up three of the four walls. Here the five hundred councilors held session.

Themistokles offered his companions a seat upon the lowest bench, while he paced before them, his footfalls echoing on the hard marble. "That cobbler knows more than us, I would say." He continued his deliberate stroll, turning and retracing his steps, stalking the Bouleterion. "It is more than jealousy, I think." He stopped. "Not only have you gained influence since your arrival, you have gained it at his expense." Themistokles looked around, making certain that no one, not a slave woman scrubbing the polished marble floor or a servant filling the lamps, hung about. "You know the Persians. You have observed their strengths. And more importantly, you understand their weaknesses."

Kallimakhos stood up. "We could never convince the Council or the Assembly that Xanthippos was anything less than upright. He married the niece of Kleisthenes, didn't he?"

"The demos would never so quickly accuse the family of their benefactor," added Themistokles. "I thought, my good Aristides, that he is a dear friend of yours?" He could not resist the opportunity of casting even this slight aspersion his rival's way.

"I do not judge a man by rumor, but by his actions," countered Aristides.

Kallimakhos moved between the two. "You forget what we have come here to discuss."

For the next several hours the four men talked of deviousness of Xanthippos, measuring what he might gain by an alliance with Persia and what he might lose by war with them. Themistokles very easily could understand Xanthippos while Aristides would not come to grips with the plain facts. Miltiades and Kallimakhos thought of the charge of treason and the hearing before the Council. This was no minor offense, to be judged by a magistrate, or even the jurors of the Heliaia. If Xanthippos could convince the Council of this charge, then the entire Assembly would become Miltiades' jurors.

✵✵✵✵✵

Hegesipyle need say nothing. Her face conveyed to Miltiades a dire concern along with the same look of isolation and regret that hung over her since their arrival over a year ago. He could not be certain her concern was for him or her fate if she was left without a husband in the alien city. The night previous she had wept, talking of her frustration at watching him here in Athens, not the master of his fate, as he had been on the Peninsula. Indeed Athens was a strange place, a place where normal sense had been turned upside down. Instead of a single strong ruler determining the fate of the many, the many held the destiny of the single man in their hands.

Miltiades took the kantharos cup from her and poured the libation, dousing the altar beneath the wooden figure of Zeus. His wife had prayed to her Thrakian god, Bendis. If he had more time he would pray to every god, Greek, Thrakian, even Persian. Illyrios, as silent and looming as ever stood behind him, waiting to escort his master to the Pynx and the gathering Assembly. Miltiades glanced one last time to his wife before pushing the gate open, but before taking another step he fingered the pouch hanging from his belt, squeezing the four knucklebones within. Relieved, he stepped into an empty, dark street, the nascent light of dawn not yet penetrating into the alleyways between the tightly packed houses of the city. Slaves, armed with rope dipped in red paint, had begun to cordon off the Agora, allowing only one avenue of exit—toward the Pynx. An old man tried to slip by them, onto the Dromos that headed to the Kerameikos. A slave lashed him with the rope, staining his legs and rear with paint. Reluctantly he reversed course toward the Pynx Hill.

Miltiades looked up to the stairs that would lead them to the Assembly, the treetops on the hill catching the first golden sliver of sunlight of the new day. Above these the semeion banner fluttered in the mild breeze, signaling that the Assembly was indeed in session this morning. At the top of the stairs he stepped into the crowded, bowl-like hillcrest, where men paused to stare and whisper as he passed by on his way to the bema. Here he could see the fifty prytaneis or presidents of the Council seated on the platform behind the bema and beside them the arkhons, Themistokles amongst them. In front of the altar to Zeus Agoraios stood several priests, their attendants and sacrifices. A young boy clad in white wrestled with a squealing pig, dragging it to the altar, where one priest sprinkled water atop the animal's head before opening its neck over the blood-stained marble. Another boy rushed forward, carrying a bronze bowl to collect the sacred blood of the victim. Over and over this sacrifice was repeated until a score or more bowls were filled to the brim. The boys then took their bowls and began tracing lines of blood around the entire Assembly, circumscribing the dusty Pynx and marking out the kartharma or consecrated ground. Other men stalked the perimeter, ensuring that everyone present stayed within the holy circle. The herald had opened the proceedings by calling Xanthippos forward.

"Relax, my friend," said Kallimakhos as he edged in next to Miltiades.

Xanthippos slowly climbed the three steps to the top of the bema, accepting the myrtle wreath before turning to face the Assembly. "I have come here today as a most concerned citizen. A citizen who fears for his city—and yours," he said drawing the last word out as he scanned the audience deliberately. "Eighteen years ago we Athenians expelled Hippias, a dangerous man—a tyrant. We all remember the fear under which we lived. Say something that displeases the tyrant and he can take away your property, your slaves and even your wife. Exhibit too much enterprise, too much intelligence and you threaten him." Xanthippos looked to the klepsydra, the water clock, being sure not to tarry too long on any one point, wanting desperately to get every thought crammed into his six-minute speech.

He glanced back to the Assembly, squinting slightly as the sun slipped over Mount Pentelikos. Now he cleared his throat. "I am sure that some recall Hippias' father Pisistratos. Some will also remember him as a good man, a tyrant, but still a good man. This memory may soften your heart. You may say that Miltiades here is a tyrant, but still a good man." He opened his hand to reveal four small cubes. Miltiades heart pounded as he rechecked his knucklebones, not letting loose his grip. Xanthippos ranted on. "Let us toss these now and see what life Tykhe, goddess of chance, shall provide for us. Will this tyrant be good, or evil?" Now he snapped his hands closed over the dice. "Athenians, I have a much better idea, one that our fathers had when they created the law against tyrants. Let us not rely on Tykhe, or these dice, or any single man, but ensure that every one of us continues to govern our city. Exclude this tyrant," he barked, pointing directly at Miltiades, "a man who has profited at the expense of others, ruling them like a king in the Peninsula, installed by the tyrant Pisistratos himself."

The crowd erupted into a sea of swirling murmurs. Xanthippos waited, letting it all simmer. As the grumbling began to subside, he continued.

"And why am I so certain that he is not only a tyrant, but one set on ruling Athens just as he did Elaios. He, together with the other tyrants of the islands, hired themselves out to Darios, the Great King, the man whose only desire is to put all of us under the Persian yoke. Travelers have told me, as they have undoubtedly told you my fellow Athenians, a vast invasion fleet is now on its way to Europe. It is convenient that this man," bellowed Xanthippos as he thrust his pointed finger at Miltiades, "is amongst us at this most critical time. But if you do not believe me, listen to these men, men who lived under the rule of Miltiades." He waved the two colonists from Elaios to the bema. "Nothing is more dangerous or more deadly to us all than rule by a single man. The law is clear in this regard, as is the punishment. Tyranny is the murder of our way of life. That is why the law will not tolerate a hint of it." His voice was powerful, yet not proud, carrying to the depths of the crowd. He paused, wetting his lips, gathering his breath for his final words. "Listen to men who know Miltiades for what he is."

He waved one of the colonists forward, handing him the wreath as he descended the steps. The man had not spoken to such a crowd before and stared frozen, like a frightened animal. Laughter started to erupt from the Athenians. Xanthippos, near the foot of the bema, seethed with rage at this bumpkin who in a single moment had undone his well-crafted argument. "Speak up man," he barked through clenched teeth.

Finally the man's face lost its paralyzed gape. Words slowly rumbled up his throat, softly at first but increasing in volume as he gained confidence. "This man, Miltiades, lived at Elaios like a king, and we his subjects," he said, as he looked down to his friend, then to Xanthippos, who nodded in return, grinning. He continued. "He traipsed about surrounded by his paid mercenaries, afraid to meet anyone face to face and on equal terms. It was by might that he ruled, just as his benefactor Hippias ruled here at Athens in years past. He is as guilty as Hippias." He dipped his head sheepishly, working to contain the smile of satisfaction that threatened to burst across his face—he had learned the lines exactly and repeated them without error. Next to ascend to the bema was his companion from Elaios. The man took the wreath and reinforced the indictment, citing an incident when the two had been beaten by Miltiades in the agora of Elaios. This tale of a brutish lord treating free men like lowly slaves instigated howls of indignation throughout the Assembly.

Miltiades shook his head as he listened to it all. He knew that amongst gentlemen he could plead his case and they would consider—and understand—but these shopkeepers, potters, fisherman and tanners, these uneducated laborers would never believe an aristocrat. By the conversations buzzing around him there was scant hope that any would listen to him. Hegesipyle was right. Athens was different. Athens was dangerous.

Kallimakhos grabbed him tightly by the arm. "Do you have any witnesses?"

"None." Miltiades said with resignation.

"What about that hulk of a slave that follows you around?" Kallimakhos words became tinged with excitement.

"He is only a slave. His word is no good amongst free men."

"His words are good. But he must be put to the rack first. The law is clear on it. Slaves must be tortured to be sure they do not lie." Kallimakhos optimism rose. "These men about us would welcome someone to refute Xanthippos' puppets."

Miltiades considered it, but only for a moment. He could not submit the man who saved his son's life to such brutality. No, if this argument is to be won, it must be done on his words alone. "No. Illyrios is no witness."

The crier snatched the myrtle wreath from the departing colonist, shouting out Miltiades' name.

He labored up the three steps as though he wore his armor, bending under its weight. With a slight tremble in his hands, he pushed the myrtle wreath down on his head and looked out at the thousand score Athenians that studied him. "To begin I would like to say greetings to the two fellows from Elaios, who had so clearly recollected past events—or so they think." He knew this trick of speaking directly to his accusers would summon anger, and put an edge to his words. "I recall the day I beat these two. Beat them until they couldn't walk." Now the crowd exploded with groans and waved clenched fists. They shouted, "Kataba! Kataba!" but Miltiades would not get down, not yet. "And fellow Athenians, what would you do if you caught a pair of thieves, their hands full of pilfered gain, fleeing from the very person they robbed?" Suddenly only the chirping of birds and the occasional hoot of an owl could be heard across the top of Pynx Hill.

"Think on this fellow Athenians—if I were indeed the tyrant that Xanthippos claims, then why, by the dog of Egypt, would I come to the very place that has destroyed tyrants? It is like a fish jumping into a net to avoid being caught. There is no sense to it." He scanned the faces, at least the ones in proximity, and they began to lose their hard-etched cynicism. *At least they are listening*, he thought. Now he gazed directly at Xanthippos. "The man who accuses me has the most to lose and the least to gain from a war with the Persians. It is amusing indeed that he implicates me of collaborating with Darios."

"And as for Darios, the Great King, I did, of course, march with his army. I, along with other Hellenes, guarded the bridge into Skythia for him. And I alone pleaded to cut that bridge and let the Great King perish amongst the Skythians. But others, men like Xanthippos, argued against such action, as he argues now against me." The last drop fell from the klepsydra ending Miltiades speech.

Xanthippos, eager to address the assembly for his final time, bounded up the steps, not waiting for the herald to announce him, or for Miltiades to lift his crown of myrtle. Xanthippos snatched it from him as he passed. "Convenient that any men who can substantiate Miltiades claims are either dead or Persians!"

The Assembly exploded with laughter. "Tell me Miltiades, if you are so virulent an adversary of the Great King, why does your son live at his court and amongst his most loyal subjects?"

Miltiades' chest collapsed from within as the breath rushed out. He could not believe these words. He certainly could not believe that Metiokhos still lived. Kallimakhos steadied his friend with an arm around his shoulder. A man edged into next to Kallimakhos, whispered to him then the two threaded their way through the press of men and out of sight.

Xanthippos knew he had delivered news unknown. He smirked at Miltiades, almost jubilant at his maneuver of rhetoric. "It is a strange thing that you cannot produce a single witness, not one you could trust with reforming the truth to suit you, anyway." He pulled the wreath from his brow just as the attendant was about to stop his speech. He flicked it at Miltiades, pushing his way through the crowd, moving to the huddle of his comrades that milled about near the steps of the Pynx Hill.

By now the sun had gained full possession of the morning sky, its heat undeniable. Miltiades swiped his forehead with the back of his hand while sighing. "My friend Xanthippos brings goods news to me. My son, Metiokhos, who I thought killed by the Persians, lives. That is information that I could never hope to gather, since it would rely on such close ties to the Persians." Men chuckled here and there at his comment, but from far at the rear of the Pynx he could see Xanthippos glaring at him.

"Witnesses that could attest to my plan at the bridge, are as Xanthippos states, either dead or Persians. Some are both." Again, the crowd laughed. From the back of the Assembly the crowd began to shiver as a small group of men shouldered their way forward. He saw Kallimakhos approaching along with several other men—and Illyrios!

Kallimakhos hustled up to the seated arkhons, and directly to Themistokles. Themistokles rose. "This man who Kallimakhos brings to us is the slave of Miltiades. He is to testify."

Illyrios did not struggle as they clamped his thick ankles to the bottom of the board with leg irons. Two lengths of rope dangled over the three-meter high board. Two men tied these off to Illyrios' wrists, while a third began to tighten away the slack by cranking the windlass. The slave's arms quivered a bit as they stretched. Sweat poured off his back as the sun bore witness to his anguish. The leg irons started to twist, cutting into his flesh as the ropes tightened and the windlass cranked.

"It's not even hurting him," yelled out someone from deep within the Assembly. Now two men leaned on the crank handle. Illyrios made no sounds, only the taut rope and stressed wooden board groaned. A court scribe leaned over to Illyrios, barking questions, scribbling answers upon a waxed tablet. Every so often the scribe dipped an earthenware cup into a deep bowl of water, then doused the tablet, keeping it cool in the unrelenting heat of a cloudless summer sky. Illyrios watched the spent water pool then painfully evaporate, wishing for only a drop to quench his burning thirst. This interrogation went on for almost an hour, the heat, the ropes and the irons tearing away at Illyrios' mantle of courage. After all this he finally let out a wail as they cut the ropes.

The scribe, satisfied with the veracity of the testimony, handed it to the crier. He stared at it for a while then took the speaker's platform. "Over and over he repeated only these words, "Miltiades alone argued to destroy the bridge."

At these words, men all through the Assembly yelled out their premature verdict, but it would not be binding until the pebbles had been tallied. Two large urns at the exit of the Pynx had been set up and guarded by officers of the court. The choice was clear, the tally made easy, for only Xanthippos and his companions dropped the black stones of *guilty* into the receptacle. White pebble after white pebble clattered into the almost overflowed urn of *acquittal*.

Miltiades did not watch as the Assembly voted. He rushed to the board and his slave Illyrios, where Kallimakhos followed. They gave him heaping cups of water, and stood over him patiently, as he slowly recovered the feeling in his arms, which until now, hung lifeless at his sides, his hands scraping the dust.

"I've sent for an iatros," assured Kallimakhos.

Miltiades looked into the glazed eyes of his slave. "I did not order this."

Illyrios tilted his head to the side, to take his eyes out of the sunlight. "I know."

Kallimakhos shrugged his shoulders. "What do you mean? Of course you ordered it. No one else can permit a slave to be tortured but his owner."

Miltiades searched the diminishing crowd for the physician finally looking to Kallimakhos. "Unless the slave impersonates his master."

Chapter 19

Shore of Mount Athos—Summer 492 BC

The gray pall of clouds had begun to retreat along with the overwhelming swells that the sudden storm had conjured. Mardonios rode along the pebble-strewn beach unable to speak. He shaded his eyes as he looked up, hoping to see the first sliver of sunlight pierce the gloom. All around him men, his men, lie face down in the surf amongst smashed timbers, tatters of sailcloth and splintered oars. High above towered stark Mount Athos, mutely defiant. The crunch of wet stones beneath feet compelled him to turn around.

"Lord Mardonios," shouted the Median infantryman as ran up beside his horse. "The count is at three hundred."

Mardonios still could not invoke a solitary word. He just nodded. The Mede spun away and trotted down the beach toward a cluster of Persian officers. Mardonios rode on. Soon he was beyond the voices of the others, where cawing gulls and the whoosh of retreating waves pulling on the gravel beach filled his ears. But the storm—that filled his mind.

His grand fleet first had taken Thasos, next Akanthos, but geography compelled him to sail east, out into the sea and away from the safety of land to avoid mighty Athos. But it was summer, and the gentle winds blew from the south, or so said his admirals. Five hundred triremes, plus a good many freighters, grain lighters and other vessels of provision, pushed free of the sheltered beaches around Akanthos and hoisted sail. Yesterday morning dawn revealed a perfect sky, azure and unblemished—not the hint of a cloud anywhere. Five hundred ships, over 100,000 men, and nothing between them and Athens but a small bit of ocean. Now he slid from his horse and began to walk, oblivious to the surf washing up and over his purple calfskin riding boots. He knelt next to the body of a Phoenician oarsman, the man's eyes still open and staring up at the brightening sky, his arms ever limply advancing and retreating with each wave. Mardonios brushed away the sand crabs that had begun to nibble on the dead man's flesh. They waved their claws high with false pugnacity, but scurried swiftly into the sanctuary of the foamy surf. The face was swollen with seawater, its bloated tongue forcing open salt-whitened lips. Mardonios began to sob. Suddenly he stood up and withdrew his akinakes sword and thrust it skyward. "It will not end this way!" he shouted. He thrust its polished blade into an advancing wave, as if to strike at the sea itself.

A squad of Persian infantry came charging down the beach, convinced that their commander had called for help. Mardonios turned calmly toward them as they poured around him, looking, listening, and anxious to carry out his slightest command. "Each body is to be collected."

✸✸✸✸✸

For three days they scoured the shores at the base of Athos, and sent smaller vessels out into this lethal expanse of sea, to search for survivors and collect what remained of the once magnificent fleet of the Great King Darios. All along the beach the twisted hulls of wrecked triremes had been piled high and the bodies, wrapped in sailcloth, cloaks, or boughs of pine, stacked atop each pyre. Mardonios solemnly approached the cauldron of sacred fire and dipped the torch, igniting the pitch. It popped and crackled with flame, sending sparks into the inky night sky. A lonely war-horn wailed; across the entire length of the beach men walked toward the pyres, Mardonios included, finally poking their torches into the kindling, instigating random flames that soon licked upward to engulf the stacks of funerary wood. The Persians stood in reverent silence as holy fire consumed their brethren. Mardonios watched as the rippling blaze threw its eerie light over the beach and the listing hulls of his fleet, casting wild shadows that magnified the height of men, stretching and distorting them into the shapes of towering monsters. Embers swirled high into the night. Mardonios prayed. He prayed to Ahura Mazda to deliver his fleet and army safely back to the Great King. He prayed too, for his wife Artozostra, his bride of but three months, left in Susa as he embarked on this great expedition. But most of all he prayed that the Greeks would not escape the wrath of Darios.

Chapter 20

Sea of the Hellenes—Late Summer 490 BC
Athenian month of Hekatombaion

Datis stood near the pilot and the small section of balustrade that flanked the high stern of his trireme, spreading his feet and facing the open sea as though it all belonged to him. He caught sight of another ship as it cut the waves under the power of 170 rowers. "And what is he thinking, Nabusera?"

"The old Greek?" His deputy looked to a bald foreigner who sat cross-legged on the top deck of the passing vessel. "Hmm. I would think he cannot wait to be home again."

"Pray that Ahura Mazda can keep old Hippias alive long enough to be of help to us, and his King. His home, if it was his, now belongs to Darios." He scanned the blossoms of sails that dotted the glistening midday swells, allowing the confidence of this expedition to gather within him. He would not repeat the blunder of Mardonios, and sail the long and circuitous route that had led to the Imperial fleet's destruction. His plan was simple and direct— a straight line from Kilikia in Asia to Greece, using the islands as waypoints, and untapped storehouses for his fleet. Each island would add to his provender, the King's treasury, and to his invasion flotilla. By the time he reached Athens, this tiny city would be alone.

"Naxos!" yelled the lookout from high atop the single swaying mast.

Datis' gaze followed the man's out-thrust arm, across the waves to a dark hazy speck on the horizon, more a mountain than island to their eyes. His officers and marines, kneeling on the twin halved battle deck, straightened their backs and craned their necks, as they too searched out this initial objective. It would late afternoon before they would land; battle, if needed, would wait until tomorrow. Minutes collected into hours, and the hours pushed the sun below the horizon to the west, leaving only the summit of the island's mountain swathed in light. Datis grinned as he watched the last sliver of day melt from the promontory. "That it named for their god, is it not?"

Nabusera moved in next to his commander and leaned upon the railing. "Mount Zeus. That is what the Naxians call it. Some men say Zeus grew from child to man on Naxos."

Datis turned to Nabusera and winked. "These men would be the Naxians, I think. Every man wishes to be favored by the gods."

Along with the day, the winds departed, allowing no rest for the rowers. They continued to heave the ship forward but to an unhurried lilt for the row-master let them chatter away—the day had been long, and tomorrow would be longer still. Suddenly the fire cauldron at the stern of the ship spit showers of embers skyward as a crewman poked its yawning mouth with a torch. A sphere of orange light washed over the pilot, the deck at his feet, and the section of backstay that extended from the mast to the sternpost. Beyond, the sea stretched inky and flat, like a great puddle of lampblack, while here and there in the purple skies above, stars flickered on, their presence left uncontested by the death of the old moon.

Datis, feet wide apart while being tested by the living sea, shuffled astern. "How much farther?"

The pilot's knuckle's whitened as he squeezed the tillers. "We turn that point of land, and you'll spot Naxos town. We'll not need its harbor. The beach is long and its bottom is sandy."

Datis stared at the finger of land. He spun visions in his mind of the town, its walls, and the inevitable fleet of warships that would be arrayed against them. He could hear the unseen waves slapping the rocks, the oars moaning as they fought against the sea and the chatter of the Phoenician rowers below his feet in the lower decks. A shout exploded from below followed by indistinct clamor.

"I'll cut it off!"

Datis knew Phoenician well. He scurried to the ladder that led into the bowels of the warship. There in a tangled heap lie three men: an oarsman, the row-master, and one of his marines. Even in the dark he caught the glint of a blade as the rower's arm flashed toward the marine. The row-master lunged, pinning the oarsman's arm upon the deck, while the marine pulled his akinakes clear of its scabbard with a thwang.

"What is this!" barked Datis as he strode forward, grinding the heel of his boot into the rower's knife wielding fingers. The man wailed. The blade tumbled to the deck, where with one fluid kick Datis sent it careening off the bulkhead. For that moment there was no sound: not a single oar cut the sea; no man spoke; all heads turned toward Datis and the men tangled between the rowers' benches.

The row-master jumped to his feet. "Lord, your marine started this."

Datis kicked at the Persian marine until he scrambled to his feet. "Up! Up!"

The Persian pulled himself straight and tall; he dipped his head saying nothing, but the Phoenician hardly exhibited such self-restraint. "He pissed all over me." I yelled up to him and he laughed at me, pissing down all the while." The Phoenician's face glistened with sweat, his eyes, white and bulging with rage as he spoke.

Datis fought to keep the smile that threatened to form submerged beneath the snarl of command. He found a bit of humor in this indignity suffered by the Phoenician, but he also knew that the rowers were pissed on, sweat on, shit on, and vomited on by their ilk that toiled above. It was nothing new to them. Now he directed his words at the row-master. "What is he doing with a knife!" Any trace of lightheartedness evaporated now with his mounting anger.

"Lord Datis, how can I tell a man he cannot defend himself? After all he fights for you. He fights for Darios. How can a man go into battle unarmed?"

Datis pondered the row-master's words. He knew the Greek oarsmen, his enemies and free men, would all have blades. But he could afford no such accommodation. His rule was known. So was Darios'. Only marines would be armed in his fleet. Less to worry about, and this incident indeed reinforced such prudence. He grabbed the row-master by his tunic, almost tearing it from his body. "Get them rowing. This—and you—shall be dealt with tomorrow."

The row-master spun away from Datis and began shouting orders. The rowers all faced astern and plucked up their oar-looms and quickly resumed the cadence. Datis climbed the short ladder to the battle-deck just in time to see the screening finger of land slip away to his right, revealing a long stretch of sandy beach that spread right up to the torch-lit walls of Naxos. Even in the dark of night he could make out figures of men scurrying about the beach, some with lamps or torches, shouting wildly, eventually melting back away from the shoreline into deep shadows, their voices divulging their presence.

"Signal the fleet to land in battle line." Datis called for his armor-bearer to bring his corselet and weapons. His Persian marines shuffled toward the bow, as the rowers accelerated the trireme toward the abandoned shore. From the walls of Naxos the blare of a salphinx trumpet, the unmistakable sound of combat, caused every muscle in his body to tense, sending his free hand instinctively to the hilt of his akinakes sword. He exhaled loudly and released his sword, turning his gaze back to the impending shoreline. Suddenly his trireme shuddered and groaned as its keel buried into the sandy bottom. The grip of land abruptly stopped all momentum of the vessel, but without restraint his marines lurched awkwardly, some stumbling, others skidding across the battle deck, while only the few along the rail managed to keep to their feet. Anxious either for combat or to escape another moment onboard, the Persians leapt from the warship into the surf, subsequently overrunning the beach up to the low scrub that hemmed in this vast crescent of sand. To both his right and his left, trireme after trireme ground ashore, spilling noisy contingents of marines onto the island of Naxos. A Persian war horn signaled them to battle array, and soon thousands of warriors seeped into formation.

Nabusera heaved through the knee-deep water to catch up with Datis. "Lord, shall I dispatch scouts?"

Datis nodded. He knew they would find no Greek outside the walled town now, but he was relentless in his thoroughness, and would take nothing for granted in any campaign under his command. His plan, so carefully thought out, would bring him great fame and favor with Darios. Like steppingstones across a muddy stream, he would use these islands to plant a firm foot, vanquish each in turn, and then add to his numbers before exacting the inevitable upon the Athenians. Unlike his rival Mardonios, he would make no premature return to his King. No unseasonable wind would deliver the Greeks. No army either. He had seen what these Greeks were made of, at Ephesos, at Lade, Rhodes, and here on Naxos. Only time stood between Datis and his victory. Soon Europe would be Persian.

Within the hour his scouts returned, and just as he had surmised the Naxians had deserted the countryside, not a single man amongst them brave enough to contest the beach, the vineyards, fields, or homes that spread across the island outside of the town. He ordered two hazarabam of Medes to advance to the town—about two thousand—with instructions to launch the assault, while he dispatched squadrons of cavalry along every road leading inland. From here he studied the walls of the town. No torches flickered on the battlements. No men peered out from the crenellations. He called for his entourage to fetch him some food and drink. Servants and slaves scurried about: some unfurled exquisitely crafted carpets; in pairs, others toted dining couches and various items of furniture; still more carted vessels of wine and provisions from a beached freighter.

Nabusera approached his commander hesitatingly, perplexed by this commotion. "Should we lay siege to the town now, before they can strengthen their defenses?"

Datis dropped into the soft embrace of a cushioned divan. "Sit down and eat, will you."

"But my lord—"

"Do you question me?" interrupted Datis.

Nabusera dipped his head into a bow as he touched his fingers to his forehead. "Truly I do not my lord. I apologize for my eagerness." Nabusera lowered himself onto a dining couch, but scanned the men around him and his commander, assessing his predicament with circumspection.

"Relax! You should study those walls as carefully as you study me." said Datis.

Nabusera leaned forward, straining to focus upon the dark battlements and towers of Naxos. Suddenly it struck him. Not a man stood atop the walls. Not a single torch flickered. He wondered now if anyone remained within the walls. He grinned. So too did Datis. Nabusera accepted the cup of date-wine from the serving boy before settling back into the silk cushions of his divan.

*****

Well before dawn the Medes had set the town alight, for Datis wished the Naxians to see the flames as they hid in the hills and gullies, and upon the slopes of Mount Zeus and in its flanking ravines, with stark clarity. The incinerating town alone would fill their eyes, the sight not diminished by a single ray of daylight. Smoke too would carry his message of destruction, a message delivered with every breath. They would know the power of Darios—and of Datis.

Unknowingly he had dozed off, mesmerized by the dancing flames that celebrated his conquest of Naxos, but as his eyes flicked open, they caught sight not of fire, but the coming day. He slipped a perfumed scarf from the sleeve of his robe and buried his nose in it—the wind had shifted now delivering the acrid haze of the dying fires of Naxos over the Persian encampment. His cupbearer hovered within reach, handing the goblet of wine to Datis as he opened his hand. He filled his mouth slowly then chewed the wine before letting it tumble down his parched throat into his anxious belly. As he tipped the cup empty he held it for a moment, a frame for his eyes as he stared at the coiling snakes of smoke above Naxos and the sprinting rider tearing directly toward him.

Nabusera slid from his horse before the animal stopped, launching him into a short sprint as his feet hit the ground. "Rowers have deserted, lord."

Without hesitating he barked, "Hunt them down. It will give our cavalry practice in rounding up these Greeks." Datis grabbed another full cup of wine and drank much less delicately now. "But do not kill them, at least not yet. We need every oar in the water."

"But my lord, one of the rowers is from your very warship."

Datis chucked the half-full goblet into the ground as he sprang to his feet. Rowers deserted, as did infantry, cavalry, archers and others. But not from the flagship of the Great King's fleet. This must be dealt with swiftly. It must be dealt with ruthlessly. "Send out the Median cavalry. And send for the row-master and pilot of my ship."

Datis flung open his robe, tossing it upon the ground as he strode away from the encampment to a suitable grove of trees. He leaned forward, one hand against the trunk of a plane tree, using it as a brace as he relieved himself of the wine. His head pounded. Before he could pull his trousers up he began yelling for his body-servant.

Three rowers had been rounded up by mid day, along with several score Naxians, of which only four or five looked like they could pull an oar, or wield a spear. Still, Datis surveyed the lot of captives deliberately, pacing up and down the line of them as they knelt in the sand, hands bound and feet by chains. He turned around to face a huddle of his officers. "You! Come here." The row-master of his trireme hurried to him. Datis pulled his akinakes sword from its scabbard, lifting the chin of one of the captives with the point of its blade. "Is that him?"

The row-master's mouth opened but no words came out. He cleared his throat then answered nervously, "Yes, my lord, that is the man."

Datis only saw the rower once, but the rage in that man's face burned an enduring image into his memory. He did not need the Phoenician to identify him. Datis, his blade still under the deserter's chin, stared at him. "Why did you run?"

The man, steel still poised to end his life, answered quickly. "To live. Your marine tried to kill me once. Only my rigger's knife saved me then. Now I am defenseless."

"And did you not know knives are banned amongst the rowers?" Datis at first thought he would indulge the man, but saw the face of the Phoenician row-master turn sour with his question. The deserter started to speak, but stopped himself. Datis turned to the row-master. "Did you not make it clear to your men that knives are banned aboard the King's fleet?"

"But, my lord, they have always carried them, I mean the experienced ones, the ones that know what happens in a sea battle." The Phoenician shrugged his shoulders as though to diminish the seriousness of his omission.

Datis pulled away the akinakes from the deserter's chin, while his eyes remained transfixed upon the row-master's face. The man returned a broken, quivering grin. That was more than Datis could endure. Rage filled him as he squeezed the grip of his akinakes sword, wanting to plunge it into the pathetic row-master's belly. He slid the akinakes back into its scabbard. "Yoke him!"

A squad of infantry sprinted away, returning with a shipwright and slaves bearing a large timber and coils of chain. The timber, upon closer inspection, proved to be an immense collar. The guards threw the row-master down upon the sand. He fought to keep from being pressed into the notches in the twin-halved yoke, but in moments they had his neck and wrists clamped securely. The yoke was obviously fashioned with a smaller man in mind—the row-master's face went from red to purple. The guards stood him up, but the weight of the heavy timber cowered him. Datis nodded. A guard flashed a curved knife, the type a slaughter-man might use in carving up the carcass of a bull. He pulled on one of the row-master's ears, drawing the blade down quickly, blood spraying across his face as he held up the severed ear. The man wailed in pain. He sliced off the other. Now the row-master sobbed. Blood splattered over the yoke and streamed over the man's neck and shoulders. It was finished when the guard carved off his nose. Now they chained the yoke to a mule and led it away, across the length and breadth of the Persian encampment for all to see.

Datis turned to the deserter. He stared back, waiting his turn. "You—go!" he bellowed at the rower. "I am certain you will tell everyone that knives are banned in the fleet." He looked at the staggering figure of the row-master in the distance. "Something he failed to do."

✳✳✳✳✳

Datis tapped his goblet of date-wine impatiently. "Well, read it back to me."

The scribe's eye's scanned the clay tablet, re-reading it all before he announced it to Datis. "In the first month of Farvardin, during the year thirty plus one of the Great King Darios, Lord of the Persians, Medes, Sakai, Baktrians, Sogdians, Ionians, Phrygians, Kilikians—"

"Yes, yes, I know all of that. Read to me the substance of my message." Datis shook his head then sipped away the dregs of wine that pooled at the bottom of the huge bejeweled goblet. His face puckered as the bitter drink hit his tongue.

The scribe began, "After sacking the town of the Naxians and burning their temples, all in punishment for their rebellion against great Darios, I Datis commanded the Imperial fleet to sail west to the island of Paros where five-hundred of the conscripted islanders took ship and joined with the fleet." The scribe halted and glanced at Datis for approval. Datis nodded, but rolled his eyes.

"Your servant, Datis," the scribe continued with his recording, "then commanded the fleet to sail for Delos, sacred island of the Greeks and their god Apollo. Here, on behalf of your imperial majesty he did no harm to the inhabitants, but rather sacrificed 300 talents of myrrh and frankincense to honor the god and exhibit the true nature of this expedition."

"Stop!" commanded Datis. He pondered the last entry. 300 talents, the weight of over 150 men in incense was no trifling amount, even to the most powerful of gods, but he hesitated in revealing his generosity to Darios. "Change that. Mark the amount of incense at 100 talents." He waited for the scribe to poke and stroke the clay, re-writing the number until it was more suitable. The scribe looked up. Datis flicked his upturned hand, "Go on. Pass the landing at Karystos, and our attack on Eretria. Just recount the tally of slaves and loot."

"We shall deliver to you Great King, from the city and lands of Eretria, Greeks who are considered to be amongst the greatest of their warriors, 5,000 captives, not counting 1,000 of the survivors of their vanquished army."

Datis stood up from his divan smiling. He summoned the wine steward, who rushed forward with a cumbersome pitcher, and expertly filled Datis' goblet, spilling not a single drop as he followed his master on his imperious stroll before the table of the scribe. Datis clapped his hands. Nabusera, pushed the tent flap aside and entered, touching his hand to his forehead while he bowed. "Bring to me the Athenians you captured." Now he directed his words to the scribe. "Read to them the tally of our enterprise so far. They will know, by these very numbers, that there is no escape from the arm of Darios. These Eretrians fled into the hills. In a scant three days they had all been hunted down. Tell these Athenians what is in store for their city then put them ashore across the Euripos. Their talk will be worth a hazarabam of Immortals." Just as Nabusera turned to leave, Datis stopped him. "Loyal and efficient Nabusera, summon our commanders. In two days I want the army to be in Attika. In three we will be in Athens."

Chapter 21

Outskirts of Korinth—Late Summer 490 BC
6th day of Metageitnion

Pheidippides bent over and heaved an enormous breath. He sucked the air in gulps, much as a thirsty man would guzzle water, for the last hill drained him. He straightened up for a moment measuring the day. This pace he would keep for at least three hours more before darkness would compel him to walk. His profession of day-runner defined his efforts, but on this day, and the next few if necessary, he would travel both day and night, in light and utter darkness, until he reached the Ephorion at Sparta.

At least now, as he burst forward again, the merciless sun began to slip behind the trees, affording him cool shadows as he sliced along the narrow road from Kenkhrai that carried him south into the Peloponnese. Off to his left the Saronic Gulf glistened. Ahead he made out the unbending pavement of the Diolkos slipway, the path for ships to be dragged from the Saronic to the gulf of Korinth. He glanced at it only for a heartbeat then focused again on the road beneath him. In his mind he beat out the rhythm of his pounding feet. Slap, slap—slap, slap, his boots struck hard upon they dusty limestone road. He kept both eyes down, watching, steering every stride to clear ground, avoiding stones, tree roots or any obstacle that could impede him, for he could not afford a stumble, miss-step or fall—-the city of Athens, his city, his family's and his tribe's, depended upon his success. Every shred of endurance, every ounce of stamina would be expended on this run.

"Where are you off to in such a hurry, friend?" quizzed a farmer as he scraped an ancient hoe along the parched furrow at the edge of his field.

Pheidippides pointed straight ahead. "Sparta!" He did not turn to see if his answer was received, but sustained his pace.

More and more, as the towering Akrokorinth grew, he blew by startled Korinthians, most plying the road to and from the city proper, all gaping in awe at his resolute clip.

A breeze swept up the scent of the sea triggering, for a moment, a vision of Phaleron Bay and the walk he took there just a few days ago. He and his son strolled along, every so often skipping a saucer-shaped stone atop the gentle swells of the bay, chatting with fishermen or sailors from the freighters, pumping them for gossip and tales of strange people from strange lands. It was from one of these fellows—a Rhodian kaleustes—that he learned of the fleet. "The Persians, why they just beached near Karystos days ago. Another day, maybe two and they'll be standing right where you are." That was all the Rhodian said as he hurried off to the quay and his ship. Rumors had of course, preceded that day, but it was this chance encounter that marked with certainty Pheidippides last moment of the serenity of routine. By day's end he had been summoned to the Strategion in the Agora. Kallimakhos himself handed him the dispatch, insisting that he read it, understand it, and compel the Spartans to do the same.

He swallowed hard. His throat burned dry. The flask of water swung in cadence with his strides, reminding him with each step that a drink hung on his hip, but he would not consider it. No, he would sip from it later, when running changed to walking, and day turned to night. Then he would also nibble away at the fist-sized hunk of bread and half onion that hid in the small sack counterpoised on his hip opposite the flask.

Twin-yoked oxen pulling a cart rumbled toward him, swallowing up most of the road. He gauged the terrain on either side: a trail of boulders bracketed the road to the left; to the right trickled an exhausted stream; directly ahead lie four piles of donkey scat. He planted his left foot into the path of the wagon, driving hard and over the scat, his right foot landing in the streambed. Two long strides and he passed the oxen. Two more and he left the wagon behind him, the empty amphorai in its bed chattering away at every bump.

"Where—?" barked the team-driver.

"Sparta!" he yelled out, abbreviating the question and the encounter.

Soon he was pounding his booted feet into the road that skirted the agora of Korinth, stunned old men jumping from his determined path, while small boys galloped along with him in short bursts, laughing until their elders chided them and cleared the way for Pheidippides. Women, mostly slaves, stared at him with mouths agape, hugging their bundles of bread or jars of oil like long lost loves. As he passed groups of men, they shouted the inevitable question, but instead of restating his destination he worked to unsettle them too. "The Persians have landed!" he bellowed more than once in his easily recognizable Attic dialect, leaving no doubt of the invaders' whereabouts.

As the day slipped away, so did the traffic. One stumble induced him to stare at the road, to the point that his eyes pained him. The second one brought him to a knee. "By Hermes!'" he spit out through grinding teeth. It bled. A stone had taken a deep gouge out of his right knee. Even in the low light of dusk, the blood glistened red, and ran hot down his shin. "Might as well have a drink." Centered in the road, he planted his arse down and pulled out the chunk of onion from the leather sack, biting into it until his eyes flooded. Quickly, he filled his mouth with bread and worked it all with his teeth, gulped it down, finally emptying his flask. *No more water, but at least the load is lighte*r, he thought. He managed to always put the best light on things. His occupation, by its very nature, deprived him of companionship, so his conversations became internal exchanges requiring the ultimate in optimism to sustain him. After a few more dry bites of onion and bread, he rose up and stared into the black of the road ahead. The sky above held a whisper of light, but not enough. "Now, we walk," he announced to aching feet and throbbing legs.

He reckoned he had covered almost 400 stadia, about a third of the distance to Sparta. This, along with impediment of night, frustrated him. He had prayed to the god, and his prayer was answered. His legs could indeed carry him on the run. But he knew, on one hand the gods provide, while at the same time they deny. Yes, his legs could run, but his eyes could not see. Next time he would be more exact in his prayers. He wriggled his shoulders, resettling the empty flask, leather sack, and his bundled himation cloak that hung suspended on a hefty flaxen rope. Mosquitoes began to swarm. "Alright, alright. I'm getting up. Tell Kallimakhos I only rested for a moment." He swung his hand in front of his face. "Now go back to Athens and torment your master."

Every so often he broken into a jog, and every so often his foot caught a stray root or stone, causing him the slow. He looked up, searching out the crescent of the waxing moon, hoping for its scant light to brighten his path, but it was still tucked away behind looming trees and hills that pressed in from either side. At night it proved difficult to gauge his bearings with any precision, but he knew he had passed the road to Nemea and Agamemnon's mighty citadel near Mykenai, so the city of the Argives should be close by. Before he spotted the torch lit walls of Argos, the stars blinked out in bands, erased by Mount Larisa that stretched into the night beyond the city. Here the road yawned wide and smooth enticing him to test a cautious jog. The moon finally had climbed above the horizon illuminating this expanse of flat fields enough to aid his straining eyes. A stabbing pain shot up from below his ribs, causing him to double over, as though an unseen spear had been thrust into his belly. He gasped and wailed all at once then clamped his hand over the imagined wound but felt no blood, only sweat, and even this would be depleted soon if he did not drink. Surrounded by a formless, murky landscape his mind began to manufacture definition that his eyes could not. A breeze fingering through the tall grasses of the fields transformed to the voices of the strategoi in Athens.

"I do not believe this Eretrian," argued Xanthippos. *"The Persians would have sent heralds to us."*

Pheidippides shook his head. The words still rang as if Xanthippos were standing next to him.

"You can wait here for them if you so desire my brave Xanthippos, but the rest of us should post the katalogos for each tribe, call up every man that can march and leave at once," Miltiades countered without hesitation.

Now Pheidippides stopped dead in the road and clamped his hands over his ears. Tears ran down his flushed and sweaty cheeks. "I will run! I will run!" He was certain these voices had been sent by Athena herself. His pace had slowed, by pain to be sure, but hundreds, even thousands of his own countrymen could be feeling the iron of Persians spears.

A dog barked as he flew past the walls of Argos but Pheidippides kept moving, propelled by his constant chants to Hermes, and began the ascent into the foothills of Mount Larisa. With each step now his legs burned and his mind whirled. He fought to keep his eyes on the road and his mind on his task. It was only when he finally had reached the crest of the last hill and felt the ease of descent pulling him forward did he rest again, coaxed by the gurgling waters of the Erasinos River to stop, fill his flask and quaff his thirst. As the cool water passed his lips he reminded himself to sip slowly, and not fill his belly. Water without wine would be difficult enough to keep down. He must, as the gymnasiarkhos had warned, be moderate in both food and drink, and not let impulse rule him. He filled his mouth once and let it flush down his throat. One more gulp and he was on his way again.

Past Hysia, then he began his climb onto the slopes of Mount Parthenios and the deep woods of Arkadia. The moon had abandoned him here, and even the voices of Miltiades, Xanthippos, Kallimakhos and the rest of the generals at the Strategion, so he chanted even louder his prayers to Hermes and Athena.

"Pheidippides!"

He stopped and spun around to catch sight of the source of his name. Something moved behind the writhing trunk of a timeworn olive tree. To him it appeared to be the head of a man, but the dark would allow no more distinction that that.

Again the voice drifted from the shadows. "Pheidippides. Why do the Athenians do not honor me? I have been friend to the men of Athens in the past and will so be in the future."

Pheidippides heart drummed in his chest. This was either a god or a dream. If a dream it could do him no harm. If a god, well, he knew he had no protection from an immortal. This thought alone calmed him. Without fear he walked toward the olive tree and the voice, but before he could look behind its wide and twisting trunk he saw the figure of a man melt into the shadows beyond. He knelt at the base of the tree, scanning the earth where narrow shafts of moonlight illuminated footprints. Pheidippides stroked the impressed earth gently. His fingers traced not the footprint of a man, but the cloven hoof-print of a goat—a very large goat. "Pan," he whispered as he searched the dark. No sound, no movement. The god had fled as quickly and quietly as he had arrived. *After all,* he thought, *he does live here.*

✴ ✴ ✴ ✴ ✴

The five Spartan ephors had agreed to meet with Pheidippides without delay. They listened to his brief, but impassioned plea for help, then dismissed him while they conferred—that was over an hour ago. By now he had eagerly consumed the ample portioned meal they had provided while a Helot versed in the arts of the gymnasion kneaded away the excruciating pain of muscles worked beyond exhaustion. Pheidippides curled himself to sleep upon the meter long marble bench in the courtyard of the Spartan Ephorion, awaiting the message he would return to his countrymen. He almost wished their deliberations would drag on, providing him with the advantage of a guiltless sleep, a reconstitution of the stamina needed to reach home as quickly as he had reached Sparta.

Someone tugged on his shoulder. He blinked open his eyes, fighting the midday sun as he tried to focus on the form that hovered over him. Slowly he rose up, shading his eyes as stared into the face of the man standing over him. First the locks of long, braided hair reminded him he was still indeed in Sparta. Next the man's chiton filled his gaze with crimson, confirming beyond doubt of his whereabouts. "You can tell the men of Athens that we will march," the ephor Euryleon stated grimly. "But not until the moon is full, six days hence."

Pheidippides bolted to his feet. "In six days the battle may be over. In six days the Persians may be on the very road I took to get here. In six days Athens may be only a memory."

Euryleon grabbed the Athenian firmly by the shoulders with both hands and gazed into his pleading eyes. "We cannot insult the gods. By then the Karneia will be over. By then—and with the gods' help—we will come."

Pheidippides knew arguing with a Spartan was like arguing with a stone. They are, to his mind, the only race of men that could close their ears to talk, like others could close their eyes to sight. He drew a deep breath as he scanned the mighty range of the Taygetos Mountains—a veritable wall of living rock that protected Sparta's western flank. He walked slowly toward the gated courtyard, stooping briefly to tighten the lacings on his boots before exiting into the agora proper. It took only moments for him to regain his bearings, to find the road north. First he would skirt the low hill of the acropolis, then cross the Eurotas continuing north toward Skiritas. Hope and the prospects of Spartan help and buoyed him on his journey from Athens. Now fear motivated him. Not the fear of death, for the pains of life inured him from that. No, he feared dying alone. He feared standing before a ruined city and the dead of his family and tribe, realizing he lived because he failed them.

Chapter 22

Plataia

11th day of the Plataian month Ippodromios

11th day of the Athenian month Metageitnion

Theolyte slowly wrapped the four onions in a wad of linen before tucking them into the wicker pack, nestling it between the heavy stone grain mill and a jar of pungent tarichos salt-fish. Before tying the pack closed she slipped in a simple clay oil lamp. She stared long into the open pack and its contents, knotting the grass cord dexterously, finally clasping it tightly to her chest as she carried it out into the courtyard.

Arimnestos stroked the black crest of his kranos helmet before handing it to Teukros his slave, who had one hand already occupied yanking on the reins of a skittish mule. Teukros slipped the helmet into one of the twin panniers that hugged the animal's back before tugging the mule out of the courtyard.

Arimnestos now looked to the blood-stained altar of Zeus Herkaios and whispered one final prayer, an entreaty to the lord of Olympos, not to deliver him or any of the Plataians readying to march to the defense of Athens from inevitable death, but to spare his home and his family. Theolyte, his wife, clung to him, both hands wrapped around his arm, her face buried into the nape of his neck. Arimnestos felt every muffled convulsion of sobs. His fingers filtered through her shimmering, raven hair. "Shhh," he whispered into her ear. "The Athenians are many. And the Spartans, too, will be on their way."

Theolyte looked up, rubbing away the tears with a loose, shivering fist of fingers. "For certain? The Spartans are on the march?" She took the carefully weaved garland of ivy and blossoms from the altar and solemnly placed it atop her husband's head.

"They have promised and they always keep to their word." Arimnestos looked to his friend Lampon with a distinctly cautionary glance, an appeal to add nothing at his comment. He knew the Spartans would indeed be there, but he and all his companions may be dead by that time and Athens in the hands of the Persians.

Lampon turned from Arimnestos and clasped both hands of his wife Kyra. Her eyes, although misty from restrained tears, held no hopeless worry, or resignation to fate. Her eyes were the steely gray of Athena's. *Her* eyes held nothing but resolve. She reached her arms around Lampon's neck, her toes barely touching the ground and embraced him—more intensely in that moment than in any other.

Arimnestos called to his small brother, a boy not yet ten years old, assigned as a runner for the army, "We must go." Mikkos plucked up his small wicker pack and bedroll. Arimnestos, with a strong hand upon his brother's back, pushed him along and out of the courtyard.

"Come on!" yelled Eumenidas from outside the open courtyard gate. Arimnestos grabbed the arm of Lampon and led him onto the road. A band of about fifty men crammed the narrow roadway—half Plataian hoplites and the other half their battle-servants, with a sprinkling of young boys to be employed as messengers for the army. Most had mules to lug their panoplies, while only a few carried their own seventy pounds of armor and weapons on this long journey to Marathon.

Arimnestos took his place at the lead of this humble column, Lampon beside him as they stepped off. He turned back only once. Just outside the gate he bade farewell with his eyes to his father, mother, and his wife Theolyte. But it was the face of his sister Kyra that compelled him to stare longer—hers was the face of courage.

Behind him, as they quickly covered the distance to the shrine, men chatted away as though they were all on the way to their annual drill, their confused but entertaining distraction that for a day or two got them accustomed to their armor and weapons, and at the very least got them familiar with their neighbors in the line of rank and file. *The Persians are warriors*, he thought, as he listened to the banter. *We are only farmers.* He wrapped an arm around Lampon's shoulder and smiled. "What an adventure, my friend. Something to tell your grandchildren. What an adventure indeed!" Lampon's face was blank, his eyes looking off to the peak of Kithairon. "We have nothing to fear. Our Athenian and Spartan allies probably will have them all killed by the time we get there. Anyway, they'll stick us at the end of the line somewhere, away from death and glory." He hoped his lie was not betrayed by his voice.

Lampon's face cracked with the hint of a painful grin. "Do you really think so? I mean about the battle being over before we get there?"

"Who knows? Does this make you feel better about it?" said Arimnestos in a most soothing tone.

"Most certainly not! I may not be the bravest, but I'll not shirk my duty." Lampon's face reddened for a moment, then he looked down into the dust of the road—an apology for letting slip this bit of emotion.

Ahead of them, nestled into a small grove of plane trees stood the marble shrine of Androkrates. Throughout the sacred precinct the men of Plataia gathered, spread like a seething, jumbled blanket upon the harvested fields. The early morning air, choked by the stench of mule dung and draft animals, hardly moved even here in the often wind-swept shadow of Kithairon. Men clustered in small groups, each and every one of them with sacred garlands upon their heads. Polyandros, the one-time strategos of the Plataians, stood before the shrine, waving to Arimnestos. "Up here!" he yelled.

Arimnestos shouldered his way forward to the small altar and the flaming cauldron adjacent. Polyandros extended both hands revealing a wad of linen. "You, Arimnestos, are the general of the Plataians now." He flicked his glance down at the bundle in his hands. A young boy pulled a reluctant, pure white goat up the four stairs to the altar, its hooves skidding on the polished marble as it lowered its back while trying to gain a bit of purchase for escape. The boy yanked even harder. The goat slid as it reached the top step.

Arimnestos peeled away the linen to reveal a gleaming xiphidion knife. He wrapped his fingers around its grip then stepped to the goat. Polyandros sprinkled a fist full of barley over the frightened animal's head. It shook every grain to the ground. Arimnestos, without hesitation, slipped behind the goat quickly, pausing for a moment as he mumbled his prayer to the hero before dragging the sharp blade across the animal's pulsing neck, opening its throat wide. He held it clamped to the marble beneath him as life quivered out with a stream of hot blood and a final gush of breath from the gaping wound. He released the now limp carcass. Blood continued to flow out, creating an ever-expanding puddle until it spilled over the edge of the step, down to the next. He rose slowly, handing the bloody xiphidion to the boy clad in white, and dunked his hands into the bowl of sacred water.

178

Although Arimnestos was no priest, he needn't look to the mantis who sliced the belly open of the sacrificial goat. He knew, no matter what the auguries, they would march. But still, in deference to the gods, he kept his station near the altar, scanning the faces of his neighbors and fellow Plataians. Most looked toward the altar and the mantis, eyes searching, anticipating. Every now and then his gaze locked upon another's in the crowd and he smiled confidently. In return he received a smile. Finally the priest, hands and arms bloodied, nodded at Arimnestos.

"To Marathon!" he shouted.

"To Marathon," echoed the voices of a thousand Plataians.

Every one of them turned to face the road south and the stout slopes of Kithairon, while the lokhagoi, or commanders of each company herded their men into order. Soon the crowd condensed into a triple column of men, with their attendants and sumpter beasts in tow. There they all stood waiting for their strategos Arimnestos to take the lead. As he made his way forward along the road, men barked out his name. He, in turn, recognized each one with a comment, a wave or merely a nod. Soon he moved to his place at the acme beside his friend Lampon and his uncle Belos. His father, past the age to fight, stood across the road from Arimnestos, shading his eyes from the gaining morning light, at the same time admiring and even envying his son.

Arimnestos, without turning around, stepped off and repeated quietly, "To Marathon."

✱✱✱✱✱

Men swarmed over the Agora of Athens, heaving forward toward the monument of the Ten. Here the katalogos for each tribe was posted, listing the names of the men to be called to action. Kallimakhos pushed through the throng of Athenians and stepped up onto the end of pedestal between the flanking tripod and the statue of Antiokhis. Kallimakhos, a tall man, still could not measure up to these slightly over-sized facsimiles of heroes past. But at least from here he gained the crowd's attention. "Men of Athens," he shouted, more than once until they grew silent. "There is no need to check the lists. Every Athenian will be marching. Only the epheboi and the men of sixty years and more will remain here to guard the walls." With these words the crowd surged toward the northern exit of the Agora and toward the Diomiain Gate. The Agora, although large, did not offer the expansiveness necessary to marshal the entire army. All advanced to the shrine of Apollo Lykeios and of his sister Artemis Agrotera.

Women lined the narrow roadway out of the Agora, right up to the yawning gate. Above them, in the towers and the along the mud-brick battlements, the oldest men and the young epheboi—the eighteen and nineteen year old recruits—gawked at them as they passed.

"Father!"

Miltiades looked up to the wall flanking the open gate, certain he recognized the voice. There, in full armor and waving his spear overhead stood Kimon. "Father!" Kimon smiled, glanced to a friend standing next to him and pointed to Miltiades. Miltiades nodded discreetly. The gathering army moved up the northeastern road, accumulating eventually into an open plain punctuated by the gleaming temple of Apollo Lykeios.

Semeophoroi, or signalers from each of the ten tribes, poked their standards high into the air, dividing the sacred precinct of the Lykeion evenly amongst each taxis. Men began to shuffle slowly toward each, much too slowly for Kallimakhos the polemarkhos, or war-leader. "Men, do not dally. To your banners!" The semeophoroi stabbed the air furiously now, hoping to incite more urgency. Within a quarter hour ten immense clusters of men milled around the standards.

Kallimakhos, as war-leader, ascended the steps to the temple, but before dispatching the victim, whispered not to the god Apollo, but to the statue of his sister instead, to the goddess invoked for a successful hunt. To him the Persians were nothing less than marauding animals. This would be a hunt, not for sport, but for liberty. "Artemis. I swear an oath to you, grant us success, and I will sacrifice a goat for each and every one of the invaders that we slay in defense of our land, our families, our temples and shrines."

Miltiades, strategos of his tribe Oineis, grabbed the standard from his semeophoron and began walking toward Mount Lykabettos and the road that would take them to Marathon, halting at the boundary stones of the Lykeion. More than 800 Athenian farmers, potters, fishermen, merchants, and of course gentlemen-of-leisure coursed around Miltiades and the banner. He stared back toward the walls, to the very heart of Athens, to the tumult of neighbors, friends and rivals and wondered how they would survive the coming days. Almost ten thousand Athenians crammed the field—ten thousand different opinions on how to deal with the Persians.

"Men of Oineis!" bellowed Miltiades. This he repeated until most turned to face him. "Men of Oineis! Athenians! Form up to march. Form up behind your lokhagos." Ten men, the lokhagoi or company commanders, shouldered their way forward, drawing with them the men of their companies. "You others," yelled Miltiades, "men with baggage, mules or carts, follow behind."

Servants, slaves and attendants of the hoplites seeped rearward, allowing the fighting men to rally around each lokhagos. "We are fourth!"

The warriors of Oineis stood by as the first three tribes of the Athenian militia marched by them toward the towering hill of Lykabettos and onto the road to Marathon. The dust, along with the stench of fresh dung from the draught animals, practically choked the breath from Miltiades and his men. He turned to his right, watching the last of the tribe Hippothontis pour by, catching sight of Aristides and his men of Antiokhis as they formed up ready to follow Miltiades' division.

Through no plan of the generals, the column began to stretch, induced no doubt, by the pall of yellow dust, increasing separation from the man or beast in front; soon it covered almost two miles of the road. For more than an hour they tromped along, passing vacant farmsteads, empty fields and abandoned villages until they came to an intersection. A runner barreled down the column, stopping at each strategos. Miltiades stepped out from his men as the messenger approached.

"Kallimakhos wants all the generals forward." He sped off, not waiting for a reply, question, or confirmation.

Miltiades' old legs ached as he began to jog down the column. While he trotted by, men started to kneel or sit, taking advantage of this pause. Ahead he saw Kallimakhos in conversation with Xanthippos and Melanthios, but before he could join them Aristides pulled up beside him. "I think there is a debate as to what road we take."

"Come, let us add our opinions to the mix," said Miltiades, grinning.

Xanthippos thrust his pointed finger toward the road on the left. "That is the shortest route."

Kallimakhos crossed his arms as he looked down the twisting road that led to Kephisia. "Xanthippos insists we take the road around Pentelikos." Now he walked slowly away from the assembling strategoi, in deliberation with himself. He spun around. "What say you, Aristides?"

"It is the quickest way to Marathon, and that is a fact." Aristides crossed his arms also, imitating the polemarkhos as he too studied the winding path.

Miltiades did not wait to be asked, but burst out impatiently, "If I were a Persian, that is the road I would hope the Athenians would take."

Xanthippos' face filled with rage. "What do you imply?" His knuckles turned white as he clenched both fists. His face, on the other hand, burned red.

"Oh come now, my dear patriotic Xanthippos. Even I know Hippias is with the Persians, and he would go first to the villages of his kin, to places where he could rally support to the Persian cause. Marathon was his first choice, a place loyal to his father. Probalinthos would be next I would think. And the road that leads to Probalinthos is to our right. The road *you* recommend would lead only to our defeat."

Aristides moved between the two. "I do not think either of you has a clear head in this matter. Common sense, though, dictates we take the shortest—."

Kallimakhos cut him short. "—Miltiades is correct, but for another reason. My estate is at Aphidna, not far from Marathon, and I would indeed take the road to Kephisia, the quickest, to reach home. But if the Persians landed with cavalry, as we know they have, the road through Probalinthos is the logical choice. It is the route the Persians must take."

Aristides nodded, standing aside as Kallimakhos passed by him on his way to the agema of the column. Motion rippled through the army. They marched to the right, towards Probalinthos. Soon they streamed through the village of Phyla. Less than an hour later they marched into Pallene where women and young children lined the route. Where also tardy stragglers caught up with the army and blended into their proper companies. Through each village, or deme as they are called in Attika, this same scene played out. The ranks swelled while the remnants of the anxious population watched their army march by before they packed up and headed in the opposite direction toward the walled city of Athens. By early evening the road swung by the sea as it approached the harbor at Probalinthos. As darkness fell, the army of the Athenians passed the flanking spur of Pentelikos, which pressed them close to the sea. At first the pungent smells of foreign spice mixed with wood smoke greeted them, but soon, as they cleared the trickling foothill of Pentelikos, the shimmering bay of Marathon yawned wide before them. The crescent shaped beach and plain glimmered with the uncountable cook fires of the Persians.

Kallimakhos waved the euzonoi, or light-armed men forward, to sweep toward the village of Marathon and contact the pickets of the invasion force. Several hundred, Illyrios amongst them, jogged into the groves and along the sandy beach, eyes wide open, nostrils flaring at the foreign smells, alert to an encounter. Not far ahead Illyrios sighted the glowing trunk of an olive tree, illuminated by a sputtering campfire at its base. Three faces seemed suspended in the gloom above the flames, their bodies hidden by dark cloaks in even darker shadow. The three began jabbering unintelligibly as they rose quickly, stumbling toward their stack of arms, one grabbing a bow, the other a short spear. Illyrios and his companions washed over them like a storm wave, dozens of iron spear points and fire-hardened ash perforating the three

Persian bodies as they sprawled on the cold Athenian earth. Across the plain the wail of a Persian alarm horn pierced the mute night. Illyrios and the euzonoi moved on, by way of the boggy glade, slicing through the tall fennel grass and on toward the village of Marathon. No Persian fires burned in the marsh, they moved quickly, coming to the small scattering of buildings of the village. Only two houses shown light from within—these were quickly enveloped by the euzonoi. Illyrios, unable to push through the cramped doorway, stood outside. A single screaming word echoed out followed the ping and rattle of spear points. The house emptied. The last of the infantry squad dragged the lifeless body of a Persian out, dropping him in the dry gutter of the narrow, twisting alley.

Athenian light infantry filtered through each and every house, shed and stable, finally spilling out of the town and into the sacred grove of the temple of Herakles. Not far off—less than three stadia—the Persian campfires grew dense marking the boundary of their out-camp. Far beyond Illyrios could plainly see the vast main camp of the invaders to the left of the dog-tail peninsula of Kynosoura. His eyes, now thoroughly accustomed to the dark, scanned the shoreline, picking out the hundreds of beached warships, some marked out by torches, others by their hulking shadows only. He reckoned from this point the Persian force to be at least four miles deep, far into the marshes of the Kynosoura and covering the two to three miles from the shore to the foothills.

Chapter 23

Marathon
12th day of the Athenian month Metageitnion

"What is he all about?" snapped Datis, motioning toward Hippias. The old Greek, on all fours, scooped up handfuls of sand, letting it filter through his craggy fingers. He brushed away the debris of the tide and squeezed the sand once more.

Artaphernes laughed. "It seems he has lost a tooth. Coughed it out when we landed and has been looking for it since."

Datis took his friend by the arm and walked him away from Hippias and toward the open plain beyond the marsh. Wild fennel blanketed the land between the infrequent patches of cultivated soil. Far beyond and across the sweeping plain of Marathon, the clear morning air was smudged by the cook fires of the Greeks. "All of Athens is marshaled there."

"And we, my friend, have three times over the men they do. Why do we procrastinate?" Artaphernes stroked his curled beard, waiting for a response.

Datis waved his hand overhead. In an instant a slave appeared with a tray containing two goblets fashioned like the guardian lions of Persepolis. He lifted one free of the tray, but did not drink straight away, preferring to trace the intricacies of the gold work on the cup with admiring fingers. He smiled then sipped slowly. Artaphernes did the same. "The old man back there, scouring the sand for a tooth, still has friends in Athens. We can afford to pause, taking measure of their influence." He swirled the dregs of his almost empty goblet before tossing them out, staining the white sand bloody with wine. "A single hand is all that is needed to throw open a bolt. Remember Eretria."

"But what of the Spartans? Our spies in Argos and Aigina say they will come to the aid of Athens."

"The Spartans cannot march until the full moon, three days hence. The Argives are certain of this. Add three more days at the very least for them to reach Athens, and another day to reach Marathon. We have the time to let the Athenians defeat themselves."

From the haze of the shimmering heat upon the plain, two figures on horseback grew as they galloped toward the Persian commanders. One of the riders circled, his arm high overhead, whip in hand and smacked his horse hard, sending it into a full sprint. Sand flew up in rooster tails from its hooves and the pounding shook the very earth on which they stood. Nabusera reined up, sliding effortlessly from saddle to feet. "Twenty-five did not return from their watches last night. Truly, the Greeks are in the town and have set their camp around the temple of their god." The three looked out toward the grove of trees just above the village of Marathon. Sunlight glinted off the bronze and iron of their weapons, but the Greeks moved leisurely about. Stationed forward in the plain and in the foothills to their right, light armed Greeks stalked the frontier of the Persian lines as scouts and a detriment to any cavalry.

Datis shaded his eyes, staring up at Pentelikos. "Keep watch upon that mountain for it will deliver a sign."

Artaphernes grinned. "And how much of the King's gold did it cost to employ such a reliable messenger?"

"None at all, my friend. None at all. Years with old Hippias and the other Greeks have revealed to me the essence of their nature. We Persians have sworn obedience to Truth, our God, and our King. Each one of these Greeks is loyal only to himself. Look no further than their greatest festival, the one held to pay homage to their god Zeus and held in Olympia. They contend with each other. Not for the honor of their country, their city or even their family. They contend in this festival for themselves and the singular glory that victory will confer upon them. Their very own gods are the models of deceit. They honor heroes that are victorious by guile and not courage. Ask old Hippias and he will tell you. The naïve admire brave Akhilles, but it is wily Odysseus who most Greeks strive to emulate. This self-interest is our greatest advantage."

$$*****$$

Kallimakhos and the generals had been up and about well before dawn, performed the sacrifice and taken their akratisma meal together as they had done so many days at the Strategion before departing Athens. Now, as the sun climbed into an unblemished morning sky, they scanned the broad plain and the thousands of Persians covering it.

Kallimakhos' eyes traced an imaginary line from the sea to the foothills, just forward of the lines of the Athenian army. "Their cavalry is of great concern," he said shaking his head.

Miltiades slipped by Xanthippos, passing him as though he was nothing more than a shadow, moving close to Kallimakhos. "We are positioned well. The sacred grove and the scattering of trees beyond will discourage horsemen." Miltiades, too, scanned the front lines of the army. Indeed the thick and contorted trunks of olive and their sprawling canopies of silver-green—gifts of Athena—did fracture and confuse the flat ground approaching the village. But still, further inland and toward the road to Oinoe, gaps appeared. Miltiades stepped directly in front of Kallimakhos, a barrier to the eyes and ears of Xanthippos, and whispered, "Send the light-armed men up there with axes." He pointed to the lower slopes of the foothills, beyond the tussocks of wild fennel, and thickets of olive and fig, to the upright stands of pine. "Cut them low and scatter the trunks, branches and all, across the gaps."

Kallimakhos nodded with a smile. He gathered the other strategoi around him and made this plan clear, and soon parties of men, some with axes and others with spear and light shield, trudged inland, filtering up the slopes and through the timber. The air thickened with the report of ax on wood, echoes rolling down the tilting foothills to the sea. Suddenly a squadron of Persian cavalry streamed out of their camp.

"Do not fret, Kallimakhos," assured Miltiades. "They are curious is all. They will not leave the broad plain for the confusion of the trees."

Most all the Athenians halted, turned and stared at the advancing horsemen. The Persians reined up at the edge of the plain, a hundred meters or so from the nearest group of woodcutters, and commenced to notch arrows. Their commander, gold flashing from his arms as he waved and shouted orders, trotted his mount up and down the line of horse-archers. In unison loaded bows swung up, level at first then arcing higher to increase trajectory and range. The commander's arm dropped. Arrows hissed deadly through the air. Suddenly shouts exploded from the wooded slopes followed by taunts. "You couldn't hit the sea if you were standing on the beach!" yelled an anonymous voice in clear Attic Greek. "Afraid to fight, face to face!" bellowed another. Again the Persians filled their bows and again they emptied then into the woods.

186

Aristides pulled on Kallimakhos' arm. "Do you hear that?" he asked as he waved with his hand for the others to quiet down.

Before Kallimakhos could answer, Stesilaos, general of the Aiantis tribe, pointed toward the road to Oinoe. "Flutes!"

The ten strategoi and their polemarkhos Kallimakhos turned, all shading their eyes, straining to glimpse the source of this remarkable melody. In the hollow between the hills flashes of reflected sunlight sparkled. The flutes grew louder. Figures of men imbedded in a veil of dust oozed into view. Suddenly a single man burst from the expanding throng, sprinting down the road towards Marathon. Now the thunder of cavalry shook the ground, and the Athenians from their locked glances. The Persian squadron clearly spotted the source of the flutes also.

"The Plataians!" The shout went up across the Athenian camp. The men in the woods cheered. Smiles of relief settled on the faces of the strategoi. Only Kallimakhos retained his grim visage.

"The sight of our ally brings you not even a whit of cheer?" asked Aristides.

"Do not misunderstand. It is a wonderful sight. For a moment though, I thought it were the Spartans marching down that road."

$$* * * * *$$

Nabusera flung himself off his horse at the feet of Datis. "Spartans! Truly, the Spartans are coming through the pass!" He stumbled, kneeling before his commander. As he struggled to master the convulsions of his breath-starved lungs, he touched his brow with clustered fingers in obeisance.

Datis, hands on hips, laughed. "Look again, man." He flung his chin forward. "More farmers, not warriors," he said contemptuously. "Plataians, most likely." Most unusually, Datis extended a hand to Nabusera, helping him to his feet. "Is their abatis complete?"

"My lord, we tried but could not attack them amongst the trees. And then, well, that column of infantry appeared from nowhere." Nabusera kept his head bowed as he spoke. "They have laced the open ground with felled trees. We cannot ride around them now."

Artaphernes pushed one of his thick gold rings up and down the index finger of his left hand. "Events, it seems, are following your scheme."

Datis nodded in affirmation. "Yes, but we must allow them time to empty Athens of anyone who can resist, and be certain also, that their entire force is gathered here. Let them settle in. They will not initiate battle. They are here merely to block the road to Athens."

Chapter 24

Athens
13th day of the Athenian month Metageitnion

Kimon rubbed the sleep from his eyes as he stared northeast toward Lykabettos, the hill of wolves, its pinnacle the final relay of any signal from Marathon. He knew that by now Athenians and Persians had sighted each other, and wondered why no battle had taken place, so he turned around and stared back into the city from the Diomiain Gate, to the vacant Agora. Here and there isolated spirals of smoke spun into the sky, the only indication of life within Athens. Beside him old Androkles snored, wrapped in his himation cloak and curled up next to the warmth of a brazier. As sunlight spilled over the northern walls it induced movement to the slumbering defenders. Kimon looked to the eastern tower and spotted two epheboi like himself, on its roof and silhouetted against the glowing dawn, searching, no doubt, for any sign or signal from Marathon. Again he scanned Lykabettos before his eyes drifted to the right, sighting the gaping field of Apollo Lykeios and the god's shrine, the very place where the army had assembled days prior—the last place he had seen his father. A single dog pranced across its uninterrupted expanse, soon melting into a grove beyond. At his feet the remnants of garlands, dried and tattered by the late summer heat, reminded him also of that final day when life still coursed through Athens. For a moment anger overcame him, an anger induced by his inaction and his station here at the walls. *Better to be there at Marathon*, he thought, *than to linger here, fate unknown.*

A slave, her head covered in a huge cloak that dragged behind her feet, shuffled from the tower doorway, two bowls of wine in hand. She did not wake Androkles, but instead placed the wine on the battlement above him. Kimon, compelled by thirst, did not wait for her to approach but impatiently lunged forward, and snapped up the bowl from her. Immediately he sipped a mouthful of warm wine, then thought for a moment about sitting, but stopped, for that would place him in cold shadows, so he instead leaned against the sunlit mud-brick, keeping warm as he dipped his bread into the wine. Too quickly he consumed it all.

Below, on the narrow street leading from the Agora, he spotted three men familiar to him. Aristonymos and his son Kallixenos hustled along with their cousin Megakles in tow. "They should be at Marathon," growled Kimon under his breath. "With my own eyes I saw them march out together with Xanthippos and the others of the tribe Akamantis." As they passed through the gate they pulled their cloaks up overhead, but by then Kimon had marked them out. Once outside the gate the three huddled in conversation, until Aristonymos turned back, heading quickly through the gate and into the city. Kallixenos and Megakles, on the other hand, continued onto the road that led to Marathon. Kimon watched them until the road curved past Lykabettos and out of view.

Androkles tossed the himation off his shoulders and sat up. "Any signal?"

Kimon shook his head. "None."

"That is a good thing. Only defeat will be signaled to us by that hill. Victory will arrive on foot." Androkles curled over his bowl, hands shivering with age as he dropped pieces of torn bread into the wine.

Chapter 25

Sparta
15th day of the Athenian month Metageitnion
15th day of the Spartan month Karneios

Helots worked the tents of ceremony, erected for dining throughout the festival of the Karneia, pulling out the supports and snapping up the turf-bound pegs, causing the linen and hide canopies to collapse slowly as they exhaled. Behind Taygetos the sun slipped away, and with it the last moments of the Spartan festival and prohibition on battle. Almost two complete morai of Spartan heavy infantry—two thousand hoplites—crammed the road north of the humble acropolis. Following them extended the battle train of Helot shield bearers, carpenters, smiths, and mule-drawn fodder wagons. Leonidas had already performed the sacrifice to Zeus Agetor, and the bearers of the sacred fire stood before him, their earthenware pots glowing, illuminating their faces and etching hard lines into the already austere countenance of Leonidas.

Theasidas, polemarkhos and commander of the expedition, stepped forward to receive his final orders from the king. "I envy you, boy," declared Leonidas. Now he leaned forward, guarding his words. "It would be me leading them out, but they won't have it." He flicked a glance at the five ephors—the supreme magistrates. "Next time, Karneia or not, I will be at the head of the army." Now he cupped his hand against his face and whispered, "They think I will turn suddenly toward Argos or Aigina, and forget the Persians." He stepped back, away from Theasidas, so all could clearly hear his words. "These men from the East, the Persians, will not honor our

190

customs of war—or peace. If they defeat us, it will be a defeat lasting all time. Remember this well on your march. Your mission is to succor the Athenians," he said almost shouting. "It is their survival—and ours that you must ensure. Your orders are simple. Your orders are clear. Return here only with a Persian defeat."

Now in complete darkness the flute players piped away, offering the familiar cadence of the Embaterion march. Theasidas jogged away from the gathering of kings and ephors toward the head of the column. Soon the two thousand streamed away from the acropolis and over the Eurotas River. Leonidas turned to his co-king Leotykhidas. "Tomorrow I must grovel before them again, or bang their heads together so they may listen to sensible talk."

Leotykhidas' placid smile melted away. "Leonidas, you have convinced them to send out the army, the first ten age-grades. The very best. Quite a feat considering most have just returned from Messenia. What else do they need convincing of?"

"Years past, when Kleomenes lived and reigned, an Ionian named Aristagoras visited Sparta. This man displayed to my brother Kleomenes an immense map—a map of the Persian Empire. I fear two thousand of our best may not be enough against the Strangers. We may be compelled to send our last man to the Isthmos for a final, desperate stand."

The songs of Tyrtaios, belted out by the departing army, echoed up the valley of the Eurotas, mingling with the gentle, fluid melody of flutes. Leonidas and Leotykhidas remained at the Babyx Bridge, hanging on to the fading hum of distant, confident voices.

Chapter 26

Marathon
16th day of the Athenian month Metageitnion

A squad of euzonoi trudged in from the foothills, complete in their task of harassing Persian foragers. Two of them dragged a man by the arms through the dust, dropping the limp corpse at the feet of Kallimakhos. He was most certainly a Persian for his long trousers were covered in emblems of the sun, repeating embroidered bursts of gold in neat columns sparkling in the light of mid afternoon. Metal glinted from beneath his tunic, but the blood was hardly noticeable, camouflaged by the deep rich purple dye of the cloth. One thing Miltiades discerned that Kallimakhos did not. "Look. He has no boots." Miltiades called for the captain of the squad to come forward. "Was this man on horseback?"

"Why no."

The answer caused them all to pause for a bit. Miltiades face grew dark-browed. "Each and every day previous, has it not been cavalry that foraged outside their camp?" Miltiades snatched a spear away from one of the euzonoi then poked the felt slippers of the Persian Infantryman. "He is not a rider." Now he looked out toward the Persian camp. "Have any of you seen their cavalry today?"

✶✶✶✶✶

Artaphernes walked along the edge of the marsh, heading for the springs of Makaria where almost two thousand horses loitered with their farriers, taking their fill of water and grain. He found Datis easily, standing high above the commotion on a jagged white boulder, surveying the preparations. Artaphernes knew the voyage, although short, would wreak havoc with the

192

horses, and this shrewd precaution of feeding and watering the animals beyond their daily rations would help sustain them once on the beach at Phaleron. "Datis, it seems the Athenians are neatly in your vise."

Datis acknowledged him with a furtive glance before barking out a string of orders to Nabusera. Soon, in small groups, horses were led away from the springs to a trail behind the main camp and toward the glistening bay of Marathon. Satisfied that the intensity and coordination of the activity suited him, he hopped off his perch and greeted Artaphernes. "By dawn the cavalry should be fully embarked. At that time the Greeks will have two choices, and neither will be pleasant. They can retreat once they discover our fleet moves on Athens, and if they do I will be behind them. Have you noticed, my dear Artaphernes, how unsuitable their armor is for combat from behind?"

Artaphernes grinned at his words, but Datis did not. "The second choice?" Artaphernes asked.

"The second choice." Datis paused for a moment then repeated," Yes, the second choice. It is the very one they have had since they set foot on the plain. Do battle. But for this they must emerge from the safety of their precious olive trees and advance over open ground. We have three times their number and in men of experience, men who have fought and won in battle." Datis snatched an arrow from the quiver of a passing archer. "We have both seen what havoc Persian arrows can deliver. Imagine the destruction that we will heap upon these Greeks as they stroll across that beautifully empty plain."

Artaphernes pulled Datis by the arm, pointing up to a rocky crest that towered behind the Greek camp. "Can you see that flashing? A signal of some sort?"

Finally Datis smiled. "When you arrive at Athens tomorrow, you will ride through unbarred gates."

Artaphernes smiled with both admiration and relief. "There is nothing left to chance is this endeavor, my friend. You have eyes and ears in every Greek city, even in the Athenian camp. You know when and where their allies will arrive. You lavish attentions not only on our god Ahura Mazda but on theirs also. Even heaven could not stand against you."

"There is one more thing that I must attend to. One final detail before battle—and victory."

✳✳✳✳✳

Every evening, as the old day faded, the ten strategoi, their polemarkhos Kallimakhos and Arimnestos, the general of the Plataians, gathered for food and counsel. Every day also the command of the army changed hands, moving from one of the strategoi to another, assuring that even in war demokratia functioned. Now by this custom Epizelos, general of the tribe Hippothontis, anxiously relinquished his authority to Miltiades as soon as the sun slipped low.

Supply wagons, which had followed the army to Marathon, arrived now in smaller numbers and with less appetizing food. Figs, usually plentiful, had become rare delicacies, and even rations of tarichos salt fish thinned. Arimnestos, sitting cross-legged before the cook fire, bit hard into an onion. His eyes watered and his face puckered, but he took and even greedier bite. The pain of hunger overwhelmed any discomfort caused by the pungent vegetable. Lampon reached for a small earthenware jar, and tapped a bit of its contents into his palm and without a word extended it toward to Arimnestos. His friend pinched some of the salt-thyme mixture, sprinkled it over the onion then bit again.

"Here," said Aristides as he passed a kothon of wine to the Plataian.

Arimnestos grabbed the cup and nodded a thank-you before dousing his throat. He wet the index finger of his right hand then tapped it upon the mostly barren grape leaf, picking up the last crumbs of cheese. "How long will they sit there?"

Miltiades spit out the remnants of the wine that clung in his mouth. "I would have thought old Hippias would have convinced them to move by now. The few Eretrians that escaped say many Persians have been left on their island to secure Khalkis. "

Themistokles stood up. "Have you tried to count them all? They are in little need of reinforcements."

"And what do you mean by this?" snapped Aristides. "Surrender to them?"

Before Themistokles could answer, Xanthippos stepped to the fore. "I think he means parley with them at the very least. Miltiades here is intent on battle. It may be a battle that need not be fought."

Miltiades flung his empty cup at the feet of Xanthippos. "Should we talk with them? Or maybe you already have? We all saw that signal from the high ground over there. It was no signal meant for us, but for the invader."

Xanthippos thrust his cup toward Miltiades, emptying it in his face. Aristides and Kallimakhos grabbed Miltiades while Themistokles gleefully halted Xanthippos' advance with a blow to his belly, doubling him over.

The shouts of a messenger caused them all to stop and gather a bit of restraint, for they detected the alarm in his voice. "A Persian herald! A Persian herald wants to speak with Miltiades of Lakiadai."

Miltiades hesitated then spoke. "You must be mistaken. Kallimakhos is polemarkhos."

The messenger shook his head. "The herald was quite clear about it. He says his master and you have met before."

"A friend from the past, perhaps," said Xanthippos with a snarl as he tugged the wrinkles from his chiton.

Miltiades said nothing. Outwardly he maintained an aspect of calm, but inside his gut tightened; his heart raced. *What would a Persian want with me?* As soon as he moved to follow the messenger Illyrios plucked up his spear and trailed closely, all three threading their way through the maze of cook fires of the camp, beyond the pickets of light infantry and toward a torchlight gathering of several men. Two he spotted immediately as Athenian light infantry betrayed by their tall spears and leather caps. In front of them a small entourage of Persians assembled. One of them, a slave no doubt, unfurled a carpet while another pair carefully positioned two chairs atop it, all this activity illuminated by four slaves bearing sputtering torches. Watching impatiently nearby stood three more Persians, two of which wore bronze, funnel shaped helmets and purple tunics, clutching short spears in their right hands and wicker sparabara shields draping lazily from their left. The third, although in Persian robes, carried no weapon. It was he who spoke first as Miltiades approached.

"You sir, are you Miltiades of Lakiadai, son of Kimon, and once ruler of Elaios?"

Miltiades paused for a moment before answering, for there was something in the tone of this Persian's voice that rang familiar. His Greek was impeccable. Not a tinge of accent. "Yes, although you have me at a disadvantage, sir."

The Persian stepped forward, reaching for a torch from one of the slaves, then held it out, illuminating his face. "Please sit." With a flourish he waved an inviting hand toward one of the vacant chairs. Miltiades shrugged his shoulders then sat. The Persian, once satisfied that his guest was settled did the same. "Do you not recognize your own son?"

Miltiades' chest collapsed as the breath rushed out of him. He stared through the torchlight, past the Persian robes, the curled and dressed beard, and the glittering bands of gold. He gazed directly into the man's eyes and found his son, Metiokhos. Instinctively he rose. So did Metiokhos. The two embraced. "We thought the Persians had killed you."

Metiokhos smiled. "If it were you they had captured, then I am certain you would be dead. Their commander, Datis, would have had no compunction in doing this. But for reasons unknown, the Great King has become my benefactor. It is through his good grace that I am allowed to come here tonight to speak with you."

Miltiades, with the flush of excitement subsided, coolly asked," And what shall we speak of?"

"Father, do you remember the very last time we saw each other? On the quay at Elaios?" Miltiades nodded. Metiokhos continued. "Do you also remember the words we exchanged that day?" He paused, waiting for an answer.

"In detail? Why that I cannot recall," responded Miltiades quite belatedly, old thoughts an impediment to speech.

"Father I stood on that quay, begging you to not abandon the people of Elaios. You argued that there was nothing wrong in this, that every man was ultimately responsible only to himself. It was an argument that I could not accept. But today, I see things differently. Today, I see that you were right."

Miltiades, for a moment felt the flush of satisfaction rush over him, but it quickly vanished. "And you son, why are you here this night to remind me of this?"

"Because it is the course that I propose to you now. I offer you—no, the Great King offers you, a place in his court, and a pardon from the inevitable defeat that will befall Athens tomorrow."

Miltiades no longer saw a son, but a Persian standing before him. Anger welled up, but he fought it back. "Son, I propose an alternative. Come back to our camp, and I will deliver you from the defeat that with Athena's aid we will heap upon the Persians."

Metiokhos' mouth hung open in disbelief. "Father, if anything I recall you as a shrewd man, not an idealist. When the sun sets tomorrow the Persians will be in Athens. There is no doubt about this. Show your canniness once more and do the sensible thing."

Miltiades looked beyond his son to the myriads of glowing fires of the Persians, to their ships on the beach and the hundreds of others in the bay, speckled with torchlight. He stared long at the ships. Then it struck him. A scant few hours earlier no ships were afloat. Now hundreds were. "And where is your Persian master sailing to?"

Metiokhos glanced over his shoulder at the fleet in the bay. "That is why I am here and why I am warning you. Their cavalry is embarking as we speak and it sets sail for Phaleron. Your army cannot be in two places at once. Athens is doomed."

196

"Metiokhos, it seems that we both have changed over the years. I have become more of an Athenian, while you have become less."

Metiokhos laughed. "You are not an Athenian, nor a Persian, nor an Elaian. You are Miltiades. It all begins and ends with you."

"There is a certain thing that Athens bestows that enriches far beyond the wealth of the Great King. It is, in this world today, a rare commodity."

"And what is this precious article?" snapped Metiokhos, with contempt.

"Liberty." Miltiades embraced his son one final time then turned away, walking quickly back to the camp. He did not turn back, but heard the chatter of Persian, the rustle of the carpet and chairs being totted off and the fading footfalls of his son's entourage. Unescorted, and without torch or lamp, he was challenged as he approached the edge of the sacred grove in the precinct of Herakles. "Athena!" shouted the sentry.

Without even thinking Miltiades barked the counter-sign. "Areia!" The guard stepped aside as Miltiades drifted by him. His walk brought him to the circle of strategoi that hovered over the waning cook fire. All faces lifted up as he approached, each bathed in the orange glow of the fire and silenced by anxiety—they wished to know, and quickly, of his meeting with the Persian.

Without hesitation Miltiades detailed his parley and departed, leaving them all to argue the consequences and their course of action. Bereft of speech he wandered back through the grove of olives, toward the vacant town of Marathon. Suddenly it struck him. The trees, the dwelling, the figures of men milling about, all cast shadows even now in the thick of night. He looked up, over the spur of Pentelikos. Above, glowing eerily, the new moon hung dominating the heavens. For a moment his spirits lifted. *The Spartans are marching*, he reminded himself.

✷✷✷✷✷

Arimnestos, Lampon and his uncle Belos huddled over the glowing coals, not for warmth but for light, as Mikkos knelt within its halo, scratching figures in the dirt. The slave Teukros poked and prodded the embers, trying to coax some flames to life. Belos drew a stone across the leaf-shaped spear-point, the metal thwanging with each pass. With each pass too, the edge grew sharper. Lampon fiddled with the string of charms that hung around his neck, staring into the mesmerizing firelight while Arimnestos fought to stay awake, an inadvertent snore breaking the silence and his drift toward slumber. His friend Eumenidas had already succumbed and lie wrapped up in his himation cloak, snuggling very close to the warmth of the fire pit.

Lampon, fingers still twirling one of the blue glass eyes hanging on the necklace asked, "Battle tomorrow? Are you sure Arimnestos?"

Mikkos stopped his doodling, cocked his ear, but did not look directly at Arimnestos.

The mellifluent, eerie hoot of an owl responded first then it was Arimnestos' turn. "Hear that? Athena has answered you," he said smiling with serene confidence.

Mikkos knew not to speak, but with the coming battle had so many questions. "Arimnestos—I mean general Arimnestos, sir?" He waited for acknowledgement or admonition. Arimnestos smiled at him. He continued. "General sir, if we defeat the Persians, what will happen?"

Lampon frowned. "Don't bother your brother, why don't you fetch some—."

"Let him talk. It may do us all some good," said Arimnestos, cutting his friend off.

Mikkos scratched the dirt with the stick again nervously. "What will happen if we defeat them?"

"Do you mean to them or to us?" asked Arimnestos.

"Both." Mikkos blurted it out quickly.

"Well, if we defeat the invaders, as I pray we shall, we will return to our farms and the Persians, I suppose will return to theirs."

Mikkos again twirled the stick in the dirt. "And if they defeat us?"

Arimnestos paused. In fact, he had never pondered what defeat would mean to them, and the Athenians. "The Persians would return to their farms."

Mikkos furrowed his brow as he waited impatiently for the rest of the answer. "And us?"

"I would think we would go with them."

His answer compelled them all to silence. The four of them sat there, ringing the fire, each in mute thought until suddenly Lampon smacked his arm. "By the Dog of Egypt!" He commenced to dig at the flesh on his arm. "Is there not enough Persian blood for you to feast on?"

Belos reached into a small leather sack, pulling out a sprig of greenery. "Rub this on your arm. It wards off mosquitoes. It may do the same for Persians." He snapped the twig of basil, releasing its potent oils before handing it to Lampon, who angrily swiped it across his arm. Belos gazed across the black, open plain to the Persian camp. Unlike nights previous, the invaders still stirred, given away by dancing torches and the braying of mules. Now he looked about, into the proximate darkness that seeped over and around their small huddle. "There will be battle tomorrow, for They are out there stalking the night, marking victims, and as I hone my blade so to do They hone theirs. Their claws will be sharp and thirsty when the sun rises."

Arimnestos and Lampon stared at Belos in silence. Neither dare say the names of these daimons—the Keres—spirits who hover above the dead and dying, waiting to snatch men's' souls.

Chapter 27

Marathon
17th day of the Athenian month Metageitnion—Dawn

The moon, the new moon, this moon full of such promise for the Athenians, had slunk below the sea, leaving the sky black and teeming with stars. Miltiades lay on his back, his mind whirling, the cold earth summoning up the pain of age in every joint in his body. Every so often he would gaze east, trying to pick out the first streak of day. An isolated cloud scudding by occupied his sight until it melted away behind the ridge. Beside the fire that was long since dead his slave Illyrios snored, one hand clutching a pair of javelins and the other a threadbare himation cloak, which he had wrapped around him as a blanket.

Miltiades' eyes blinked closed, only for a moment it seemed. When he opened them he saw the river Ister, fog creeping up its banks, his bridge spanning it. The thunder of hooves echoed from the far bank, compelling him to rise. Before him the fog seemed to part, as though at his command, to reveal Darios and the Persians preparing to cross. He looked around. Men from the past, dead men—Histiaios, Aristagoras and other Ionians—stood beside him. He could not speak, but only pleaded to them with his eyes. The shades, devoid of any expression, stared at him. A cock crowed.

"Master it is time." Illyrios loomed above him, jerking his shoulder, trying to break the grip that slumber and the god Morpheos had exerted over him.

He shook his head, trying to clear it. He clamped both hands over his face, expelling a great sigh. As he peeled away his hands he looked up, expecting the black night sky, but instead he saw Dawn rising to the east, but dressed in robes of war. The horizon glowed blood-red, low clouds burning crimson as though they were alight. A lone eagle patrolled the sky above the bay to his right. Both Illyrios and he smiled at the omen.

The strategoi and their polemarkhos gathered as they did every day at the altar in front of the small temple of Herakles, its twin columns of marble standing tall, buttressing the carved pediment above. Just now the orange tiled roof began to catch the new day's light. Kallimakhos and the mantis performed the daily sacrifice, but before the generals took their breakfast Miltiades called them to council. He climbed up the two steps and framed himself between the columns. Behind him the burning tripod cast whirling shadows within the small temple porch.

"Gentlemen, you know that today we decide on our immediate course of action."

Xanthippos spoke first. "While you slept, we debated. And watched. We watched as the Persian transports emptied the beach of cavalry. And if what you say is true, we have only a single choice. We retreat to Athens. We must be there to defend our homes." Beside Xanthippos four other of the strategoi nodded their heads in affirmation. For Xanthippos the night was well spent.

Miltiades looked to the others, to Stesilaos, Themistokles, Aristides and Epizelos. They neither confirmed Xanthippos' plan, nor did they challenge it. Kallimakhos stood apart from them all in silence too. "This is my day to command," said Miltiades, "but I will not force my decision on all of us. We must, as a council, decide together. We have two choices. The first is to attack the barbarians now and place our fate in the hands of the gods and our skill at war. If we do this and prevail, we can then march back to Athens."

"That is what they want us to do. If we are here we cannot defend our city." Xanthippos bounded up the stairs, taking his place next to Miltiades rudely stepping in front of him. "At least by marching home we give Athens a chance."

"And when we turn our backs and run, for that is your plan," said Miltiades as he moved chest to chest with Xanthippos. "What will stop the Persians from attacking us in the rear?" Miltiades hustled down the steps of the temple to stand with Aristides. "What is the count now? Who wishes to follow this plan of Xanthippos?"

Xanthippos and four others shouted, "Yes!" The rest looked to Miltiades. Aristides spoke. "It seems we are at an impasse. Five wish to retreat, while five wish to fight."

Miltiades turned to face Kallimakhos. "It is now in your hands, Kallimakhos, to either enslave Athens or to make her free. If we refuse to fight, as Xanthippos suggests, I have scant doubt that bitter dissension will undo us." Miltiades turned toward the Persian camp and the open expanse of the plain. "But, if we fight before the agents of this dissension can sew their rot, then we give Athens the best chance. I cannot predict victory or defeat in the coming battle, but I can easily foresee defeat without one. Kallimakhos, the decision is yours."

*****

Artaphernes entered the sprawling tent of Datis, both flaps held wide by servants, the flanking cauldrons of fire fluttering at the sudden admission of the breeze. Datis stood motionless, clothed only in embroidered trousers of gold and purple, as his body-servant sprinkled him with sacred water, water carried with them from far off Persepolis along with the holy fire that burned in the sacrosanct receptacles. Two other servants approached him, each carrying different articles of accoutrement. One slipped a thick, padded tunic over Datis' head and pulled it taunt, while the other held out the leather and bronze scaled armor before him. Datis thrust his arms out in front of him as the two servants surrounded his chest with the armor, securing it with leather lacings that joined at his back. Once fastened, they covered this with a tunic of deep, shimmering purple. A young boy shuffled forward holding a tray of glittering, silver and gold bands. One by one he slid these onto Datis' arms until all ten had been emptied from the tray.

"The ships are ready, my friend," said Artaphernes, his voice laden with both anxiety and anticipation. "Now we must both do our parts."

Datis calmly settled into a deeply cushioned chair while his body-servant continued with his ritual, carefully lining his master's eyes with inky kohl and rubbing red ochre upon his cheeks, both meant as antidotes to age. Once complete the two commanders and friends stepped from the lamp-lit tent into the gloom of early morning. A salphinx—war trumpet of the Greeks— blasted from the far end of the plain, overwhelming, for a moment, the drone of activity in the Persian camp. "They are forming up for battle," said Artaphernes, as he looked across the misty plain. "Or they are preparing to withdraw?"

Datis, his face betraying neither satisfaction nor concern, calmly stated, "Either way Athens will be ours." Now he walked toward the sacred fire of his god, two Magi trailing behind solemnly. He plunged his arms skyward, looking up and began to recite, "O Ahura Mazda! When wicked persons torment both me and my followers, who is our protector from Angra Mainyou and the minions of evil? There is none other that Thee. Do Thou evoke and give rise to such thought so in our minds we may obtain courage and strength in this coming battle." He scooped a generous handful of incense from the casket that a Magus held and tossed it flamboyantly into the crackling flames, sending a cloud of billowing consecrated smoke skyward.

Datis left the holy fire and the obligations to his god behind him as he walked to the tent where the commanders were assembled. The hum of chatter ceased as soon as he strode in. Thirty men, each a commander of a hazarabam, or regiment of one thousand, began to gather around him. Their plan of battle, although reviewed time upon time, would again be detailed. Datis stepped upon a short stool, just enough in height to bring all the faces of his commanders into view. "The plan is unchanged," he commenced his briefing, hands on hips, chin thrust forward confidently. "Two hazarabam of Lykians will deploy to the far right flank, past the stream." His eyes locked on Spitamenes. "Your three-thousand Sogdians will form up next." One regiment after another, one commander after another, he marked out positions, skipping over Nabusera and his six hazarabam of Persians and Sakai that would comprise the center of the battle line. Finally he singled out his trusted subordinate and captain of his finest regiments. "The Greeks cannot match our line. To equal us in length they will sacrifice depth. If they maintain depth then we will turn their exposed flanks. This is the formula, simple and straightforward. You, Nabusera, and your six thousand will hold the key. In the center, drive the Greeks back. Your archers alone will do this. Most of them shall perish without coming to grips. Look at that plain." He jumped from his stool and led them outside, and pointed toward the Greeks with his akinakes sword. "It stretches empty for a mile between their lines and ours, a fine killing ground for your arrows. Once their line is broken we will pour through the gaps. We have the advantage in speed. They, on the other hand, are tied to the earth, anchored by their ponderous armor."

* * * * *

"I pray for an ill wind, friend," said Aristides as he watched the last Persian transport slip out into the bay.

Miltiades clamped an assuring hand on Aristides' shoulder. "It is a full day's sailing from here to Phaleron. If the gods are with us we will have the time." Miltiades, knees and back still stiff from the damp ground and lack of sleep, hobbled over to Kallimakhos.

Eukles, a lokhagos of the Aiantis tribe, laughed at him. "Those old legs will not carry you far."

Miltiades was quick to respond. "Running is only for the defeated. Give me a man like that old Plataian over there." He pointed to Belos. "A man with legs bowed and thick is impossible to move. That is whom I want next to me in the phalanx. No quick, nervous feet for me."

Kallimakhos waved the ten strategoi to surround him, for one final council. "Remember the signals. When the salphinx blows once we step off, advancing at a walk. Two blasts and we run." He turned his glance to Miltiades. "This will be the deadliest time for us, while they pour their arrows into us." He stepped slowly over to Arimnestos, and embraced him. "Your Plataians are the end of the line. If they turn you, all is lost." Then he winked and said, "Three blasts from the salphinx and—"

"I shall not forget," assured Arimnestos. "We will not fail you."

Kallimakhos stepped before the army and scanned the lines, the waving, undulating ranks of farmers, potters, carpenters, men with ancient wooden shields, battered kranos helmets, some with bronze corselets, others with body armor fashioned from glued layers of linen, and still others with nothing more than a thin wool chiton separating vulnerable flesh from the sharp metal of war. Gentlemen too, like Miltiades, Aristides and Xanthippos populated the files, but these men were resplendent in polished armor, helmets made tall by crests of fine horse hair and bronze faced shields bearing expertly painted devices, insignia of their deme, phratry or of the daimon they invoked for protection. But one thing they all wore, and which caused no distinction from farmer to aristocrat were chaplets of flower and vine, woven into crowns atop their helmets in honor of the gods. Behind the ranks of hoplites, scattered in front of the sacred grove of Herakles marshaled the light infantry, men too poor to afford armor and shield, too vulnerable to fight within the shock of the phalanx, but who would, if all things turned against the Athenians, be the last men to stand between the invaders and their homes.

Kallimakhos held his xiphos sword high over head, presenting it to both the gods and the army, then wrapped his left arm around the neck of the pure white ram, kicking its back legs out, pinning its convulsing body to the earth.

"To Herakles and Pan!" he shouted as he plunged the blade into the rams' throbbing neck. The beast kicked and bucked, and bleated until the blade cut clear through the windpipe. He held it firm, watching the blood course from the wound onto the dry, thirsty soil of Marathon.

The mantis leaned over him, studying the pooling fluid of life, a smile spreading quickly across his face. The men in the front ranks cheered, even before the proclamation was made. "The blood flows well!" bellowed the mantis.

Miltiades grabbed at the leather pouch of knucklebones and muttered a prayer to Tykhe, for luck was what they needed this day.

*****

Nabusera spun around as the roar echoed from the Greek lines. He stared, a puzzled look upon his face, as he strained to see what caused this commotion.

"They cheer a sacrifice, superstitious Greeks!" assured Datis. "They look at tree or a rock, or a stream and see a god there. Devil worshippers! There is only one true god." He pulled hard on the reins, causing the gold spikes of the war-bit to dig into the war-steed's toughened mouth. "Praise to Ahura Mazda and to our lord Darios." He rode off, down the ranks of his army toward the bay.

Nabusera slid from his horse and began stalking the front line. "Plant your shields here," he instructed, drawing and imaginary line with the tip of his akinakes. Archer after archer plunged the spiked bottom of his wicker sparabara shield into the parched soil of Marathon, presenting a wall over a mile long to the Greeks beyond. "Bring the caches forward," yelled Nabusera. From deep behind the lines, at the edge of the Persian camp, slaves hurried forward with bundles of arrows, for the gyrtos quivers would be emptied before the Greeks even reached them. Nabusera nodded as he perused the inventory list handed him by the scribe. "Twenty arrows for every Greek," he said under his breath with a muffled laugh. Suddenly a blast of wind stirred up the dust and toppled a few of the shields in the front battle line. He pulled his silken scarf across his mouth. In the bay the water turned white tipped, and to the west a bank of clouds rolled across the horizon, dark, thick and billowing. The sight made him pause for only a brief moment—the tasks of battle occupied him once more. He remounted his horse and rode to the captain of the Sakai cavalry, the only horsemen left, for the rest were headed for Athens along with Artaphernes. The conversation was fleeting: his contingent would only enter battle if the Greeks ran or if their flank could be turned. Satisfied that all was in order he trotted over to the center of the battle line. There he pulled a handful of figs from a leather satchel; figs scavenged from the groves of Marathon, and held them out for his horse to nibble on. A single trumpet blared from the Greek formation.

Chapter 28

Marathon

17th day of the Athenian month Metageitnion—Mid Morning

"That is the signal!" yelled Arimnestos. To his right the taxis of the Athenian tribe Erekthis stepped off. To his left the foothills seemed too far, offering scant protection from a Persian move to his flank, but he gazed across the plain, clearly marking out the end of the Persian line—only infantry and they stretched no further than his Plataians. Motion rippled from the center toward his flank, causing him to step forward tentatively. He heaved his shield high, dropping its deep, concave inner rim upon his shoulder, relieving his arm of the weight. He kept his helmet propped up off his face, the gesture unknowingly imparting confidence to those around him.

Belos nudged him with his shield. "Remember; tuck yourself into the belly of it." He grinned. "Keep moving and do not fall. If we stand together, nothing can break through our shield wall."

Now the voices of thousands rose up and across the advancing phalanx of Plataians as they sang the paian, the sacred hymn. The Athenians quickly joined in. Across the plain the battle lines of the Persians seethed, throbbing with wild activity, but still only a mob, individuals coalesced into a froth of humanity. With each step forward his legs wobbled, either from fear or the weight of seventy pounds of armor. Every so often his advancing ranks encountered a small tree or bush, causing them to break apart their shield wall as they swirled around the obstacle. This sight unsettled him, and drove home the simple advice his uncle has imparted to him. The cool wind had faded, leaving them devoid of relief from scorching sun of late summer. "Stay behind me," he barked to Lampon.

"Where else would I be!" he shouted back.

Arimnestos turned around and saw his brother-in-law, head encased in an ancient bronze kranos helmet, his eyes wide and white within the dark slits, sweat dripping from his beard. Behind him six more ranks of his fellow Plataians marched, faces deep in the shadows of their helmets, shields bobbing with each stride, crests wobbling frantically.

Facing forward now he began to mark out individuals in the enemy line, recognizing not Persians, but Lykian warriors, conscripts of the empire, their identity revealed by the gleaming curved blades of their murderous war-sickles. Pouring through gaps in their ranks, archers rushed out and planted shields. He pulled his helmet down, not bothering to secure it with the leather laces. Once inside its confines, every breath became magnified—and so did the heat. Sweat streamed down his forehead, stinging his eyes and filling his mouth with its salty tang. The salphinx blared out the signal.

✳✳✳✳✳

Kallimakhos pumped his spear high overhead for all to see as he began the charge. The Persian lines, buttressed by deep rows of planted sparabara shields, bristled with arrow-strung bows. A single command bellowed from Nabusera. Twenty thousand and more archers drew their bowstrings back against their cheeks. Another command echoed, and twenty thousand arrows lacerated the morning air.

"Spears up!" shouted Kallimakhos. Men within earshot swung their spears up, while others quickly imitated them, all the while jogging forward, trying to keep abreast of the man right and left. Kallimakhos did not look up, but followed the shadows of the barrage as they streamed over the barren, ever diminished landscape between the two armies. What started as a mild rumble, like the sound of a brook or rivulet of water, built in volume until the sky above them howled with death. Suddenly bronze arrowheads hailed down, pinging off their helmets, upturned shields and rattling in amongst the forest of spears. An arrow had sliced through Kallimakhos' linothorax, penetrating only slightly into the flesh of his right shoulder. He wanted to reach up and pull the shaft free, but dare not release the grip of his shield or spear. Instead he focused ahead, counting in threes with each footfall, inhaling and exhaling in perfect synchronization, watching the archers' killing field shrink. He reckoned two more volleys.

*****

Themistokles' legs burned as he picked up the pace, clearly noticing the center of the Athenian line bowing inwards—a koile phalanx—the very maneuver Miltiades had detailed, but to his concern too pronounced. "Faster!" He burst forward then glanced back to be sure his men followed. Behind him a boiling cloud of dust churned, flashes of metal flickering through the murk, men still belting out the paian. To his right stormed the ranks of the tribe Oineis, Miltiades taxis, doubled in depth to his four ranks. Nearly at the very center of the line Aristides led his division. Ahead Persian archers huddled behind their shield wall, launching thick and murderous barrage after barrage into the charging Athenians. This headlong dash, it seemed, had caught the Persians unprepared, for their aim was high, an underestimation of the Athenian pace; the poise that the King's army had so often exhibited evaporated quickly. Still many shafts found their marks. The air sizzled, followed by a cacophony of thuds as the razored bronze arrowheads buried deep into shields, armor, bone and flesh. Themistokles heard the searing flight of one arrow as it hurtled from the closing barrage. Thwack! He turned to his left and saw Melanthios head swing back, the fletched shaft of an arrow springing from his eye, blood pulsing in gushes. He crumpled into the dust, trampled by his own men as they advanced relentlessly.

Themistokles focused now on the Persians. "So many!" he repeated over and over. The distance had diminished to less than one hundred meters. The once thunderous barrage now sputtered as the enemy front rankers prematurely abandoned their bows for dagger-like akinakes swords. What began as a growl exploded into a roar. At the far flanks, the twin horns of the Athenian lines smashed into the Persians. Bronze upon bronze, man upon man, the clash produced a deafening yet indefinable tumult, a sound so thick, so loud it appeared to manifest itself as a solid, adding to the turbid haze of the dust churned up by the struggle. Themistokles swung his spear up to an overhand grip. What at first were indistinct blurs, rushing figures, and animated shadows crystallized into men. He saw faces emerge. Worried eyes, eyes of fear and others of ferocious intensity glared at him. The enemy front ranks swelled into tight formation, officers barking commands, the final barrage launched then bows cast aside for spear and sword. From all around now he heard the battle cry well up.

Chapter 29
Marathon
17th day of the Athenian month Metageitnion—Mid Morning

Nabusera's horse twirled about as he fought to keep it reined in and facing the advancing Greeks. He glanced quickly, right then left. Both flanks had already engaged, lost in a storm of dust. Before him his six hazarabam of Persians and Sakai wedged behind their shields and braced for the charge. Across the field the rumbling lines of the Greeks closed in. "Ala, ala, aleu!" This the Greeks screamed over and over. He waved his spear. Rear-rankers, men armed with whips, raced forward and began flailing their own men to keep them in formation and moving ahead. "They are insane," he said as the last sliver of open ground became swallowed up by the charging Greeks. "They will have nothing left."

The impact caused his horse to rear up, almost tossing him. It was not the sound, nor the sight, that startled the beast but the bone-shaking thunder of collision, transmitted through the very earth, that panicked it. Nabusera could not hold his place so he kicked hard, sending the animal into a gallop along the rear of the Persian center. Every so often a single distinct cry pealed above the din, a warrior in hideous pain, only to be quickly muffled by the roar of battle. He raced up and down the ranks, shouting to his men, but blind to the real progress of combat. Suddenly a stiff wind rolled up from behind, whisking away the dust, exposing the whirling entangled mass of Persians and Athenians. The Greeks showed courage, pushing their thin line into the throbbing block of his Persians and Sakai, but as they fought, they fell. The momentum of the charge had been expended, and the sheer mass of the

209

King's army began to absorb the assault, finally reversing it. "They are spent," he shouted. "Advance! Advance!"

A Persian war horn wailed. A cheer exploded from the ranks as step by step the Greeks stumbled backwards. Nabusera exhaled long, pursing his lips as the breath whistled out of him. He saw it. He felt it. He prayed to Ahura Mazda that it would continue. The Greek center, although not collapsing, was in retreat, and his men, encouraged by the diminishing resistance, surged forward. On either flank the battle was still heavily contested, neither side able to gain any advantage, but here in the center, he could deliver victory. He smacked his horse hard, sending it into a sprint, his squadron of Sakai cavalry streaming behind him, spilling into the void created by the advancing infantry. Once in amongst his men he led no longer but was carried along, like a leaf in a raging stream, pushed, pulled and buffeted by the inexorable currents of battle. Men from either flank began flooding into the deflating Greek center, confident they rode the tide of victory.

✳✳✳✳✳

Datis arched his back in an attempt to gain every bit of height possible, to see into the froth of battle from atop his horse. "They are breaking in the center," he said, pointing with gauntleted hand, directing Metiokhos' line of sight.

Metiokhos watched, as he once did from the tower in Elaios, the very same event repeating itself, but here no sudden loss of a tribal chieftain would deliver the Athenians and his father. "He would know better," he mumbled.

"Did you say something?" Datis pulled on the reins as he slid forward on the horse's white and gold caparison.

"I cannot believe my eyes," Metiokhos answered shaking his head. "My father knows that the strength of your attack will be against the center, yet that is where the Athenians are at their weakest."

Datis spoke, expressionless, "You Greeks only know one way to fight— on level ground against men similarly armed. We employ various weapons and a multitude of tactics. The Greeks had little choice in their deployment, and no flexibility." He pointed to the right, to the far flank and lower slopes of the foothills. "They fear our cavalry sweeping around behind them. This would be more disastrous than any numbers taken head-on, so they strengthen their wings. Arrayed such, as I knew they would be, I need no cavalry. My infantry will crush their center while the Greeks cling to the flanks, checking a maneuver that will never come."

Metiokhos lips betrayed a covert smile. "I am not a military man, so I defer to your skill and explanation." He touched his brow with his hand in the Persian style. "I beg your leave, for although I am indebted to both you and Darios, I do not wish to see the destruction of my countrymen. In this I hope you will understand and grant me indulgence. I would take ship now and meet you in Athens."

Datis nodded with no other acknowledgement of his departure, instead barking an order to one of his lieutenants. "Have the ships ready to launch. I would expect the Greeks to be in full retreat soon." He stared at the swelling void in the center of the battle line as it swallowed up more Persians, Sogdians, Baktrians and Medes. *One final push and it will be over,* he thought, before slamming his whip hard into the horse's flank.

Chapter 30

Marathon
17th day of the Athenian month Metageitnion—Late Morning

Aristides shuffled backward, trying to keep within the shadow of the shield of the man to his right. The Persians crashed into his front rank, hurling their wickerwork sparabara shields into the bronze of the Greeks, flailing wildly with their short spears and even shorter swords. By now his eight-foot long spear had snapped in two, so he jabbed and pumped its remnant, capped with its bronze butt-spike, into the Persian advance. Thrust after thrust, lunge after lunge he heard the discouraging crackle of his spear penetrating only wicker. Suddenly a blind plunge buried deep into flesh. Less than a foot in front, a Sakai infantryman clutched the shaft with both hands as his eyes rolled back into his head, trying frantically to pull the bronze spike from his throat. Aristides twisted it, enlarging the wound and freeing his spear.

A succession of blades rattled off his shield as more Sakai pressed forward, sagaris war axes flashing wildly. With each blow his left arm weakened until his shield dropped, exposing his head and neck. For a moment a bright light flashed across his vision before all went black. He staggered back, his skull concussed by an ax strike that spilt his horsehair crest, but failed to penetrate the thick bronze of his kranos helmet. Furiously he squinted and blinked, inducing tears. He prayed to Apollo to restore his sight, if only for moments, till the battle is ended. Summoning every last ounce of strength, he leaned hard into the bowl of his shield, using his shoulder to take some weight off his failing arm, but try as he might, he could not hold his ground without becoming enveloped by the Persian horde. Discouraged, he continued to back-step. His men on either side, without normal depth of file, had no chance to push back against the overwhelming weight of the Persians. For fleeting moments though they dug their heels in and lowered their shoulders, but the sheer mass of the enemy skidded them rearwards until they began to stumble again.

Two of the enemy, encouraged by a gap to his left, rushed forward. Aristides intercepted them with his shield, but the impact snapped his shoulder, dislocating it. Although adrenaline overwhelmed the pain he could not maneuver the shield to deflect any aimed blows. A quick backwards glance afforded him scant comfort. Originally four men, deep the files were now worn shallow through the attrition of combat, leaving only a single rank to cover his back. Directly behind him Anytos saw Aristides plight and strode forward, shoving him rearwards while fending off the emboldened Persians that moved in for the kill.

As the Athenians reeled, they began to trip over the spent arrows of the Persian barrage, this marking clearly the start of their charge. They had given up over two hundred meters of ground, for most all of them here in the center were either wounded or exhausted, and this with exhaustion came thoughts of relief, delivered by a quick and painless death. Some of them broke formation, heaving themselves into the Persian line. Aristides relinquished his shield, for his arm now hung limp from a mangled shoulder, but now, at least, he could wield his sword unimpeded, deciding to exchange his life unevenly with the invaders.

Gradually the disintegrating Greek center collected into small pockets of hoplites forming distorted squares and circles as a last ditch effort of defense. If they ran they would be supremely vulnerable, burdened by armor and unable to cope with a foe equipped for speed. The Persians swarmed around and by them, intoxicated by victory and the prospects of looting the Greek camp. Over the roar of combat three quick blasts from a salphinx trumpet cut through the air. Almost overcome by his wounds and fatigue Aristides fell to one knee. *The Keres—they must be coming for me*, he thought. *For I can hear their cries.*

✳✳✳✳✳

Illyrios heard the crescendo of the roar before he saw the Persians explode through the center of the Athenian lines. The euzonoi around him shuffled nervously, glancing at each other for assurance, or some look of confidence that would compel them to hold their ground against the enemy charge. At the very same time a blast of wind struck them head on, as though the gods carried the Persian advance upon wings, but it unsettled Illyrios for only a moment; he knew this wind, the Etesian as it is called, and it picks up in late summer. Dust buffeted his eyes causing him to squint. He turned away and rubbed them clear before transferring all but one javelin from his right to left hand.

As the Persians grew closer a few of the light infantrymen bolted—they had hardly expected to confront the full force of the invading army, being assigned to guard the camp and the Temple of Herakles. As though an invisible hand tugged him backwards he began to retreat, but quickly gathered himself, crouched low and extended his throwing arm behind him as he slipped his index finger through the javelin's throwing loop. *If I run now I am free*, he thought. More around him dissolved into the groves of olive and fig, thinning the already meager ranks of euzonoi.

Someone shuffled in beside him. He turned to find a young boy, one of the Plataian messengers, standing next to him, brandishing a xiphidion dagger and biting his lower lip so hard that blood trickled down his chin.

"Run!" he growled at the boy. The Plataian shook his head violently. "Then stay behind me!" He strode in front of the boy, sweeping him backwards with the edge of his small hide shield.

Illyrios had most certainly seen the Persians fight before, but never from this vantage, eye-level and directly in their path. They did not run, but neither did they dally, but pressed forward as fast as their light weapons and armor, all designed for warfare on the plains of Asia, allowed them without tiring them. They advanced in clusters—squads of infantry—some Persian, but others he easily recognized as Sakai, marked out by their tall, pointed caps and flailing sagaris battle-axes. These he feared more than the Persian infantry, armed with short spear and akinakes sword. His shield, although thin by Greek standards, could adequately absorb the blow from sword and spear if wielded with dexterity, but the sagaris, well the sagaris ax would slash through his pelta shield with a single blow.

The Persians and Sakai closed in. More of the euzonoi filtered back through the trees, leaving only a dozen or so—Illyrios and the boy amongst them—guarding the main approach to the camp. Suddenly Illyrios' arm exploded forward, launching the javelin, his index finger snapping the throwing loop hard, imparting a tight spiral to the shaft. One of the lead Sakai jerked backwards; he folded violently at the waist as the javelin bored into the soft flesh of his belly. Other javelins spun through the air, thudding into the Persians, perforating their sparabara shields easily at so close a range.

Purely by instinct, the remaining euzonoi edged closer together, trying to protect their flanks, and any attack from the rear, but as the first wave of Sakai crashed into them these fierce warriors from the northern plains of the Empire slashed furiously away with their axes, pulverizing the shields of the euzonoi.

One after another Illyrios flung his javelins until his hands held only pelta shield and dagger. He focused on one of the Sakai charging forward and intercepted the swiftly descending ax arm with his left hand, halting the blade just inches from his scalp then, exerting every last bit of energy, managed to drive the Sakai's arm back, over his head, continuing the arc rearwards until he heard the ligaments and sinews snap. The man howled. Illyrios plunged his dagger deep, almost lifting him off the ground as it penetrated just below the ribs. Now he was bumped and jostled as the dwindling band of euzonoi came together under the Persian onslaught.

$$***** $$

Miltiades shouted his order again after the third blast from the salphinx. "Wheel left!" He pumped his spear into the back of a fleeing Baktrian and yelled again, "Wheel left!" The three taxies to his right had already spun toward the center after driving off the Baktrians and Medes opposing them. Half of the Persian army retreated while in the center the other half pursued an illusory victory, severing the once contiguous formation into fragments. "Synapismos! Lock shields!" The ranks compressed together, men sliding close and into the protection of their neighbor's shield. Miltiades started the battle cry again. "Ala, ala, aleu!" Fatigue proved fleeting for they were imbued with the spirit of the goddess Nike, advancing with savage efficiency as they slammed into the withering Persian center. Screened from each other by the billowing dust, the Athenians, almost shoulder to shoulder, heaved inward. On the far flank the sturdy Plataians too moved on the signal, routing the Lykians before swinging right toward the sea.

As they advanced, they trampled over the dead and the dying, plunging the butt-spikes of their spears into the writhing bodies of the invaders, and stepping coolly over the bodies of their own men. Miltiades began to slip, the normally firm, dry earth had become slick with blood, piss and vomit. With every step he cleared mounds of shit, intestines, severed arms and legs—this once pristine field was now covered in the grotesque blanket of Ares, stitched from the flesh of his victims.

At first the Persians and Sakai in the center turned bravely to hold back the twin jaws of the Athenian vise. Nabusera, his horse cut out from under him, had grabbed a discarded Greek shield and hid in its deep belly, delivering furious blows with his akinakes while withdrawing. Miltiades spotted the single bronze aspis amongst the dwindling enemy formation and thinking it a fellow Athenian about to be overcome, pushed forward. He tossed away his shattered spear, drawing his two-foot long sword from its scabbard, almost wounding the Athenian next to him as the blade whizzed by.

He wanted to advance quickly, but whenever he expanded his stride the uneven slippery ground frustrated him. Haste would indeed bring him low, and once off his feet, his own men might even kill him inadvertently. One by one the enemy in front either fell or fled until he was almost on top of what he thought was an Athenian in the midst of Persians.

Nabusera, desperate to escape, swung his head side-to-side, searching for a pathway to the clear. Infuriated, he slashed wildly at the Greeks around him, delivering and taking blows. In this crazed frenzy he turned away from Miltiades, revealing not the linen armor of a Greek, but trousers and a Persian tunic.

Miltiades strode forward, pushing hard off his right foot as he swung his sword hand overhead, arcing his blade down powerfully, slicing deep into Nabusera's right shoulder, driving the Persian to his knees.

*****

Arimnestos, blood running down both legs from wounds in his groin, kept to the advance, carving a path through the crumbling Persian ranks. Suddenly he felt the facing of a shield bury into his back. He looked over his shoulder to see Lampon, framed by the aperture of his own kranos helmet, stumbling over the human debris spewed across the earth. "Keep to your feet!" he yelled to his friend.

Ahead the scene was so different from their initial advance. There were no Persian arrows blotting out the sun, no hordes of brightly clad infantry charging confidently at them, no fierce squadrons of cavalry pummeling their flanks. In front of them whirled a maelstrom of filth and death. The once ubiquitous and thirsty dust had been quenched by blood, the earth churned to knee deep, crimson mud. It covered the sprawl of wounded and the slain, and even those still clutching to their last moments of life as they fought hopelessly on. "Keep close!" he yelled. "Keep slow!" No prospect of victory must allow his men to charge and cut down easy victims as they fled. "Keep to formation!"

The front ranks of the Plataians undulated, swerving forward in places only for moments until men who kept their heads and heeded Arimnestos pulled the enthusiastic back into line, offering not the slightest rift to their shield wall. They walked over slaughter, driving their spears into each and every enemy body, living or dead. Any cries for mercy were met with sharp iron. Their own men upon the ground they dispassionately ignored. Now the dwindling haze of battle revealed what remained of the Persian center: strange men, dressed strangely, formed a crumbling storm of movement, the pressure of the wheeling Greek flanks squeezing them out toward the marshes. Beyond this swirling mass Arimnestos saw the familiar horsehair crests of hoplites seep into view, bobbing wildly with their advance. Only handfuls of Persians remained in the gap between the Plataians and the Athenians now, inciting a charge. Bands of Athenians swarmed over the remnants of the enemy, overcome with rage that took precedence over rational action and the orders of their lokhagoi.

Prompted by this, both the Athenian wing and the division of Plataians abandoned closing the vise and transformed from a cohesive formation into a profusion of mobs, bursting recklessly toward the Persian camp—toward loot and easy victims.

Chapter 31

Marathon—By the Ships
17th day of the Athenian month Metageitnion—Midday

The Persian command staff started to run toward Datis as he galloped hard through the sea-soaked sand, the horse's hooves tearing chunks of it high into the air. He reined up in knee-deep surf, his captains and servants surrounding him in panic, desperate for orders.

"Take him first!" he bellowed. Carefully he helped slide the facedown body of Nabusera from his horse. The blood soaked through his gauntlets and smeared the brilliant white caparison red. "Easy!" he yelled. Five of them gingerly cradled the limp form, and as they repositioned their grips Nabusera cried out, bringing an ephemeral smile to Datis. "Carry him to the ship."

One by one the Persian triremes slid backward off the shelf of the beach and into the bay. Orders echoed from their decks and quickly oars plunged into the sea. Datis spun his horse around to face the oncoming Greeks and the refugees of his army. From here it all seemed to slow down, losing the frenetic pace of combat. Persians sprouted from the melee, for they were hardly encumbered by the weighty armor of the Greeks and streamed quickly by. The Greeks, on the other hand, barely jogged, and appeared content with the determined pace of a march. Further inland the right wing of his army lost touch, and filled with blind terror, poured into the marshes near the Makaria Springs, their figures quickly swallowed up by the high fennel grass. Several columns of Greeks gave chase.

"Archers forward!" the small company of bowmen raced after him as he rode toward the oncoming bands of disordered Greeks. "Form up!" The archers planted one sparabara after another, hastily slapping together a shield wall as they attempted to repel the impending Greeks. His own retreating men trickled by him: some, gripped by shame, turned and fell in behind the archers, but most, weaponless and bloody, splashed through the surf only to clamber aboard the dwindling number of triremes. As the Greeks approached, the fever of victory soon became stifled by the sight of the Persian shield wall. They slowed to a walk. For a moment Datis' spirit lifted. Although the rampaging Greeks slowed their advance, it gave them time to reform, dress their lines and absorb more of their comrades, swelling the ranks of the nearest enemy contingent to well over one hundred. Datis, with little calculation, knew his scant wall of thirty shields would swiftly be overcome.

Around and by the advancing Greeks, surviving Persians sprinted, tossing away their short spears, bows and sparabara shields, escaping to the last of the departing ships. Volley after volley of arrows screeched through the air, raining down upon the heavily armored Greeks. The barrage only slowed them, but he could see more and more Greeks emerge from the cloud of battle—a battle that was once a conflagration and now had become nothing more than the last sputtering embers of combat.

Datis scanned the melee, watching the heavy streams of his men shrivel to nothing more than a trickle, hoping for more, but seeing less and less. He stared out, disheartened.

The captain of archers barked his command, "Loose arrows!" then calmly walked to Datis, grabbing the horse's reins to steady both of them. "Lord Datis, you must take to the ship now."

Datis wanted to speak, but either the heat of battle had dried the spit from his throat or the utter poise and courage of this man who had just spoken with him stole his words. He simply bent low and kissed the captain of archers upon his forehead and nodded. Suddenly, above the incessant roar of battle, the cries of hundreds pealed from deep within the marshes, fusing with pleas of mercy in Persian and Sogdian. Datis slid from his horse, pausing for a moment as he eyed the caparison stained with the blood of his friend. From the deck of the trireme men slipped a bow-plank over its edge fast, letting it splash hard into the swells, Datis bounded up and onto the deck. The row-master waved for oars to be readied. As soon as the rowers had cut the surface, the clang of hammer on bronze began to beat out the cadence. Datis watched helplessly as the Greeks inundated the tiny band of archers. Other Greeks stormed by, racing headlong for his embarking trireme.

Datis knelt next to his friend Nabusera, cradling his head as he tipped a small flagon of wine, letting a bit trickle into his mouth. Nabusera swallowed painfully while grinning. "Truly, I pray I have done honor to Darios?" He licked the dried blood from his lips and took another swallow of wine. "But, my friend, what is more important, did I do honor to you?"

Datis fought back the mist that threatened to cover his eyes. "You are victorious, this day. For me there is no greater honor." Then he thought to himself, *if the others had only fought as bravely.* Gently he lowered Nabusera's head. "Rest now. Tonight we will be in Athens."

A Baktrian marine raced forward to the bow, followed by others, and prepared to repulse any boarders. A single Greek splashed through the surf, and sprinted for the wavering bow-plank. He strode up the wooden plank, hefting a fractured shield upon his left shoulder, its lower half wobbling as though it pivoted on a hinge. One of the Baktrians charged at him, swing his sagaris ax, splintering the shield and leaving only the bronze arm grip spinning on the lone Greek's wrist. The Greek, desperate now to keep his footing as the retreating trireme lurched violently with the draw of oars, grabbed hold of the balustrade. The Baktrian, with another swipe of his battle-ax, severed his hand clean off, sending him tumbling into the waves.

✷✷✷✷✷

Aiskhylos plunged the leaf-shaped blade of his hoplite sword deep into the Persian archer's chest, planting his foot on the now lifeless corpse as he withdrew its blade. At that moment he looked up and saw his brother, completely alone, charging up the brow-plank of a Persian trireme. He spun quickly around and swung his shield up, and sprinted toward the last ship. Before his feet felt the cool water of the bay he watched as his brother collapsed into the sea, followed by the discarded brow-plank. Without thought he flung away his shield and sword, running with every last bit of energy that his body could summon, but with each advancing stride he slowed, legs surrounded by the ever-deepening sea. Kynegeiros disappeared beneath the surface, weighted down by his armor. "Brother!" Aiskhylos cried out. He probed the foaming waters with out-stretched arms. "Brother!" he yelled again. He stumbled. He groped beneath the swells and latched onto the scabbard strap, pulling in desperation until his brother's head popped above the surf. He gathered him up in his arms and trudged out of the water, crumpling to his knees upon the sand, exhausted. Anxiously he tore the kranos helmet from his brother's head, wiping the seawater from his face.

Kynegeiros coughed. He coughed again then sucked in a chest full of breath. His eyes blinked open. "We have won, brother," whispered Kynegeiros. Seawater foamed from his mouth as he coughed one final time before his eyes locked forever on the face of Aiskhylos.

*****

Arimnestos stood up to his thighs in the dank water of the marsh, eyes searching for any last Persian survivors. He trudged forward deliberately, flanked by other Plataians of his company, hunting down any of the enemy that still lurked in the tall grasses near the Persian camp. No one talked. The only sound audible was the gurgle of water as it swirled around the legs of the hoplites as they cautiously swept through the marsh. As he approached the far side of the swamp, indicated by the thinning grass and the lake beyond, the ground opened up into a vast meadow. To him it looked like a scene from Hades Hall, grim hoplites stained dark by the filth of combat stalked the expanse gloomily, as though they themselves were shades of the dead. At their feet and sprawled over the boggy earth lie thousands of brightly appareled corpses—Persians, Medes, Baktrians, Sogdians, and Lykians— the litter of flesh, muscle and bone discarded by Ares.

Chapter 32

Marathon
17th day of the Athenian month Metageitnion—Midday

Miltiades stood upon the beach staring out at the last of the Persian warships as they slipped out of the bay and into open sea. He had little time to savor this brief victory, for if Metiokhos did indeed tell him the truth, the enemy fleet's course would bring them to the harbor at Phaleron, propelled fortuitously by the stiff Etesian wind that still swept over the battlefield and undoubtedly the waters off Attika. His fatigue was indescribable, but his spirit remained buoyant. He strode up the gentle incline of the bay, scanning the battlefield, seeing corpses strewn thick in the center for almost a full stadion. Carrion crows and gulls had already bravely descended to peck away at their meals. As small groups of surviving Athenians approached, the birds burst skyward, cawing and flailing their wings, climbing just high enough to stay out of reach but near enough for another foray into the harvest of corpses. His men staggered about, bodies expended and minds in utter shock. He recognized one man cradling another in his arms.

"Aiskhylos!" No response. He yelled the name. And again. Finally Aiskhylos drifted toward him, arms still full, carefully settling the body of his brother Kynegeiros on the sand at Miltiades' feet. He grabbed Aiskhylos by the shoulders and shook him. "Aiskhylos, we must rally the men."

Aiskhylos cocked his head as he looked strangely at Miltiades. Miltiades heart sunk in desperation. Suddenly Aiskhylos blinked then asked, "Athens?"

Miltiades nodded. "We have to arrive in the city before them."

"You are wrong, my friend. Not Athens. We must get to Phaleron before them."

Miltiades quickly realized what he said to be true. Reaching Athens itself before the Persians would be a prodigious feat, considering the day's work so far, but to march on another four miles beyond the city to the harbor would be nearly impossible—but it would be the only place to take on the Persians as they landed. Miltiades swallowed hard. "Help me gather them up." He looked down at Kynegeiros, his ashen face locked in eternal serenity, sand clinging to his sea-soaked chiton and linothorax. For a moment he envied him. "We shall take care of him," assured Miltiades, "and all the others." He caught sight of some of the euzonoi as they stalked amongst the Persian dead hunting for loot. "You!" All five turned as he called. "Come here!" They hesitated briefly before jogging to Miltiades. He sent four to find the other strategoi and one to seek out Kallimakhos and the trumpeter, for the only quick way to rally them was by salphinx call. Instead of waiting Miltiades, along with Aiskhylos, patrolled the battlefield, instructing men where to assemble while they hoped to find the rest of the generals still living. As they walked inland they came to the center of the battlefield, the span contested by the Persian elite against the divisions of Themistokles and Aristides. Here very few men walked about—most either sprawled about on their backs or bellies, their wounds so severe they could not rise. The ones that could, filtered amongst their comrades, offering water, wine or just words as they sought to comfort them.

"Over here!" A kneeling figure waved at them. It was Themistokles.

Miltiades and Aiskhylos trotted over to him. They found him with Epizelos, one of the generals. They stared at him in silence. Epizelos lay on his back, his eyes open and staring nowhere. "He cannot see."

Epizelos rocked his head back and forth. "It is true," he said. "In the midst of it all my sight deserted me." Miltiades, hardly a trusting soul, waved the edge of his shield over the man's face. Epizelos did not flinch, nor did he blink. "Is it getting near dark?" he asked. Miltiades lifted the shadow of the shield from Epizelos' face. As Miltiades looked up he spotted another group, but not euzonoi. These men were heavily armored hoplites and they meandered slowly their way. "Are you wounded?" bellowed Aiskhylos. They did not answer. They all shuffled forward except one. One man, with his left shoulder drooping unnaturally, tried to hurry ahead, but his legs wobbled until he collapsed into the dirt. Others hustled to pick him up.

"That must be Aristides," remarked Themistokles as he rose up. "Only he could afford such armor."

Indeed Aristides did stumble his way forward assisted by others of his taxis of Antiokhis, the men who took the brunt of the attack. More and more survivors of the battle trickled around them until finally the signaler, salphinx in hand, sprinted toward the gathering. Miltiades expected to see Kallimakhos with him, for the trumpeter, by custom was always at station near the polemarkhos. The man shouldered his way through the throng of warriors, stopping out of breath before Miltiades. Before the question could be asked he spoke. "Kallimakhos is dead." He drew a deep breath and repeated it. Men all around began to mumble words of denial. Others lowered their weary heads.

Miltiades could not delay. "You must signal for assembly."

The trumpeter's face contorted in disbelief. "Why? The battle is over."

Aiskhylos looked directly at him shaking his head. The others around him, ones who easily saw this, appeared stunned. Miltiades answered him. "Yes, this battle is over, but there is another one waiting for us." Now he singled out Eukles. "You told me once before how valuable swift feet are in war. Now is the time to prove it to me. And prove it to them." He swung his arm out pointing to the assembling and battered remnants of the Athenian army. "Run back to the city and tell them what has happened. Tell them to hold on. Tell them we are victorious."

*****

Arimnestos did not linger in the Great Marsh. He heard the salphinx blare out the call to assemble and began the long trek back across the battlefield toward the temple of Herakles. Already slaves stalked amongst the Persian dead, stripping away anything of value and helping any wounded Athenian or Plataian. As he stepped, the bloody muck that was once an expanse of harvested fields, slowed him, especially in what was the center of the clash. The hot sun thickened the mud—and the stench.

By the time he arrived at the outer precinct of the temple of Herakles, the ground had mostly re-hardened. As he scanned the bodies he noticed that here most were Hellenes, but not heavy infantry clad in bronze. Here the fallen proved to be the light-armed euzonoi. Some of the survivors, along with the marshalling hoplites, formed a ring around a pile of Persian bodies, obviously viewing some spectacle. They crammed in closer, tightening their ring around the heap of corpses, pointing down and chattering. Arimnestos, at first not at all interested, lumbered over to the crowd. As he approached he saw what they all stared at—in the center of the pile lay the huge body of one of the euzonoi, sprawled face down. He shouldered his way to the center. There, lying next to the body of the light-infantryman was a young boy. Scattered around them were the bodies of nearly twenty Persians and Sakai, some with javelins sprouting from them, others displaying enormous, gaping wounds. All were quite dead.

"What is everyone looking at?" asked Miltiades as he tugged on Arimnestos' shoulder while peering over it. He too looked at the pair, and their apparent handiwork. He dropped his shield and sword, pushing several men aside as he moved forward and kneeled. Then gently, almost reverently, he turned the corpse of the man over, certain he recognized him. Illyrios, his beard stiff with coagulated blood, stared at him with lifeless eyes. In one hand he held a dagger; the other, it appeared, he had used along with his thick arm, as a shield for the boy.

"By the gods, he slaughtered them," remarked Lampon as he squeezed into the circle. Lampon suddenly lost his grin of admiration. He drifted forward and crouched over the body of the boy. He gazed for a moment at his face before turning to find his friend.

Arimnestos shook his head, "No!" he screamed. He shoved men aside, bursting by Miltiades and Lampon. He flung the arm of a dead Persian from the neck of his brother and scooped Mikkos up. His face was chalky, his body cool.

Suddenly he opened his eyes. "Brother?" The single word, a simple question, stunned Arimnestos.

The men started chanting prayers, some searching for their lucky talismans, other spitting into their chests to ward off evil, convinced that only sorcery could have delivered him from death.

Mikkos painfully tilted his head to look around. "Where is he?"

Arimnestos knew precisely who he asked for, so he turned allowing Mikkos to see Illyrios.

"He must be the bravest in the world," stated Mikkos.

Miltiades pulled the small leather pouch from his belt, the one containing the very same knucklebones he had liberated from Xenias at the bridge so many years before. He slid the dagger from Illyrios' hand, replacing it with the pouch.

Chapter 33

Temple of Apollo Lykeion, Athens
17th day of the Athenian month Metageitnion—Afternoon

Eukles smiled as he raced into the precinct of the Lykeion, knowing that in minutes he would be at the Diomiain Gate. From here he could make out the towers, and was convinced that men moved about in them. Suddenly pain tore through him, just below the ribs and spanning the width of his abdomen. Wincing, he clamped his right hand over his side, and drew it away. His palm glistened with blood. "Just awhile longer," he said. "Just awhile longer."

From his post in the tower Kimon spotted the runner. He scrambled down the rickety ladder, jumping past the final four rungs onto the dusty ground. One of the twin doors had been pushed open slightly, more than enough room for him to slide through edge-wise and onto the road. He broke out into a sprint. About a hundred meters from the gate, just after a twist in the road, he spotted a lone figure, slumped over, both knees planted in the dirt. Kimon skidded to a stop.

Eukles coughed, bloody spittle hung in gobs as he bent over, both hands palm down upon the earth. He spit then tilted his head to look up at Kimon, an odd smile erasing any sign of pain. "Nike!" He coughed again. More blood foamed out his mouth. "Go now and tell them."

Kimon hesitated, reluctant to abandon the messenger, but knowing also he must complete the man's task. He bounced to his feet and sprinted toward the gate, turning back only once. Eukles had collapsed.

Kimon exploded through the gateway. Men above, in the towers and on the battlements, leaned out. "What has happened," more than one yelled as sprinted toward the Agora. They abandoned their stations and swarmed after him as he sped toward the Strategion, not even slowing as he bounded up the broad marble steps. He pummeled the door, the rapping echoing throughout the small building. Still no one came. He pounded again—and again. By this time the squads of guards comprised of the old and the very young epheboi began to collect around him. "Where is Androkles?"

From the bushes adjacent to the Strategion a shaky voice answered, "Who calls for Androkles?" The old man stepped into view, pulling his chiton straight.

"He was taking a piss," remarked one in the crowd, inciting a ripple of laughter.

Kimon turned. "We have won!" The guardsmen pressed closer, shaking him, tugging him, and shouting questions. "It is Eukles. He is near the Lykeion." Kimon flew down the steps, retracing his strides, out of the gateway and down the road that snaked toward Lykabettos. As soon as he spotted Eukles, he accelerated.

A mob now flocked around the messenger. Kimon lifted his head, and brushed away the coating of dust that encrusted his sweat-soaked face and beard. Someone handed him a water flask. Gently he coaxed Eukles to wet his lips and swallow a bit; the water revived him. He fought to open his eyes and squinted through nothing more than pain-wracked slits. "We have won." His last breath rushed out of him with those three words.

Chapter 34

Cape Sounion

17th day of the Athenian month Metageitnion—Late Afternoon

The wind, which Datis interpreted as a blessing from Ahura Mazda, suddenly petered out as they approached the stony promontory of Sounion on their way to the harbor of Phaleron. Another good sign. From here they would row and the fleeting breeze would have slowed them when they changed course, but more good fortune traveled with them. Not far ahead he spotted the transports of Artaphernes, all laden with his powerful cavalry. In a few short hours they would be in Athens.

The water here was clear as crystal, and the high jagged cliffs appeared beautiful, but imposing. He laughed a bit as they cruised by a ragtag fleet of fishermen. The men onboard each small boat erupted into a panic for they were caught at sea and much too close to such a large flotilla. The fisherman steered for land, finally slipping into the perceived safety of the serrated coastline.

High above, perched on a finger of land, he spotted various constructions: rows of partially built columns fashioned from marble drums; patchworks of stone and mud brick walls; smaller dwellings capped with red-orange roof tiles. *A temple to one of their gods,* he mused. Then it struck him. The sight of this rocky, empty shore that he watched slip by for the better part of the afternoon, exhibited nothing worth the cost exacted so far in gold, time, and in subjects of the Great King. *Why would old Hippias want to return?* he thought, shaking his head. He stared down at the balustrade and the deep cleft in the wood stained red with blood. He wondered for a moment, *Greek or*

Persian? As he dragged his gauntleted hand over the darkly blemished wood his gaze returned to the supine figure of Nabusera and the three physicians that tended to him. His friend slept, inured from pain by the brew of poppy and date-wine. One of them kept murmuring the chants necessary for healing; another peeled away the cloak, revealing the blood-soaked linen dressing swaddling his shoulder.

The sun hung low in the west, kissing the hills of the Peloponnese. Ahead dark hunks of land floated in the waters of the gulf. One of them, the island of Aigina, would receive preference, being of assistance to the Great King during this campaign. Datis had already begun to form his list of delegations—which city of Greece would be invited to become the capital of the satrapy of Greece? Would he choose Athens? No, he could not, for Darios was clear in his commands—the city was to be put to the torch, its inhabitants removed to the mainland of the Empire, most sold to pay the expenses of the expedition, while a select few were to be sent along to the court at Susa.

For a moment he admired the courage of the Athenians, men from a tiny city standing defiant. Then he thought of Nabusera and the others, thousands of his men left at Marathon. A very high price indeed to pay for this negligible stretch of rocky land. "Argos!" he said, drawing the attention of his marines. Then he said under his breath, "that will be my capital."

"Ho!" bellowed the pilot as he pointed landward. "That is their harbor."

The invasion fleet approached Phaleron, fanning out in a broad arc to envelope the port; the transports slipped forward after the scout ships had signaled it empty of Athenian triremes.

Datis turned to one of his marines. "Get me one of the rowers. The best swimmer of the lot." He returned quickly with a Phoenician. "A purse of gold for you when you return," he said squeezing a leather pouch full of coin. "Swim ashore and scout the beach." The Phoenician plunged into the dark water of the gulf, for night had fallen, and revealed nothing of the shore. Datis leaned over the balustrade, listening to the Phoenician splash toward land. Soon he heard nothing.

*****

Metiokhos strolled across the mildly pitching deck toward Hippias. The old man stood at the railing, staring at the night-shrouded coast of his homeland. "I do not see it," said Hippias in between pathetic coughs.

"What?" Metiokhos immediately gazed out toward shore, looking for something but did not know what.

"The signal." Hippias collapsed to his knees under a fit of coughing while he wheezed to gain a breath. "There should be a signal."

Metiokhos pulled a handkerchief from the sleeve of his Persian robe and gave it to Hippias. "You are wracked with the delusions of old age. There is no one at Athens that would welcome your return. If this new Athens made a patriot of my father—you look for a sign from a traitor that does not exist."

* * * * *

Amply past the first watch, Datis heard the approach of a small boat, rude oars slapping the water noisily. Men yelled up, others from his trireme responded, tossing several lines overboard. One line pulled taunt. He heard the smack of feet as someone scaled the hull, barefoot. In moments the head of the Phoenician swimmer bobbed into view above the railing. Two of Datis' marines reached out and heaved him onboard by the armpits, unceremoniously dropping him on the deck at their commander's feet. The man slowly craned his neck and looked up at Datis.

"Well?" Datis growled impatiently. "Is the harbor clear?"

The Phoenician, his eyes filled with fear, merely shook his head.

"How many?" Datis motioned for his marines to stand the Phoenician up.

The Phoenician, head down, eyes still locked upon the deck answered. "Thousands."

Chapter 35

Phaleron—Precinct of Kynosarges
18th day of the Athenian month Metageitnion—Past Midnight

A ribbon of moonlight danced over the swells of the harbor of Phaleron, while beyond, signal lamps on board the vessels of the Persian war-fleet twinkled like a blanket of stars brought to earth. All around him men collapsed into pools of spent flesh, exhausted from combat and their grueling race from Marathon. They thanked the gods for this night—this one last night they would live as free men—before the Persians attacked. Many of them succumbed to sleep. Miltiades, though, sat facing the sea, the moon, and the anchored Persian fleet, rubbing his sore knees. Kimon knelt beside him.

Themistokles lumbered over to Miltiades and dropped to a seat on the small hill that sloped gently toward the harbor. "Without a fleet we will never be safe from them," he declared.

"We still have a chance. When they land we must attack. Do not let them disembark their cavalry. That will be the key," said Miltiades.

Themistokles laughed. "Can you not see, man? They have given it all, and have nothing left." He spoke of the Athenians scattered across the precinct of Kynosarges. Indeed, if the Persians landed, few if any of them would be fit to challenge them.

"I wonder if the Persians know this?" asked Miltiades as his head dropped forward against his pulled up knees. "It would have been better if Aristides was here." Another 800 would make a difference, but he thought about it again. Aristides and his Antiokhis taxis had been shattered—most every one of them sustained gruesome wounds, unable to walk much less run from

Marathon to here—to Phaleron. He drifted in and out of sleep, awaking every so often to the sight of the invasion fleet filling the horizon, praying to Zeus, Athena and Poseidon for deliverance. He prayed also that the Persian commander Datis proved to be a sensible man, a man of prudence. He prayed he would be satisfied with his gains, even if these did not include Athens.

"Father, the day is breaking," said Kimon as he looked over his shoulder to the east.

Miltiades smiled. "It will be a glorious day, my son." He fought his aching muscles attempting to stand. Kimon propped him up, handing him his spear to use as a crutch. Miltiades leaned hard upon it. Suddenly he seemed quite old to Kimon. As the sun rose and light began to filter over the heaps of sleeping Athenians, one by one they rose up and began to fit their armor with poignant resignation.

Themistokles handed both Kimon and Miltiades a fig. "That is the last of them," he said as he dropped one into his mouth.

From across the water the same fearful wail of war horns echoed from the Persian fleet as they did from their land army the day previous. Miltiades reached for his battered shield. "Get up men!" he yelled.

Now he heard shouting from the far flank of the army, the wing that spread north toward the small village of Piraios. Cheers erupted next. A boy came barreling down the road screaming Miltiades' name at the top of his lungs.

"Over here!" He waved, and others pushed the messenger toward Miltiades.

"They are coming!" The boy shouted over and over.

Miltiades looked to Kimon. "Son, when it starts, stay behind me."

The messenger skidded to a halt in front of Miltiades. "They are coming," he repeated. Oddly Miltiades detected a grin that stretched quickly into a smile on the boy. He opened his mouth but not a word slipped out. The boy drew a deep breath then jumped up and down pointing north. "The Spartans! They are coming!"

"Form up!" barked Miltiades. He glanced at the anxious messenger. "And how far off are they?" He scanned the Persian fleet hoping to see masts wobbling atop each ship, a sure sign that they prepared to sail and not fight, but the triremes, freighters, and troop transports jockeyed about, preparing to execute their final maneuvers before landing.

The boy shouted, "Listen!"

Miltiades, Themistokles and Kimon faced north, straining to hear what the boy announced. The almost serene notes of Lakonian flutes wafted from the hills beyond, intermingling with buoyant voices all singing as one. Into view marched a column of scarlet clad hoplites, their polished bronze armor set ablaze by the morning sun. Again the Persian war-horns moaned.

Kimon pulled on his father's cloak. "Look!"

Miltiades, Themistokles and the rest turned to the harbor, to the source of the trumpeting. Out there sails blossomed like flowers, filling quickly with the offshore breeze. They watched as the fleet melted into the haze of the distant horizon.

Chapter 36

Marathon
18th day of the Athenian month Metageitnion

The Spartans did not linger at Phaleron once the Persian fleet had set sail, but asked permission from Miltiades and the other Athenian commanders to continue on to Marathon, to view for themselves the handiwork of these exhausted, courageous men. Theasidas, their commander, knew quite well that he and his countrymen would inevitably face these Persians on the field of battle, so he would become acquainted with this foe and see if the Athenians related their valor accurately or with exaggeration.

By mid afternoon they had already passed through Probalinthos, the yawning bay of Marathon coming into view not long after. The sky above was crammed with carrion birds and gulls, the plain flat and grimy. To their left, as they passed the village, they sighted the smoldering remains of a massive funeral pyre. Continuing on, they threaded their way through the sacred groves of Herakles, and to the plain beyond, where slaves tossed weapons onto a huge pile of Persian arms—the tropaion, or trophy—the point where the battle had turned. Once upon the battlefield, the Spartan columns, so disciplined until now, broke up into wandering bands of men, some accompanied by proud Athenians as escorts to the grisly scene, all gawking at the thousands of slain Persians. They had never seen men dressed so oddly, with trousers, thick slippers or boots on their feet, and armed with effeminate bows. Stranger still was their headgear. Some had sensible metal caps, although hardly as substantial as the Spartan closed-face kranos helmet; most lay there with nothing more than a swirl of linen or felt atop their heads.

The Spartans scoured the plain, reconstructing the battle from the position and number of Persian dead, reckoning the apparent errors and the unmistakable accomplishments of the Athenians.

Theasidas stood near the Charadra stream, assessing the battlefield, when he spotted one of his eirenes, a warrior from the first age grade of twenty, maundering about with an Athenian, Persian akinakes sword in hand. "Amompharetos," he called out. The young man jogged smartly to him without a moment of hesitation, followed slowly by the Athenian. "What is so interesting?" he asked.

Amompharetos turned the dagger-like sword in his hand, studying the jeweled hilt capped with twin snarling lions, eyes fashioned of burning red rubies. He offered the sword to Theasidas. Next his slid his own short sword free of its scabbard and measured both with his eyes. "The Persian blade is not much shorter than mine," he said thoughtfully. He reached to the ground, lifting a battered Persian sparabara shield. This too he compared with his own heavy oaken aspis shield. He ran his fingers over the bronze skin of his shield then poked a finger through one of the multitude of perforations in the Persian wicker sparabara. "Odd combination," he stated coolly. "A short blade and a flimsy shield."

The Athenian offered his open hands to Amompharetos as a gesture to accept the Spartan sword. Amompharetos smiled and placed it into the Athenian's anxious grip. "The only difference I see is in ornamentations. Your sword has none, while the Persian blade sparkles with gems."

Amompharetos retrieved his sword. "Only two things may adorn a Spartan sword—my hand at one end and the enemy's blood at the other." He slipped his sword back into its scabbard and plucked up his spear where it had been implanted in the packed soil of the battlefield. Suddenly the Spartan's face went dark.

"What is so unsettling?' asked the Athenian as he easily discerned Amompharetos' change in demeanor.

"A day," answered the Spartan. The Athenian's brow wrinkled into a look of confusion. "Pardon my manners, but I have not asked your name."

"I am Myronides, son of Autolykhos." He extended a hand. So did the Spartan. "You said a day?'

"I regret that we arrived a day too late." Amompharetos wrapped his arm around Myronides and walked him toward the remains of the Persian encampment. "Come. Give me the grand tour of the barbarian camp, for I may never see a Persian again."

Chapter 37

Susa—Court of Darios
Autumn of 490 BC

The members of the Persian court were arranged perfectly, radiating from Darios' throne in order of rank and importance. Immediately to the king's right sat his son by his wife Atossa, Xerxes. Next to Xerxes sat Artabazanes, grandson of Gobryas. Flitting amongst these three was Bupares the eunuch, his ever-present flywhisk snapping lazily, held by trembling, aged hands. Mardonios ranged between two thick cedar columns, pacing like a caged animal. They all awaited news of the expedition. Unbeknownst to them the final battle had been fought a week earlier, and soon—so very soon—the fleet messenger service of the Persian Empire would traverse three months of land routes in barely seven days with this vital message.

Outside the apandana, or main hall, musicians, dancers and jugglers queued up, along with scores of multifarious other entertainers, ready to enter on command, to initiate the splendid celebration commemorating the conquest of Greece.

Darios suddenly convulsed in a fit of coughing. A Magus rushed forward with a burner of incense, an attempt to ward off bad air or devils. Darios, with a furious backhanded wave, sent him stumbling away. "Get that out of my face!" He stuffed his face into a large silken handkerchief, one retrieved from the sleeve of his robe, muffling the last of his coughing.

At the far end of the apandana two of the Immortals smartly slipped their spears into the left hands and pulled in unison on the huge door rings. The pins squealed, and the heavy bronze and cedar doors groaned, as they swung open. A single man stood on the threshold, hesitating, only a dark figure devoid of any detail, silhouetted by the intense daylight behind him. Bupares clapped his hands twice. The man began his long, stiff and overly proper march the length of the apandana. He passed ranks of courtiers and scores of fire cauldrons, hustling beneath dozens of hanging oil lamps on his way to the throne of Darios. At the foot of the half dozen stairs that elevated Darios, he halted. He knelt. Finally he bowed, pressing his chest upon the carpeted floor, stretching out both arms, one hand empty, the other clutching a curled dispatch. Bupares shuffled forward indignantly, annoyed at having to bend so low to retrieve the message. He straightened up very slowly, and equally slowly climbed each step before coming between Darios and Xerxes. He snapped the scroll open, breaking the Royal seal and began to read—and shake.

Chapter 38

Athens—House of Aiskhylos
480 BC—Late Summer

"No doubt the Spartans will hold them," assured Aiskhylos. He presided over another gathering of his dining club, although now not for entertainment, nor diversion, but to discuss the unraveling of recent events—events that ten years past they would have never thought possible. "But still, it would be better to have Aristides here—and your father."

Kimon nodded. "Xanthippos, in an attempt to improve his position, has managed to weaken Athens immensely." He leaned back into his couch, lifting the kylix to his lips, staring for a moment at the dance of reflections in the wine. The empty couches in the andreion cried out, the ones once occupied by Aristides, Kynegeiros, Kallimakhos, and his father Miltiades—heroes of Marathon: "Look now and see who does not attend." He motioned to the vacant couches. "Whom do we blame? The Great King? Or is it someone much closer? My father did not die at the hands of any Persian."

Aiskhylos lifted himself up. "Wounds slew Miltiades."

"Wounds sustained in the service of Athens. Xanthippos, though, managed to reshape the truth, convincing the Assembly to fine my father for not subduing the Parians, a fine so exorbitant, he could not pay—and so he wasted away in prison. Would he not be alive now if it were not for Xanthippos?" Aiskhylos could only arch his eyebrows, and dared not interrupt his friend. "He turned Athens against my father, and now he has managed to do the same to Aristides."

"Oh come now. It is the long-standing quarrel between Themistokles and Aristides that culminated in our good friend's exile. You cannot blame Xanthippos for every unfortunate circumstance."

Kimon shook his head in disbelief. "Do you think that even half the men who voted could write—*Aristides*? Xanthippos, I would suspect, handed out those shards with our good friend's name already etched onto them."

Aiskhylos grinned. "There was no issue with Kallixenos, or Megakles, thanks to you. Everyone knew how to scribble their traitorous names for the ostracism."

"Regrettable that we could never connect them with Xanthippos. And now everything rests with Themistokles and the fleet," admitted Kimon reluctantly. He cared little for the navy. But still he knew Themistokles to be a patriot, and would not engage in the sort of political sniping that had ultimately killed his own father. That is why, to the amazement of his friends, he led a procession to the Akropolis days previous, to dedicate his horse's war-bridle, exchanging the accoutrements of a cavalryman for the shield of a hoplite and marine, urging other aristocrats to do the same.

The door creaked open slowly and in walked Praxis. He slipped his himation cloak free of his shoulders and draped it on a peg behind an empty couch. Not waiting for his slave, he kicked his sandals free and collapsed into the caress of the divan, an empty hand outstretched until the steward filled it with a kylix of wine. "Gentlemen, I have just come from the house of Myronides," he announced before quaffing the wine. "The news I bring is not good."

Aiskhylos swung his feet to the floor, leaning forward. Kimon propped his head up with his left arm, still reclined as he was amongst the embroidered Carthaginian pillows on his divan. Kimon spoke, asking the question that Praxis silently demanded. "What is this news?"

Praxis gulped another portion of wine. "Leonidas is dead. The Spartans are dead. The Persians are coming—again!"

Author's Note

I have unapologetically portrayed the Athenians as heroes in this story, since they were not the aggressors. Admittedly it makes for a better plot, but I maintain that the contention between Xanthippos and Miltiades is historical and can be supported by Herodotus' account of events. As to whether Xanthippos was connected to the elements that were for appeasement with the Persian Empire, no one really knows, although Kallixenos, a member of his tribe, was ostracized later.

The one aspect of the battle of Marathon that seems to have been retold inaccurately is the run of Pheidippides. Most often he is portrayed as the runner to bring word of the Athenian victory, when in fact it was another named Eukles who made this famous run. Why did Eukles die after running only 26 miles when Pheidippides ran over 300 miles in four days and apparently survived? I chose battle wounds as the cause.

Another component of this battle, and others from this era, concern the deployment and involvement of light troops. I have found it difficult to reconcile light infantry and attendants being intermingled with the heavy infantry, especially considering the very nature of hoplite combat, and chose instead to borrow plausible scenarios from Alexander's conquest of the Persian Empire, employing these elements as scouts and camp guardians. I do apologize to the long dead vase painters who have depicted things otherwise.

The main character of Arimnestos the Plataian is found in Herodotus' account of the battle of Marathon, and he fought again at the battle of Plataia in 479 BC. In my first novel, *In Kithairon's Shadow*, which is about this battle, I made no mention of him because one of the pivotal Spartan figures of the battle was also named Arimnestos.

Glossary

Agoge   The state sponsored education system of Sparta, focusing primarily on military development, thought to begin at age seven, continuing to age eighteen.

Akinakes   Persian short sword.

Akratisma   Breakfast.

Andreion   The men's dining hall in a Greek home.

Aspis   A shield; the hoplite shield was constructed of a bowl shape wooden core with an offset rim, and was often covered with a thin facing of bronze, although leather was also used; it was held with the left arm by a central armband that moved the weight from the wrist to the forearm, while the left arm gripped a handle just inside the rim.

Chiton   A tunic made from two rectangles of cloth pinned at the shoulders.

Daimon   A spirit.

Dathabam   Persian military unit of ten warriors.

Deipnon   Supper.

Ekthesis   The act of exposing an unwanted infant.

Embaterion March   Quick-paced march of the Spartan army, often accompanied by the singing of the paian.

Hazarabam   A Persian regiment of one-thousand.

Himation	A long cloak.
Histion	The large, square main sail of ancient Greek ships.
Hoplite	A Greek heavy-infantryman equipped with a bronze helmet, an aspis, bronze or linen composite body armor, greaves, a sword and his primary weapon, an eight foot long spear.
Iatros	A physician.
Kaleustes	The seaman in charge of the rowers on a Greek ship.
Kopis	A thick-tipped chopping sword.
Kylix	A shallow wine cup, often fashioned with a stem.
Lokhagos	In the Athenian army, the commander of a unit (*lokhos*) of one-hundred hoplites. In the Spartan army, a commander of a unit (lokhos) of 512 hoplites.
Mora	A division in the Spartan army consisting of two lokhoi (1024 hoplites)
Nautai	Rowers on Greek ships.
Omphalotomos	A mid-wife.
Paradeisos	A Persian garden or park.
Penteconter	An ancient warship with twenty-five rowers per side on a single level.
Petasos	A broad-brimmed felt hat.
Pirradazis	A Persian way station on the Royal Road.
Pynx	the hill in Athens where the people assembled to vote and debate proposals.

Sparabara	A Persian shield constructed of interlaced wicker and leather.
Spartiate	A male citizen of Sparta.
Sphagia	The blood sacrifice carried out before battle.
Stadion	A distance of approximately 185 meters.
Stoa	A long building with a series of exterior columns on one side and a wall on the other.
Strategos	In the Athenian army, a commander of one of the ten divisions based on the ten tribes of Athens.
Symposion	A drinking party, usually hosted by the affluent.
Trireme	A square-sailed warship propelled by oarsmen (nautai) positioned in three banks per side; the crew consisted of 170 nautai, 20 epibatai (marines) and several officers.
Xiphidion	A short sword or dagger.
Xiphos	A sword.

Printed in the United Kingdom
by Lightning Source UK Ltd.
131551UK00001B/86/A